Clouds Over Katahdin

A Johanna Kincaid Mystery

Anneka Lowrie

STORMVIEW MOUNTAIN PRESS

Certified
Non- Ai

Stormview Mountain Press
14 N. Reamstown Rd. #44
Reamstown, PA 17567

Praise for Clouds Over Katahdin

The Johanna Kincaid Mystery Series offer readers tightly woven storylines that are vivid and engaging. Lowrie's use of descriptive language allows readers to crisply visualize the settings and immerse themselves in the story.

– Erica Shay, Author of the Tarot Mysteries

I couldn't put it down! Really strong characters. Lowrie's best yet!

– Advance Reader: Claire Wagner Kimball

Clouds Over Katahdin is a deep dive into the unthinkable. I honestly didn't see it coming. Johanna is truly a force to be reckoned with. Outstanding.

Advance Reader: Gayle Andrew

A portion of the proceeds from the sale of this book will be donated to The Boundary Mountains conservancy project.

The Boundary Mountains Preserve in Maine is located within the Appalachian range, a top global conservation priority for The Nature Conservancy. This range stretches from Alabama to Canada and is one of the most resilient, diverse and carbon-rich landscapes in the world.

Project:

https://bit.ly/BoundaryMountains

Make a Donation

https://bit.ly/NatureConservancyDonation

Dedicated to Lisa

who brought me
buttercups and pussy willows
and who shall ever be found at Parson's Meadow
in the spring listening to peepers and wood frogs

Jameson - Minsky Family Tree

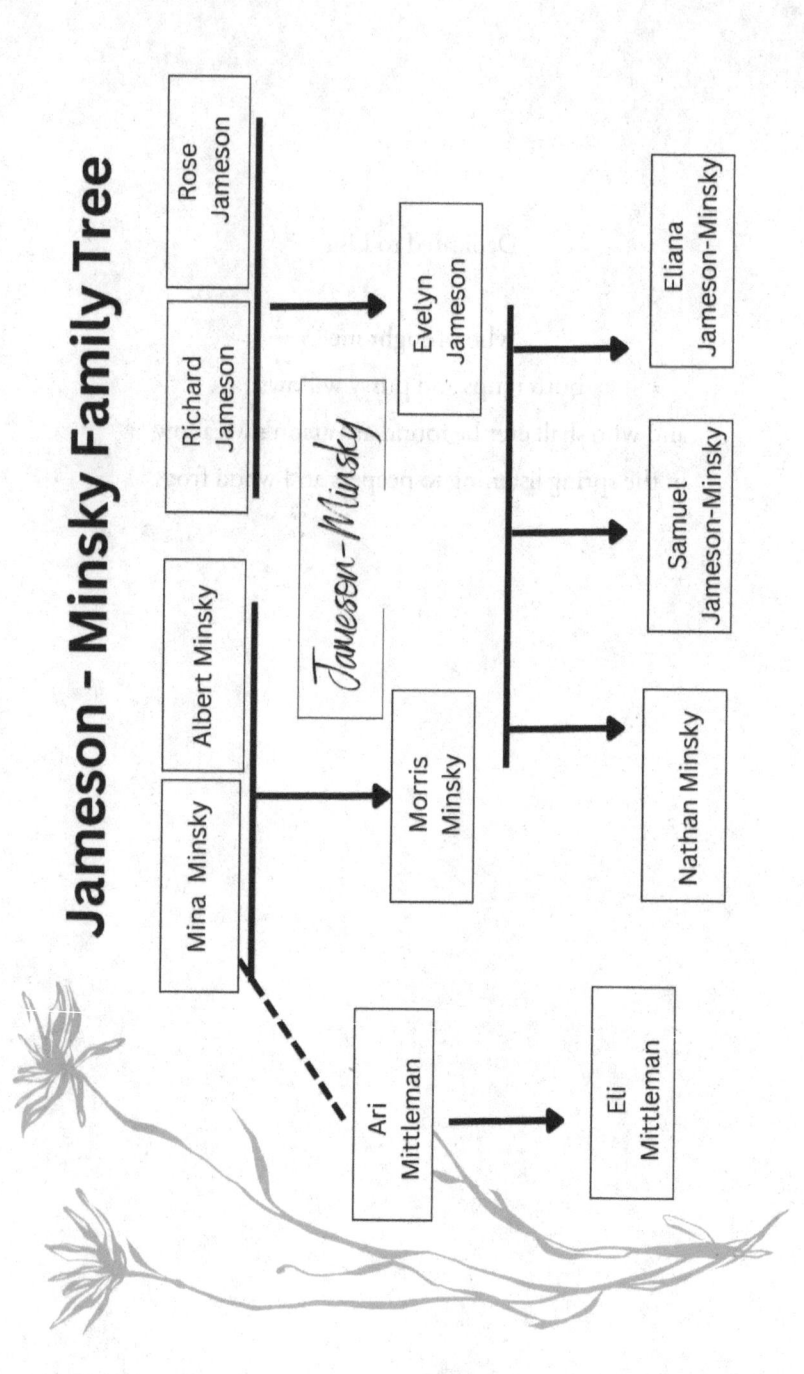

Contents

Prologue

J ohanna braced for impact as Scott swerved abruptly, nearly hitting the plumber's van ahead of them. The Subaru careened across the breakdown lane and came to rest on a grassy embankment. They heard the sounds of multiple collisions. There was a solid ribbon of red taillights further up Interstate 95. Traffic was now at a standstill.

This was not how Johanna and Scott Kincaid planned to spend a vacation trip from their solar farm in Cross Fork, Pennsylvania. Scott retrieved his cell phone from the floor of the vehicle where it had landed and placed a call.

"I'd better tell Scrag we're going to be late," he said. "This doesn't look good."

Moments later, they heard emergency vehicles heading to the scene. A state police officer driving up the breakdown lane stopped when he saw their Subaru.

"You folks ok?"

"Yes!" Johanna shouted.

The trooper waved and sped off. Scott left a voice message for his uncle in Belfast. The traffic incident had occurred on the last leg of a long journey to the Maine coast, just north of Portland. Scott jockeyed the Subaru Crosstrek back onto the highway, as a fellow motorist waited patiently for them to rejoin the line of vehicles.

Johanna leaned back against the headrest and thought about the start of their day at Elk Run Farm. It had begun with packing and a troubling conversation with an old friend.

Harvest

"Something's wrong with Norah. She doesn't sound at all like herself." Johanna put her cell phone in her backpack and turned to face Scott.

"What's the matter?"

"I'm not sure. Her voice was shaky, and she had completely forgotten she invited me to come stay with her at the herb farm."

Scott set his duffel bag on the kitchen floor next to their backpacks and looked at Johanna. Her long silver hair was folded in a soft, thick layer of braids that trailed down her back. He ran his finger along the curve of her jaw, feeling the softness of her skin. Her storm-gray eyes were still vibrant, though crease lines had formed at their edges. It gave her gaze a deceptive sharpness that belied what he knew to be a gentle, compassionate nature.

She was still attractive to him, though much older than when they had first met. Beautiful then and now, he thought to himself. She wore faded jeans and an oversized grey flannel shirt he suspected had once been his. She had a perplexed expression on her face and sounded very concerned.

"It's a good thing you called her before we left."

"After I reminded her I was coming to help with the herb farm, she remembered. She was very nervous during the entire conversation. Then she said that knowing I would spend a few weeks was a relief."

"Now that does sound odd," said Scott. "Norah is one of the most decisive, independent and pragmatic older woman I have ever met, yourself included."

"She is over ten years older than me," Johanna responded curtly.

"You know I am only teasing." He smiled.

"Your flirting could stand a little improvement." She flashed her eyes in a signature no more nonsense manner. What else are we bringing?" she asked, swiftly changing the subject.

"I think we should bring our pistols and field bags in case we have the opportunity for some target practice."

"It's a perishable skill," she responded. "It's best to keep up our training."

Scott nodded. In the mountains, wild animals had as much right to the terrain as humans. It was the intersection between those territories that dangerous encounters often occurred and a certain level of preparedness was necessary. Scott carried a pistol at all times. Johanna did not.

The transition from intentional target shooting to carrying a concealed weapon was a difficult one for Johanna, who had spent her career as a psychotherapist. She strongly believed in non-violence after many years of seeing the effects of cruelty, trauma, and abuse first hand. She was Buddhist and a vegetarian who would not even kill an animal for food and wasn't sure she could do so, even to save her own life.

It had been hard to reconcile the paradox of 'do-no-harm' with 'self-protection' in her mind. She struggled with the conflict by choosing to fire her pistol only at a gun range. A paper target was not a human being, she rationalized. She had carried her pistol concealed only once and luckily had not needed to use it to defend herself.

Scott placed the last of the duffel bags and backpacks in the trunk of the Crosstrek. It amazed him how much they could fit in Johanna's small Subaru. Their duffel bags nestled up against Johanna's camp kitchen box and the tent bag. All the camping supplies they would ever need stacked nicely in her car. He looked up at the pink and grey streamers that spun across the sky like the wispy strands of a spider's web. Dawn rose softly in the mountain's eastern sky. They had already covered over the gardens for the fall, harvesting and storing all the vegetables in the root cellar.

They had grown enough staple foods for the entire winter. Johanna had spent the month of September canning and dehydrating their spring and summer plantings. Organic butternut and acorn squash were lined up on the rafters of their solar farmhouse.

They had stripped corn from their cobs, dehydrated it along with peas, potatoes, celery, and carrots, then packaged them in vacuum-sealed packets for winter soups. Jars of canned vegetable broths, along with tomato purees and pickled cucumbers, lined the storage shelves in their walk-in pantry.

Johanna was doing a final walk-through before they closed up the farmhouse. She adjusted the controller for the solar charged batteries that supplied all their electrical needs and lowered the thermostat for the heating system. In case her daughter, Kaye, and her husband, Rob decided to stay on the mountain, she left fresh towels and sheets on the bed. She had carefully placed written instructions for using the farmhouse's solar power and propane backup systems on the kitchen table.

Overlooking the southern gardens, the kitchen was the largest room in the house. They had designed it as a working farm, so there were two kitchen sinks, one for food preparation and cleanup and another deeper sink with wooden counter tops for washing vegetables harvested from the gardens.

The wash sink was connected to an outside grey water tank to be filtered back into the gardens. The previous weekend, Scott had emptied the tank for the winter while irrigating the empty rows. They had spread quarry dust to enrich the soil and mulched the beds with leaves Scott had run through the chipper last fall.

Next year, Scott thought as he closed the Crosstrek's back hatch, we need to build a hydroponic greenhouse. We could eat fresh salads throughout the harsh, cold winter. As Johanna locked the front door, his cell phone buzzed, and he answered.

"It's Dennie up at the top," he told Johanna. "She wants to know if we want to stop by for breakfast on our way out. Pancakes."

"I'd love to," responded Johanna. "We are taking our time with this trip, no rushing."

Their granddaughter had parked her RV camper by the barn at the top of the mountain earlier that week. Elk Run Farm, a series of swales and man-made ponds, was carved into the side of a two-thousand-foot mountain in the Wilds of Pennsylvania. The upper pond drained into the middle pond about one hundred feet lower, which fed the lower pond by the farmhouse. The ponds served as irrigation sources for the lower gardens, which were planted on terraced swales and a summer swimming hole by the farmhouse.

Scott cultivated sea-buckthorn berry and elderberry bushes along with apple trees, forming a juice bearing forest along the ridge-line. The barn housed the processing machines that stripped the berries, prepared and bottled the juices for sale. Their granddaughter ran the fall juicing operation, working with migrant farmers. She managed the packaging and shipping of the finished products.

Elk Run Farm supplied medicinal quality organically grown elderberry and sea-buckthorn juices to companies that re-bottled them under their own brand. Dennie managed the extraction and packaging in the fall and the website ordering division during the rest of the year. Scott tended the berry and apple growing throughout the spring and summer.

Minutes later, they joined their granddaughter in the RV's mini kitchen. She had a plateful of freshly cooked pancakes beside her propane stove, ready to serve. Dennie was in her late twenties and nearly as tall as Scott. She got her height from her mother and her dark curly hair from her father.

Her college studies focused on accounting. She completed her degree but chose not to work for a firm. The idea of working in an office all day was not appealing to her. She would rather use her knowledge to run her own business. Before working the berry juicing operation with her grandfather, she managed a horse farm. It was an outdoor life she sought.

The two of them had number minds but sun-drenched bodies, as Johanna liked to say. Neither liked the fluorescent world of business. Years of working outdoors on building projects reinforced a desire for ceilings made of sky for Scott. Dennie simply disliked the feeling of being socially contained within four walls on someone else's schedule.

The RV was a self-sufficient mobile office and living unit. Dennie could conduct business anywhere. She loved to travel during the year. She spent one summer in the Grand Tetons, hiking and camping, while managing the berry juice sales using the RV's satellite Wi-Fi.

The RV was now hooked up to the water and septic line Scott had installed at the barn. Solar panels mounted on the RV's roof provided electricity while propane supplied hot water, heat, and cooking. Dennie stayed in it during the fall berry harvest. It was a time-consuming operation but well worth the reciprocity of earning one's living by giving to and receiving abundance from the earth.

Scott was preparing his granddaughter to take over the entire business one day. He was hoping she would want to learn how to grow, trim and tend the berry bushes. It was not a life for everyone. But he felt true freedom and independence were worth stepping back from modern lifestyles with their frantic, harried pace and lack of sustainability.

Dennie offered plates of warm, fragrant pancakes to her grandparents. She had brewed a pot of coffee as well.

"There is a Mason jar of syrup on the table," she offered. "It's a new brand from my friend's maple syrup farm in Vermont. We are trying elderberry infused maple syrup. I hope you like it. It took a few trial runs to get the optimal amount of elderberry, so it tastes right."

"Interesting idea," Scott responded, as he poured a small amount onto his pancakes. He wasn't as adventurous as Johanna regarding new flavors.

"If it's good enough," said Dennie, sitting down with them, "the maple syrup company will order about a hundred gallons this year for their product line. If that's a good seller, they will increase ordering next year by double. We would be the sole source for about five years while they developed their market."

Johanna took a bite of her liberally covered elderberry and maple syrup pancakes. "This is delicious!"

"Not too sour?

"Not at all," responded Scott, finishing his plate. "It's definitely a distinct flavor, different from plain maple syrup. It's not as overpowering as I thought it would be."

"The idea was to create a fresh taste and be able to market the health attributes of elderberry."

"Well, it's definitely a fresh taste," responded Johanna. "it's not like blueberry maple syrup at all."

"Great," said Dennie. "This means about a five percent increase in sales this year alone."

"We can afford to put in a hydroponic greenhouse and give you a raise," said Scott.

Johanna gave her granddaughter a warm hug. She placed a spare set of farmhouse keys on the small table. "Your mom and dad might spend a weekend down below. You are welcome to use the hot tub or spend some time in the farmhouse if you need a getaway from the frantic packaging."

"Thanks," Dennie said. "I definitely have my hands full. But don't worry," she turned to her grandfather. "I have you covered. By the time you get back, we will be done and all buttoned up here for the winter."

"Where are you headed afterwards?" asked Scott.

"I have some plans to head west again," she replied. "Montana. Big Sky."

"We will check in with you when we get to Maine," said Johanna. "Say hi to Richard for us. We are sorry to have missed him."

Richard was a biker friend of their granddaughter. He often joined her RV excursions. They were never sure if the relationship was romantic or platonic. They suspected both.

Moments later, Scott had driven the Subaru Crosstrek out of the entrance to Elk Run Farm and descended the mountain road to Cross Fork. They would stop in town to have their mail forwarded to a post office in Maine before taking the back road to Elmira, New York. They would be gone for about six weeks.

They faced a lengthy journey, covering almost 650 miles to Belfast, Maine. Their plan was to drive to the Berkshires in Western Massachusetts, then head northeast through New Hampshire's White Mountains range. They would enter Maine in Fryeburg and travel north to Augusta before heading to the coast.

They both loved the Belfast area. Coastal Maine, with its rugged harbors, was home for Scott. His family had settled there a few generations ago, and he had grown up with many opportunities in the ship and house building trades. They planned to spend a couple days so Scott could visit his uncle, Scrag Baker, a local lobsterman.

After their brief visit on the coast, Scott would travel to the Maine Organic Farming Institute in Unity for a month long training in straw bale home building and off grid projects. He was borrowing his uncle's truck so Johanna could continue on to Tiadaghton, a small town near Mount Katahdin. It was there she would help Norah on her medicinal herb farm and help package herbal teas for her mail order business.

Rear View Mirror

Traffic on the interstate moved slowly. As they drove by the scene of the accident, Johanna could see a tractor trailer in the center median and a totaled Mercedes SUV that someone had towed out of the fast lane. The driver of the tractor stood by his rig, unhurt, while the continually flashing lights of the ambulance seemed to indicate that the motorist was injured.

"Road rage?" Scott pointed to the Mercedes.

"He probably tried to speed past the truck, then cut back in too close," suggested Johanna.

"Looks to me like the trucker was trying to change lanes when the Mercedes sped up beside him and cut him off. Did you see the skid marks?"

As the long line of traffic came back up to highway speed, Scott concentrated on driving and Johanna returned to her thoughts.

The road they had initially traveled from their farm into New York had wound through the same mountains and along the same meandering creeks that Johanna had traveled with Angelique, her friend and mentor, when they went to Nadine Thunderchild's farm the previous spring, over a year ago. That escapade had resulted in a dangerous adventure involving a sex trafficking ring and the rescue of an abused child.

A few months after Johanna and three other women interfered with a high profile human trafficking and murder operation, she told Scott what had occurred. When he learned about her role in the intervention, he was angry they had left him out.

With the help of private detectives Marti O'Neil and Jayne Cullen, they had involved law enforcement without revealing the location of one of the trafficked girls. That girl now lived with Nadine Thunderchild on her farm with a new name and a new life.

Scott understood the necessity of anonymity and the importance of Johanna's involvement. But he made her promise she would never again leave him out of her decisions to assist in dangerous matters.

"We are a team," he had said solemnly. "We can't keep secrets from one another or this will never work. You could have been killed."

He was referring to the fact they had divorced years ago after a bitter separation. While many of their friends and family believed they had remarried, they hadn't. Although they repaired the layers of distrust and betrayal that pulled them apart over the years, they realized theirs was a fragile relationship. It still had hard edges and moments of pain and sadness. It was a tenuous relationship, often fraught with painful memories.

One such memory intruded on Johanna's thoughts. A few years after their breakup, she and Scott had been separately invited to a friend's wedding. If she had known he would be there, she remembered thinking at the time, she would have declined. The mood was joyful as their friend was getting remarried after losing his beloved wife to cancer years prior. It was a celebration of a return to happiness. She remembered seeing Scott dance with a bridesmaid, talking animatedly with her and laughing. Her heart sank, though at the time she could not say why. He seemed happy and she, herself, was so very sad.

Her eyelids teared up with the vividness of the memory. She looked at Scott, realizing how far they had come. A team, indeed. A lifetime spent together and ten years spent apart. In those years of separation they mended the wounds they had so carelessly inflicted upon one another. They had found a path back to a level of devotion rarely matched by others their age. Together, they had weathered storms that had crushed many other couples beyond repair. They believed the key to being together was to never think they were so rock solid that their love was unbreakable. They agreed to always remember how fragile love was, if not embraced with more courage than confidence.

Johanna's thoughts turned to her her old friend. Norah Jordan-Minsky was a former professor of botany and environmental science. Johanna had first met Dr. Minsky and her husband, Nathan, when she was studying clinical psychology at the University of Maine. Nathan was one of three grandchildren of Albert and Mina Minsky.

Nathan's grandfather had started a logging company similar to the one his family had in Germany. For that endeavor, he needed land, and according to Nathan, lots of it. They settled in the north Maine woods, where Albert eventually built a financial dynasty and a railroad to Canada. Mina created a family herb garden at their first homestead farm in Tiadaghton. Over the years, the herb garden became a business in its own right. This was the property Albert gifted Nathan, and it was Mina's medicinal garden business he had sought to bring back. Nathan and Norah had worked together to make Minerva's Meadows and Tea Gardens a successful internet enterprise as well.

But Nathan had been killed in a kayaking accident last year, leaving Norah to manage their business alone. Now that Nathan was gone, Norah needed help. Johanna would be a working guest, helping her friend get the fall tea catalog packaged and shipped. As a therapist, she knew firsthand the effect of losing a life partner on a woman's soul and would be a source of support during this period of her friend's grief.

Minerva's Meadows

Norah hung up her phone. It was the third time this week she had tried to call her mother-in-law. Each time, it rang once and went immediately to her voice mail. This time it returned a beeping noise indicating her mother-in-law was talking to another caller and then suddenly disconnected without going to the voice mail.

She had received an invitation to attend one of Evelyn Jameson-Minsky's fall garden tea parties. It was to be held that afternoon at the mansion. The handwritten invitation had come by postal mail earlier that week requesting a confirmation by phone and listed her mother-in-law's new private cell number.

In the past, she was invited not only as a guest but also as an expert speaker. She was usually expected to present a talk on whatever plant Evelyn wished to showcase from her extensive botanical collection. This was the first occasion the request of her presence did not include a performance as well.

"It's at 4PM," Norah said to herself, looking at the wall clock in the farmhouse kitchen. "Four hours from now. I should just go. She expects me there."

She sighed. The days now always seemed overly long and very lonely. Losing Nathan when they had expected to have so many fine years left together was excruciatingly hard. He successfully reached his goal of not only bringing back his grandmother's herb farm business but also expanding it.

Besides her own personal loss, his expertise as manager of the family investment and holding companies was lost as well. Nathan had graduated at the top of his class at Harvard Business school with a prestigious MBA. He possessed a brilliant mind. His grandfather had chosen Nathan as successor trustee of the Albert and Mina Minsky Legacy Trust, when the previous leadership under his nephew Eli

Mittleman was to be transferred. This was a source of irritation to Nathan's younger brother, Samuel, a Yale Law graduate who had expected to be selected. Albert had charged Nathan with the Trust's control of the logging, land, and railway logistic empire.

Norah not only inherited her husband's share of the family fortune, Nathan had named her the successor trustee in the event of his death. The details of the Trust were a closely held secret and no one else in the family knew she had been named. Eli had stepped back into his previous role of trustee after Nathan's death until he could train her in the Trust's oversight and management. At that time, the announcement that Norah was taking over the directorship would be made.

Samuel was now vying for that position again by right of succession now that Nathan had died. He counted on Norah's board seat vote to name him to the role. Eliana Jameson-Minsky, Nathan's sister, was supportive of her brother's desire to be placed in control of the family legacy Trust operations.

"I'm not ready to face that confrontation," Norah thought. Her husband had often confided his concerns to her about his brother's desire to control the Trust. He maintained Albert was not only wise in his business dealings, he was a keen judge of character. He had entrusted his brother-in-law, Ari, with overseeing the family Trust instead of his own son Morris, whom he considered a shallow excuse for a man. Each trustee was given the responsibility and a secret set of guidelines to train their successor trustee. Albert had instructed Ari to cultivate those skills in his own son Eli, then Nathan, again bypassing his own son.

Nathan's father Morris was no slouch in the brains department either, Norah remembered. He just didn't have the integrity to go along with the gift of a sharp mind. Integrity, Nathan had told her, according to his grandfather, was defined by what you would not do. It seemed his own father's character was questionable for reasons he never learned. Neither Mina nor Albert allowed any talking down of a family member in their presence. So one person's indiscretion never became a source of ridicule. Respect and honor in all things was the Minsky way.

What brought Norah and Nathan together was her relentless search for scientific truth and his desire to make the world a better place through wise and fair business practices. They had fallen in love with one another's minds and shared sense of integrity. It was Nathan's dedication to doing the right thing, which both Albert and Mina recognized and valued in their oldest grandson.

Norah remembered the day Mina had given her the herbal book of medicinal recipes that had been in her family for generations. She had translated it from its original German and Yiddish, handwriting it in her uniquely beautiful European English script.

The tooled leather-bound book bore the original title in German, Buch der Gartengeheimnisse. It meant "Book of Garden Secrets" in English and the first page was an introduction in Yiddish, welcoming the reader, who was about to learn how to become a Gortn Meydl, a garden girl.

It was the same day Albert had conveyed the deed to the Tiadaghton homestead property and the dormant business of Minerva's Meadows to Nathan. He offered the Trust terms of agreement to him, the signing of which constituted a commitment to the contingencies of the deal. A formal business plan to be presented to Albert with quarterly and annual financial statements. There were stipulations that the property and business would never be offered as collateral for any personal credit. The Trust would decide and fulfill any operational loans needed. Nathan and Norah could draw a salary from operations, but neither the business nor the property could be sold without first refusal from Albert or the Minsky Legacy Trust.

"He's a real Mensch," Mina had confided to Norah that day. It's not that she favored Nathan over his brother and sister, it's that she appreciated his honesty and trustworthiness.

"He vill make a success of this," she said in her heavily accented English, "because you are already a true Gortn Meydl. Hier, let me show you the secrets of the book."

While Nathan and his grandfather had discussed and signed a multitude of contractual agreements, Mina turned the fragile pages of the hand-bound leather book. She pointed out notations, soil preparations, seed gathering and propagation methods. Norah saw time-honored techniques learned by trial and error through generations of women, skills she, herself, only knew by training and research. It contained accurate line drawings of each plant, herb, or flower. These women were the true environmental scientists, she acknowledged at the time.

Minerva's Meadows, Herb and Tea Gardens were far more than a farm business. It was a legacy of trust handed down with a grave responsibility.

Garden Party

"**I** think you should leave now," said Eliana. "Isn't it bad enough you neglected to respond to Mother's invitation but to arrive an hour late to her party and expect to be seated is pretty arrogant, don't you think?"

"But I did respond or tried to," answered Norah, near tears. "The line was either busy or no one answered."

"What do you mean, busy? The invitation clearly said to respond by email. Everyone else did. The voice mail hasn't been set up on her new phone line yet. She was counting on you and had to get a garden society presenter, all the way from Bar Harbor, at the last minute."

Norah was confused and disheartened.

She had arrived at Evelyn's residence, the Minsky Mansion she and Morris had inherited after Mina passed away. Elegant botanical gardens had replaced Mina's careful plantings. Groundsmen labored throughout spring and summer to create a cacophony of colorful, unusual flowers not native to the Maine landscape.

The last event of Evelyn's garden season always included a horticultural presentation and concert performance. Norah was wearing a dress made of elegant black wool with a saffron colored silk scarf and carried her coat across her arm. She was prepared to speak if Evelyn still needed a presenter.

She had arrived at precisely ten minutes to five. For some reason, her kitchen clock was an hour off. She knew she was late when she glanced at her watch, but there was nothing to be done about it. She was well aware Evelyn would be gravely disappointed, but she never expected to be turned away.

Lisette, Evelyn's housekeeper, had answered the door when she arrived. She was formally dressed in tailored black pants and a white, linen blouse, her hair wrapped in a sleek chignon. She asked Norah to wait in the mansion foyer.

She returned quickly with Eliana, who proceeded to berate Norah. Lisette stood off to the side of the foyer, eyes downcast, and a neutral look on her face. Norah focused her gaze on the ornate woodwork in the entranceway of the gilded age mansion as her mind began to shut down under the barrage of accusations.

"I am so sorry, Eliana. Surely Evelyn must know it wasn't intentional. My invitation clearly said to call," she struggled to assert. "There has been an unfortunate mistake."

The gentle notes of Debussy's piano solo Clair de Lune began to fill the foyer with its precise yet touching beauty. The botanical presentation was evidently over.

"Show me your invitation," Eliana demanded, holding out her hand. "I personally hand wrote them myself and I am sure I wrote Mother's email address on each one."

"That's the thing," Norah said apologetically, "it's gone. I must have misplaced it."

The younger woman rolled her eyes. "Really?"

Lisette shifted uncomfortably.

"Norah," Eliana continued, her voice somewhat softer, "we all know this past year has been hard on you. But you aren't the only one mourning Nathan. My mother lost a son. Nathan was her rock, as you very well know. He was my big brother. We all loved him very much. This has been hard on us as well."

Norah saw Lisette look down suddenly, her hands held tightly together, her shoulders stiffening.

"I know, but...." she started to say.

Eliana held up her hand like a stop sign. "Mother is very worried about you. Living alone, unnaturally prolonged grief, unusual behavior, memory lapses. She has left it up to me to tell you her concerns. Maybe you should get professional help," she said in a low voice.

"I understand," responded Norah.

"Do you? Do you really? It's best you leave now. Mother has guests she must attend to. We are all just getting back to normal here, but your selfishness is just too much to tolerate."

"Please give her my sincerest apologies," mumbled Norah, "it won't happen again, I promise."

As she walked to her Jeep, her body began to shake with growing shock. Oh no, not now, she thought as she felt her heart begin to race and her mind begin to freeze. Everything around her was speeding up and everything within her was shutting down. It was like being in a slow motion spiral with everything outside her tunneling away.

As she tried to close the vehicle's door, wondering if she dared to drive, there was a movement beside her. She jumped.

A soft hand gently touched her pale wrist. It was like an electric shock at first, then swiftly accompanied by a flowing warmth of affection. She calmed instantly.

"I am so very sorry, Miss Norah," Lisette said.

"It's ok," she responded, "it's just going to take me a while to get used to his being gone."

"No, I mean, I am sorry Mr. Nathan is gone too," struggled the petite woman, "but Miss Eliana told me to come get her if you arrived. I would have made sure you had seating, but she would not let me. I am so very sorry."

She smiled at Lisette. "Thank you. You are such a kind person. Please, just call me Norah. I don't stand much for the Jameson family formality."

"Here," the housekeeper offered a card with her cell number written on it, "if you need anything, please call me. Now I'd better get back before Miss Eliana notices I am not at my station." She sighed.

Norah squeezed Lisette's hand. "That goes both ways. If you ever need a nice tea break or a walk in a fragrant garden, just come by. Standing invitation. No call necessary."

Lisette nodded and stepped away from the vehicle as Norah drove away. Her hands no longer shook, her heart rate was calmer. She thought it was all just a big misunderstanding.

Nathan had tried to tell her years ago his parents were pretentious when he introduced her to them. But his grandparents, the Minsky's, were real down to earth good people.

Tears fell softly from her eyes as she drove back to Tiadaghton. Nathan would have never let Eliana speak to her that way. Not in a million years. Her heart sank as she turned onto the farmhouse road, seeing the painted sign Nathan had hung years ago. It swung on its post in a stiff wind that carried a flurry of golden-red oak leaves, spinning in the crisp autumn air.

She entered the homestead through the kitchen door and glanced at the wall clock. It was the same time as her watch.

How could that be? she thought. I must be losing my mind. She stood in shock, staring at its hands, leaving the door open behind her.

A gust of wind blew through the door and lifted a yellow card off the kitchen table. It fluttered to the floor.

She picked it up. There, clearly written in Eliana's elegant penmanship, was her request to respond by email. The door slammed shut, and she sank into a chair, clutching the invitation with hands that had suddenly grown cold.

Her whole body began to shake again.

This is unreal, she thought, fighting her panic.

Johanna is coming. Her shoulders relaxed. She will know what's to be done. She began to sob with a weariness that bordered despair.

Local Color

Belfast is a seaport on the rugged coast of Maine on Penobscot Bay. Along with the Front Street Shipyard, a custom yacht and shipbuilding company, there were a few other boat building and repair companies along its docks. The harbor had become a boating attraction for weekenders and had even been listed as a cruise ship destination. Which meant it was a busy port that posed challenges for the pace of its growth and economy. It'd been a working waterfront and mercantile support for generations of local fishermen and lobster-folk. Belfast was an old town with some brand new paint.

Scott drove along the familiar streets and found a parking spot in front of Rollie's Bar and Grill. They walked down to the commercial fishing wharf at the landing where his uncle had a slip for his lobster boat, the Mary B. It was a bustling dock with scenic tours, a bay-side trail and an expansive walking bridge spanning the Passagassawakeag River that drained into the head of the bay.

The Mary B was in. Scott waved to his uncle, who at that moment was off-loading his gear for the day. They had timed their arrival perfectly. When his in-country tour of duty in Vietnam ended over fifty years ago, Scrag Baker returned to the sea in the grand tradition of his family. He became a lobsterman. He found it difficult to be among too many people, even harder to take commands from businessmen he deemed foolish or worse. The sea healed wounds too deep to reveal and too harsh to share.

Scrag returned the greeting after putting his gear down dockside. He scratched his head, pushing back his red woolen cap, and waited for Scott and Johanna to join him by the old boat. He wore a tattered brown and yellow plaid flannel shirt with its sleeves pushed up, revealing tattooed arms and bright yellow Helly Hansen bib overalls hoisted by thick black suspenders.

"I'd hug ya," he announced, "but then ya'd smell like fish!"

"Glad to see you too, Scrag," said Scott.

"Same here... and you Johanna, you're younger than ever!"

Johanna grinned at Scrag's backhanded compliment and stood back while Scott approached his uncle by the stern of the boat. For a man in his mid-seventies, he was fitter than many and pricklier than most. He got a kick from shelling out insults, some of which stung and others that were merely amusing. "At the end of the day," Scott had told her when she first met his family, "if something goes bad, Scrag's the man you want standing beside you."

"Why don'cha take the house keys and get settled into the cottage? They're under the driver's seat of my pickup."

"Thanks!"

"I'll be right along. Johanna, there's a pot of corn chowdah sittin' in the fridge. Warm it up on the stove. Jest vegetarian, I promise," he said, holding his arms up in mock defeat. "There's a Bassett clam pie in there too, if you can bear to heat it up for me."

"Thanks, Scrag," Johanna laughed, remembering the scene in his kitchen years ago when he tried to serve her clam chowder. He vehemently disagreed that anything other than meat or fish could be one's main fare. Punctuating his fervent conviction, he hoisted a wooden spoon as if to harpoon her. Undaunted by his dramatics, she grabbed a rolling pin and they sparred across the linoleum floor.

"Park by the Tahoe, plenty of room for your little rice grinder in the drive!" he abruptly waved them off and returned to his offloading.

They picked up a few loaves of French bread, grapes and a block of cheese at a local market, then headed back up the Belfast Road, the same way they had traveled into the city.

Scrag lived in an old cottage in Morrill, right on Smith Mill Pond. Scott had grown up in that house under the care of his uncle and aunt.

It was a long and painful story. Early in their relationship, Johanna learned about the loss of Scott's mother in childbirth and the subsequent handoff of his newborn baby sister, Louisa, and himself to be raised by his mother's brother Scrag and his wife. Mary Stiles Baker was the only mother his sister ever knew. She was childless herself but loved her niece and nephew as fiercely as if they were her own.

Scrag was willing to take on his sister's children, but forever held a grudge against Bruce Kincaid for abandoning his children. Baker grudges were palpable and relentlessly renewed, lest the regard soften. Once Scott turned twelve, he spent summers on Nova Scotia with his father. That was how Johanna and Scott met.

It seemed such a long time ago, when she had left her home town of Bucksport at eighteen and lived with her grandparents for a year in Nova Scotia. It was a year of discovering her Scottish heritage before entering the university; a year of avoiding small town gossip.

Scrag's cottage was small but comfortable. He had done little to change it in the ten years since Mary had passed away, other than keeping it well maintained. It was said that he ran a tight ship, both on and off the water. That was evident in the efficiency of his kitchen and the comfort of his small living room with its woodstove and peaceful view of the pond through a sparklingly clear bay window.

His uncle had stacked the wood pile for the winter against the south wall of the garage. Scott grabbed some logs to stoke a fire in the stove while Johanna took the large stainless steel pot out of the refrigerator. Within a few minutes, the woodstove was going with its expanding circle of warmth. The corn chowder was heating on the kitchen's old propane stove as she put the pan with its rich pie of buttery sea-clams in the oven.

She set out plates, bread, and a bowl of grapes on the table. While she sliced the cheese into small pieces, Scott brought their duffel bags and backpacks into the house.

Scrag's guest room was Scott's old bedroom, remodeled years ago by his sister Louisa when he left for college. It had a sturdy double bed, a desk, chest of drawers and bookshelves with a braided rug on the floor. Its only window faced the pond. He set their things on the bed and took some books from the shelves. His old textbooks from college were interspersed with Louisa's collection of literature, poetry and plays. She had been a drama major who followed behind her brother's studies of economics and fine homebuilding.

Louisa lived in Brooklyn with her partner, an older woman with whom she shared her life. She was a professional actress with a successful stage career and more recently taught drama at Columbia. Scrag missed her, as she had filled the void left by his beloved Mary.

Johanna made a pot of coffee and sat at the table while the chowder was heating. Scrag pulled into the driveway a few minutes later. They heard him turn on the outdoor shower; a brisk challenge in the chilly October air. The old man did well for himself, Johanna thought. He lived a spartan but healthy life and didn't seem to mind his time alone.

Moments later, he came into the kitchen wearing blue jeans and a clean flannel shirt. "Won't be able to do that much longer," he said matter-of-factly. "I see ya got the woodstove cranked."

"And the chowder is nearly ready. You want coffee?" Johanna offered.

He nodded and sat at the table, taking some cheese and bread.

"Thanks for having us, Scrag," said Scott, sitting down in his old chair at the table.

"Wouldn't have it any other way. Straw bale, ya say? Wouldn't think that'd stand up to a cold Maine wintah."

"You know how it is in Unity. Innovation and sustainability. It's gotta stand up," Scott said.

"New fangled but tried and true," the old lobsterman acknowledged. "We'll see."

While the old man grumbled, he also grinned, thought Johanna. For a man who'd seen far more harshness in the world than he'd cared to, Scrag Baker maintained a positive outlook, a rugged charm and a teasing attitude.

He enjoyed hurling well-placed insults at locals, and he expected the favor to be returned. He made regular appearances at Town Meetings, according to him, to keep the board of selectmen on their toes. Scott could think of a few townspeople who urged him to run for office, but Scrag refused.

"My job is to keep 'em straight, not join the bandits and bastahds," he had told Johanna in years past. The only person he truly disdained was 'the damned Scotsman,' Bruce Kincaid. She suspected it was more from habit than any current provocation. Scott's father left Maine and moved to back to Nova Scotia after Addie died in childbirth. It was an ongoing relationship of mutual disrespect. Scott made peace with his father and finally understood the fundamental reason he made the decision to leave.

He was heartbroken when Addie died and could not bear to see her bright blue eyes in their children's faces. Many years later, his father confessed he had made the wrong decision but knew in his heart Scrag and Mary would raise his children better than he ever could have done.

Louisa barely knew her father and did not know the man was in the audience watching her performances as often as he could. "She is the image of her mother," Bruce had told his son, "with the dramatic flair of the Scots."

On the walls of Scrag's living room were four theatrical photos of Louisa. One was her first high school performance in Ibsen's A Doll's House, obtained from the local newspaper. Over the couch, Mary had hung a professional cast photo of the college musical Grease when Louisa landed her first lead role. There was a large photo of the expertly choreographed dance routine of 'Money' from Cabaret in which she played a decadent showgirl in the pre-war Berlin Kit Kat Club, hanging by the dining table.

On a far wall, by a bookcase, was a spectacular picture of the off-Broadway hit, Hair, in which Louisa, in her lead role of Sheila, sang "Good Morning Starshine." Johanna and Scott had joined Scrag for the show in New York City. Forever after, Louisa was called "Starshine" by her uncle.

That Scrag doted on Louisa did not surprise Scott. Both his father and his uncle adored Addie Baker Kincaid, and Louisa was by far her mother's daughter. What one could not forget, the other could never forgive.

Scrag's formal education had ended with the war and began in his self-collected library of philosophy. His bookshelves contained poetry by Gary Snyder and Rainer Maria Rilke. Sun Tzu's Art of War formed the brusqueness of his attitude on life. Marcus Aurelius, Plato, Nietzsche, Beston, Emerson and Thoreau shaped the depth of his mind into contours of intellect and understanding. He had never written an essay or research paper, but he understood a poet's innuendo of disaster the way he knew the underbelly of an armored tank and the interweaving of a lobster trap netting. He knew it intimately.

As they ladled the creamy corn chowder into large bowls, the kitchen smelled of goodness, love and family, or so it felt to Johanna. She had placed the dish of clam-pie on the stovetop, whereupon Scrag helped himself to a large portion. Scott distributed chunks of bread for dipping, with a smile of contentment on his face.

For some people, she thought, coming home must feel like this. Warm and familiar. For her, going back home was a dread she avoided at all costs. Her parents had passed away a few years back, one and then the other, so she was saved from the inevitable conflict. If she never returned to the town in Maine where she had grown up, it would be too soon. The past was best left forgotten, she thought sadly. Unfortunately, it was a ghost as well.

"How long ya staying, JoJo?" asked Scrag, jolting her back to the present. His nickname for her was intentionally irreverent. Sometimes he called her "Dr. Jo."

"I am headed out on Sunday morning," she responded.

"How about a trip to the gun range tomorrow?"

"That's a great idea," said Scott. "We can always use a little more practice."

Johanna smiled. Maybe, she thought, I can shoot some holes in my past while we're at it. The feeling of growing up in a place where she never fit in haunted her. The thing about target shooting, she acknowledged, was that you had to abandon all your emotional defenses and focus only on the task at hand. Denial was the anthesis of situational awareness. Clearly, she needed the practice.

Later that evening, she and Scott attempted an outdoor shower under the full moon. They burst back into the kitchen, cursing and shivering. Scrag was relaxing by the woodstove with his long legs resting on a leather ottoman. He looked up from a book he had read far more than once. "Wind, Sand and Stars" by Antoine Saint Exupe'ry.

"Ayah." He nodded and went back to his book.

The road to the local gun range wasn't as well-maintained as Scott and Johanna's sports club in Cross Fork. But then, this club was a closely held membership in a rural town that tried their best to keep out-of-staters from becoming property owners.

A dilapidated, abandoned dwelling was on the corner of the access road. Its poor condition made the road to the range even less appealing. A weathered sign painted with the splotchy words, G_n Club was nailed to a tree in the overgrown yard. If the road ever had a name, no living person remembered it.

Scrag drove up the bumpy, pot-holed dirt road which became bumpier as it narrowed to the width of two tire tracks weaving haphazardly like a drunken sailor had carved it out of the forest. Johanna gave Scott a look somewhere between alarm and amusement. She knew this was the place he had learned to shoot when he was a kid.

They came around a bend and the road opened onto a paved parking lot. There was a clapboard club house, out-buildings that housed tractors for mowing the fields and the range. The stands were equipped with flat tables, rifle rests, trash barrels for spent shells and push brooms to collect them with.

At Johanna's look of surprise, Scrag shrugged. "We have to keep out the riffraff somehow."

They took a cooler of food, water and two stainless steel thermoses of coffee from the Tahoe, setting them on a picnic table. Johanna had filled them back at the cottage under Scrag's express direction; one thermos was labeled "strong" and the other "strong ++." 'Strong' was freshly brewed, full-bodied coffee, rich with cream. The other was pitch black. "Straight from Davy Jones' locker," Scrag informed her. He had warmed it up after leaving it in a pot on the back burner of his stove for a few days.

"It'll wake the dead," he had proclaimed proudly.

The gun range was a football field's length of grass. It had standing barriers at ten, fifty and seventy-five yards, to which one could staple targets. The back wall was a hundred yards out, with wooden stands for targets. The earthen embankment was filled with lead from bullets fired over decades of use. This was a place where families gathered, contests were held, picnics shared, and shooters honed their skills.

They brought their field bags containing firearms, extra ammo and magazines to the shooting platforms. A shingled roof shielded each platform and had a designated area that accommodated up to six shooters and their gear. No one else was at the range that day, which put Johanna more at ease.

She wore blue jeans, one of Scott's old sweatshirts, and a khaki colored quilted vest. She used an old ball cap to pull her hair back and secure it. Handling and firing ammunition exposed people to lead residues and gun powder that got on your face, hands, clothing and hair. She found it easier to wear a ball cap. It kept her hair cleaner and sometimes shielded her face from hot shell casings ejecting from the gun's chamber. She wore eye and ear protection, as did Scott and his uncle.

"It's one of the few rules we have here," said Scrag. "Don't want any injuries we can avoid. Gun safety is everyone's responsibility. Besides, it's embarrassing to get kicked out of this club. No one will ever let ya live it down."

They each staked out their place on the shooter's stand, arranged their magazines, boxes of bullets, and cleaning supplies. Johanna owned a 9 millimeter Sig Sauer 938 pistol. The quality of its German engineering was so precise, it was said, you could drop it on the ground and it would not accidentally fire. The coating on the Legion series allowed it to be immersed in water or dropped in mud and still function accurately.

Those were not the reasons she bought it at the gun shop. She liked its feel. She could wrap the fingers of her left hand securely around its trigger guard stabilizing the weapon's powerful kickback when fired. Its grip fit her hand so well she could easily re-aim for the next shot. Her hands were small, and she appreciated the placement of the magazine release button, which afforded her a one-handed discard, therefore she could quickly use the other hand to reload.

The Sig was semi-automatic. Meaning the shooter had to press the trigger for each shot as the spring- loaded magazine automatically popped another round in the chamber. It was limited to a seven round capacity which required re-inserting a new magazine after it fired seven times.

Scott and Scrag had already stapled some targets to the stands out on the shooting range. Hers, a classic bulls-eye target with concentric black and luminous yellow rings, was positioned about ten feet away, directly in front of her shooting stand.

Scott and Scrag set their targets upon posts a hundred yards down range. Scrag had brought his rifle with a mounted scope. Scott unpacked a 9 millimeter caliber Sig Sauer, p226 from his field bag. It was a full size Legion firearm favored by Navy Seals.

They shot their weapons at will and the sound of gunfire filled the air like a shooting gallery at a county fair, only a lot louder. The bursts died away as they reloaded. She focused her attention on the target, took aim, and pressed the trigger twice. Her gun instructor at the Sig Sauer Academy in New Hampshire trained his students to take a shot, hitting anywhere on the target, then placing the second shot inside the first hole. She shot seven rounds, pressed the magazine release and went to reload.

"Put your gun down." Scrag had come up behind her. She did so, placing its barrel in such a way that anyone could see it was unloaded.

"You would be a much better shot if you stopped anticipating the gunfire and closing your eyes," he said. "Can I help you out a bit?"

She nodded as Scott put his firearm down on the stand without re-loading to watch the lesson.

"You're afraid of your weapon. Imagine how more afraid you would be of an attacker. You need to make fear your ally," he said firmly.

Johanna respected his opinion and nodded, though she was skeptical fear would ever be on her side.

"You've heard the female of the species is deadlier than the male, right?" he continued. "For a man to kill, his fear has to become anger. If he acknowledges his fear, he knows he is already dead. He drops down into his anger and rage, knowing that's what it takes to defend his family. That's how gov'ments get eighteen year old boys to join up, ya know. They instill the idea they're gonna be heroes for defending their families and their country. They use the most primal instinct on the planet to turn boys who love their families and would defend them to the death into sharpshooting killers on command."

Johanna shifted uncomfortably. She looked at Scott. He shrugged.

"Now I know what you're are thinking, women aren't built like that. And ya might be correct. But right now you're terrified of your weapon and that can gitcha' killed. The two biggest obstacles to functioning under attack are the inability to use your firearm and your fear. Only your mindset can turn both of 'em into allies."

"Let me tell ya a story. There was a village under attack from the Vietcong and my recon team was on-point with orders to observe the hostility but not engage. An enemy soldier walked up to a village woman, a girl really, aimed his machine gun at her child. She grabbed a knife and ran at the guy. He mowed 'em both down."

Johanna felt tears burn at the corner of her eyes.

"I see your empathy," said Scrag. "This woman, like most villagers, was likely Buddhist. She prob'bly practiced compassion every day, pretty sure. But when the soldier threatened her baby, she dropped down into something more primal than anger. She became fearless. She automatically protected her child. It was the fiercest act of bravery I have ever seen."

"But they died."

"Look Johanna, you think your gentleness is not capable of harm," he said brusquely. "I beg to differ. The best trackers in the animal world are the females. They track and kill prey for their babies every day. From a panther to a sparrow, they bring the food. For many men hunting and killing can be a sport or a business, for the female it's driven. I ask you, Johanna, who becomes a more formidable adversary when food and babies are concerned?"

Johanna nodded.

"A woman will become a banshee if something threatens her loved ones but often becomes a paralyzed victim if they themselves are the target. Men defend - women protect. It's a different mindset. Wanna test my theory?"

"Sure," she responded, but her voice wavered with uncertainty.

"Scott, come and stand about three feet behind Johanna while I change out the target."

Scrag took down her bulls-eye target and moved the stand closer to the shooter's platform but not to improve her aim. He stapled a black, silhouetted target resembling the threatening outline of an intruder to the stand, then joined them behind the firing line.

"Your pistol is empty, Johanna. I want you to drop down and give me five pushups."

At Johanna's shocked look, he said, "fuckit, make em girlie pushups, I don't care."

"Smarty," she responded, then lowered herself to the ground and quickly performed a series of pushups.

"There's an intruder in your home," Scrag shouted, "Scott's down, he's been shot. Now jump up, load, rack, and fire two rounds at the threat."

Johanna leapt to her feet, popped the magazine in her Sig, racked it, and fired two rapid shots. There were no bullet holes in the target.

"Well that there's a bust." Scrag said, "The adrenaline gotcha. Think about it. Your mind knows this is a drill, but your fear is still affecting your aim. Remember, an attacker already has rage and anger on his side. You only have one defense: you go to the range and drill, drill, drill. You invent scenarios. You practice often and you carry your weapon all the time because it's your first ally."

She looked at Scott, thinking, *I can't walk around with a gun in my pants.*

"I know you can do this," Scrag said gruffly. "You have it in you, but you're actually more afraid of your own lethality than you are of your weapon. I've seen grown men, big ones, burly guys, cry like a baby when their face got hit with hot brass. They flinched whenever they aimed. I see you shoot, no flinch. Why hell, you get hit with brass in the face and you ignore it. There's a shell stuck on your neck right now. Don't tell me you can't protect against a threat. Let's try it again."

Johanna sighed, swiped the shell casing onto the ground, and stepped back up to the shooter's bench.

"Unload your weapon, pop the round out of the chamber, and put the mag on the table. Scott, come here." Scrag signaled him over and whispered.

Scott returned behind Johanna, but this time he dropped onto the ground.

"Same scenario, JoJo, but now I'm gonna time you. Give me a double tap, only. Try to put a second bullet in the first hole, just like you've been training." He pulled out his cell phone and set a timer.

"Go!" he shouted.

Johanna quickly dropped to the ground, did five push ups, jumped up, loaded her magazine, racked her pistol and aimed. Scott moaned. She fired twice.

There was a single hole in the target square in the middle of the hooded figure's silhouetted form.

"Put your weapon DOWN!" Scrag shouted. Johanna put her gun down on the stand, barrel pointed down range. "STEP AWAY from the platform." He retrieved the target while Scott stood up and dusted himself off.

Scott looked at it. Both rounds had entered the same hole. "Jesus, Johanna."

"Yep, sometimes even a blind squirrel can find a nut," said Scrag. "Can you do it again? And again? Up till now, all you've done is target practice. Woman, you are ready to drill and train."

"What was her time?" asked Scott.

"I started the timer when she reached for her pistol, five and a half seconds!"

"Fast enough."

"You have to learn to carry your weapon racked, Johanna, one in the chamber." said Scrag. "You may find five seconds is too slow to save your life. Remember, an attacker is always ready to shoot."

The smell of exploded gunpowder filled her nostrils with its sharp, metallic scent, the same smell that hung in the air after fireworks. Even through her ear protection, the sound of the muted gunfire still echoed in her ears. She had seen the blue flame burst out of the barrel as the bullets fired from the chamber at nearly twelve hundred feet per second. Her heart was racing. Not good.

Cleanup was quick as they wiped down their weapons, then packed and stowed all their gear in their field bags. Scrag passed around the residue wipes to remove gunpowder from their hands and faces. He and Scott took off their jacket outerwear and left them in the back of the Tahoe before heading to the picnic table. Johanna removed the khaki vest and put a woolen sweater on over her sweatshirt.

Scrag broke into the cooler and took out some turkey subs, leaving the veggie wraps for Scott and Johanna.

"Ya did good, JoJo," he said, reaching for the 'strong ++' thermos.

Scott sat next to Johanna and hugged her shoulder. She passed the wraps and snacks to him. She was more quiet than usual, lost in thoughts about her own capacity to be lethal. A history of rebellion and insurrection wove through her Scot's ancestry like the dyed strands in their wool tartan plaids. Her father's people from the Hebridean Isles always blamed their Viking blood for the momentary flash of temper that seemed to dwell in their lineage.

She believed it needed to be vanquished. But as a psychologist, she knew the ultimate price of suppression was costly. So she practiced meditation, not to quell her impulses, but to inform and transcend them. Target-shooting was an acceptable rationalization she felt she could manage. Training to shoot another person was a different matter. Making fear her ally seemed beyond her capability. Fear was primal, automatic.

"Most people," Scrag said, interrupting her thoughts, "they come to a range, shoot a box of rounds and call it a day. But others, they're serious about improving their skills, sharpening their minds."

"Heightened fear can become heightened situational awareness under the right conditions," said Scott. "Becoming intentionally aware of your surroundings is a good thing. You can avoid deadly events by knowing when to not be around them."

"It's like the first level of Aikido," said Scrag, "Train so you don't need the last and most lethal level. All martial arts have a basis in meditation and contemplation. No kidding, those Kung Fu Buddhist monks could deal a death blow in the blink of an eye!"

"You need to learn to smell danger and get focused," added Scott.

"I don't know if I could actually kill someone," responded Johanna. She set her mug of 'strong' coffee on the picnic table.

"You're not a sociopath or a mercenary, JoJo. They kill," said Scrag. "You aren't a cop or a soldier, they defend. You are a kind and caring person. If ya say the word 'kill,' ya won't be able to aim your weapon at another human being. What you are really doing is stopping the threat."

"How horrible, Scrag, for you to see that girl and her child blown apart."

"I saw many people blown apart, JoJo. Hell, I blew people apart. I had body parts blown on me. Once, I survived by hiding under the blown apart bodies of my friends. War is horrible, Johanna. Don't let anyone tell you it isn't. They're liars. I hunted men, and I killed them."

"I am so sorry," Johanna said.

Scott got up from the picnic table and took the cooler back to the Tahoe.

"Tell the truth?" said Scrag, his voice lowered. "What nobody knows is me and that damned Scotsman, Bruce, had an agreement. If the gov'ment still drafted boys for cannon fodder when Scott turned eighteen, I was to drive him to the Canadian border before he could sign up for selective service. There is a river crossing we all know about. Kincaid would be on t'other side, take Scott, and he'd never set foot in this country again. Sometimes, the appearance of animosity is a cover-story for an unholy alliance."

She didn't find the other brass casing that had dropped down her shirt and stuck to her breast until later.

A Proper Cup of Tea

It was a three-hour drive from Belfast on the coast to Maine's inland lakes and mountains region. Johanna drove nearly due west for about two hours before the road turned in a northerly direction. The state bordered New Hampshire on what was fondly called its "west coast" by Mainers. Yet Tiadaghton was far enough north that the western edge of Maine was a boundary of mountains between Canada and the United States.

Norah and Nathan's homestead was nestled in the shadows of Mount Katahdin. They could see its snowcapped peaks in the distance from the high meadows behind their home. Johanna was very near the turnoff exit to the county road that led to the small town of Tiadaghton. Minerva's Meadows was on its outskirts along the Carrabec River. She and Scott worried about Norah because of its remoteness now that she lived alone.

To Johanna's knowledge, her friend's only remaining family was Nathan's mother and his two siblings, a brother, and a sister, and their families. Norah and Nathan had no children of their own and her parents, the Jordans, had passed away years ago.

Norah Jordan-Minsky's doctorate in botany had led her to do groundbreaking field work in ethno-botanical traditions which had resulted in her popular book about indigenous plant medicine. She introduced Johanna to Nathan many years ago when she was a keynote speaker on sustainable agriculture at the Common Ground Fair. Johanna had taken one of Norah's classes in eco-psychology. She had attended the fair at her instructor's invitation.

After the presentation, while Norah attended a question-and-answer session, Nathan and Johanna waited for her in a local coffee shop. One of the first things she learned about Nathan was he not only admired his wife, he adored her. Her brilliant mind did not intimidate him. In fact, he told Johanna over an espresso; it utterly captivated him.

"How did the two of you meet?" She remembered asking him.

Nathan had leaned back in his chair and glanced out the cafe's red checker curtained window for a moment as he gathered his thoughts. "It was at the University of Maine in the fall of 1970. They were drafting young men into the Army for the Vietnam War. It was a scary time. I was a senior majoring in engineering with a business minor. I had an early acceptance at Harvard to complete my MBA. It was Norah's junior year, but she was already involved in writing her thesis. She was a botany major back then and had just taken a class in ecology."

"Understand it was a brand new course offering," he had continued, sipping his espresso. "The first Earth Day celebration had only just occurred a few months before in April. She was excited about the prospects for the future. She wanted in on the ground level. I had never met a woman so passionate about her work before, other than my grandmother."

"Don't tell me you were a hippie!"

Conservatively dressed in a casual suit and tie, his carriage and demeanor gave an impression of an impeccably dressed executive who presided over multi-million dollar business deals. He had a calm and focused demeanor that exuded confidence and success.

"I wouldn't go that far, but worn-out, patched jeans, t-shirts, sandals and long hair were standard wear, for the times," he laughed. "There was a protest at the campus ROTC building that day. Word had gone out to show up on the protest line with signs opposing the idea of taking war classes for credit. Lots of students showed solidarity by simply skipping class."

He continued, "No one wanted another Kent State situation with the National Guard, so we accepted that if you didn't join the protest, you would just head to Lucerne Lake. I carried an Army issue canvas backpack filled with a bottle of cheap wine, a loaf of bread, and a block of cheese to share with friends at the park. There was no way I was going to lose a chance at Harvard by getting arrested."

The waitress came to the table, and Johanna had ordered a second coffee. Nathan raised one eyebrow quizzically and smiled at her.

He had a rakish grin she remembered as she drove the Subaru onto the exit ramp and continued for several miles on a well-traveled thoroughfare. He had been an attractive man, personable and kind. Norah had described him as a genius with numbers and with an uncanny ability to predict which investments would be successful and which would not. Gentle with the people he loved, he had the reputation of being formidable in the boardroom. For all his financial acumen he was, she had said, admirably honest, with a level of integrity that dwarfed other men's.

The country road came to an intersection at a four-way stop. A sign informed her that the town of Tiadaghton was to the right. She turned the car in the other direction and continued driving. Tall pine trees lined both sides of the winding back road. The air was much cooler here and she could feel the elevation rising slightly over the miles as she drove. Her thoughts turned back to Nathan's story.

"I was walking by the chemistry building when this girl came stumbling out of the bushes by an entrance door. I will never forget the look on her face. I was the last thing she expected to see."

"Norah?"

"Oh yeah. She had sneaked into the labs to rerun a botched experiment defying the class walkouts. She thought the coast was clear and suddenly there I was, a witness to her defection."

"I asked if she wanted to join me at the park so she could say that was where she had been if anyone challenged her. She agreed. I never met up with my friends that day," he said, looking out the window again.

"We started talking. The more I learned about her, the more I wanted to know. I think I fell in with her over a bottle of Mateus and a loaf of bread," he said softly. "She was passionate about studying ecology. It was a perfect combination with her study of botany. I remember watching her face light up as she talked about her thesis. Like today, at the podium, she still loves to talk about cultivating traditional plants and herbs."

"She's brilliant, you know," Nathan added wistfully. "She's socially awkward, it's true, but I adore her mind."

What he meant was that Norah was often oblivious to social cues and had an unusually authoritative manner of conversing that was occasionally off-putting.

"Numbers speak to her," he said with admiration in his voice. "She sees things in patterns and layers. She can analyze how objects or ideas fit together or oppose one another. She understands their form and function with a far greater breadth of association than other people can. And she has an encyclopedic memory."

"You're a numbers person too, aren't you?"

"Yes, of course," he laughed. "I think that's why we got on so well at first. Then there were the times, the state of the country being at war. She was passionate about scientific truth. I wanted to make the world a better place."

"Wasn't that your generation's cultural view?"

"It was more than that for me," he said in a somber tone. "I'm alive because my grandfather was an intuitive businessman who survived the holocaust by leaving Germany well before Hitler sent people like me to the concentration camps. He disagreed with the monetary policies of the Weimar government."

"My grandfather persuaded my grandmother to leave their home," he continued, "and travel half a world away because he believed they were on the brink of catastrophe. Their families thought he was a fool. But his discernment and business acumen turned what seemed to be a mistake into a substantial family fortune, not to mention escaping the rise of the Nazi regime and the holocaust.

"You're Jewish?"

"Yes. I had to register for the draft in the late 60s like all the other guys my age. My grandfather impressed upon my brother Samuel and myself to use our minds to further our education or else we would end up cannon fodder. He told us the family legacy depended on our contributions."

"What a choice!"

"If you were enrolled in college, you qualified for a deferment, so you weren't as likely to get sent to Vietnam. In my case, getting an education was a matter of survival. It impressed upon me the severity of the situation. I couldn't afford to be a protestor or a college dropout."

"It was a tough time for an entire generation," Johanna remembered saying.

"That's why Norah was such a sparkling light in a dismal world. War and death hovered over us all, and yet she was excited about a new world of sustainable living on an abundant planet. The overwhelming confusion, drugs, constant rioting and violence did not daunt her. In a world profiting from the development of plastics and chemical products that poisoned the earth, she wanted to forge a road to sustainable solutions using science rather than an empty philosophy of greed. We waited til she got her doctorate to get married. Dr. Jordan. She worked so hard for it. She continues to inspire me."

He had glanced out the window again. Johanna would never forget seeing his face when he glimpsed Norah across the street. His eyes grew soft, and he smiled with a warmth that was reserved solely for the willowy woman walking toward the cafe.

Even now, in her seventies, Johanna thought, Norah had a way of walking through a space as if every muscle in her body moved with fluid purpose. She was decisive in her motions but as graceful as a dancer. Her expressive face constantly revealed the changing temperature of her thoughts and moods. She was the epitome of intelligence and integrity, which was probably the source of a great deal of professional jealousy from those who tried to compete with her meteoric nature. Johanna suspected she didn't have a mean bone in her entire body and didn't understand anyone who did.

As long as Johanna had known them, Norah was passionate about ecological sustainability and Nathan's passion in life was reserved for her. How could such a powerful and loving man as Nathan Minsky be gone so soon from a world that sorely needed his kind?

The road crested as she drove around a curve, and suddenly the forested road dropped away to reveal a spectacular view on the right. A snow cragged mountain ridge in the distance rose like a translucent mirage from the plains of a wide valley. The bright morning sky was cerulean blue, capped with white cumulus clouds that gathered along the Katahdin range as if they were snagged on its sharp peaks.

A brilliant morning sun illuminated the glittering edges of those clouds and bathed the south basin in a halo of golden light. Mirrored lakes splashed across the floor of the valley like sparkling gems.

Even more stunning was its uninhabited wild terrain. Perhaps the valley was too rugged to build on, too remote for even the hardiest of homeowners to consider or simply too fierce to be tamed by men, she reflected.

A steep rock face on the left side of the road rose sharply with small rivulets of runoff water cascading over its sides, plunging into a deep culvert. Johanna inhaled as if she could take the ancient landscape into her body. She wished she could share the gentle sense of peace and wild beauty she was feeling this moment with Scott. Though she had been out this way before, many times, the contour of the land never failed to stir her soul.

She saw the sign for Minerva's Meadows Herb and Tea Gardens ahead. It hung from a post that allowed it to swing freely. The familiar white flower with dark green leaves that curled around the edges of the gold lettering gave the entire logo the appearance of vitality and growth. She would have to remember to ask Norah what kind of flower was depicted on the sign.

The access road was on the left, winding its way up the steep mountainside. Within moments, she passed the first garden with its autumnal yellow, orange and white chrysanthemums. She could see an old stone wishing well, in the distance, beyond the trimmed boxwood bushes that bordered the driveway. Rose bushes, still in bloom, and meandering stone walkways led to the ornamental gardens. She had never viewed the gardens and thought she might explore them on this trip.

Mina created the original landscape designs. It had taken years to build the scree and rock gardens while cultivating all the plantings. Norah told her Mina had planted ornamental flowers of ever blooming seasons of colors based on the planting instructions from the family garden book she had brought with her from Germany.

She said it was an honor to restore the gardens and to add plantings of her own. Johanna had never met Mina Minsky, but she suspected she and Norah were kindred spirits.

The herb shed, greenhouse and barn were on her left as the driveway ended in a wide parking area for guest tours. She parked the Subaru by the barn and looked at the familiar homestead farm on the right side of the property. The single floor, ranch style homestead was originally built in the 1920s and was later partially renovated by Nathan.

It stood quite a distance away from the barn and outbuildings, making use of an expansive lawn to create privacy from the business operation. There was a small sign pointing the way to a rock strewn mossy path she knew led to the mountainside wildflower meadows. At this point, the carefully cultivated gardens ended and a wild, natural world began.

Field upon field of wildflower pollinators grew here, ever repopulating themselves and giving way to the absolute wisdom of nature. This was Norah's crowning achievement. Yet few visitors cared to leave the cultivated beauty of the ornamental gardens to discover the lands for which they named the farm.

The medicinal tea gardens grew within the wild meadows of the higher elevations. Lavender fields with meadowsweet, feverfew and camomile blended with calendula that burst with seeds in the fall and were carried by the winds perpetually replenishing the earth's own pharmacy. There were Minsky lands for as far as the eye could see on this side of the road, down to the river, up over the mountain meadows and across the right of way. A dynasty had begun here in this tranquil yet rugged slice of land.

She had come to the farm a few times in the summer months over the years and at least once during the winter for a ski weekend on the cross-county trails behind their property. But she couldn't remember a single time she had visited in autumn.

She texted Scott; '*arrived*' before gathering up her backpack. As Johanna closed the car door, a light wind blew through the yard, skittering autumn leaves in a swirl that spun around her legs. *Ah, she thought, the Wind Sisters are here.*

"For a shaman," her indigenous friend Angelique had long ago instructed her, "there are no unintended connections. Spirit communicates by using natural means. Pay attention or you will miss it."

The particular connections she referred to had a sensory feeling attached to their appearances. In the beginning of her shaman apprenticeship, the unmistakable sensations were both startling and uncomfortable. But now, they were like old friends weaving through her life, side by side, with normal human experiences.

She retrieved a small gift box of elderberry and sea-berry juices from the car seat and walked toward the back gate. The house was built at an angle to the driveway, the front door and hydrangea-lined porch faced the main road. In spring and summer, the grounds literally burst with blooms and colors, but now they were simply green fading into brown or leafless branches. The back entrance faced toward the steep slope of the mountain that rose behind the property. Visitors always went to the front entrance, while guests knew to go to the back.

The gate opened into Norah's backyard, which was bordered by a ten foot high lilac hedge enclosing her private gardens. Johanna walked along the paved walkway which led to the brick patio and kitchen door. When he was a child, as the story went, Nathan had named his grandmother's backyard, The Secret Garden.

In the spring, snowdrops bloomed first all along the pathway, then after them, a row of yellow daffodils would soon follow. After their brief season passed, it was a row of bright red tulips that would rise to complete the pathway's magical carpet of color. The effect was a gradual widening of the path as flowers burst into bloom.

Though the spring and summer flowers had long since passed, she could still see why a child might have felt such a place was full of wonders. Once the pathway burst into color, the branches of the forsythia bushes would turn sun-drenched yellow before fading back into their leafy green robes. Then the French lilacs would arrive; towering perimeters affording a backdrop of color for the rest of the garden. Each spring Norah gathered spires of fragrant purple blossoms with their signature scent as bouquets to sell in the local farm market.

Lush pink peony bushes along the lilac hedge marked the beginning of early summer, with their soft petals appearing to flutter tenderly in the breezes. As the summer progressed, the Moon Garden would take center stage. White Arabian Jasmine and splashes of color from the petals of the Four O'Clocks grew at its base while vines of pale blue morning glories spun up the lattice, intertwining like secret lovers with white moonflowers that bloomed in the dark of night. It made for heady scents under the evening stars, Johanna remembered.

Off to the side, closest to the patio, a tiered rock garden was still producing kitchen herbs; marjoram, chocolate mint, chive, tarragon, rosemary and lemon basil grew with a cheery yellow marigold border to keep insects at bay. Nathan had installed a small waterfall that splashed down the rocks and irrigated the herb garden when needed. The source of the waterfall's benevolence was a rain barrel situated under the back eves of the farmhouse and a stone paved channel that ran like a stream-bed to the top of the rock garden. The soothing effect had reminded her of the rain chain that hung in the gardens of Elk Run.

Norah's autumn flowers now graced her private gardens before the season would unfold into winter. A just bloomed sea of Montauk Daisies quivered in the gentle, cool wind that filtered through the backyard.

There was a break in the lilac hedge forming a natural opening that led to the vegetable gardens beyond and wild flower meadows up on the hillside. A few years ago, Nathan began reconstructing the vegetable gardens into a series of raised bed plantings with gravel walkways and deer fencing. It was to be the beginning of a farm overhaul to help compensate for their aging bodies.

As Norah had told her, the days of bending and crouching to tend the vegetable garden would soon end. Johanna hoped to see their modifications as Elk Run Farm was becoming more physically demanding each year.

Norah waved as she opened the kitchen door. The two women hugged one another and Norah sank into her arms. In that moment of intimacy, Johanna sensed her friend's depth of sadness and relief at her arrival. She felt Norah surrender herself to a will greater than her own that demanded she carry on despite her loss.

Johanna had a reputation of being exceedingly kind and patient with her clients without a single strand of judgment. Known for her genuine sincerity, she met her clients with encouragement and acceptance. Wherever they were in their journey of recovery, she held a space of deep healing.

Johanna also had the gift of Second Sight, as her grandmother termed it. It gave her unexpected insights into situations that had proven useful in her clinical practice. She used these abilities skillfully and her clients thrived in her healing environment as much as Norah's flowers thrived in the rich soil that nurtured them.

With her friends, Johanna combined those therapeutic skills with affection and familiarity. These were qualities Norah both recognized and needed. Many people did not realize vulnerability was the true strength behind their adaptability. Unlike many trees whose branches whipped around in a storm, the willow could bend dramatically without breaking. Powerful emotions could be tolerated without snapping a person's mind if one knew how to harness their wisdom.

Yet Johanna could feel Norah was close to breaking. She smiled gently as she handed her friend the gift box of berry juices and entered the kitchen.

Norah sighed as tears welled up in her eyes. A moment of fragility gave way to a sense of purpose. For all her losses and disappointments, Norah Jordan-Minsky had a lot to live for.

"I've water boiling in the kettle and I baked lemon-walnut muffins," the older woman said. "Thank you for this!"

She placed the gift box on the counter.

"Come, choose a tea and sit at the table!"

A wide pine farm table stood in front of the bay window. It afforded a stunning view of the backyard gardens. There was a shelf by the old gas stove with rows of Mason jars, each bearing a name of a Minerva's Meadows specialty tea.

Johanna chose a Jasmine and Wild Bergamot blend along with a Royal Albert bone china teacup from the glass-fronted tea cabinet. This was a well-practiced ritual with which Johanna had often taken part throughout their years of friendship.

Norah placed a plate of fragrant muffins on the table.

"I baked some dandelion bread yesterday. Try a slice with some rose petal jam. I am trying out some new recipes. If they are good enough, I am adding them to the food section of Mina's garden book."

Norah chose a blend of nettle leaf, ashwagandha and lemongrass for herself, then handed Johanna a small metal strainer to brew her tea. She went over to the tea chest and selected a Wedgwood Hummingbird design china teacup and saucer.

For as long as Johanna had known her, Norah continued to add fine bone china teacups and dessert plates to her collection. The translucent fine china tea-ware included such delicate designs as flowers and birds hand painted by generations of artists adept at crafting scenes. From the Wedgwood Wanderlust series with names such as Emerald Forest, Waterlilies, Pink Lotus to its famous Royal Albert Old Country Rose teacups and the gold-rimmed Hummingbird and Wild Strawberry collection, Norah's tea chest was full of vintage, elegant tea-ware.

"Anything new?" Johanna nodded toward the tea chest as the older woman poured boiling water through the tea strainers. Norah looked wistfully at her tea chest and shook her head sadly.

She referred to the things she collected, such as the tea-ware, out of print books, Bauhaus furniture and abstract geometric art as her 'special interests.' Her home was a unique blend of the odd and unusual. She collected both objects and information, making her an inexhaustible expert in her areas of interest.

Nathan had always enjoyed the contradictions between the austere Bauhaus furniture with its earth tones, wood and metal construction that were juxtaposed with the large art paintings with their vibrant hues of orange and blue, yellow, red and purple geometric forms. Johanna remembered when he bought Norah a numbered print of a huge Georgia O'Keefe poppy. He joked it took her a month to get used to it because it did not feature any hard geometric lines. Now hanging over the sofa in their living room, the scarlet petaled painting dominated the room.

Norah joined the younger woman at the table, spreading some rose petal jam on a slice of dandelion bread, while waiting for their tea to steep.

"I'm so glad you have come," she said. "So much has been happening that I don't know where to start."

"Let's just visit over these fabulous muffins and jam, like old times. I have never eaten dandelion bread before. Who knew dandelions were edible? I have heard of rose hip jelly but not rose petal jam," said Johanna as she tasted the bread and jam.

"Yes, let's!" Norah sighed with relief. "Let's have a proper cup of tea." They sipped their teas and talked about the food section of Mina's garden book.

"Playing with new recipes is keeping me on my toes and not dwelling on Nathan. I can just see him rolling his eyes over the dandelion bread," she said with a laugh.

"It's delicious! So like you, Norah, to serve something so homey as lemon walnut muffins along with bread made with weeds!"

"Ah, but one person's weed is another person's wildflower."

"The Jasmine-Bergamot tea is perfect. I know the benefits of nettle tea, but what is ashwagandha?"

"Well, as you know," began Norah, "nettle is an immune strengthener, and it's packed with vitamins. Ashwagandha root is an adaptogenic. Its scientific name is *Withania somnifera*. I grow it here on the farm, dry it in the dehydrators and grind it up. It helps the adrenal system. Too much cortisol due to stress, and it serves to lower the strain on the autonomic nervous system. Too much fatigue and burnout, and it can help revive the adrenals. Ayurvedic medicine has been using it for thousands of years to manage stress and anxiety, but western scientific literature has shown it useful in reducing inflammation."

"Your Mason jars just name the ingredients. Do your product labels explain their benefits?"

"We are not allowed to make claims of medical benefits. We can, however, suggest how they have been used in traditional settings. It helps to have my credentials on the official website as an ethno-botanical researcher."

"I always put a teaspoon in my coffee maker with a little cinnamon," she continued. "Nathan loved the taste of the coffee brewed with ashwagandha. He said it was a necessary prelude before analyzing financial statements. But I think he was putting me on."

"Well, the rose petal jam on dandelion bread is a real hit," said Johanna. "Nathan would have loved it."

Norah smiled and leaned back in her chair.

She had not changed a single thing in their home since Nathan's death. The kitchen was exactly the same, perhaps because of its efficient design, thought Johanna for a moment. But the rest of the house was as it always had been. Norah had not rearranged anything. Nothing had been added or removed.

Johanna knew from her years as a practicing psychotherapist, there were many ways to adapt to the loss of a life partner. Many of those left behind removed all signs of their partner's life. Changing wallpaper and furnishings and giving away their loved one's clothing put painful daily reminders at a safe distance. For some people, it was often easier to deal with loss by creating dramatic changes in their living arrangements. This, they felt, was the only way they could move forward with their lives.

Some, like Norah, left everything just the way it was while their partner was still alive. It was as if they needed to feel their loved one had just left the room and would soon return. There was no right or wrong way to manage grief, Johanna mused, but denial was a definitely a much longer road to acceptance.

The constant reminders of personal items, clothing, and frequent use of their loved one's name in conversation seemed to many people a sign of unnecessarily prolonged grief. Yet, Johanna knew it was that very devotion that had the power of making acceptance even more attainable. People who were willing to dwell so acutely in their loss could often sustain a bond with their beloved that surpassed the apparent finality of death.

Many years ago, Angelique had said of her people's beliefs, "it is said, after death, the spirit remains to help with the healing." But even with her gift of Second Sight, Johanna could not feel Nathan's presence. She worried about Norah's isolation here on the farm. It was good she was there to listen to her friend's longing reminiscences about her dearest love.

"My in-laws think I'm peculiar," said Norah. "Nathan always used to say he loved my oddness. It built character for those who had to deal with me. He said it with great affection."

"You have always been singularly unique," responded Johanna. "It's part of your charm."

"When I speak, I am describing images I see in my mind," Norah confided. "I thought everyone saw things in their heads. I even see the letters of the words I am speaking. I've been told it's bothersome to people when I don't get to the point right away. But I am simply describing what I see."

"I've attended your lectures. You are concise and yet always blend a story into your presentations. People get the entire picture!"

"But that's the problem, you see. When people ask a question, I assume they want the answer. In a class setting, this works rather well. But in social situations, I just can't find the right ratio of facts to pleasantries!"

"I totally understand," laughed Johanna. "You are the consummate professor. Try being a therapist. When people ask me about human behavior in a social setting, I practically have to pinch myself so I don't launch into some insightful theoretical explanation. They really want the short version."

"What's a short version?" Norah chuckled. "Nathan was my saving grace. He always jumped in at family gatherings and interjected with 'do you really want to know?' That let everyone off the hook, me included. He was tired of seeing their eyes glaze over when I provided some unappreciated depth of explanation."

"He was your champion, Norah. He loved you so much."

"I know," the older woman responded softly. "I never knew sorrow could cut the edges of your heart like a razor blade."

The two women sat silently for several moments with their individual sadnesses. One woman's loss now in reparation and the other's poised perilously close to the silvery edges of despair.

"But these days I'm afraid it's way beyond missing social cues. It's my memory that worries me. I think it's going."

"How so?"

"Somehow, earlier this week," Norah related, "I misread an invitation to my mother-in-law's annual garden party. I honestly thought it said to reply by phone. But she never answered, so my participation wasn't confirmed. They turned me away on the day of the event. She had to get another speaker. I always attended and gave a botanical presentation, you see. When I got home, I re-read the card. It clearly stated to reply by email. How did I get that wrong?"

"Wait," interjected Johanna. "No one in your family contacted you to see why you hadn't confirmed?"

"No. There is more. A few months ago, I clearly remember throwing a charity solicitation letter in the trash. Then a month later, I found I made a donation for over a thousand dollars to that same organization. It appeared in my credit card statement. I have no recollection of doing that. It wasn't even a charity I would have supported."

"It goes on," she continued. "I keep losing the keys to the farmhouse, but never the herb shed. The last time I had Don at the hardware store, make me five copies of the kitchen door keys. Two weeks later, they were all gone. Can't find them anywhere. Is this how your mind slips away?"

"You have lived a very healthy lifestyle for many years. You've used herbal medicines and homeopathy rather than overly relying on prescription medicines," Johanna said thoughtfully. "The type of memory loss you are worried about is caused by inflammation in the brain. Your body likely has little inflammation compared to many others your age. I think this is just a sign of normal aging."

"I know," said Norah, "but stress plays a big role in memory retrieval and I certainly have been through a lot. I question my ability to step up to the helm of the Minsky Legacy Trust. Even though Nathan named me his successor trustee, Eli Mittleman has taken the interim role."

"Who is Eli Mittleman?"

"Eli is the son of Mina's youngest brother, Ari. He is in his eighties, now. Ari was Albert's choice for trustee, which, according to Nathan, royally annoyed his own father at the time. But he was Albert's right-hand man and groomed to run the legacy businesses. He was the obvious choice. He named his own son, Eli, to take over in later years."

"Eli tutored Nathan, because Albert named him the successor trustee, when Eli retired," she continued. "Nathan has been including me in all the decision making ever since he took over."

"Does Eli think you are ready?"

"Yes. He meets with me monthly to go over the books and discuss business strategies. Last month he said I should announce my trustee position at a family board meeting. The entire structure is very complex. I simply can't see myself functioning as trustee if I can't even remember where I put my keys."

"There are layers to memory issues, many of which are simply age related but are not any indication of dementia," offered Johanna. "We need to account for the quality of your sleep, for example."

"Lately it's been fitful."

"Memory consolidation occurs at night during deeper levels of sleep. Let's start there. Improve depth of sleep and if you see improvement, well, that's it then," said Johanna confidently. "There's nothing wrong with your long-term memory, I can assure you."

"Maybe I should use my own sleep enhancement tea blend," said Norah with a laugh. "Valerian and sweet violet in a green tea base that has L-theanine."

"Doesn't that increase alpha waves?"

"Yes, it does, and the valerian helps relax the mind."

"Alpha waves are the first stage of sleep, so that's a plus!"

Johanna smiled at the older woman. She had her own concerns about her friend's emotional stability, but memory wasn't one of them. There was a big difference between forgetfulness under stressful situations and the onset of dementia. A signature diagnostic feature of the first was knowing one had forgotten something and the struggle to recall it. In dementia, one didn't even know one had forgotten something and as the disease progressed, one no longer recognized the names of familiar objects or people. As far as running a business was concerned, mild cognitive deficit was more an annoyance than a diminished capacity to perform.

"I suppose I should use my relaxing bath bombs, too," Norah said. "I make them with magnesium and essential oils."

"Bath bombs?"

Neither woman had heard the Range Rover pull into the driveway, but they both heard the knock on the front door.

"Who could that be?" Norah said as she stood up. Looking out the side window, she smiled. "It's Samuel, Nathan's brother. He always comes to the front."

Norah opened the door as Johanna stood behind her. A tall, distinguished older man entered. He was slender with an athletic build and casually dressed in a pair of beige slacks with a powder blue Polo sports shirt under an expensive leather jacket.

"I was on my way to town and I thought I'd drop by to see if you needed anything," he smiled, looking directly at Norah. "I'm sorry. I didn't know you had guests."

He looked at Johanna as if just noticing her presence, though he had clearly parked by her car.

"This is Johanna Kincaid, an old and dear friend of ours. She was a student long ago, but we have become very close over the years. Johanna, this is Samuel, Nathan's younger brother."

A shadow of consternation flickered briefly across his face before he stepped forward to shake Johanna's hand vigorously.

"It's kind of you to visit. She has been going through a difficult time."

Johanna returned his handshake with a smile as sensations flooded her body. Though she could see a vague resemblance, she immediately realized he seemed to be a very different person than his brother. He was far more reserved, his posture more stiff and formal than Nathan's more easygoing, calm and confident demeanor.

"Johanna came to help me complete the fall orders and cover over the last of the gardens. She has extensive garden experience. She will be here for several weeks," responded Norah. "Come join us for some tea."

"Sure, if your guest doesn't mind my intrusion."

"Not at all," said Johanna, "it's nice to finally meet another member of the Minsky family."

"We are a complicated lot."

He removed his jacket and draped it over an armchair that was, in Johanna's memory, the one Nathan always favored. He followed them into the kitchen, where he sat in the chair that had been Nathan's place at the table. Johanna watched Norah's shoulders tighten and heard her shallow intake of breath as she retrieved a mug from a kitchen cabinet.

"What would you like, tea or coffee?" she asked.

"You know me. Just coffee and light cream."

As she turned on the coffeemaker, her brother-in-law addressed Johanna.

"Where are you from, if you don't mind my asking?"

"Well, originally from Maine. But my husband and I own an off-grid solar farm in Cross Fork. The Wilds of Pennsylvania. We make organic elderberry syrup and sea-berry juice."

"Married?" He said unnecessarily.

She nodded, wondering where this peculiar conversation was going. She thought he was merely being protective of his brother's wife, but her gut instinctively tightened for reasons she could not explain.

Norah handed Samuel a cup of freshly brewed coffee and sat down at the table.

"She is too modest. Johanna is a retired clinical psychologist. She worked for many years at The Glen in the Berkshires. It's a health and healing spa for the rich and famous."

"I've heard of it. Never been, myself. That must have been an interesting career, being privy to the secrets of world dignitaries and celebrities."

"I wouldn't put it quite like that," Johanna said, sipping her tea. "It was a very meaningful time in my life. I am as passionate about human behavior as Norah is about regenerative agriculture and medicinal plant traditions."

He nodded casually, as if he had suddenly lost interest. Then turned his gaze to Norah.

"I heard there was a mixup at Mother's garden gala. I'm sorry Eliana treated you so harshly. "

"It was very distressing," she responded, nodding her head. "I was so sure I needed to confirm to Evelyn by phone."

"After that incident, Mother set up her new voice mail greeting right away so it wouldn't happen to anyone else," he said kindly. "I'm really glad Nathan devised the franchising plan for the Minerva's Meadows brand. It was the right time to sell the idea, so the bulk of all that work wasn't on you."

"It was ingenious." Norah turned to Johanna. "Nathan created a business plan in which some items in his grandmother's garden book could be farmed out to other businesses under the Minerva's Meadows label. It generates exclusive rights for some of those products."

"How does it work?" asked Johanna.

"For example," she replied, "when it's perfected, I will add the rose petal jam recipe to Minerva's Meadows Chutney, Jam and Jelly line. A woman in Bangor owns a wholesale business making jams and jellies. She bought the exclusive rights to use our label. She has access to all of Mina's jelly and jam recipes as well as mine. Her company will produce them in bulk. The Minerva's Meadows Trust receives ten percent of gross sales in perpetuity. If she drops the line or goes out of business, the Trust takes back the label and all its rights."

"That is quite a forward looking strategy."

"Are you going to offer the tea blends for franchise this year?" asked Samuel. "I am happy to draw up the agreements for you."

Norah smiled. "I might be ready to do that. It's kind of you to offer. But please, no gratis. Nathan would want you to be paid."

"Of course he would have insisted. I would have expected nothing less from Nathan," Samuel nodded and he leaned in toward his sister-in-law.

Johanna observed the lines around his mouth and the muscles on his forehead tightening. His gesture implied agreement, but his face implied conflict. Years of biofeedback with her clients drew her precise attention to muscle tension and expressive body language.

"Do you practice intellectual property law?" she asked.

"Business law such as contracts, trusts, wills and real estate law, mainly. I can do intellectual property agreements in that mix."

His monotone voice sounded disinterested with the discussion, she noted, but with Norah, his entire demeanor changed. He became animated. She sipped her Jasmine-Bergamot tea and leaned back in her chair as all her observational skills went into high gear.

"I recommend you increase the initial cost to franchise the rights to the Tea Garden label. It's a much bigger line that has had a great deal more sales exposure throughout the years." He finished his coffee. "Nathan sold the rights to the Jams and Jelly line cheap at $50,000, thinking the percent of sales would be the bulk of the income."

Norah was listening intently. She leaned forward as he spoke and nodded. Samuel smiled and nodded in return.

"I recommend you offer exclusive label rights to Minerva's Meadows Herbal Tea line for half a million dollars with a 1% annual profit percentage. Then we court Lipton, Bigelow and Celestial Seasonings for the buy. See who nibbles first."

"I need to think about that, Samuel. Nathan made sure the deals required a commitment to non-GMO, organic and sustainably sourced ingredients. He felt we could not trust the big commercial players to honor that."

"I can review his wording to ensure that requirement is stated precisely."

"Who verifies the quality of the ingredients in the end product?" asked Johanna.

Norah smiled and reached across the table for Johanna's hand. "Nathan believed in doing business with people who had honest reputations. He valued trust in business agreements and always honored a handshake. But he was no one's fool. He did his due diligence as well. He retained the right to an independent quality control lab that randomly validates the contents to be free of contaminants both genetically and chemically."

"As I remember," Samuel interjected, "the consequences of falling afoul of that requirement resulted in a stiff penalty and losing the label rights."

"Wow," responded Johanna. "He thought of everything."

Samuel stood up. "I should be going. Let me know what you decide. I say, go for the big potatoes with the same restrictions."

"I will think about it." Norah stood up from the table to see her brother-in-law to the door.

"I need to get my duffle bag," said Johanna. "This is as good a time as any." She followed them to the front door.

"Thanks for being concerned and for all your suggestions, Samuel. I know you are thinking of me and how much work I am facing. It's a good idea, and I am sure we can come up with a plan."

Samuel and Johanna went out into the driveway as Norah closed the front door against the brisk wind that blew across the driveway.

Johanna opened the Crosstrek's back hatch and pulled out her canvas duffle bag and yoga mat. Samuel rested his hand on his driver's side door, then turned to her.

"Do you have a minute, Johanna?"

"Yes, of course." She placed her things on the driveway and walked over to the luxurious steel gray Range Rover.

"I know you are a friend and you know Norah very well. But we are very concerned about her state of mind, her mental health. She has changed since we lost Nathan. I understand that profound grief can account for a lot. It's been over a year since Nathan died. Surely by now…" his voice dropped away.

"A loss like that changes everything," Johanna offered. "There is so much to get used to and it's all new. If you are asking my professional opinion, I can only say she is right where she should be."

"It's just that she isn't the person she was before. She is forgetful. She often seems confused. We were thinking she might benefit from an evaluation. Having someone like you here to both help and observe is a good thing."

"Thanks for your confidence, but I can tell you that grief has its own path. It's different for everyone. She is just finding her way in a world without Nathan."

He nodded and smiled as he opened the vehicle door.

"I'm sorry for your loss, Samuel. Your brother was a good man."

"Everyone thought highly of him," he responded after a moment of silence. "Even his business adversaries respected him."

As she watched him back up and drive away, she felt uneasy. But she couldn't put her finger on it. Contrary to what most people thought, Second Sight or pre-cognition, as it was often referred to, didn't always kick in when you would like it to. It had its own time and space. And this wasn't it.

She dropped her duffle bag on the guest bed in the spare room and returned to the kitchen. Norah was standing at the kitchen door gazing into the backyard.

Johanna took a bite from a lemon walnut muffin on the table and joined her friend at the door. Norah leaned her head on the younger woman's shoulder.

"It's not as hard as they think it is to keep up with the gardens," she said softly, as if she was thinking aloud. "I have the Unity College interns who help with the spring plantings, trimming, mulching, and watering schedules. They stay for the September harvests. They work in the herb shed, cleaning, labeling and packaging the seeds for next year's annuals."

"I have the UMaine horticulture students who get credits for taking my hands-on classes here in the ornamental gardens," she continued. "They do all the weeding, caretaking, pruning, watering and gathering."

"Years ago, Nathan contracted with the school board to have the Tiadaghton High students earn community service points for helping to maintain the property. I have a lot of support."

"He truly thought of everything," Johanna said, taking the older woman's hand within her own.

"I can't let go of the tea blending. I just can't. It's all I have left of him. We always did the ordering, blending and packing ourselves."

"You don't have to decide now. I am here as long as you need me."

"Oh Johanna, how am I going to go on without him?"

And then Norah cried.

A Bodhisattva's Vow

Johanna woke to the sound of a hawk's raspy cry in the distance through the open window of Norah's guest room. It was still dark in the early autumn morning. She lay in the soft bed listening to the sounds of the mountain waking up. A late season cricket or two chittered and a solitary tree branch creaked.

Crows called back and forth, and a cool breeze flowed into the room. Johanna liked to keep her windows open as long as possible before the colder temperatures of the season dictated otherwise. She stretched her legs and thought of coffee.

Coffee and yoga. She started her day with meditation and a few yoga poses that kept her mind free and her body limber. When she arrived, she had propped her yoga mat against the chest of drawers.

Norah's spare room was comfortable and welcoming. Next to the kitchen, it faced the back side of the house with a wide, double-hung window overlooking the gardens. A vase of cobalt blue glass containing a bouquet of dried hydrangeas rested on the chest of drawers. Their pastel hue made a soft complement to the pale yellow curtains and the multi-color country quilt on the bed. The room had a wide-armed, mustard yellow armchair with a reading lamp and a bookstand beside it. Her jacket hung on a coat tree by the bedroom door.

Meditation first, she thought, then coffee. By then there should be enough daylight for a little yoga outside on Norah's patio. She stacked the pillows on the bed for support, sat up, and folded her legs under her in tailor fashion. She focused her attention and watched her thoughts begin to spill from the part of her mind that constantly chattered. Still the mind, she thought, do not try to erase it.

First Norah's concerns about her memory failing tumbled forth, followed by a sense of uneasiness about Samuel. She missed Scott and reminded herself to text him again. Her thoughts turned to Dennie as she noticed herself wondering about the syrup and juice processing at Elk Run Farm. She released the chattering of thoughts in her mind, opened her eyes, and focused entirely on her surroundings.

She noticed the chirping of birds and focused on the patterns of their calls. Two chirps, pause, then one chirp followed by a distant bird repeating the pattern. Listening to the sounds and sensations of her own breath entering and leaving her body, she noticed the silences between her breaths. She heard the songs of the birds and the whispering of gentle winds flowing through the open window. They bore the sound of autumn flowers fluttering in the morning breeze and touched her face as if to softly kiss her forehead. *The Wind Sisters, again.*

Through the window facing the bed, she could see the last of the moon garden's offerings; leftover moonflowers beginning to close their petals in the growing light of dawn. A few remaining bright blue morning glory buds would soon unwind to greet the day. The air felt fresh to her, cool, then she smelled the lightest scent of rose wafting through the open windows.

The rose garden was located in the ornamental gardens, on the opposite side of the property, beyond the barn. Where did the unmistakeable scent of rose come from, she wondered, as she ended her meditation.

Fragrant fingers of dawn pierced the shadows on the side lawn and a gentle wind ruffled the moonflower vine, causing the last of the flowers to flutter before they closed in the sunlight.

She pulled a sweatshirt over her head and traded her nightwear of sweatpants for yoga pants. Wearing socks, she walked quietly into the farmhouse kitchen. The night before, Norah had prepared the coffeemaker, adding ashwagandha and cinnamon on top of the fair-trade coffee grounds.

Johanna smiled and pressed the brewing button, then opened the back door. The cool, pure mountain air greeted her like an old friend. Its crispness carried memories of her childhood. A unique New England signature bearing the promise of pumpkins and squash. Memories of apple picking in orchards with the thick, sweet scent of fallen apples; intoxicating to the heart of a child. She was thinking of apple pies when the coffeemaker beeped.

The smell of the coffee was rousing, and she poured a generous amount into a mug, adding a liberal splash of cream. Wrapping herself in an afghan throw from the living room couch, Johanna stepped out onto the patio and sat in a white Adirondack chair. She curled her feet up under her and sipped the coffee. A curl of steam rose from the hot liquid as she held the warm cup in her hands. It was a fragrant daily ritual that invoked a fierce pleasure in an ordinary act.

The ashwagandha root added a frothy texture and a smooth taste to the cinnamon-flavored coffee. Who knew health could taste so fine, she thought. That was really the secret to Minerva's Meadows tea blends. Sometimes the healthiest of earth's pharmacy tasted bitter or too strong. But the complementary blending of other crushed herbs created a synergy of flavors. Valerian was an acquired taste, she remembered, and its smell was singularly unpleasant. But blending it with the sweet smell and taste of violets changed its appeal.

It was a double whammy; she realized. Norah blended the respiratory benefits of violets with the calmness of valerian. Mina's garden book of secret remedies was brilliant. The nighttime tea was a blending of peacefulness and ease of breathing.

She placed the empty cup in the kitchen sink and retrieved her yoga mat. Glancing in the bathroom mirror, she glimpsed her face. It looked rested in the natural light of morning. The lines that had recently formed were receding into a softness, as if they too momentarily succumbed to the peace in which her mind and body now dwelled. Mountains had that effect on her.

Johanna entered the backyard and placed her indigo blue yoga mat on the grass by the Moon Garden. At the base of the moonflower lattice with its twists of morning glories, a flowerless night-blooming jasmine shrub stood beside the faded remnants of Four O' Clocks that had retreated from the summer's pallet, a few wild bergamot fronds remained with their pale lavender spires wavering amongst an undergrowth of purple violets.

Bergamot was both a pollinator and a mosquito repellent which, like marigolds, protected the gardens from predatory pests. While the lattice vines spun twists of white and blue blossoms, the base was an unbroken mixture of leftover lavender and purple hues.

She stood on her mat amid these fragrant floral offerings to the wind and moved into mountain pose with arms outstretched to the sky. As she lowered into a gentle, slow forward bend, she had a sense of surrendering to the earthy presence of the surrounding gardens. She moved down onto her mat into plank pose, rose up into downward dog, then completed a series of cat-cow bends which gave strength to the core of her being.

She lay face down on her mat, being utterly aware of her fingers gripping its surface with her hands splayed out. There was a sense of coming home to herself through the familiarity of the mat and the thousands of poses she had done on it. Her mat was a symbol of her soul's home and her natural place in the world. It gave rise to the truest essence of her being, which within the vast Buddhist tradition to which she belonged, was that which had never been born and could never die.

She stood up into mountain pose again, lowered her arms then raised them in a sweeping sun salutation greeting the eastern dawn, poised amongst the cycles of plant growth, decay and regeneration. Again, she smelled the lightest scent of rose. A fragrant moment of absolute peace wafted in the cool air as she sat back onto the rolled afghan, her impromptu meditation cushion. She pulled her legs into easy pose, tailor fashion, and raised her hands above her head, interlaced her fingers into prayer pose rising in seated mountain.

She brought her clasped hands down to the level of her forehead, "clear mind," she chanted aloud, then exhaled, moved her hands down to her throat, "right speech." She exhaled and brought her prayer down to her heart, "compassionate action."

"Let my mind give rise to enlightened attitude so that I may be a benefit to others," she continued her prayer. "and may all beings be free from suffering and the causes and conditions of suffering, without exception." *Let this become, she thought, the aspiration vow of a Bodhisattva.*

She then leaned forward into child pose, placing her entire body onto the mat and extended her arms forward, fingers still clasped in prayer pose. It was a sacred posture of complete surrender. Resting her forehead on the mat, she exhaled and ended her practice before the lattice, listening to the gentle sound of fluttering flowers.

As she rolled up her mat, she saw Norah standing at the open kitchen door with a mug in her hands. Dressed in an old pair of jeans, she wore a dark blue, long-sleeved T-shirt adorned with a Local 222 Teamster logo.

Norah smiled as she held the door for Johanna. When she turned around to close the door, Johanna saw the message on its back, "In Unity, there is Strength: Stay United."

"How does French toast with blueberries sound?" she asked.

"Utterly delicious. You spoil me," Johanna replied. "What's with the Teamster shirt?"

"A pipe-liner gave it to me about ten years ago. I was asked to speak about land conservation in Colorado at the University in Boulder. When I was done, a heavyset man approached me. He waited until everyone else had finished speaking to me. He handed me his card identifying himself as an environmental inspector for the pipelines."

She took a loaf of sourdough bread from the pantry, cinnamon, and a bottle of olive oil, then continued as she whisked milk and eggs.

"He showed me a manual of environmental standards for the pipeline industry and an invoice listing the kinds of grasses they used as covering on the completed construction areas. This man described the efforts made for erosion control and the miles of webbing used along the construction pathway to soak up any accidental spillage."

"He told me they hire environmental engineers to bring the pipeline safely under a river or creek," she continued as she cooked the French toast on Mina's old propane stove.

Norah recalled how he praised the safety measures in place due to environmental scientists like her, and then said something that profoundly affected her.

She stacked the toast on the serving dish and placed it on the table.

"He said industrialists only care about making money. He'd been in that line of work for decades and oil and gas were getting increasingly difficult to drill. Now it requires the use of caustic chemicals to extract it from deep within the earth."

"I remember him saying," Norah continued, "at the rate they're going, the profits will dwindle too much for them to bother. That's when you'll see them invest in solar, wind, thermal and biomass. They count on activists agitating. They are letting environmentalists like you do their upfront marketing for them so the investment bankers will cut loose with the billions of dollars necessary to develop a profit chain but they won't be any cleaner in that industry than they are now."

"He handed me this shirt and said, the drivers, machine operators, and construction teamsters will still provide the labor to get the job done. He said he was a Christian man and that he respected God's creation. So when the time came and the industrialists swung their attention to sustainable energy, it would take someone like me to keep them in line."

A few minutes later, the two women sat at the pine table with a stack of steaming French toast slices before them. Sliced oranges completed the breakfast.

"He told me to get ahead of the safety curve for the sustainable energy projects before the industrialists could lobby the government for whatever they wanted. I wear his shirt to remind myself of the power of conservation, that greed often overrules sensibility and that when people come together with a common purpose, they can set a higher standard for such operations."

"Did you?" asked Johanna. "Did you get ahead of the safety curve for the solar production?'

"Yes," Norah responded. "A team of us met at Unity College and drafted a safety guide for solar panel installation and land management procedures. Like the man said, if the energy companies could exploit its construction and the workers on their projects, they would."

Johanna sipped her coffee with a dreamy look on her face.

"I love the ashwagandha coffee. It's so smooth. This is my second cup!"

"I know, little secrets make all the difference. Coffee can be so bitter and acidic," the older woman commented. "Want a garden tour before Herbary visit? I always go on a morning walk up the hillside. Exercise is so important."

"Of course. I want to see Nathan's raised vegetable beds."

"We can start there and head up the hillside."

They placed their breakfast dishes in the porcelain sink to soak while Johanna went to the bedroom to change. When she returned, Norah was wearing a red and black plaid Mackinaw jacket and held another in her hands.

"It was Nathan's. I hope it's not too large. It holds in body warmth and it's a great wind barrier."

"You honor me," responded Johanna as she slipped her arms into the sleeves. A musky deep woods scent embedded in its woolen fibers rose around her, remnants of campfire smoke and a bittersweet reminder of its owner. No wonder Norah kept articles of his clothing. She surrounded herself with the scent of his strength.

Lay of the Land

Warm streams of sunlight pooled on the patio and filtered through the border of trees between the homestead and the main road. The enclosed private garden still received an abundance of early morning light, yet the autumn air was chilly. They walked around the far side of the house as Norah pointed out the high deer fencing that surrounded the property.

"I've never seen the fall flower beds before," mentioned Johanna. "They are such a blast of color in the spring and summer."

"Yes, some of them still bloom late into September and October. Most of the Moon Garden and the kitchen herbs still produce. Nathan built a tall stockade fence around this side to separate the front of the house from the side-yard. It has a gate with a latch on this side, so we could maintain privacy when people toured the ornamental gardens."

"We have a few apple trees over here," she continued. "We get a couple bushels a year but a lot of ground fall. Nathan loved to lob them over the deer fence. An offering to the forest, he always said."

As they came back around to the backyard, the Moon Garden was now a sporadic splash of blue, lavender and purple from the newly bloomed morning glories, bergamot and violets. The last of the white moonflowers on the vine had closed up for the day.

The break in the lilac hedge opened out into the vegetable gardens. It was a working farm with a permaculture inspired design for sustainability and regenerative no-till practices. Norah explained the benefits of not turning over garden soil at the end of growing seasons. Johanna was surprised to learn it prevented soil erosion while increasing organic matter and encouraging biological activity from beneficial bacterial growth and the vital presence of earthworms. The high deer fence continued along the edge of the forest and around the entire quarter-acre gardens, protecting the inner vegetation from foraging intruders.

"What do you do about groundhogs?" asked Johanna.

"There is a six inch concrete footing under the ground around the perimeter. We built the fence line on top of it. So far, it's been a good deterrent from burrowers."

"Over there are the raised beds we are building to convert from planting vegetables in the ground. Work in progress!" She pointed at a series of stainless steel troughs and three foot high wooden planters filled with soil.

"What's that?" Johanna pointed to a platform structure with a large plastic barrel on it. There was a long, black plastic pipe connected from the bottom of the barrel, running all the way to a metal tank by the gardens.

"One of Nathan's inventions. He was a bit of a MacGyver when it came to jury-rigging. That is a gravity fed, rainwater containment system. The spring and summer rains fill it and the water runs down, as needed, into the holding tank, where it builds up some pressure."

Norah showed her how the piping entered one side of the metal tank that sat on a flat concrete pad and a series of black garden hoses exited the other end.

"We laid the garden hoses along the ground in the planting beds. They have holes punched in them, so when we open the sluices, rain water from the tank sprays the plants or gently irrigates them."

"Sluices?"

"Yes," laughed Norah. "Another engineering design by Nathan. Come look at this."

At the top of the plastic pipe by the containment barrel there was a joint with a small piece of flat metal sheeting, spade shaped, fixed in place. Norah pulled the grip handle and the stop-gap opened. Johanna could hear water trickling through the pipe.

"It will fill the tank and build up pressure. Then when we want to water the gardens, we open the sluice on the other end of the tank." Norah demonstrated by walking to the tank and pulling a grip handle on the second sluice. The water gently sprayed out onto the ground through the garden hoses.

"We need to empty the containment barrel and put the hoses away for the winter, so I will just let it run dry now."

"What if you have a dry season?"

"There is an artesian well over there in the back section of the property." She pointed to a corner by a shed. "We have a small pump house by the wellhead where we can connect the hoses. It all works quite well. Nathan studied mechanical engineering before he went to business school. He loved tinkering around," she said wistfully.

"He was a genius," remarked Johanna. She noticed her friend's casual transitions from present to past tense. She flipped up the jacket's collar against a stiff breeze.

"I will need a little help to put the beds to sleep. Are you game?"

"Yes, of course. I can help with that. Do you mulch them over?"

"Yes, we have one more leaf blowing weekend coming up. Jost Bergman comes over with his chipper and runs them through. Then we spread them."

"We mulch with fallen leaves up on the mountain, too."

"Trees have so much to offer. There is a lot of nutrition in their leaves. Trees pull their nutrients from the soil during the active season and then transfer it into the leaves. In the autumn the dry, fallen leaves replenish the soil. Best to put that goodness back in my gardens. What we don't spread in the gardens we pile over there," she indicated a patch of ground by the deer fence. "We layer straw, green compost, grass clippings and autumn leaves. It decomposes into rich dirt over the winter."

"I had no idea!"

"Where do you think the forest floor comes from?" laughed Norah. "Come, let me show you the lay of the land."

Johanna followed the older woman out of the gardens through a back gate to the path leading to the wildflower meadows. The gentle incline meandered up along a hill that was filled with the remainders of all kinds of flowers and plants.

Some splashes of summer color still punctuated the fields like vibrant exclamation marks within the subdued and fading ground cover.

On both sides of the hill, the forest displayed trees with vibrant yellow and orange autumn leaves woven through a sea of still green branches, highlighted by the sudden brilliance of red spires. In another week, the leaves would turn more rapidly as the angle of the sun changed, the days became shorter and the evening temperatures dropped. The maple and birch trees were the first to change, and as they did, the sunlight filtering through their leaves caused the brisk air to appear more vivid and sharp.

"Every meadow is a storyteller," said Norah. "Long before I met Nathan or his grandmother, I fell in love with nature. I was reading Aldo Leopold in high school when other students were learning the art of non-violent protest. Rivers and streams conduct symphonies while trees compose epic poems and tall grasses recite a gentle haiku. The birds, of course, are legendary song masters. But it's the flowers of the meadows that produce the sagas of the mountain highlands, the prairies, and rolling hills. These meadows are no different. I've been listening to their tales for years."

They had walked up the hill far enough that they could look back over the lilac hedge into the backyard. They could see the parking area, the barn and the back entrance of the greenhouse that connected with the Herbary. A dirt road behind the barn led to the river.

"Where is your medicinal herb garden," asked Johanna, "or did we pass it already?"

Norah laughed, put her arms on Johanna's shoulders, and gently spun her around in a circle. "You are standing in it."

"Hyssop, meadowsweet, feverfew, calendula, lavender, all of these are in the meadows," she said gently. She swept her arm as if introducing the cast of a play. "Milk thistle, burdock and wild dandelion will make their appearance next spring on the far side of the meadows."

The hillside became a little steeper. They came to a ridge of wild rugosa rose bushes. Petals still fluttered to the ground, revealing rich, rose hip knobs full of vitamin C.

"I gathered the rose petals for the jelly while they were still attached to the hips. Not all, I only take some," said Norah. "The student harvesters will be coming out in a couple weekends to gather the hips."

As they walked on, they heard the morning birds call to one another. A brisk wind swept across the meadows and leaves of gold swirled in the sky. Norah stopped at an overgrown stone path that wove through the fields and led into the woods on the side that faced the river.

"I need to get the students to cut back some of that undergrowth," Norah said. "Nathan always trimmed it during the summer. Echinacea will be waving in the wind with the native grasses all along the stone path to the river, next summer."

"The last incline is a bit strenuous," she said as they climbed the steepest part of the hillside, "but the view at the top is worth it. So is the exercise."

"I've been meaning to ask you, what kind of flower is on the Minerva's Meadows sign? I don't recognize it."

"It's a gardenia. Believe it or not, magnolias and gardenias are my favorite flowers, but they simply won't grow here. So I settled to use their images on our labels. I carried gardenias in my bouquet when I married Nathan. They were astoundingly fragrant, and I'm sure it took days to clear their scent from the banquet hall."

"Gardenias have a distinctive scent to be sure," laughed Johanna.

They arrived at the top of the hill at a plateau that stretched for miles beyond. Mountain laurel and hawthorn bordered the ridge of the overlook. Norah sat on the ground facing the downward slope and Johanna lowered herself beside her. Behind them were the blueberry barrens that continued up to the logging roads, which led deeper into the forest.

Looking down the hillside, the Carrabec River was on the right. It was a flowing border that began up in the northern mountains, curled around the vast

Minsky land holdings and meandered to the town before branching into streams and creeks.

Before them, for miles beyond the meadows, beyond the farm and the road to Tiadaghton, rose the Katahdin range in the distance, piercing the blue skies with its grey pinnacles of sheer cliffs.

"It's a million dollar view," Norah swept her arm around the vista that lay before them. "Nathan cleared a space up here for a sitting bench. He would have installed it this past summer if he had lived," she said wistfully.

Johanna put her hand over her friend's. "Scott would be happy to do that for you next spring."

The older woman covered Johanna's hand with her free hand in a gentle clasp. "Thank you, I would appreciate that."

For several minutes, they sat together on the hill overlooking the utter wildness of the meadows. Then they headed back down the hillside.

Boat House

When they reached the overgrown path, Johanna suggested they continue down to the boathouse. "I can tell Scott what needs to be done. He'd be happy to help."

"I really appreciate it," Norah replied. "Likely I can get the high school students to cut it back. It's not much. You'll see."

They stepped onto the path that cut across the meadows and led into the forest. Within a few minutes, they left the fields and entered the cool stillness of the woods. Here, the pathway became a natural passage. A trail strewn with pine needles and freshly fallen leaves guided their way through the trees.

The sounds of the meadows became muffled by the dense woods. Even the sounds of their footsteps were muted by the thick forest floor. A squirrel chittered. A blue jay complained. The soft rush of flowing water became louder as they got closer to the river.

The trail led down to the river and continued along the water's edge. They stopped by partially submerged moss-covered boulders. Norah sat down, leaned over and let rivulets of clear water pour through her fingers.

"He knew the Carrabec intimately, every season, every mood and every twist and turn it took," she mused. "He and Samuel canoed it with their grandfather from the time they were young boys. They loved the river."

Johanna sat on a flat rock that jutted out into the water. The river was low, but she could see the water line on the opposite bank. A good six feet of rise. It must be wide and swift in the spring run-off, she thought.

"Samuel felt he was to blame, you know," Norah said. "He said he should have talked him out of it. But they knew every inch of the river. They cleared the path

of the Step Falls portage when they were teenagers, so white-water canoeists and
kayakers could retake it over and over. They cut in the portage for the Thresher
Falls so no one would get caught in the swift-moving water and get sluiced over
it. No one knew that river better than the two of them."

"We made a day of it, every year," she continued. "Samuel and Ann in one
canoe, Nathan and me in another. We called it the annual spring river run. A
picnic lunch at the Step Falls rapids while we took turns shooting the falls. We
called it the 'Stairs' because the river dropped five times over a series of ridges.
The perfect whitewater rapid run. Right now the water is so low at Step Falls you
can walk across the river on the same stones you have to shoot in the spring and
summer."

Johanna put her hand in the water. It was bracingly cold. She bet it was even
colder when the snow melted in the spring. *We think of it as three things, she
thought. A river. A mountain. Snowfall. But it's all one thing. The liquid tears of
a mountain stunned by the solemn beauty of the earth awakening in the spring.
Where did I hear that? Gary Snyder's poetry?*

Norah's voice suddenly brought back her attention.

"They called it the Thresher. In the spring runoff, it's deafeningly loud. It's the
only real dangerous part of the river. You hit the narrows first, it's a chute of fast
water. A wild ride, for sure. Then the river widens and slows down. Nathan said
the river was deceptive there. It's much faster than you think. There is a tendency
to want to paddle out into the wide bend. But that's a mistake. You have to hug
the left bank quickly or you can get swept over the cliffs. That's where they built
the portage. About two hundred feet before the Thresher. The portage is a little
long because you are avoiding a steep elevation at the cliffs. But it's good because
you put in again at the bottom of the falls. There are a lot of great rapids to run
there. Samuel named them the Cascades when he was a kid. Lots of opportunities
to bend sideways and draw with your paddles when the river is high."

A gust of wind blew down the river, using its unfettered path as a channel
for cold air, and whipped around the rocks. Both women drew their Mackinaws
tighter around their bodies.

"About a mile beyond the Cascades, the river turns again. Nathan's grandfather cleared a picnic area on the banks of the river bend so Mina could sit and watch the boys shoot the last of the rapids before coming into the Tiadaghton fishing pier, a couple more miles of just flat water. She wasn't one to get out on the river. There is an access road to the picnic area."

She looked out across the river and sighed.

"Norah, what happened that day?"

She crossed her arms as if to brace herself from within.

"I was giving a presentation at a conference that weekend out in Unity. It was a Friday, and I got an early morning phone call from Nathan. He said he was going to meet Samuel to discuss some business classes he wanted to offer high school kids on making sustainable, profit-making business plans. I guess he felt he needed legal advice."

"He said Samuel was meeting him at the boat house around 9AM to canoe the annual spring river run together, then have a lunch discussion at the Carrabec Tavern."

The next day I went to the conference expecting he would call or text me, but he didn't. Sunday afternoon, while I was attending a presentation from the crew at the research station, Samuel and Ann showed up at the college to bring me home. I will never forget his words, "we've lost him. Nathan's gone."

"I think I must have gone into shock. He showed me a series of text messages from two days before." Norah pulled her cell phone from her jacket pocket. "Here, he made a snap-shot of the text conversations and shared them with me. Read for yourself."

She looked through her photos, then handed her phone to Johanna.

Samuel: [Fri, Apr. 14, 2018, 11:14AM] Can't make the river run. Got an important call. Let's do it another time. Meet me for lunch as planned?

> Nathan: [April 14,2018, 11:18AM] I left my Jeep at the pier to bring us back after the run. Jost gave me a lift up to the farm. I'll just take a kayak. It's a beautiful day for a river run. Meet you at the pier.

> Samuel: [April 14, 2018, 12:34 PM} Where are you old man?

Johanna handed the phone back.

"When he didn't show up at the pier, Samuel tried calling him, but it's often hard to pick up a signal on the river. After he was three hours overdue, Samuel went to the sheriff's office, and they organized a search party. They found the kayak overturned on some rocks down river from the Thresher rapids. They found his body on Sunday morning at the river bend. That's when Samuel and Ann came to get me."

"No one called to tell you he was missing for over twenty-four hours?"

"They thought he might have been stranded."

"Did they do an autopsy?"

Norah looked surprised.

"It was an unattended death," responded Johanna gently.

"The sheriff and rescue team said it was clear he drowned after being thrown out of the kayak. He must have gone over the Thresher cliffs. Samuel did the identification."

"Eliana and Evelyn went to the funeral home on Sunday morning while Samuel drove out to Unity to get me," she said slowly. "They requested a cremation. That was in Nathan's last wishes. By the time I got there, they had already sent him to the crematory."

Norah looked away again. She stared at the river as if it had answers to questions she dared not ask.

"You didn't get a chance to see him?"

"No, they all felt it would be too hard. They wanted to spare me. He was so damaged, you see."

Johanna considered her next question before asking.

"Wouldn't he have told you he was making a river run by himself?"

"Yes, usually," responded Norah, "I thought that was odd. But he knew I was speaking at the conference. He probably didn't want to worry me. He was such a considerate person."

"Yes, yes he was." Johanna took her friend's hands and held them within her own as they sat quietly for a few moments. A single vermillion colored leaf spun on the river water, got caught in an eddy between two rocks and swirled at the river bank by their feet. How could such a beautiful thing as a river cause such a horrible tragedy, she wondered. Yet she knew. It had been a spontaneous decision to run it alone. It was the fragility of human confidence to think that familiarity could over-ride danger. It had cost Nathan his life and Norah her deepest love.

"I never got to say goodbye. Don't you think I should have, Johanna?"

"Sometimes people do what they think is best without fully considering the impact. I'm sure they meant to spare you." But inwardly Johanna wondered why they waited so long to tell Norah he was missing and not long enough for her to say goodbye to the man she loved.

"What was the last thing Nathan said to you?"

"Oh, here." Norah flipped through her messages. She had saved all the texts from Nathan and held the phone out to Johanna.

> Nathan: [Fri, Apr. 14, 2018 8:30 AM] I love you so very much.

"He sent it before he left in the kayak," said Johanna. Maybe you were never meant to say goodbye to one another. Maybe a love like yours can't be defeated by death."

Norah nodded, stood up, and helped Johanna get to her feet.

"Let's go to the boat house. Someday, I will have to get back out on the river again."

Wild-Crafting

T he next morning, Johanna and Norah prepared for a day of tea blending in the Herbary. They entered through the greenhouse and walked along its flagstone pathway. Flat tables for starting vegetable and annual seedlings in the spring lined the sides, doubling as a harvest collection center in the autumn. It was empty now, but by March the tables would be full of plant pots and grow lights. A connecting door at the end of the greenhouse opened into a large room with wide counters lined with dehydrators and bins.

This room had once been a shed with skylights and a high-pitched roof on which Nathan had installed solar panels. In the spring and summer, strong sunlight filled the room, warming its rafters and surfaces with passive solar heating. The solar panels provided electricity to power the dehydrators. In the corner was a freeze-drying machine for large bulk processing. One of the counters held large individual container bins labeled nettle leaf, meadowsweet, and hawthorn root, wild bergamot and milk thistle. Bins containing more aromatic herbs and flowers, like valerian and lavender, were doubly wrapped in black plastic.

"Here's the rose petal bin," said Norah. "Still plenty left for some rose tea blends and filling a starter box to send to the jelly vendor in Bangor. I'm including a sample jar of the jam, too."

"It was delicious. I hope you have a jar I can bring Scott. His favorite is orange marmalade but I have a feeling he will develop a taste for roses."

Norah laughed as she picked up the bin of dried rugosa rose petals. "We'll look at Mina's garden book in a few minutes. Rose petal jam is just one of the unusual recipes. The entire garden book contains the culmination of more than a hundred years of medicinal trial and error. The tea blends are specifically measured for optimal results."

"Is that why it's called Garden Secrets?"

"I guess you could say it's filled with secret wisdom, but it's far more than that," responded Norah. "See that opening in the wall at the far end of the dehydrator counter? Nathan cut a hole in the shed wall wide enough to pass the bins through. That way, we can work with the contents of one tea blend at a time."

She led Johanna through a set of double-swinging doors that looked as if Nathan had salvaged them from a restaurant remodeling project. They entered another small room with wide countertops, huge metal bowls, measuring spoons, cups, and long metal stirring rods. There was a porcelain sink, dish washer and two long oak tables.

"This is the wild-crafting room," said Norah.

"Is it a lab or a kitchen?" asked Johanna. She pointed to the beakers and tall graduated cylinders of different sizes lined up on the shelves.

"Well, it's a hybrid lab of sorts. Normally in a chemistry lab, those tall cylinder containers are used to measure liquid volumes but we use them for a different purpose in wild-crafting."

The rustic timber walls and plain wide-pine flooring gave the room a warm earthy feel. But the metal bowls, beakers and stirring rods gave the feel of a lab; precise, hygienic, efficient.

"This entire farm is home for my soul. Gardens, meadows, land and the fixings of a good laboratory," said Norah. "I spent as much time as possible in here after Nathan died. This room soothes me. See, the natural world teaches us how to find the wild spaces in our own minds. It's not susceptible to social media influencing."

Norah sat down on a tall stool by the wide countertop where she crafted the herbal blends.

"Nature has no paradigm," she said, brushing a grey streaked curl from her forehead. "It's not subject to the whims or pressure of human ideas. The wildness of nature, juxtaposed with its precise and calculable ways of being, is the simple evidence that all things are interdependent with one another. Crucially so."

"I remember your joking in class once." said Johanna, "You said, '*humans really aren't the top of the food chain when it comes to intelligence.*' It wasn't well received."

"Of course not. Inconvenient truths rarely are. When I see this as a laboratory," Norah continued, "my mind becomes structured, sequential, methodical. But when I begin blending tea formulas from herbs, flowers, roots and leaves, something in me leaps outward and becomes part of what is being crafted."

"You found your wild place."

"Ah, you get it. Not just me, though. We all have a touch of wildness within our minds."

"It's not just an inconvenient concept, Norah, it's a formidable truth. Society won't have it. Even the field of psychology wants to tame that wildness, label it, and, worse, treat it. No wonder it slipped into the unconscious. What a great hiding place. But oh, so dangerous there."

Norah placed the rose petal bin on the counter.

"It's more than that," Norah explained. "See, when you run your fingers through these rose petals, you combine your energy imprint with the energy field of the plant. You can feel its wisdom. When you drink the rose-infused tea, you get the energy patten of a wild thing. Its wisdom becomes a part of you. Maybe that's what's necessary to keep our minds a little bit wild, too." She shrugged her shoulders. "I don't know."

"Plant-spirit medicine?"

"Or quantum physics. A formidable truth, indeed. Its power is never diminished by what society believes or doesn't believe. Hubris doesn't matter because pride and ego can only change human perception, not the truth of something that's beyond our imagination."

"Like wildness in a human mind," responded Johanna.

"Indeed," said Norah. "We need to blend some loose teas today. I have some orders to fill and we will stock any left over remainders in the Herbary. Follow me."

She opened a wooden slider door that led into the Herbary's shop. Along one wall were tall cabinets with shelves containing boxes of tea packets and loose tea blends of all sorts from the Minerva's Meadows catalog. There was a display shelf of soaps, tinctures, salves and lotions.

"What's this?" asked Johanna, taking a pump spray bottle from the shelf. "Pest Be-gone?"

"Another secret from Mina's garden book. It's a non-toxic pet spray that mosquitos, fleas, ticks and other insects find repulsive. It's safe for humans too. Take one, there're plenty of them."

"The pack and mail center is over there, by Mina's old-fashioned cash register and the landline. It's a working antique on the apothecary counter," said Norah. "We pull an order box from the wild-crafting room. We get the mailing labels from the office over the barn. We match the order box to a customer invoice."

Johanna picked up a roll of packing tape and held it up with a smile and raised her eyebrows.

Norah seemed not to notice. "Next, we seal the box and add the mailing label. I bring them to the post office in Tiadaghton."

Johanna smiled, "I get it." Once her former professor was on a roll, she wasn't easily deterred or side-tracked.

"The most fun is the tea blending," said Norah. "At least I think so."

They returned to the wild-crafting room, where Norah handed Johanna a white lab coat. She took Mina's large leather-bound book from the bookcase and carefully handed it to Johanna.

"Look at it," she said. "Get a feel for the generations of women, called garden girls, who contributed to it over the years. It's fascinating. It's pretty heavy too."

Johanna opened the cover to find the first page on which was handwritten a Yiddish greeting on yellowed vellum. A separate piece of paper, not bound in

the book, had been inserted. It was an English translation, rendered in a delicate
European script and signed by Minerva Mittleman.

[*Greetings, young Gortn Meydl. Sit down with a cup of tea and see what we have
here for you. So many secrets, such wisdom from the world of growing things.
From gathering seeds, to planting and harvesting by the phases of the moon, to
making healthy soil, adding minerals, growing good food to feed your children,
we will share our secret knowledge. Take what we have learned and always add
to the pages in this book. Food is medicine, you will see, and a healthy life makes
one as wealthy as a fortune of gold and silver. Between these pages, you will find
more treasure than ever you could imagine.*]

How do you add pages to a bound book, thought Johanna as she gently opened
the section on preparing the gardens for planting.

"Mina painstakingly translated every page into English, by hand, then bound
them into this book. An intern of mine created these binders," said Norah,
retrieving two three-ring notebooks. She placed them on a blending table. "They
correspond, page by page, to all the instructions, planting and harvesting guides
in one notebook and all the herbal blending recipes in the other."

The notebooks contained computerized printouts of the instructions. They
were as distinct and concise as the Old Farmer's Almanac Johanna used for the
Elk Run farm.

"If you look in the old book," said Norah, "it's broken into two sections.
Growing, harvesting, and drying procedures in the beginning. Then, medicinal
uses, blending instructions, and herbal recipes blending about halfway through."
She opened Mina's book to the page that separated the two sections. "See?"

It was a line drawing of a water fountain with the statues of three women
in separate poses. One leaned back against the fountain's column and looked
dreamily at the sky. The second one was partially submerged in the water of
fountain's base. She looked toward the first statue. The last statue held up the top
bowl of the fountain with one arm and looked back over her shoulder.

"Mermaids?'

"Rhinemaidens," responded Norah, "Mina loved them. In fact, there is a full-size replica of this fountain in the ornamental garden. You'll have to see it. I'll pass the Lady Evelyn Assam and the Dandelion Detox herb bins through the dehydrator room window so we can get started." She left the room.

Johanna turned some of the pages in the old book. From the drawings alone, she could see the book described how to gather seeds from various herbs and flowers, wrap them in folded butcher's paper, then label and store them in a cool, dry place. She had never thought of gathering her own seeds. She always bought them from heirloom, non-GMO sources, but here was a complete guide to gathering and storing them.

Johanna could identify the flowers by their meticulously rendered drawings alone, as they were botanically correct. Mina had added their names in both German and English. Here was dandelion and nettle, side by side, not in alphabetical order, as they would have been listed in a modern compendium. *Lowenzahn und nessel.* She compared the pages to the blending notebook. The pages of both books were arranged in order of their medicinal benefits. This was a materia medica, a book of plants and their medical effects. It was the first of its kind crafted entirely by women, as far as she knew.

Johanna felt a familiar tingle pass through her finger tips as she turned the pages of the old book. It was a sensation she had experienced often since childhood. The rocks and stones she collected as a young girl told her stories when she held them by showing her images in her mind. They began their stories by tingling her fingers, then sending shivers throughout her body.

In her mind, she saw wrinkled hands sealing two pages together over a thin slip of paper with an image drawn on it. She could not clearly see the flowers drawn on the pages. She could not tell what image was being sealed between them, nor what type of sealant was used. She felt a furtiveness in the old woman as she pressed the pages together. There was an urgency to her actions, almost fear. But who? Which one of the garden girls had hidden something in the book, what was drawn on the hidden page, and why?

"Johanna, can you pull these bins through and put them on the blending table?"

She quickly placed Mina's garden book on the counter and slid the bins through the opening onto the blending tables. She put the containers of dandelion, feverfew, and milk-thistle on one table and the containers of mint and lemongrass on another. Norah brought the last bin of dried, wild bergamot through the double doors and placed it by the rose petal bin on the counter.

"We'll blend the Dandelion Detox and Lady Evelyn's Assam first," instructed Norah. "Then we'll make the two separate rose and wild bergamot batches after we wash down the blending tables. I keep a close eye on cross-contamination."

"Find the recipe for Dandelion Detox in the binder," instructed Norah, as she slipped a lab coat over her sweater. "I'll get the beakers, cups, and bowls."

Johanna found the section for detoxification, anti-inflammatory, and liver cleansing. There were several blends to choose from; Dandelion Detox, Tulsi-Nettle Breathe, Ginseng-Turmeric Stress Relief. She laid the notebook flat on the table.

"Read the ratios first."

"Equal parts dandelion root to milk thistle, blended four to one with feverfew, with one quarter lemon rind," read Johanna.

"So, take two cups of dandelion root from its bin and put it in the tall beaker. Then add two cups of milk thistle from its bin. That's right, use your fingers to gather it up. Add it on top of the dandelion in the beaker. Now add a cup of feverfew to the top of the beaker. You can see the layers in the right ratios. Now pour the contents into the big metal mixing bowl."

"That's right," said Norah. "Now take a stir rod and sift them altogether."

As Johanna stirred and sifted the herbs together, their individual scents combined. A feeling of goodness flowed through her body. She began to feel a gentle sense of peace when she suddenly saw the image of the sealed pages in the book in her mind again. It was accompanied by the same feeling of urgency.

Norah opened a cabinet drawer beneath the blending table. "We store all the bulk additives in these drawers, dried crushed lemon rind, orange peel, ashwagandha, dried honey, green and black teas."

She filled a quarter cup of the dried lemon and added it to the mixture Johanna was blending. "Voila," she announced. "Five cups of Dandelion Detox, fully blended. Now put the bowl on the other counter, get another metal bowl and do it again!"

Johanna repeated the ratio process again and stirred the mixture as Norah added another quarter cup of dried lemon rind to the second batch.

"What's dried honey for? asked Johanna.

"It's the secret ingredient for some of the more bitter blends," responded Norah. "Sweetens just a little, not to mention the anti-bacterial benefits of honey. We are going to try it in the new Lady Evelyn's Assam."

They made ten bowls of the Dandelion Detox blend before storing the rest away in plastic bags. "Sometimes, I put the leftovers in individual tea bags when we don't have enough left for a blend. We put them on the sampler shelf in the Herbary Shop for giveaways."

Norah went out to the shop and returned moments later with a container filled with empty boxes. The label for the Dandelion Detox box was the line drawing from Mina's garden book, reproduced in full color, along with a milk-thistle and a sprig of green feverfew leaves, along with the Minerva's Meadows logo.

"Now we each take a measuring cup, fill it with one cup of the blend, add it to a plastic bag, twist the tie and put it in a box." She demonstrated. "Seal the box. Done." She then placed the finished product in an empty order container.

Within half an hour, they had boxed the contents of the all blending bowls. Johanna brought the container of Dandelion Detox boxes to the pack and mail center. When she returned, Norah had already put the beakers, bowls, and measuring cups in the dish washer and wiped down the blending table.

"Lady Evelyn's Assam is a new blend," Norah said. "So we need to experiment with the ratios. We craft a few different blends and test them out. See which one is the best. For this, I use Mason jars and label them with the different ratios and ingredients. I have a friend at the Farmer's Market. I always give her a few samples. She is an herbalist, and she casts the independent vote."

"Not exactly a double-blind study," remarked Johanna, "but definitely a scientific approach."

Norah laughed. "Mina's marketing strategy. We ask the testers to rate them on a scale of 0-5, for overall best flavor."

"Aha. A statistically valid Likert scale."

"Of course. Now for this we use the graduated cylinders. We will add different ratios of herbs, starting with the base, which is Assam tea. It comprises the greatest amount. Then we experiment with different layers or ratios of lemongrass to mint and dried honey. Let's make three unique blends."

Norah took three graduated cylinder tubes and placed them on the table while Johanna got the bins of lemongrass and mint.

"Start by filling the base of each tube with one cup of Assam loose tea from the bulk tea cabinet. Then we will choose different combinations of lemongrass and mint. I'll record the ratios. We add about two teaspoons of dried honey on the top, leaving one tube without."

As Johanna filled the tubes with the different measurement combinations, Norah suggested.

"Why are you calling it Lady Evelyn's?"

"Evelyn is Nathan's mother. She has anxiety and high blood pressure. She loves her morning coffee, but her doctor wants her to cut back. At ninety years of age, habits are hard to change. Assam is a black tea that's high in caffeine, but we are adding mint and lemongrass for digestion, immunity, brain boosting. These blends are antihypertensive, but not relaxing. They produce a natural alertness and clarity of thinking."

"At her age, she won't change her caffeine intake, but she might be willing to drink a modified blend that's healthier," said Johanna.

"Right. It's Minerva's Meadows response to Earl Grey tea," laughed Norah. "But Evelyn might enjoy it being named for her, besides she likes Assam tea."

Johanna completed the three blends, then topped two of the tubes with dried honey. They poured the mixtures into three different mixing bowls. As Johanna stirred the blends, Norah labeled the Mason jars with the three different ratios. They completed the process by filling each of the jars with the newly blended loose tea.

"I'll make a sampler for the Farm Market test later," said Norah. "Let's go over to the barn office and print out the invoices and mailing labels for the tea orders. We can return after lunch and blend the Wild Bergamot and Rose tea and the Tulsi-Nettle blend.

Johanna put the Mason jars in a basket as Norah swiftly wiped down the blending tables and put the mixing equipment in the dish washer, turning it on.

"It's like a chemistry lab," said Norah. "We always clean up between batches to avoid contaminating the blends. We only use the herb bins for one blend on a table at a time. Nathan would blend one on that table while I worked on another over here."

"It's methodical and precise."

"If you bring Mina's garden book, we'll head over to the office."

Johanna took the leather-bound book along with the planting binder and followed Norah through the shop and into the parking area.

Secrets of the
Garden

A door in the back of the barn opened onto a hallway and staircase that led to a screened porch on a landing overlooking the back slope of Minerva's Meadows. Norah opened the dutch door to the apartment over the barn.

"This was once the original office of the Minsky logging and farm businesses. We kept the inner office as it was but remodeled the rest as an apartment. It has a full kitchen, living room and bathroom we used for graduate interns who were learning certified organic farming practices. They stayed here for their internship. We got valuable, skilled help, and they got an education."

"What a beautiful space," remarked Johanna. They had painted the walls of the open kitchen and living room area a light color that added to its spaciousness. A hammock was strung from the post and beam rafters, and the ceiling had two skylights with large windows in the kitchen area that looked over the hillside leading to the meadows.

"I will give you a set of keys. You and Scott are free to come anytime, no notice needed. It would be great to have someone on the property again. The bedroom and bath are rather unique."

They entered the office, which seemed to transport them back in time. An old roll-top desk stood against the far wall beside file cabinets of oak. Investment and business books lined a bookshelf, along with old gardening journals. Johanna saw The Wealth of Nations by Adam Smith, Silent Spring by Rachel Carson and The Good Life by Helen and Scott Nearing, side by side. Old seed catalogs were stacked on another shelf.

"This is Mina's desk," said Norah, pointing out a wide pine table. "We commandeered it for the landline phone, fax machine and computer. Accessing the internet was a modern necessity we found useful in resurrecting Minerva's Meadows herb farm. It has proven priceless."

A cranberry colored Persian rug woven with a pale blue center covered the floor. Paintings of the Rhine River and the Black Forest hung on the walls. Above Albert Minsky's desk, there was a sepia tone photograph of a locomotive hauling flat cars filled with logs.

Norah opened a folder on Mina's desk and pulled out a sheaf of customer orders. She turned on the computer and loaded blank sheets of labels into the printer.

"I'll only be a minute. Why don't you explore the bedroom and bath area? There's a sitting room I designed for a study area. It has a little tea-stand with an electric kettle next to a really inviting couch."

Johanna walked down a narrow hallway that led to the bedroom. The room appeared to take up the entire front section over the barn. A comfortable queen size bed with a dark blue Amish, Mariner's Star quilt was situated under a wide skylight. Two old steamer trunks with lamps on either side served as rustic night stands. In the back of the room, a doorway opened into a spacious bathroom with yet another skylight. This one was over a deep clawfoot tub with a shower attachment. The entire apartment was as private and as luxurious as a premium AirBnB vacation listing.

Johanna sat down on the couch and opened the planting and harvesting notebook. She looked through soil preparation and seed starting instructions. These pages did not have any drawings on them, just computer generated printouts of the instructions. She opened the leather-bound book and found a page that corresponded to the one in the planting guide. The drawings included landscaping layouts, depths, designs and measurements.

When she came to the middle section and touched the drawing of the Rhinemaiden fountain, a shiver ran through her body. She examined it, but could see no evidence of it being glued to another page. The back of the Rhinemaiden drawing was blank.

But still her body shivered again. Second Sight worked differently for those that had it. For Johanna, feelings became facts. These sorts of facts differed from insight formed from a logical stream of thoughts. She had honed her clinical judgment through years of analytical reasoning. But the information given to her in images and sensations was definitive and often punctuated with an emotional jolt. She saw things in her mind she could not possibly have known beforehand or deduced.

When she was a young child, she would see random disjointed images, out of sequence. It was unnerving when she first experienced her gift. Later, she experienced feelings, motivations, and underlying mental states that were clearly not her own. They usually came from touching something. She would feel a powerful attraction to something she, herself, didn't care for or a sudden revulsion for something she liked very much. She felt other people's desires and fears. None of these experiences came because she sought them out. She had learned over the years, these experiences had a purpose all their own.

Her cell phone buzzed with an incoming text. It was Scott. The signal in the barn loft appeared to be a lot stronger than in the farmhouse.

> *Can Norah do without you this weekend? I got a campsite for us up in Baxter State park. Pick you up Friday, midday?*

She placed the leather-bound book that contained far more than garden secrets on a lamp table by the chair. She returned his text.

> *Will confirm. But sounds good to me :)*

"I see you found the sitting area," said Norah as she entered the room. She held a packet of mailing labels and customer invoices.

"Why don't you leave the garden book here? You can come back whenever you want to study it. You can make photocopies of the binders, if you like. There's a copy machine in the closet in Mina's office."

"I'd love to have a copy," responded Johanna. She needed to sit alone with the leather-bound book and explore what the *Sight* wanted her to see and why.

Norah heated a pot of potato leek soup on the farmhouse stove, adding fresh marjoram and chives as she stirred. Johanna noticed her friend seemed more relaxed since working in the wild-crafting room. The mountains and the meadows brought them both a sense of peace.

She looked out the back window as she sliced the loaf of artisan bread. The midday sun filtered through the trees with a subdued autumn light, illuminating the gardens with a pale golden hue. It would take time and the turning of seasons to dull the ache of losing Nathan. The breadth of the love they had held between them formed the depth of Norah's grief.

"I got a text from Scott earlier," said Johanna. "He got reservations for a camping trip this weekend. Can you do without me for a couple days?"

"That would be fine. We can finish all the tea blending by Friday. Then we can pack and mail them all out on Monday and Tuesday." Norah turned on the electric kettle and opened a jar of loose nettle leaf tea.

"I was thinking about the tea business. It seems the main focus of the current blends is on immune boosting and wellness," said Johanna. "What do you think about featuring a winter health blend?"

"What do you have in mind?" asked Norah. She ladled two bowls of soup and brought them out to the dining room table.

Johanna followed with a basket of bread and two tea mugs.

"I'm wondering about a package of Minerva's Meadows nettle tea along with a bottle of organic elderberry juice? Elk Run can supply the bottles with a Minerva's Meadows label. It could feature the anti-inflammatory benefits of nettle mixed with the immune boosting, anti-viral benefits of elderberry."

"Hmm, a winter health blend? Nettle Elderberry? Sounds interesting. Why don't we experiment now? The kettle is hot, so let's add some elderberry syrup. Soup first, then a tea trial."

"Norah," said Johanna softly, "you are aware I know things sometimes, right?"

"I always thought you were a very intuitive woman."

"Mina's book of garden secrets is a lot more than a horticulture compendium, more than a materia medica. I think Nathan's grandmother hid something in the book itself."

"Are you referring to the cryptic little notes she tucked into the margins throughout the pages?"

"What? I didn't see any notes."

"You need to look for them. Her original handwritten translations included drawings. When I had the grad student transcribe the instructions on the computer, Mina was on hand to answer any questions. It was a long and tedious process. Mina would often write or draw something on a notepad then insert it in the garden book."

"I haven't seen any."

"Ah, you need to go through the garden book, page by page. Tell me what you think they are. I've always thought they were just little remembrances or her personal point of view, but secrets for real? I never thought of that."

"Years ago, Nathan told me about his grandfather's immigration to the states, but I'm not sure I know the full story," said Johanna, thinking Norah's version might reveal more about the old book's significance.

Norah dipped bread in her soup and nodded. "It goes back to 1914, a time of great upheaval throughout Europe and the beginning of World War 1. Albert's family owned lumber mills and railways in Germany. They were forced to support the war efforts. There was a growing fervor for nationalism, in those times. No one went against the Kaiser. After Germany went off the gold standard to pay for the war, inflation became rampant. Albert was the manager of his family's business in those days. He realized that simply printing money would bankrupt the country. It was called paper money or 'papiermark.' Mina told me he tried to convince other family members that money made from paper was not money at all, but they wouldn't believe him."

"That was a tragic choice because it provoked his decision to leave the family business, take his savings and his bride, Minerva Mittleman, and leave for the United States. Her younger brother, Ari, immigrated a year later and became Albert's right-hand man in building a business here."

"Nathan once told me his grandfather's family thought he was a fool."

"They certainly did. But it was clear to Albert the stability of gold and silver was dependable and the resources they backed would hold their value. Not so with paper or fiat currency. He took bars of precious metals and hid them in the false bottom of a travel trunk. Mina filled the bottom of her trunk with seed packets and the garden book. They left Germany before the Kaiser's folly broke out in full force. As you know, that set forces in motion that led to the rise of Hitler and the Third Reich. Mina's entire family, except for her younger brother, as well as Albert's family, died in the camps of the Holocaust. Tragic and horrible."

"Albert used his gold to buy forested land in Maine. He did what he knew best," she continued. "He bought forests for logging, built lumber mills, and railways. But that was just the beginning. Nathan told me his grandfather was a genius in business."

"So he built an empire and Mina built gardens?"

"I'm pretty sure she started with vegetable gardens for family food in the early days. She must have gotten her inspiration for the wildflower meadows from the garden girls book. She completed the ornamental gardens and had barely begun planting the meadows when Albert built their mansion. They left the homestead to start a family."

"She gave birth to Morris, their only child, in, oh, 1925, I believe. Then, when he was a young man, Albert and Ari took him into the family business right before World War 2 broke out. But something happened after the war. Bad blood, as they say, between Albert and Morris. Mina wouldn't talk about it."

"His only son and a rift like that. It had to be big," said Johanna.

"I imagine it was because Albert created the Minsky Legacy Trust, which owned all the business enterprises but then completely edged Morris out. He and Mina gave their son the mansion and a steep allowance as sole inheritance, but no control over the business investments. Next, he devised a plan to determine which, if any, of his grandchildren were suitable to take over the Trust.

"He deeded three properties to them, prior to his death, to circumvent a dissipation of the family wealth due to Morris and Evelyn's lavish lifestyle. Eliana got the hayfields and blueberry hills, Nathan got the homestead farm and Minerva's Meadows and Tea Gardens, and Samuel got the textile operation Albert bought when the Jamesons fell on hard times."

"The terms of the gifts were based strictly on their abilities to manage their properties," said Norah. "The only stipulation was that each grandchild increase their personal holdings to prove their ability, or lack thereof, to manage the Trust. As I understand it, he did not mean them to compete with one another. They simply needed to increase their own holdings and be good stewards of their shares."

"Nathan's management success of the homestead farm and Minerva's Meadows won him the appointment of trustee to the Legacy when Eli became too old. I'm pretty sure Samuel felt he was the better appointee, but there was no arguing with Albert or Ari. There is a family board of directors for the logging and railway businesses. Evelyn, Eliana, and Samuel are all members. I took Nathan's seat, by right of survivor. What they don't know is that Nathan appointed me successor trustee of the Legacy Trust or the financial worth of its vast investment holdings."

"So the trustee is fully aware of the extent of the family fortune?" asked Johanna.

"Yes. Believe me when I say, its shockingly vast."

"Perhaps it's best what happened between Albert and Morris is lost to the past," said Johanna. "Maybe that's one legacy no one wanted to pass on."

Gilded Age of Misfortune

"I keep telling you Morris," said the old man harshly, "the Trust isn't a bottomless pit of money for your poor decisions. There are no bailouts, only buyouts. You know the terms of our agreement and the time is up."

"Then I want out of the loan obligation with impunity. Jameson himself couldn't make a go of the mills. Whatever made you think I could? Was it all a setup?" yelled the younger man as he pounded his father's desk.

Morris Minsky was a tall, handsome man with a well-groomed appearance. He spared no expense in his attire. Extreme anger marred his normally congenial attitude. He loomed over his father, a shorter, heavier man who still wore his sleeves rolled up in case he needed to help in the logging mill yards.

"You will have to turn over ownership to the Trust for defaulting on your loan," said Albert. "The business was always its own collateral. The Jameson Textile Mills returns to the Minsky Legacy Trust and I will hire Joe Ferman to straighten out your mess."

"So be it," shouted the younger man. "Do I get to keep my seat on the board or is Joe getting that, too?"

"You're a bright man, Morris," said the old man. "It's too bad you aren't a good one."

"What kind of father offers his son a nearly bankrupted company and an operational loan to make it profitable, then makes him pay it back when it all goes downhill, huh? I'll tell you. A bad one!"

"You knew the terms, you had a good strategy, but you made bad decisions."

Morris Minsky slammed the door as he left his father's opulent office in the Minsky office building. Albert Minsky lowered his head, clenched his fists in fury while his eyes burned with unshed tears. He had given his only son the best education, a privileged life and a vital position at his company, where its wartime contracts shielded him from active military duty. Despite that, Morris didn't have the mental fortitude or the integrity to chart a profitable path.

Was he hard on his son? Yes, undoubtably. Morris took to wealth like he was born to it. Because he was. But his honor was always negotiable. Power, greed, and social access continued to sway his actions.

Sadly, the old man thought, his son was a spendthrift socialite who enjoyed attending parties with his wife's influential connections rather than cultivating worthwhile business liaisons and capitalizing on opportunities. To be fair, he had set the bar very high. But he had a standard and his son failed miserably with the only values Albert and Mina held dearest; that of honesty, generosity, and razor sharp business acumen.

And this was, regrettably, the real test his son had failed. There was no way now he could put such a man in the leadership position of the Minsky Legacy Trust. He would have to find a suitable trustee to manage the empire he and Mina had built. The fortune was vast, far larger than anything their son could have imagined. It went beyond the obvious forests, lumber, real estate and railway businesses. There were investments, many of which were international. The entire Minsky holdings were known only to himself and Mina. It was time to find a successor, and he had a good idea who he would approach.

He sat down at his desk and gathered the papers Morris had flung at him. The Jameson Textile Mill business plan clearly stated the strategy his son had deviated from when the revenues faltered. Scattered in the pile was the violated loan agreement from the family trust.

When his son's executive plan fell apart, he sacrificed his skilled labor force to undercut the losses on the financial sheet rather than stick to the business plan. The result was a deceptively good first and second quarter earnings report. But later, when he landed two major contracts, he no longer had the means to fulfill them. He had fired half the mill's production staff to make the books look good rather than strategically laying them off.

In Albert's eyes, if you took care of your workers, they would take care of you and make your profits soar. But Morris adhered to a different management style. He let the contracts stall while he took his wife and family on a cruise.

When he got back, he attempted to rehire his former production crew, but they had gone elsewhere. He complained to his father about the dismal lack of employee loyalty and resented having to pay his remaining staff to work double shifts with overtime pay. Still, two contracts defaulted because he couldn't deliver on time. He had no choice but to return substantial deposits on his failed obligations and ended up with raw fabric inventory he could not resell.

The result of those decisions caused the textile mill to renege on the loan set in place to bring the struggling company back in the black. Something a brilliant business major from Colby College and his grand business plan should have been able to achieve, thought Albert. All that was bad enough, but his son had also given himself a raise in the meantime.

"Profligate!" He slammed his hand down on the papers.

The Jameson Textile Mill had been in Richard Jameson's family since the mid 1880s. It had grown to be a thriving business, with national business contracts that provided the Jameson family a seat at the Gilded Age table and a luxurious, summer cottage in Bar Harbor. When your family came from textile mill barons, Albert thought, it wasn't hard to be socially well connected.

Morris had met Evelyn Jameson at a cotillion while attending Colby College after the war. A war he didn't have to fight because, as his father's only son, he could sit out the battles in a boardroom. At eighteen years of age, Albert appointed him vice president of the railway business, that transported important military supplies from locations around the country to be shipped to the Allies. His job was logistics for the Canadian rail line his father had built. He was good at it, remembered Albert, extremely good.

"What happened to my son?"

The lure of unearned power, lavish wealth, and social access without social responsibility had turned Morris Minsky into a Shanda, a man who brings shame on his family's honor, thought the old man, wearily.

His thoughts turned to the war and all it had meant that he and Mina, then later Ari, her younger brother, had come to this country when the Weimar Republic faltered economically. His ability to foresee the trouble ahead enabled him to prevent their deaths. They had lost the rest of the Minsky and Mittleman families in the Holocaust of World War Two.

Could his son not see how God had favored them by delivering them from such horrors? Their lives and fortunes were a rare blessing that he, Albert Minsky, had chosen never to forget.

When Richard Jameson sought government contracts to supply military uniforms at the onset of the United States' involvement with the Allies in 1941, he believed his mills would make a fortune. But he was wrong. Textile mills in Massachusetts had won those bids. The Jameson Textile Mills fell on hard times. Albert knew the tragedy well.

Jameson needed a loan or he would become insolvent and lose the money train his grandfather had established. No bank would issue Jameson credit because they had reserved funds for much-needed, rationed supplies. Jameson's mills were no longer a part of that supply chain. He approached Albert Minsky for a gentleman's loan.

Morris' turn at the helm wasn't the first time the mills had failed to pay back a loan. When Jameson couldn't repay the war time loan, Albert made him a generous offer. For the price of the outstanding loan, which in 1944 was considerable, and an additional large sum of money, Albert bought the entire textile mill enterprise, hence its first buyout.

Richard Jameson thought Albert a fool, yet eagerly accepted the offer. The money he invested in war-time company stocks resulted in substantial profits for years to come. He invested in war efforts, industrials, technologies, and manufacturing. He amassed a greater fortune than the mills could ever have achieved, and his social status grew even more influential.

But Albert Minsky knew he had a gold mine in the struggling company. He knew where the world was headed, and had used the strategy of owning struggling companies outright, without leveraged debt many times before. He rarely accrued debt himself as he bought struggling assets with cost heavy managements in which he saw a potential of high returns. Albert's business acumen relied on selling those businesses after turning around their profit-making capabilities. He was a man who had an instinct for timing.

Evelyn Jameson knew where her wealth came from and how her father secured the fortune he would eventually pass on to her and her two sisters. She knew exactly who had saved her father from an embarrassing liquidation. Yet, her father had no sons to take over the investment business he had built from the proceeds of the sale of the mills.

When she met the son of Albert Minsky after the war while attending the same prestigious college, she found his business success impressive. She fell in love with him, knowing the level of wealth his family had gained, which made the relationship even sweeter. The debutante's beauty and attentiveness blindsided Morris. He fell, and he fell fast. They decided a union of their families was only natural under the circumstances. But Morris had been under no illusions her father would accept him as a suitor.

Evelyn was a woman caught between two social eras. She was smart and she was educated. She graduated top of her class and her academic standing surpassed those of the men with whom she studied international affairs. Yet the business world she was stepping into would offer her no more than a secretarial position, regardless of her capabilities. While many women who came of age in the 1950s believed they could rise through the ranks to top level management, Evelyn Jameson knew better. She knew the cards were stacked against her achieving more than a well-positioned marriage.

Albert realized his son was willfully ignorant of Evelyn's ability to influence him. He saw how easily she used her negotiating skills to channel their business success through the use of prestigious social connections. Her own mother had set the bar for social climbing via extensive philanthropy, participating on the boards of hospitals, and her involvement with the Boston Symphony Orchestra. Evelyn leveraged his son's brilliant mind with the twisted social headwaters in which her family swam like sharks. Denied a chance to achieve wealth and position on her own merit, she was not above using ruthlessness to compete in a new social world her parents could no longer navigate. It was the end of the gilded age money barons and the beginning of corporate influence and control. Morris was an easy man to manipulate and Evelyn knew opportunity when she saw it.

Sitting at his desk in the office where he had negotiated so many lucrative business decisions, Albert painfully acknowledged that Evelyn Jameson was indeed her father's daughter. When she told her father Morris Minsky had proposed to her, two days after they both graduated from college, he reportedly "blew a gasket" or so his son later reported.

"He's a Jew," Jameson stormed. But his daughter had remained calm. She had learned how to pitch a deal at an early age.

"Daddy," she said, "he has old world charm but new world mannerisms. He's brilliant. Even before entering college, he was the vice president of his father's railway company. He graduated *Magna Cum Laude*. What do you think his father will offer him next? You don't have any sons, but I can give you grandsons. Grandsons who stand to inherit not only the Jameson fortune but the Minsky millions as well. Think of it. The return of the mills to the Jameson family and then some."

"You drive a hard bargain, Evelyn," Jameson reportedly said. Then he made his counteroffer. "If he will consider changing his name to Jameson-Minsky, tell him he can ask me for your hand in marriage. I will agree."

The old man's thoughts turned again to his son. It was a low blow the day he married Evelyn. But he and Mina accepted his choice and welcomed his bride into the family. He still had bright hopes for Morris then. But today the financial report his son submitted showed a company in ruins and a man who had no intentions of taking responsibility.

How can I tell Mina her son is a disgrace?

He needn't have worried, as she already knew. When Albert returned home to the mansion home he shared with the love of his life, it was she who comforted him instead.

"I knew who Morris was when he married Evelyn and I saw then the man he would become. When that goy implied the Minsky name wasn't good enough for them, I knew what would come of it. This. A man with no honor."

"Mina, he is paying a high price for his stupidity. I am a man of my word. God help me, I am holding him, my only son, to the terms of our agreement." Albert lowered his head.

Mina took his hand, lifted her husband's chin and looked directly into his eyes.

As he gazed into her face, he saw her eyes were still as bright as the day he had fallen in love with Minerva Mittleman, the green grocer's lovely daughter. She had aged elegantly. Her soft features now shone in a face that bore the lines of a life well lived. Although she had a heart of gold, she was never known to tolerate a fool.

"All is not lost, Habibi," she said softly, using a Yiddish term of endearment. "We have three fine grandchildren. Turn your attention to them. We cultivate and nourish their souls like the flowers in the meadows. We see what we shall raise!"

He nodded. "Das ist gut," he murmured.

"No one really knows what happened between them," continued Norah. "Morris eventually took a job with Evelyn's father at the Jameson Investment and Securities Company. He apparently did quite well for himself and amassed his own private fortune. Nathan, Samuel and Eliana were born into the kind of wealth few people can imagine."

Johanna thought of her work at The Glen in the Berkshires of Massachusetts. She could well imagine that kind of wealth. But she knew firsthand money was no guarantee of health or happiness. How did the conflict between Albert and Morris affect Mina, or their grandchildren, for that matter? Was it Mina's hands

she saw, pressing the pages of the garden book over a secret image? What notes
did she leave behind, and why?

Norah poured boiling water over nettle leaves in a Wedgwood china teapot
delicately hand-painted with waterlilies. She added a tablespoon of elderberry
syrup and let it steep several minutes before straining two servings into the mugs.

"Long ago tensions," she said, "and more to come when Samuel and Eliana
realize I will be taking Nathan's place."

"You've decided to do it, then?"

"Eli said I'm ready. You say my forgetfulness is just a matter of natural aging.
Nothing serious."

"Yes. As long as you feel you want the responsibility, there's no reason not to."

Norah sighed, then smiled. "It's another way to feel close to Nathan. He shared
so many details with me, as if he was mentoring me all along."

"In what ways will you have authority over Eliana and Samuel?"

"They have to submit quarterly and annual financial reports to the Legacy
trustee. Right now, that's Eli. They don't seem to object. The percentage of their
legacy allowance depends on the profitability of their businesses. According to
Mina, gaining profits for stability in hard times and for generosity in good times
is the Minsky Way. She often said, a Minsky gives back."

Johanna sipped her tea, wondering what else the Minsky Way included.

"Delicious, not too tart. I think we have a new winter health blend," said
Norah. "Are you ready for an afternoon of tea blending?"

Farmer's Market

Norah and Johanna were sitting in Adirondack chairs on the front screen porch, discussing the camping trip, when Scott arrived in Scrag's Chevy Tahoe. After he parked next to Johanna's Crosstrek, he joined the two women. Norah greeted him with a powerful hug.

"It's so good to see you again," she said, smiling. "I see you have roof racks on that old buggy. Why don't you take our canoe? You never know when you'll get another chance. The lake waters up at Katahdin are flat and serene. Nathan and I really enjoyed it."

Johanna went into the house to get a cup of coffee for Scott as he sat down on a wide couch that served as an extra guest bed during the summer months. When she returned, the older woman was telling a story about a white-water canoe trip she had taken with Nathan many years ago, on the East Branch of the Penobscot River.

"It was the first day of a three-day trip, oh, maybe in 1978," Norah said. "There were no cell phones back then. If you got into any trouble on the river, well, one of your party had to hike out for help. There's no turning back on white-water. Rivers only run one way."

Scott listened intently. He had met Nathan and Norah years ago when he accompanied Johanna for snow-shoeing on the old Minsky logging roads that wound through the northern forests. He, too, had fallen for Norah's charm, her hearty cooking and her thermoses of hot cocoa with amaretto served on a high snow trail. His admiration for the older couple included their way of life and close affection for one another.

"It was a great time to be on the river. Spring run off and the water was high. Just like the Carrabec, here, with fast water and some excellent rapid running. We had four canoes, eight paddlers, and it was great fun. However, on the first day of the trip, right before we got to the portage site at the Hauling Machine Pitch, I slipped on wet rocks while portaging through water and broke two bones in my right hand."

Johanna handed Scott a mug of ashwagandha infused coffee and sat back in an Adirondack chair to hear the rest of the story.

"What on earth did you do?" asked Scott.

Norah laughed. "Nathan duct-taped my hand to a block of wood and I could paddle for the rest of the trip. It hurt terribly, but there was an osteopathic doctor in our canoe party. He set my hand and then we outfitted the block to fit the handle of the paddle."

"What luck for you," said Johanna.

"It was. By the time I got to a hospital, my hand had already started to mend. They just put me in a half-cast and let my body do the rest."

Scott took a sip of the coffee, and Johanna could tell he enjoyed the taste. She made a mental note to plant ashwagandha in next's year's kitchen garden.

"What adventures the two of you have had," remarked Scott.

"We did, indeed." Norah looked wistful. "We really loved camping, backpacking and outdoor living. Please take our Old Town canoe. It's in good shape and the paddles are new. There are life jackets, too. All stored in the boathouse."

"I don't see why not," said Scott, smiling at Johanna. "We have both kayaked and canoed for years. It would be fun."

"In the spring, you can come back and take it down the Carrabec. There are rapids you can shoot and come back up a portage path and then shoot it again." A faint shadow crossed Norah's face. She looked away. Johanna reached over and took her friend's hand.

Scott looked down at the porch floor.

"He was a good man," he said softly.

"The best," she nodded. Then she tightened her shoulders and stood up. "I will go down to the boathouse with you while Johanna grabs her things. The sooner you hit the road, the faster you can set up your campsite."

"I need to transfer the camping gear from the Crosstrek to the Tahoe," said Scott. He stood up, stretched his legs, and handed his cup to Johanna. "That was one fine cup of coffee."

Minutes later, they drove down to the boat landing in the Tahoe while Johanna washed the dishes in the sink. She stowed a fresh pair of jeans, extra shirts, and two sweaters in her duffle bag. Along with hairbands and a brush, she included toiletries in her backpack. Finally, she added the bottle of organic insect spray Norah had offered her.

A shiver of apprehension ran through Johanna's body. Norah planned to go to Tiadaghton for supplies on Saturday. There was no reason to feel uneasy about leaving her friend alone. Just a couple overnights, she thought. Norah should be fine.

The Tahoe came up the access road with the canoe secured to its roof rack. Scott had packed it with their tent, camping gear, and double sleeping bags. It had been a long time since they had camped out. They should have taken advantage of the summer nights on Elk Run under the star trails of the Milky Way. *Next year, she thought.*

"I've got the missing key problem solved," Norah said before they left. "I put a spare under a cedar shingle to the right of the front porch. I scratched an "x" on it with a pencil."

Johanna and Scott left the farm to drive the nearly four-hour trip to Baxter State Park and Mount Katahdin basin campgrounds. The park was unique, both in its sizable acreage and the manner in which Percival Baxter, the state governor in 1924, had gifted the state over a hundred and fifty thousand acres to be used as a wildlife preserve. He also set aside nearly thirty thousand additional acres for the Scientific Forest Management Area dedicated to sustainable forestry practices. The acquisitions began in 1930 and continued through the 40s and 50s. He developed the park with over forty peaks, campgrounds and over two hundred miles of developed trails to be held in trust for the Maine people.

Scott remembered Nathan saying his grandfather had met Baxter in the early 1940s. He was so impressed with the man's vision he transferred the deeds to nearly ten thousand acres of his own forest holdings to the state. This acquisition significantly expanded the western border of the park.

With so many campgrounds to choose from, Scott had selected South Branch Pond for their tent site. There was access to trails that were not too strenuous. The aim was enjoyment not challenge; he mentioned to the Ranger when he booked ahead. It included ponds they could canoe and day excursions they could hike. October was the best time to view the mountain range garbed in its peak autumn colors.

He looked across the seat at Johanna, who was leaning back against the Tahoe's headrest, her eyes closed and face profiled against the scenery rushing past the windows as he drove. He stole a few more glances at her as he drove onto the Maine turnpike ramp headed north to Millinocket.

She had always been a beautiful woman; he thought. The soft lines around her eyes and gentle wrinkles forming on her forehead reminded him of all the years they spent together, not the ones they spent apart. They had seen good times and bad times together.

A shadow of concern passed over his rugged face. Things had happened when they separated. Things that changed them and had driven a chasm in the affection they had once felt for one another. For a period of time, they had been worlds apart. He sighed.

She reached over and took his free hand in hers. Still, her eyes remained closed. He held her hand tightly, as if that alone made it possible to hold on to the woman he loved forever. He felt an emotion he could not name fly through his body like an electric arc, an unexpected jolt so fierce he nearly jumped.

I was such a fool, he thought.

Johanna sighed and looked at him with a smile of contentment that immediately dissolved his self-criticism.

We are together, he thought, and that is all that matters.

Norah put groceries in the back of her Jeep Cherokee. The village stores were well stocked for the most part, but as long as the weather held, the locals favored the outdoor farm market. It was at the fairgrounds on the outskirts of Tiadaghton. In the past summer months, the market was open every weekend. Beginning in September, it was only open once a month. She planned to drop off the tea samples she and Johnna had blended to a woman who sold botanical products. Susan Chambers was a fellow herbalist who had very high standards.

She greeted Susan, who, at that moment, was setting up for the day. She was a young woman with spiky blonde hair and boundless energy. At midday, she was going to give a probiotic beet kvass demonstration, and Norah planned to see it.

She gave her friend the box of tea-samplers. Susan stocked Minerva's Meadows Teas in her farm market stall. She bought them wholesale in early summer and made a brisk profit from locals and tourists who frequented the weekend venue.

"Here are some samples of the new offerings for next year's shelf," said Norah warmly. "Lady Evelyn's Assam and Dandelion Detox. We are working on a winter health blend. It's nettle tea with lemon zest packaged with a bottle of organic elderberry syrup."

"Norah, you need to get more creative with these names. The word 'detox' isn't a real people pleaser," her friend laughed. "They sound fabulous to me, but people like catchy names."

She set the sampler box on the display table she had just covered with a French linen tablecloth painted with bright pink roses. She adjusted an apron made of the same rose-painted linen over her jeans and tied it around the back of her waist.

"Hey, do you have any more anti-tick and bug sprays left up at the farm? I sold out a couple weeks ago."

Norah was hoping she could persuade the herbalist to market the Minerva's Meadows line of soaps, salves, tinctures and lotion products. This was a franchise opportunity she was actually ready to part with. The pet spray formulation contained citronella, cedar-wood and eucalyptus combined with rosemary and lemongrass essential oils in an aloe base. People really liked its fresh, pleasant scent and moisturizing effects. It was safe and effective for both people and their pets.

The formula Norah used came from Mina's garden book, but she purchased the ingredients from other organic sources rather than investing her own time in producing essential oils.

"There are a few bottles left in the Herbary," she replied.

"I will take all you have."

While she waited for the kvass demonstration to begin, Norah wandered the market. She enjoyed the many booths and offerings displayed at the market, which often felt more like a county fair. There would be one more open air market in November, weather permitting, and then it was closed until spring. This was a good time to stock up some essential oils and products to experiment with over the winter.

She was approaching the garden supplies vendor section when she saw Eliana unloading vases of freshly cut flowers from her car by the Botanical Society booth. She waved tentatively.

Eliana smoothed her curly hair with the back of her wrist and walked over to her sister-in-law.

"I need to apologize for my reaction at Mother's garden party," she said. "It's just that we are so worried about you."

"It's alright," Norah responded. "This is a tough time of transition for all of us. It looks like there is going to be a presentation."

"Yes, Mother donated a large variety of ornamental flowers for a talk on autumn floral arrangements today. Afterward, they are gifting all the floral designs to a nursing home in Bridgton."

"What a nice way to brighten the day for some shut-ins," said Norah, "but isn't that rather far away?"

"Yes, somebody knows somebody who, well, knows somebody there." Eliana shrugged. "Looks like I'm the one who will transport the arrangements after the presentation. Long day for me."

"I have a friend staying at the farm who is helping me package the fall orders. We are working on some new tea blends. One of them is Lady Evelyn's Assam. I wanted to get Evelyn's final approval before we made up the labels."

"She would feel honored!" Why don't we arrange an afternoon tea gathering? Your friend would be most welcome," said Eliana. "I will talk to Mother and have Lisette call you to confirm a time."

"Wonderful," said Norah. "I will see you then."

After she purchased a selection of essential oils at a vendor's table, Norah returned to Susan's booth. She was feeling much better about her sister-in-law. *It was a misunderstanding after all, she thought. They really care about me.*

A small crowd had already assembled for the kvass demonstration by the time she arrived. Susan instructed the group in preparing a simple fermented fruit or vegetable drink that served as a probiotic for a healthy immune system. Norah took the recipe handout, thinking it would be a good addition to her personal health regimen. It was easy to make and offered many health benefits as well as its taste.

Heading back to the farm at the Meadows, she decided to spend the rest of the day baking bread. She parked by Johanna's Crosstrek and carried her packages through the backyard toward the kitchen door.

It was wide open.

I know I locked it when I left, she thought. I wouldn't have left it open. She distinctly remembered pulling the door closed. She had put the key in her shoulder bag after locking up.

Norah fumbled in her bag for the key and found it in the side pocket. She walked into the kitchen and slowly set the supplies and shoulder bag on the table. She opened the tool drawer and saw that all the extra keys were still there. The door did not look forced.

She had an eerie feeling as she approached the living room.

There on the floor of the hallway lay the cut crystal chandelier, its small prisms scattered, some shattered from its fall. She looked up. Electrical wires dangled loosely from where it had been suspended from the ceiling.

Mina had imported this antique European chandelier decades ago. It was irreplaceable. Who would break into her home and destroy a lighting fixture? Why?

A violent shiver ran through her body, and she looked wildly around the room. Nothing else appeared to be damaged. Neither she nor Nathan kept a firearm in the house. One of Albert's old shotguns was in the barn, but she doubted it was useable. She didn't hear anyone in the house. But could she trust that?

She rushed out of the house and ran to the Herbary where she could safely call the sheriff's department from the landline. She stopped suddenly. That door was wide open as well. What if there was someone in there? There were so many places an intruder could hide in those rooms.

She ran back to the kitchen, slammed and latched the door. She grabbed her shoulder bag. Why didn't she think of this before? She pulled out her cell phone and frantically pressed the buttons for 911. No signal.

She forced herself to think rationally. There is never a good signal in here. She grabbed the keys to her car and ran through the back garden. Shaking, she locked herself in the vehicle and looked at her cell phone. Barely two bars. She texted Samuel.

I've been broken into. Please come quickly.

She dialed the emergency number.

"911, what's your location?" responded Bertie, the part-time dispatcher.

"It's Norah at Minerva's Meadows. Someone broke into the farm!"

"Where are you?" asked Bertie.

"I locked myself in my car in case they are still here."

"Norah, drive away now. Come here to the office. I am sending a deputy out, but it's going to take him a while to get there."

"I can't," sobbed Norah, breaking down. "I can't drive. I'm shaking too hard."

In that precise moment, the adrenaline that flooded her body shut down her mind. She could hear Bertie's voice distantly, but could not understand what she was saying. She felt herself stiffen. Then a wall of paralysis swept through her body, eliminating all physical sensations.

When Samuel arrived, he found her sitting behind the wheel of her car, staring blankly ahead. He knocked on the window and she jumped. He helped her out of her car and into his Land Rover while they waited for the deputy to arrive.

The tent stakes were firmly driven into the ground and the rain fly was in place over the tent's skylight. Scott hooked up the inverter to the Tahoe's battery. Johanna smoothed out the air mattress in their tent and Scott powered up the inflator. For many years, they had slept on the ground in comfortable sleeping bags. But now, they admitted, it was far less jarring to their bones to use the air mattress, especially after a day of hiking.

Next, they would set up the screen enclosure, which served as a cook tent. Johanna kept an entire outdoor kitchen in a sturdy camp box. Pots, pans, dishes and implements along with a collapsible Coleman propane stove, biodegradable soap and her camp coffee pot were stored in the box year round. She had even stowed away a cast iron stew pot she used to make everything from steamed rice to hearty soups.

Whenever Johanna camped, she brought her vegetarian cuisine along. She excelled in stir-frying over a camp stove. Scott had stocked the cooler with vegetables and other perishables that Johanna would use to create healthy camp-side meals.

Within a couple hours, they were sharing veggie burgers and pan fried potatoes with steamed green beans, sitting comfortably in their camp chairs. Scott stoked the wood in the fire ring so they could share the rustic pleasure of sitting by open flames in the rapidly cooling night.

The sky was clear, and the stars began to show themselves within the deepening expanse of darkness. They held hands by the fire immersed in a silent, elemental connection with a wild and timeless beauty that was greater than the whole of humankind. Scott entwined and tightened his fingers around the hand of the woman, who held his heart within her own.

There were times she frustrated him beyond reason, as he had fought to find control and mastery over the unexpected curveballs he felt life kept throwing at him. And yet she had the uncanny ability to drive him beyond himself, to find a wildness in his soul in which desiring her defined the only thing worth being.

Losing her to her work again was not an option, he thought. When she retired from the demanding profession, she had struggled so hard to develop; she surrendered her relentless drive and ambition to excel. She turned the force of her elegantly analytical mind to the uncertain exploration of their relationship. He knew the sacrifice had cost her dearly. He knew he had to honor the fact that Johanna was a gentle gift, restored to him by a providence beyond his understanding.

As he watched her face gaze into the streamers of starlight that made up the Milky Way, he knew he would give his own life to defend hers. Paradoxically, he knew she would always wonder if he truly cared for her. She had told him she would never be sure enough of his love to take it for granted again. Things can change, she had said. It was a knife edge on which perched a love like no other and a maelstrom of secrets they never spoke about.

She sighed and smiled at him. His heart beat faster and he smiled back. Their affectionate gazes were a dizzying foreplay heightened by the memory of a thousand intimate embraces. There was contentment, sometimes, in just knowing they desired one another. And this, he thought, a younger man would never understand. He had once been that younger man.

They watched the fire die down to embers, then went into the tent.

Clouds Over Katahdin

S he woke before dawn and lay by her husband's side. She just naturally thought of him this way. But we aren't married anymore, she reasoned. We both need our freedom. We are two independent people choosing to spend our lives together. We are not trapped in some socially prescribed, obligatory marital relationship.

She zipped open the tent fly and stepped out into the shadowed silhouette of pre-dawn. The stunning quiet of the still darkened earth filled her with peace. She looked to the west and saw a glimmering trail of three bright stars poised like the shaft of an arrow on the ridge of Black Cat Mountain. Orion's Belt rested on the rim of the earth as the eastern sunrise cut a swath of pink light between the trees. It traced a luminescent arc toward the shield of The Hunter and illuminated the world with the solemn stillness of morning.

She stood within a great and nameless presence. She felt she was an extension of a deep reverence. No need for yoga, she thought, for the earth itself had formed a soundless, ancient incantation that enveloped her within its powerful embrace. She felt utterly absorbed in a vivid awareness of being alive. The natural world immersed her in the subtle movement of tree limbs and skittering light fractals framing tiny halos around a million flickering leaves in the pale dawn.

Sighing, she broke the forest's hold on her attention. She entered the screened cook tent, quietly opened the bag of free-trade coffee and turned on the propane stove. The rush of igniting gas was a seamlessly familiar sound, blending with rather than disturbing the fragile filaments of a new day. The distinctive aroma of coffee soon wove itself amongst the sweet scent of pine and the soft earthy smell of the forest floor.

She heard the tent fly zip open as Scott stepped out. She turned toward him, noting how relaxed he seemed. His mind had finally slowed down. He had realigned himself within the solitude of nature. She knew he wanted no part of businesses built on wielding schemes. He no longer wished to compete in a world where a handshake no longer meant anything and integrity was sold on social media to the lowest bidder. He had known better times.

She handed him a metal cup as he sat down in a folding chair. A curl of steam rose from the cream-splashed coffee as if that simple human comfort was an offering for the day. He stretched his long legs out in front of him, sighing as he crossed his ankles. His rugged face carried the years with soft lines and his once wavy blonde hair was now white. He wore it cropped short.

She remembered snorkeling with him in the barracuda grottos of Xel Ha during a vacation to Mexico. His face streamed with glittering droplets as he broke the surface of the water, his wet hair plastered to his forehead. His intense, blue eyes reflected the same hue as the Caribbean sea and sky. Memories of a lifetime spent in love were now crowding out the years of anger and separation, healing the pain and distrust.

She sat beside him and turned to gaze at the mirrored surface of the pond beyond the row of quiet tents. It was a bowl-shaped basin filled with lake waters at the foot of the granite crags that shaped the Katahdin range. Its north rim was still cloaked in night and crowned with fading stars. She saw the individual elements of morning as one thing. Orion chasing Taurus in the western sky as the sun pierced the new day with promise in the east. The scent of coffee mixed with the natural smells of mountain, moraine and marsh; the pungent presence of humans mingling in the wilderness terrain.

He leaned over, wrapped his fingers in her tousled hair, and pulled her closer as he kissed its soft, silky strands.

"Shall we hike a trail first, my love," he whispered, "then canoe the ponds this afternoon?"

She nodded, breathing in the smell of his body. One more element to add to the surroundings. Everything is really just one seamless thing, she thought.

"I'll cook you breakfast," he said.

Within the hour, they had eaten, cleared their dishes and packed the cook box and the cooler in the back of the Tahoe. It was best not to tempt wildlife with the scent of human food. While Scott tucked snacks and water bottles into their backpacks, Johanna applied Norah's bug spray to their jeans, shirts, shoes and arms. The sharp smells of eucalyptus and citronella filled the air, followed by the entwined scents of rosemary and lemongrass like an aromatic afterthought.

Scott took a sturdy oak walking stick from the back of the Tahoe. "Scrag said we're gonna need this." He handed the stick to Johanna as he hefted the backpack to his shoulders and buckled a waist strap to stabilize it. Johanna carried a lightweight nylon backpack containing an emergency medical kit, the pest spray, and several packages of homemade trail bars.

He took his gun from the center console of the Tahoe and secured it in its holster on his leather belt. Beauty and danger were as inseparable a juxtaposition in the Maine wilderness as their mountain home in Pennsylvania. He handed over her Sig Sauer. She checked its safety was on before strapping the holster to her belt. "*One in the chamber,*" *she thought.* This had become her mantra for remembering she carried the power to do grievous harm.

"Can you carry the bear mace too?" he asked. "It's quicker if I grab it from you in a hurry rather than fumble with a pack on my back."

"Sure." She turned around so he could fit the can into a mesh side pocket. "Better tuck the water bottle on the other side to keep me balanced." She pulled her long hair into a pony tail and secured it with a black elastic band.

The South Branch Pond Trail began in the campground and curved around the ponds before ascending the South Branch and Black Cat Mountains. The entire hike was a little over six miles and rated easy to moderate. It was a clear, cool day, perfect for exploring the woodland trails. Johanna brought her cell phone for both photography and any necessary emergency calls, though she doubted the signal would be consistent.

The previous night, Scott had downloaded a trail app onto her phone, but he preferred a paper map. He considered it not only more reliable, but a necessary level of preparedness. His years of white water canoeing and extreme outdoor adventuring had made backwoods safety second nature. He had sealed his map in a plastic bag and bungee-corded to his backpack.

According to his map's description, the trail began at an elevation of nearly nine hundred feet above sea level and would rise another eighteen hundred feet over a distance of three miles before leveling off at the peaks, then descending. They would complete a loop around both ponds while climbing the north peak of South Branch Mountain, then descending to the trail that led to Black Cat Mountain. They would have to hike the ridge line to reach its summit. The Pogy Notch Trail would return them to the campground along the opposite shore of the ponds, under the shadows of the Traveler Mountain range.

As they entered the trail head by the Lower Branch Pond, they could hear other campers begin to stir and prepare for their day. They were the only hikers on the trail this early. The sun was just now breaching the upper branches of the trees; a ball of golden light fracturing into jagged shards of shimmering silver beams. Full sunrise comes late to higher elevations, so they walked in the pale shadows of dawn.

Their sneakers crunched on the gravel as they approached the Trailhead's check-in post where they wrote their names, contact information and time of departure on the ranger's clipboard. Leaving the campground behind, their footsteps soon became muffled, then silenced, as the forest floor absorbed the alien sound of humans.

After crossing a small stream, they headed into the woods on a slight incline, following a trail that was nestled in the stand of trees that bordered the pond. They could hear the gentle lapping of the basin waters as it tickled the rocky shore line. To Johanna, it sounded like laughing. How like this hike to carry the curious reality of a shaman's vision journey, she thought.

Johanna's cell phone had a bird identification app. She had been looking forward to using it on the hike. They shared their home on Elk Run Farm with mourning doves, crows, blue jays, hawks, and eagles. Their songs and calls accompanied her work in the gardens. Rather than blending into the background, she became aware of their varied symphonies, solos, and duets. Here, on another mountain, she wanted to explore the sounds of different winged singers. She opened the app's recording feature so it could collect and identify the various calls as they walked deeper into the woods.

Looking up through the lower branches to the heights of the upper canopies and blue sky beyond, they could see thousands of leaves fluttering in the gentle winds. The trees stood still, tall trunks unwavering, yet were alive with the movement and play of winds rustling their leaves. Laughing and tumbling like children in a school yard. They glimmered and fluttered in the playful winds.

Scott sighed and looked at Johanna with a contented smile. "I always feel better in the forest," he said. "Maybe it's just people in general that get to me."

She returned his smile with a sharp grin and smoothed the strands of hair that had escaped her pony tail.

"Tell me more," she said, using a time-honored therapeutic technique that invited her clients to access meaningful insights.

"It's so peaceful and quiet," he offered. "Hiking reminds me of being a kid playing in the woods. Anything was possible and everything was fresh. The outside world is whirling with ambition and betrayal. People watch such stupid things on social media. It makes me furious. No one knows how to think for themselves anymore. They are always being told what to think and do by some influencer."

"You sound annoyed."

"I am. But even more so with myself for taking my frustration along on this hike. It's like carrying a brick in my backpack."

They walked in silence. Scott was lost in thoughts that seemed to have the force of stones tumbling down a cascade in his mind. His formerly relaxed mood seemed to have evaporated. Johanna looked up the trail to a bend in the path. It was taking them away from the edge of the pond, away from encampments and the sounds of people. Fern and wildflowers wove shadowed patterns on the forest floor. She searched the woodland ground cover for Lady Slippers. But it was too late in the season for the presence of the wild pink-veined orchids.

She remembered feeling delighted as a young girl when she first discovered them during her walks in the forest. Their pale beauty fascinated her. She always felt tempted to pick one, though she had been cautioned they were endangered. She used to believe beauty was often paired with fragility. But, in the case of Lady Slippers, it seemed beauty was paired with a heartiness that if left un-picked would flourish of its own accord.

The smell of the earth was rich with the comforting scents of pine and balsam. Johanna inhaled the sweetened air that tenderly intertwined with her breath and circled within her body. She remembered Norah telling her trees emitted airborne aerosols called terpenes and phytocides. These phytochemicals were both anti-viral and antibiotic. Trees produced their own natural protection from invasive insects, viruses and bacteria. When people spent time in the woods, she said, their bodies responded to these airborne chemicals by increasing the amount of their own white blood cells, specifically their natural killer cells. Forest dwelling causes both plant and animal bodies to increase their tumor and virus killing abilities. Being within and amongst trees improved the human immune system because of this rare reciprocity of nature.

That moment, she felt a light breeze touch her face like a soft caress. The scent of pine was strong. She could not tell if it was a Wind Sister or Tree Spirit. Her shaman training was poised alongside a precise scientific framework; both were equally valid in her mind. It was impossible for her to separate ancient wisdom from the field of scientific inquiry.

She had learned the art of 'land-speak' from Angelique. Listening to the land had shaped her understanding of vital forces unexplored by the disciplines of western science. This shared wisdom had guided her training in the more-than-human world and gave insight to a performance of power unlike anything her culture could truly understand.

Angelique taught her to greet the day with prayer and a tobacco offering. As the smoke rose from a wampum seashell filled with burning tobacco, her friend had said softly, "this smoke is my prayer rising to the Creators. We offer our gratitude before we receive blessings. Their ways are beyond anything we can imagine them to be. It is by listening, we can learn our part in All That Is."

The silence around them sang with forest breezes and the subtle whispering of leaves. Perhaps poetry was the only reasonable form of communication between landscape and person, she thought.

A twig snapped in the thicket.

The forest answered her thoughts, or so it seemed to her.

The path curved again to the left. Sentinels of spruce and elder balsam firs, both descendants of the boreal forests that had risen after the glaciers receded, led the way. One bird chirped, and another quickly answered. Blue Jays. But Johanna didn't need the app to tell her that. She carried her cell phone in one hand and gripped the walking stick with the other. She looked up into the trees that towered over them.

The Acadian forest of red spruce and yellow birch, sugar maple and white pine, sheltered the ancient and weathered mountain ranges that had been born of ice sheets twelve thousand years ago. These mountains were the northernmost stretch of the Appalachians. They were home to raptors and small birds, bobcats and Canadian lynx, beavers, deer and moose. The rich undergrowth provided food in a wide variety of vegetation, an abundance of insects and the inevitable chain of predator and prey.

It was impossible to walk in the embrace of a forest and not encounter both its other-worldliness and its strong familiarity. The wilderness of the landscape evoked an unexplored wildness in her own soul. She wondered if Scott felt the same.

"Was there ever a time those frustrations did not weigh you down?"

Scott stopped walking and looked at her. "I was just remembering that. When I was a kid, we all played in the woods. We blazed our own paths, but now I think we just followed natural openings between the trees. We stumbled over tree roots and dug up mushrooms. We made fans out of ferns and cedar branches. We built forts of fallen tree limbs. Everyone had their own special tree."

"Really?" They began walking again.

"Oh yeah. Mine was special. I can still remember every foothold on every broken branch stub. I climbed until I got to my sitting limb. I could stay there all day. What a sight we would have made if our parents had ever ventured into the woods to find us. Kids all over the place sitting in the branches!"

"We had a swamp to play in," said Johanna. "One of the older boys threw ropes over the limbs of an old oak. Someone tied a board with holes to the ends of the ropes and made a swing. We could swing out over the swamp. I remember quite vividly smelling of skunk cabbage when I went home!"

"Did you get in trouble?"

"My brother and I had to hose off in the garden before my mother let us in the house. You know, I went back to that swamp years ago, and they had plowed it down. There were condominiums built over it."

"Skunk Cabbage Condos," Scott joked.

They stopped at a tree with a marker. South Branch Mountain. North Peak. Elevation 2,599 feet. A narrow path began the summit trail.

"Funny thing," said Scott as they began the ascent, "I went back to that woods many years ago. It was still there. But it seemed so much smaller than I remembered it. Don't you think it would have grown after all those years?"

"Did you find your tree again?"

"Nope. Never found it."

"Maybe it fell down and became the forest floor. They do, you know. Norah told me."

A bird's call pierced the surrounding air, loud and insistent.

"Field sparrow," announced Johanna, looking at her cell phone screen. Another bird chittered in the distance, the pattern somewhat different. "Song sparrow."

"Want to rest for a minute?"

"I'm good," Johanna replied. "Let's take a break at the top."

The trees appeared to be shorter now that they were gaining elevation. The way became more strenuous and rock strewn. Johanna turned off the birding app and tucked her phone in a back pocket. She needed both her arms and hands for balance as she leaned into the mountain. She was careful placing the walking stick on uneven ground.

Scott took the lead as the trail narrowed. When they crested a rock formation of boulders and sharp crags, they could see soft shimmering glints of sunlight on the waters of the ponds below.

They were above the tree-line.

Then, almost suddenly, the trail opened up onto the rocky outcrop of a wide summit. Below them wavered pine spires framing a basin of green forest and above them a cloudless ceiling of Kashmir blue sky.

It was utterly quiet.

They set their backpacks on the ground and sat down by an outcropping of striated rocks. They drank cool water from their thermoses and ate trail bars as they looked at the vista below. There was no need for words. The silent beauty of the mountain, the wind, water, and forest immersed them in a sense of wholeness.

Scott reached for Johanna's hand and held her fingers entwined within his own. She felt his love for her sweep through her entire body. Laying back on the ground with her back against its rocky surface, she felt every bump, every ridge, every hollow as a solid boundary between human and earth.

Then the wild scree of a hawk broke the silence. It circled above them on updrafts of wind.

She felt the boundary edges dissolve and could no longer detect where her body ended and the mountain began. Scott tightened his grip, raised her hand, and kissed her fingers. Part human, part mountain, part sky and half wind. The word 'complete' formed in her thoughts, then was suddenly swept away, leaving her mind completely silent.

"I love you," he said, "as endless as that sky as forever as these mountains."

She could not speak. She tightened her fingers on his own. Tears slid from her eyes and ran down her face onto the ground. And the mountain absorbed her love like rain.

They could have stayed much longer, but after half an hour, Scott got up. "We should head over to Black Cat Mountain, over the ridge."

Johanna reluctantly stood up, stretched, and put on her backpack. They would follow the summit trail back down to the main path and continue for another half a mile. Scott adjusted his backpack and handed her the walking stick.

They slowly made their way down the rock-strewn path, leaning back into the mountain to keep their balance as they made the descent. Mountain ridges surrounded them on all sides and the view of the ponds gradually became obscured by the land. They continued along the forest trail.

They saw a weathered sign nailed to an old post. It was secured by a pile of rocks at its base and nestled amongst elder pines. It pointed the direction to the next summit path. Black Cat Mtn. Elev. 2585 ft. They continued on and after a short while they were, once again, above the tree line. This time Johanna led the way. The summit of Black Cat was a peak at the end of a ridge line.

It's one thing to climb a mountain trail to reach the summit. It's quite another to walk across the stark backbone of the mountain itself. As they made their way along the narrow rock path, Johanna stopped. She put down the walking stick. She removed her backpack and let it slide to the ground. They were the only humans in this terrain for miles around. A solitary man and a woman standing on the mountain's ridge. They were balanced between two great downward forces on either side as the ground dropped away to shape the steep body of Black Cat Mountain.

Scott watched quietly as Johanna lifted her right leg and braced it against the inside calf of her left and balanced her weight on her standing leg. She lifted her arms in a circle over her head. She imagined tendrils of energy extending from the bottom of her downward foot, like roots, into the solid rock. Tree pose. Yoga on a mountain top. A light wind flowed around them, yet did not disturb her balance.

She stretched her right arm behind her as she lifted her right leg into the air and grasped her foot. Arching her back, she found her balance point again as deftly as a ballet dancer. She stretched her left arm out in front of her as if asking the mountain for a blessing. Shiva Nataraja, the dancer pose. She slowly tipped forward and bowed to the mountain peak.

Scott admired the fluid grace of her form. He affixed her image in his memory like a wildflower pressed between cellophane pages. The outline of her body blended with the blue sky and became part of the timeless shape of the surrounding mountains. She was indelibly carved in his mind. Forever, beloved.

She lowered her legs and arms. Human again in a sentient world. She put on her backpack, gathered her walking stick, and began the approach to the peak. They had not spoken since they came to the ridge-line.

Cross winds blew across Black Cat summit in both directions and they could see all the peaks of Katahdin. Clouds formed over the distant range, appearing like smoky prayer offerings to the sky. These were not peaks to conquer. These were ancient extensions of an abundant world with a living consciousness all their own.

The descent was steeper than they thought it would be. Coming down to Pogy Notch, they struggled with both fatigue and exhilaration. The hike was a culmination of extreme effort and rare beauty. The trail brought them back along the shore edges of the ponds. From above, on the mountain ridges, the Traveler range seemed to be just rolling hills. But now, as they hiked back on ground level to the campsite, the Traveler Mountains rose above them like a watchful guardian and seemed to follow them around the pond waters as they walked.

A bright yellow pine warbler skimmed through the branches of the trees, chittering as it flew across the trail. Within a few minutes, they reached the boat access at the Upper South Branch Pond and saw a few canoes and kayaks out on the water.

"Lunch first, then we canoe the pond," asked Johanna.

Scott nodded, exhaling a deep sigh. She could feel his body and mind at peace again, and this allowed her to relax even more. A vigorous hike dispelled negative moods, bringing one's body-mind into alignment. From that point of reference, she knew, thoughts could become less constrained, more free to arise naturally in one's mind. She had always believed the best therapy occurred in gardens or trail walks and not contained within office walls, no matter how well appointed. This was the pinnacle of Norah's early influence on Johanna's understanding of eco-psychology.

They entered the tenting area of the campground. Scott brought the canoe over to the landing in the Tahoe while Johanna prepared a light lunch. She brewed a pot of nettle leaf and lemon tea on the camp stove to serve with veggie wraps, apples, and sweet potato chips. She put some chocolate chip cookies on the picnic table alongside the metal camp plates. Just as she took the teapot off the burner, Scott parked the Tahoe by their tent.

He sat down in a canvas camp chair, stretched out his long legs, tilted his head back and closed his eyes. His hands lay folded in his lap and he looked to Johanna like he was about to fall asleep.

She sat down at the picnic table. "Lunch is ready when you are," she said as she sliced her apple.

"Be there in a minute. I just want to soak this up."

She smiled, knowing full well what 'this' was. For a man who was constantly on the move and who judged his worth by what he could accomplish in a day, sitting quietly and doing nothing was the height of laziness. Johanna had learned the value of balancing doing with not-doing through years of practicing yoga and meditation. She knew insight rises in a quiet mind and she was reluctant to disturb his.

She ate her wrap and listened to the surroundings. The noise of campers, car doors closing, tent zipping and laughter intermingled with the chittering of chickadees. She filtered her attention between the sounds of humans and the sounds of nature in her mind. The wind played through tops of pine trees and she could hear paddles bumping as boaters pulled their canoes onto the landing. Humans had a collective gathering time for sustenance, the same as the animal world.

Scott joined her at the picnic table and poured a cup of tea. "Have you seen all the kayaks and canoes in Norah's boat house?"

"No, we walked by, but didn't go in. There were a few kayaks lined up on the racks by the river. Three, I think."

"There were a couple more Old Town Penobscot canoes inside the boat house. I would say from the 1970s. Those canoes'll last forever. Between the rack and the boat house there are five relatively new solo seat kayaks, Jackson Zen's. Very sturdy and comfortable. Werner Shogan paddles. They are very dependable in the water. Nathan was a serious boater."

"Yes, I believe he was. Norah said he and Samuel white-watered with their grandfather since they were young boys."

"What I am getting at is," he said carefully, "that outlay is a serious investment. Very high end gear. Nathan wasn't some occasional recreational kayaker. He was an outdoorsman."

"He was good at a lot of sports," she replied.

"A guy like that doesn't make mistakes in judgement very often."

"Probably not. That just adds to the tragedy, don't you think?"

"In orienteering, rock climbing, outdoor sports of any kind, over-confidence is usually the biggest threat to safety. He would have been aware of that."

"What are you saying?"

"It shouldn't have happened."

"I think Norah would agree with you," she said softly.

Johanna filled a bucket with fresh water from the spigot and added hot water from a pot she had boiled on the propane stove to make a rinse tub. She washed her plate and tea cup with a squirt of liquid Castile soap, rinsed, then left them to dry on a cloth she had placed on the picnic table.

"I left the flotation vests on the back seat," said Scott, getting up from the table to clean his dishes as well.

Within a few minutes, Scott retrieved the canoe paddles as Johanna zipped up a grey DBX vest and snapped its closures. It had bright blue stripes, making it easy to see in the water if one capsized. Scott's had vertical orange stripes that stood out brightly against the backdrop of the forest and tents.

A flurry of orange and red leaves blew through the campground as they walked to the boat access. They flipped the canoe over, put the paddles in the center section, and carried it to the water's edge. It was made of a structural material Old Town Canoe offered years ago that was superior to plastic. Rather than hitting a submerged rock and scraping along its hull, this material offered a hit and bounce quality, adding to its overall reputation as a durable canoe. One always carried a roll of duct tape regardless of flat or white-watering. Scott tossed the roll under the back deck.

They positioned the front end about three feet out in the water and Johanna took her position in the bow seat, reaching behind her for the shorter of the two paddles. Scott pushed off, then clambered into the stern end. Johanna waited for him to retrieve his paddle before placing hers in the water.

They glided through the mirrored, still surface of the pond, she paddling on the right side of the canoe and he on the left. In this manner, they kept a straight path as they skimmed effortlessly across the water. Both flat water and rapid running were physically demanding on a river, but a pond surface was less strenuous. They could paddle like this for hours.

Canoes differed from kayaks in many ways, but the most noticeable was the height above the water one sat when paddling. In a canoe, either in the seat or kneeling, a paddler was well above the water. From that vantage point they were able to read the river, finding the quickest current flowing through a series of rocks. The angle of the paddle to the water was top down from the paddler's shoulders. To shift direction in a canoe required the use of a single paddle blade to draw or cross draw and essentially using one side of the body more predominately than the other until fatigue required a change.

A kayaker sat deeper in the water because of differences in hull design. Holding the double-bladed paddles lateral to their shoulders, the kayaker had the sensation of being in the water rather than above it due to the low seating. For this reason, many canoeists initially felt uncomfortable in a kayak, believing it capsized more easily. They were not being used to using both sides of their bodies, at once, to guide their crafts. A seasoned boater was more adaptable, using these differences to their advantage on whatever water they traveled.

Johanna and Scott fell into a natural rhythm of movement as they glided through the water. The only disturbance was a ring of ripples as they tipped their blades in the pond with each stroke and water droplets falling like black pearls from the momentarily suspended blades of their paddles.

The mountains and clouds above them were perfectly reflected on the surface. As Johanna dipped her paddle in the water, it was as if she stirred up the clouds, as if she guided the canoe through the sky and not a lake. It was like a Sky Journey, she thought. If only people could truly see the world in this way. Perhaps they would put down their cells phones, pay attention to the lands, oceans and air. Perhaps they would preserve rather than drain these precious resources.

She knew that bothered Scott. He needed time away from a society that ran at such a fast pace that self-destruction was inevitable. She could feel the peace that was now overtaking him, rendering him an integral part of the landscape of water, sky, mountain and clouds. Hiking a terrain afforded an objective participation with nature; paddling the waters a more direct immersion. The boundaries of separateness between the human and more-than-human worlds blurred in such moments. The wisdom offered could only become embedded within a mind unwilling to do harm.

These were soul moments with elements of distinction that were piercingly clear. *Be, don't think*, she heard in her mind. She let go of her need to analyze.

"Shore your paddle," Scott said. She put her paddle across the bow. Turning around was not possible. The canoe barely moved. She placed her hands on the paddle and leaned forward toward the bow. She could hear just the slightest of sounds between the water and the hull. They were in the middle of the upper pond, illuminated by sunlight. The water reflected clouds all around them.

"We're floating on clouds," he said. A light wind blew across the expanse of water. Sunlight shimmered between the reflections of the clouds, like thousands of lake-born diamonds twinkling around them.

She heard a sharp intake of his breath. This was the more-than-human shamanic world she entered, yet in real time. This was the consummate middle-world journey in which one realized the sentient force of a living planet was brimming with conscious intent. To realize one is an integral part of such timelessness changes everything.

Johanna felt a depth of serenity, unearthly yet tangible; as real as the rocks she laid upon at the South Branch summit.

"This morning we were at the top of that mountain," said Scott, "and now we are at the bottom, in its heart. But it's all one thing, isn't it?"

"Our minds want to make it two things, two labels," she responded, "but right here, right now, our bodies say otherwise."

"We were meant for one another, my love," he said softly. "We are as unbreakable as these mountains and these waters. We may never come this way again, but it will always be inside us."

She nodded, inhaled, and felt the thin hull boundary between her feet and the waters dissolve as if her body itself was floating.

"I wonder what it's like to actually know it's the last time you are doing something, like white-water canoeing or shooting falls," he wondered.

"Or to hike to elevation like the time we snowshoed Poudre Canyon at eleven thousand feet in Colorado."

"One day, only one of us will be here and the other…"

"…will have walked on… as Angelique would say."

"I like that much better than saying died," he said.

Pain ruptured her peace as sharply as stepping on shards of glass. We will break one day, she thought. When one of us walks on and leaves the other behind.

"But we will always carry the other inside us," he said, as if he heard her thoughts. "That's the unbreakable part."

Orion's Belt

The night sky was moonless and startlingly clear. Scott had removed the tent fly so they could gaze up through the domed skylight. As their eyes adjusted to an inky black darkness, they could see the sparkling trails of millions of stars that made up the Milky Way. Bundled together in their double sleeping bag, they lay comfortably in the tent. The star patterns appeared; turning, rolling, twisting and unwinding across the sky as the night deepened into a three-dimensional depth of gaseous colors and glittering points of light. In a world troubled by uncertainty and confusion, they both felt there was no greater peace than this.

Scott was tired from the exertions of the day and was the first to nod off. Soon after, Johanna fell asleep in the crook of his arm. The temperature outside the tent fell to a brisk fifty degrees while their mutual breaths and down-filled sleeping bag kept them comfortably warm. The stars wheeled overhead as night winds moved through tall pines, rustling the branches. Creatures of the night made their way quietly through the forest.

In the utter silence of night, the loud crack of a tree branch snapping in the woods awakened Johanna. She looked up through the skylight and saw the star-studded belt of Orion directly overhead, glimmering in the sky above their tent. She wanted to see the full expanse of the star formations. She knew the constellation Taurus should be near Orion, identifiable by its bright star Aldebaran and the familiar cluster of seven stars known as the Pleiades.

Slowly, she unzipped her side of the sleeping bag and pulled on her socks and jacket. Soundlessly slipping her feet into her sneakers, she grabbed Scott's flashlight and opened the tent flap.

Moments later, she stood alone in the darkened campsite and looked overhead. The sky was cloudless and the air so cold her nostrils burned. She scanned the dark night sky. The time was shortly after midnight. Orion was directly overhead, its glittering string of stars would dominate the heavens until March. She looked at the grouping of three bright stars in a row, unmistakably Mintaka, Alnilam, and Alnitak. She softened her eyes. Below and off to the right, another star shimmered like a blue-white diamond, the brightest of the night sky. Rigel, the right foot of Orion the Hunter, glowed one hundred twenty thousand times brighter than the sun, though it was eight hundred light years away. Above the sparkling shaft and to its left was a lone red star, Betelgeuse.

She could not find the constellation Taurus, which should have been nearby. The Milky Way, which should have cascaded across the sky as it had earlier that night, had disappeared, leaving a blackened universe. Only Orion shone above. *How can that be, she thought.*

The waters of the pond basin gently licked at the shore.

A cool wind swept through the campground and swirled around her.

A twig snapped in the forest.

An acrid animal scent filled her nostrils.

She spun around and dropped the flashlight.

Standing at the edge of the forest, illuminated in a halo of pale silver light, was a glittering golden creature. A mountain lion. She panicked. It stared at her, then sat down on its haunches.

She knew she was not dreaming. A few years ago, Angelique sent a spirit teacher to her, a mountain lion. It announced its presence by leaving a single paw print in the dirt. But this was the first time she had actually physically seen the creature. She realized she was seeing it through vision eyes. But this was no visionary journey. It was in real time.

Long ago, Angelique had taught her about the three sacred worlds of the shaman; the under-earth world, the sky world and the middle world. She had taken underworld and sky vision journeys for years. She had experienced a middle-world journey when this very spirit teacher had shown up over a year ago. Using its shamanic skill of shapeshifting, the mountain lion helped Johanna find a hidden compound where girls were being held prisoner by sex traffickers.

A middle-world journey was indistinguishable from one's day-to-day life. As a psychologist, she knew her culture labeled such experiences as delusional or as drug-induced hallucinations. In a different culture, one that valued altered states as spiritually informed visions, middle-world journeys were reserved for accomplished shamans. They were so familiar with otherworldly terrains they were not in any danger of losing their minds when faced with tangible sensory experiences that seemed to be really happening.

Abruptly, the creature turned around and moved toward the pond. Johanna followed in the darkness. A glimmering pool of light illuminated the mountain lion as it entered the path leading to the trailhead. Johanna soon found herself on the upward incline to the peak of South Branch Mountain. It was the same trail she and Scott had followed earlier that day.

From time to time, the mountain lion would stop and turn its head as if to be sure Johanna was still following, then continued on. The range of mountains around her were dark shapes against the shadowed backdrop of glittering stars. But the shapes of the mountains had changed. This was not the Traveler Mountains. It was not the Black Cat ridge nor the peak of South Branch summit. These mountains were familiar, but in a strange and disturbing way.

The shadows lifted as the pale yellow glow of dawn revealed a rugged coastline in the distance and a sharp, snow-capped mountain range before her. The mountain lion had disappeared, leaving her alone in a forested glen. She had seen this place before, long ago in her father's family picture album. This was the Isle of Skye and the mountain range was the rocky crags of the Cuillin.

She smelled the pungent scents of heather and Scottish broom. The scent of roses, once again, filled the surrounding air. She turned.

A young woman stood beneath an arch of curved tree branches that lead into the woods. Johanna knew the legends of the Gaelic speaking peoples. This was a portal gate to the land of the fey-folk. The woman wore a simple linen dress and a long shawl woven with the ancient MacIntosh tartan. The plaid pattern was distinctive;

crossed reddish orange lines, squared off in a field of hunter's green. A silver Clan Chattan broach that bore a purple amethyst, and a raised arm wielding a sword was clasped to her shawl. She knew the words carved upon that crest by heart: Touch Not The Cat, Bot With a Glove.

It was her grandmother Aila MacIntosh who had long since passed away. She appeared young again, as she had been when the pictures were taken so many years ago. She smiled and held out her hand.

"A ghraidh," she said softly [dear one]. "Come with me."

Together, they walked to a small cottage by a stream. A garden circled the building and to its side were tall, wooden racks from which bundles of herbs hung drying in the breeze. There were three willow baskets on an oak table in the garden. Aila led Johanna to the table. Fabric packets tied with different colored ribbons filled each basket.

"These are blessing bundles," she said softly. She picked up one wrapped in white lace, a cluster of yarrow, tied with a white ribbon. She opened it. Inside was a small golden citrine stone and several packets filled with herbs, wrapped in twine. "It's a tea for new mothers. It helps increase milk production for their babies. The yarrow is for protection and the deepening of marital love."

She handed it to Johanna who immediately smelled the familiar maple syrup scent of fenugreek, fennel, and the faint smell of licorice, anise.

Aila picked up another lace bundle, bound with a red ribbon and a sprig of gypsophila; baby's breath. A black obsidian stone spilled out from the wrappings along with three small packets of herbs. "This tea helps bring on menses in case they have stopped."

"Why baby's breath?"

Aila smiled. "Notice it's slightly green."

"Not fully bloomed?"

"Smell it."

Johanna could smell its musky scent. She looked up quizzically.

"Angelica. To fool the priests. Its dried, crushed roots, along with bog myrtle and mugwort, other potent herbs, bring on strong uterine contractions, especially when

mixed with brandy. Many women suffered miscarriages and died because their bodies could not fully expel what had already died within them. Oh, and it's always good to sprinkle some of the dried flowers in a corner of one's cottage to ward off evil gossip." Her grandmother's blue eyes sparkled like quartz crystals reflecting the sunlight.

"We have made these bundles for generations of women here on the Isles and in the Highlands. They are medicine for teas and poultices. We had to be very careful to make them look like little gifts. Some, the ones with the blue ribbons, are simple tea. Not medicinal. If the clergy or English officials stopped us, they would imprison us if they found our herbal medicines. So we kept the plain ones in case they stopped us on the road. In the past, they burned our healers as witches for having these medicines."

There were two bundles remaining on the table, both wrapped in tan muslin, bound in yellow ribbons and tucked with a tiny branch of leaves, red berries and white flowers. "These are for you. To help with grief and heartbreak." She opened one bundle to reveal a piece of green jade and a packet of herbs. "Hawthorn to mend the heart, dried rose petals and lavender for peace and happiness."

Johanna held the bundle to her face and inhaled the delicate scent of rose.

"One is for your friend who has suffered a terrible loss. The other is for you, because you are holding onto your sadness. You fear you will lose him again, and this holds you back from trusting the true happiness that is meant for you."

"Make a tea with the herb packets. Light a candle in a dark room. Drink the light along with the tea. Love is the strongest force of all. You think it's just in your earthly world. It originates in the world of spirit and flows back and forth into the world of form. Love never ends, mo' chroie." [my heart]

Her grandmother clasped her hands around Johanna's as she held the small bundles. Warmth passed through her hands. She kissed Johanna's forehead. "Bring these blessing bundles back into your world. Remember how to make them. Plant your medicine garden accordingly. This is ancestral knowledge. It's in your bones, I promise you."

Aila stepped back. She seemed to shimmer. "I am always with you." Johanna reached out to her, but she was gone.

The sky above her began turning dark. Johanna was standing outside the tent again, alone in the dark, cold night. Even Orion was gone. Her hands were empty, but she would remember the healing ceremony her grandmother had just given her. She knew precisely how to make the blessing bundles. She entered the tent and crawled into the sleeping bag by Scott's side.

Later, he reached for her in the night, but she had already fallen into a dreamless sleep. Her body was cold, so he curled his around her, pulling her close. He clasped her hand against his chest, against his heart.

At the edge of the forest, she crouched and watched the campground, a spirit sentinel. Seen or unseen at will, she flicked her long tawny tail and blinked her golden eyes, sharpening her focus. Leading her student to the Isles was easy, following her back to the campground undetected was a little more difficult. Even for her.

The woman could now smell a spirit trail and notice her presence. She was learning at a much faster pace than expected for a non-blood. Oh, this is going to be good.

A Meeting of the Minds

Breaking camp the next morning after a breakfast of coffee and granola bars was a quick affair. The previous night, they had packed the cook tent and camp box in the Tahoe. That left only deflating the mattress, folding up the tent and packing it in its carry bag. They quickly surveyed their site for trash, raked the coals in the bottom of the fire ring, and headed for the park entrance.

Scott drove south on the Interstate toward Waterville, where he took the exit that led to Skowhegan. They drove nearly thirty miles on a country road headed northwest toward Kingfield. The Blueberry Hill Cafe was nestled in the countryside, a harbor of good food for locals, hikers, and winter skiers alike.

It boasted delicious homemade pastries, a sandwich cafe, and a well-stocked organic market for local farmers. As the name suggested, they were best known for their blueberry muffins and scones. It was here Johanna would meet Angelique, who was driving northwest to Moose River to visit her brother on Passamaquoddy lands. It was near the Boundary Mountain Preserve, a section of land within the two hundred and sixty thousand acres of protected forests stretching from New Hampshire and western Maine into Quebec.

As they pulled into the parking lot of the renovated cafe in an old Victorian house, Johanna saw Angelique's red pickup truck parked along the crowded side road. Her friend sat on the wide verandah, waiting for them to find a space to park.

Scott quickly transferred Johanna's backpack and duffel bag to the back of Angelique's vehicle, then turned to greet the tall indigenous woman who had not only been a family friend for many years, but had helped to reunite him with Johanna during their painful separation.

Angelique Boudreau was the retired director of a non-profit agency that offered shelter, resources and counseling to battered women and survivors of incest and sexual assault. She sat on two tribal councils and was actively involved in her community. Johanna had worked with her years ago as a staff therapist.

She was a dark-skinned woman with long black hair, streaked with white strands and bound in a tight braid that swirled down her back like a tumbling waterfall. She tied it back in a rosette hair clip, beaded in the design of a dragonfly. Wearing black jeans, a tan buckskin jacket and suede boots, Angelique was a striking woman for her beauty and her bearing. Because of her gift of understanding land-speak and her intuitive wisdom of spiritual matters, some people might have called her a shaman. It was a term she publicly disavowed.

Johanna knew otherwise as her dear friend was also her mentor in earth-based wisdom practices. It was a mystical path of training that informed the unique skills of two women from distinctly different lineages. The elders in her community supported Angelique's gifts as a natural relationship with the more-than human world. Joanna's gifts were not equally valued in her culture.

Though her Gaelic speaking ancestry believed a spiritual understanding of the world around them was a natural awareness, no one gave it any credibility in the modern day. Angelique's take on the situation was pragmatic.

"People won't steal from you what they do not value," she told Johanna years ago. "They won't understand how you know things. Best to keep this knowledge to yourself."

It was said of Angelique that she gave the best hugs, and Scott knew this to be true. Her affection for the people she cared about was unquestionably genuine. She gave Scott a strong hug and laughed.

Scott hugged Angelique warmly in return.

"Well, I am off to Unity to start the workshop in building straw bale homes. We end the training by completing a build on an actual job-site," he said. "Are you sure it's no trouble to take Johanna on to Tiadaghton?"

"Not at all," Angelique responded. "It's on the way to Rangeley Lakes. From there northwest to the Boundary Mountains. It works out rather well."

Scott brushed back Johanna's silver hair tenderly and kissed her forehead. "Miss you," he said softly.

"Be safe," she responded. "Let me know when you get there, ok?"

He nodded, then drove away in the Tahoe, the canoe secured to its roof. He would return it to Norah's boat house when it was time for Johanna to leave Minerva's Meadows.

Johanna and Angelique entered the market side of the cafe where they could order food. The familiar smells of vanilla, cinnamon and freshly baked bread greeted them. The rustic shop with its wood-paneled walls and many shelves of locally branded items was like an indoor Farmer's Market. It was stocked with items that supported a widespread cottage industry of homemade products. There were several brands of maple syrup on a shelf. Johanna made a mental note to tell Dennie it might be a good place to market her friend's elderberry infused syrups.

A plaque on the wall listed all the scones, cookies, and other homemade pastries that had literally put this store on the map. Angelique ordered a dozen blueberry muffins, to-go, along with a croissant and a cup of coffee. Johanna bought a banana-nut muffin and a cup of hot tea. They entered the dining area and chose a secluded table in an alcove in the back of the dining room.

One of the endearing qualities of the Blueberry Hill Cafe was its furnishings of odds-and-ends. Every table was different. From round and square shaped metal and natural wood, each individual table also had a different tablecloth pattern and unmatched chairs. The room was a wild mixture of colors, shapes, and configurations. Mugs of unique designs and colors, all of which competed with or complemented one another, lined the shelves. The only standard, it seemed, was an abundant supply of blue-dotted plastic plates.

"Yard sale or antique store?" whispered Angelique as they sat down some distance away from a crowd of exuberant travelers.

"Probably both," responded Johanna. She picked up her mismatched fork and spoon and saw the stamps showing the utensils were genuine silver. "Flea markets and estate sales too."

The old friends sat silently for a few moments, taking in the cafe's atmosphere and its unique combination of patrons. There was a cacophony of well-dressed tourists, tattered hikers, and camouflage-clad hunters shopping, eating and conversing loudly. It had been several months since they had last met, so this unusual opportunity was a pleasure they both valued.

"How is the medicine garden coming along?" asked Angelique. "Will Norah's design plan grow at higher elevations?"

She was referring to Elk Run Farm's regenerative mountainside landscape and its height of nearly two thousand feet above sea level. Her brother's land was also at nearly that elevation on the western border of Maine and Canada.

"Yes, I believe all the plants will do well there," responded Johanna. "I can email you a list."

"Thanks, I will give it to my brother on the reserve. They are integrating new permaculture techniques with old practices. I am sure the elders will be interested."

"How is Norah?" asked Angelique, aware of Nathan's death and the other reason for Johanna's visit to Minerva's Meadows.

"She is doing as well as anyone might expect. The unexpectedness of Nathan's death made it even more traumatic. She is devastated but trying to move forward with her life."

"Adjusting to that kind of loss takes time, many seasons. You may miss a loved one every day but each time they are not there for a holiday celebration is like the first time without them, all over again. It's like a punch in the gut."

"She is anxious about her memory. She has been forgetful and confused lately," Johanna said. She told Angelique about the garden party incident, misreading the invitation's instructions to confirm, continually losing her house keys and forgetting Johanna was going to visit. "Her in-laws seem very concerned as well. Nathan's brother, Samuel, seemed to think she needed a psych evaluation."

"That sounds serious. What does your clinical judgement tell you?"

"She is in her mid-seventies. Forgetting keys and misunderstanding instructions are all normal age-related issues. No dementia involved. She can remember complex details that are familiar to her and recalling those things aren't a problem. But it's more than that."

"How so?"

"In her case, I can explain forgetting things that happened the day before, misplacing things, and missing appointments with the trauma of losing Nathan. The way he died was horrifying. He was an accomplished white water canoeist. Kayaking that river was second nature to him. It shouldn't have happened. She isn't sleeping well, hence her memory consolidation is impaired. She is hyper-vigilant, and she experiences moments of panic."

"Like PTSD?"

"Not like," Johanna acknowledged, "it actually is post-traumatic stress disorder. You don't have to see someone killed in order to suffer a trauma reaction. Losing someone in a horrific accident, having a serious medical procedure or even a painful divorce can cause it."

"You don't have to tell me," smiled Angelique. She brushed her dark-skinned fingers across the top of Johanna's pale hand, then held it.

Johanna was silent for a moment as she looked at the blue butterfly tattoo on her friend's hand. She felt the sudden warmth of the spinning healing energy coming from Angelique's palm. She felt her heart rate slow down and breath becoming more even.

"That's right," she said. "You know that better than most people."

"We know PTSD complicates memory and impairs brain functioning," said Angelique. "How can you relieve her concerns and help her family understand what she is going through?"

"Well," began Johanna, "there's another complication."

That moment, one of the wait staff, a short heavy-set woman, approached their table in the corner. Angelique withdrew her hand.

"Would you care for a carafe of freshly brewed coffee? It's a local brand. We offer an endless pot of coffee and tea for those who are socializing here," she offered.

"That would be wonderful," responded Johanna.

"I'll be back with a pot of hot water and a box of teas, too." The woman smiled and swiftly walked away.

"I wonder if there are any Minerva's Meadows in the selections."

"I doubt it," said Johanna.

"You were saying?"

"Norah is a brilliant scientist, and a thoroughly trained horticultural expert," Johanna began. "But her brain wiring is unique. She is autistic. I picked up on it while teaching post grad at the same university she taught botany."

"Does she know?"

"No. She is very skilled in compensating. Neither the administration nor her students ever knew because she could mask her differences, but not her eccentricities. Her mind sees things in layers, like 3D chess boards. Numbers speak to her and literally tell her stories. Words have a shape to them that are pleasant or unpleasant to her. She doesn't understand common social cues or what people may mean when they speak in colloquial phrases. Forget sarcasm. She doesn't understand it at all. She takes everything literally."

"Somewhere on the spectrum, then?"

"I wish they hadn't termed it like that in the Diagnostic and Statistical Manual. A spectrum in physics has distinct frequencies, such as individual colors. Autism isn't really like that. It's more a gradient with a lot of overlapping. It's hard to identify a female with autism, let alone diagnose one. Most clinicians are more familiar with the characteristics of male autism. There're a lot of differences."

"What tipped you off?"

"Most clinicians follow the theory of mind approach to autism, where accurately predicting others' thoughts or feelings is seen as empathy. People with autism rarely think about another person's perspective. Therefore, autistic people are thought to lack empathy."

"Seriously? Can anyone truly understand someone else's thoughts? "

"Well, neurotypical people, who are not on the spectrum, believe they can accurately guess. Neurodiverse individuals rely on explicit information and observable actions. They, themselves, can't lie and believe others to be the same. They take things literally. The theory suggests the capacity to distinguish between spoken words and underlying thoughts is an indicator of empathy in neurotypical individuals."

Angelique's shoulders tightened and a momentary shadow passed over her sparkling, dark eyes.

"Norah has difficulty deciphering the meaning of facial expressions. She doesn't factor in that information when talking to someone. But I have also observed her incredible skill in understanding what people are actually feeling. Even if they are so defensive, they have denied those feelings to themselves. She sees the whole person, all at once. It's an autistic superpower. Some have it, some don't. Her students adored her for it."

"That sounds like an advantage rather than a deficit. The emotional awareness part anyway."

"I believe the difference, at least in her case, is that she intuits other people's emotions through her own sensory experience, not deduced through the ability to predict someone's intention from their behavior."

"Neurodiverse people experience a wide range of incoming sensations without the ability to filter the intensity," Johanna continued. "Her brain interprets sensory information and categorizes it quickly according to associations she has developed over her lifetime, without the reference points that neurotypical people use. She has a refined ability to see the big picture and the details simultaneously."

"This is sounding very much like acculturation to me," responded Angelique tightly. "Like requiring a person to adopt certain features and customs of a different society rather than respecting the differences. We believe in the uniqueness of minds."

"Norah sees patterns," explained Johanna. "She observes people the same way she scientifically examines the natural world. She assesses what she calls their true natures, how they fit together or how they oppose one another."

"These labels for autistic distinctions seem one-sided," Angelique sighed. "My people address all their relations; the winged, four-legged, standing nation, the winds and the thunder beings, along with two-leggeds, when they speak. We listen at the same time. It's how we show respect. Unlike your people, sadly, who only speak to one another or should I say speak 'at' them."

"If I am talking," she continued, "and I pause when a Wind Sister has touched my face or my hair, it's because I am listening to their words. If I didn't, it might take a stronger message to get my attention, such as an elder sister gust or grandmother gale-storm. When a hurricane uncle shows up, it's a clear message people are missing the boat, to borrow one of your people's phrases. Would psychologists diagnose our silent pauses and outward reflection as Attention Deficit Disorder?"

The staff woman returned with two carafes and a wooden box, which she sat on their table. She opened the box and smiled.

"If you need anything, just let me know," she said, then hurried to wipe a table.

"You bring up a good point," offered Johanna. She selected a packet of jasmine tea.

"Our brains are wired to think about the interconnectedness of things and their impact on future generations," explained Angelique. "We need to make decisions that do not adversely affect all our relations. I think the Maori word *Takiwatanga* best explains the gifts your people label autistic. It means one is in their own time and place."

"That's a beautiful word, very respectful of the differences in brain wiring and individuality of interpretations," said Johanna, taking a sip of her freshly steeped tea. "My biggest concern was that Norah might have early onset dementia due to shock, a severe stress reaction to Nathan's tragic death."

"And now?"

"I believe it's the effects of severe trauma on an autistic brain, which processes sensitive somatic and emotional responses more dramatically."

"How so?"

"Autistic people have what they called melt-downs. Complete shut down of their compensation skills. Sometimes it affects their motor skills as well. Like the inability to speak or move or, conversely, flailing about and abruptly reacting to sounds, particularly loud ones or even florescent lighting. When they are experiencing those disturbances, they can no longer process thinking or communication effectively. It can look like a panic attack to others, but it's actually a shut down. She is concerned she does not have the mental fortitude to take Nathan's position at the helm of the family trust."

Angelique was silent. She reflected on the concerns Johanna presented. She removed a fragrant blueberry muffin from her bag and offered one to Johanna before speaking.

"They added lemon zest to their blueberry recipe. Try one, they are delicious." She sighed. "My people believe in the power of medicine stories. As you know, we were both trained in grad school to listen to trauma stories and notice the development of cathartic relief through their repetition. Therapeutically, we are supposed to support changes in their stories' contents, narratives, and tones over time, eventually leading to an acceptance."

She ate some of her muffin, then continued speaking again, "My people don't believe in that so much. The repetitive, unchanging story of an experience is actually a healing in and of itself. We call it narrative medicine. We believe Spirit is involved in the original storytelling of traumatic events and we should not change the words. Many times, one person's healing story becomes the many-times-told story of her people. So far back in ancestral wisdom, no one knows who it actually happened to. It can then become a teaching story. Why don't you just let Norah tell her medicine stories as many times as she needs to?"

Angelique leaned back in her chair and brushed aside a long, dark strand of hair that had escaped her braid.

Johanna nodded, sipped her tea quietly, and took a bite of the blueberry muffin. "Norah is a genuinely good person," she said. "I remember back in my undergrad days when I took one of her new eco-psychology courses, I was having a tough time understanding the connection between the two disciplines. In those days, the fields of psychology and human behavior were strictly based on the medical model."

"She took me to her agricultural labs at the greenhouse research station. The first greenhouse was growing food using strictly organic practices. All the fertilizers and insecticides were natural, based on companion plantings, pollinator supports, Castile soap sprays and other natural ways to deter insect infestations. She showed me the Three Sisters; corn, squash and pole beans."

Angelique grinned. "I am very familiar with them. Corn is the elder sister. She grows on tall stalks, providing guidance and support to her younger sister, the pole beans that wind around her and give her strength. The youngest sister, squash, grows at the base, providing protection and nourishment to her elder sisters. Each sister supports the growth of the others by providing different nutrients that enrich the soil. What one plant takes from the soil, the others return."

Johanna nodded. "Norah explained that plant-spirit-medicine provided the molecular bio-chemistry of practically every known pharmaceutical medication. So besides giving our body's health in the form of nutritious foods, the plant and mineral worlds provide medicines that heal sicknesses."

"Then she took me to another other lab, a test greenhouse for large-scale agribusinesses," Johanna continued. "We had to put on haz-mat suits and wear respirators. We entered the greenhouse through a locked door and an air-lock room. They used fossil fuel fertilizers, glyphosate-based insecticides and growth hormones on the vegetables. She explained that the weed killers would kill all plants that were not genetically modified to withstand the poisonous chemicals they used, not just weeds. I will never forget what she said when she showed me the corn room."

"This stuff isn't real. It's genetically different from the original corn. It has partial DNA strands from insecticide resistant bacteria spliced into its genes."

"Their stalks grew in dirt that was lifeless sand, not dark rich loam. She told me it was originally the same soil they used in the other greenhouse, but over time, the weed killer applications stripped the nutrients and it became this color.

"How can a human body consume poisoned food and not become inflamed and sick?' she asked me. Then she took me back to the organic test greenhouse and picked an ear of corn off a Three Sisters stalk. She handed it to me and said, "Shuck the leaves, boil the corn for nine minutes. Eat it without butter. Then give me a two-page essay on what you learned. You could use some extra credit for your grade."

"And that's how she taught me the interconnectedness of all things."

"And...."

"It was so sweet, I could taste its goodness!"

"You honor her," said Angelique. "There is a word in the Ojibwe language for wise elders like her. *Giche-Aya'-aa*. It means "great being." I think the Creators designed her mind to help your people learn truths necessary for survival and put that wisdom into a scientific language they could respect."

Johanna nodded. "And now she is suffering because the very nature of her gift is a unique mind that can't wrap itself around a world without Nathan."

"Sounds like people labeled autistic see and experience the world differently," Angelique said softly. "I think Nathan loved Norah dearly and saw the world through her eyes. Only you, Netuksq, love and respect her enough to do that, now. Understanding her may be the single most effective way to help her through this. Her extended family may never understand her. Maybe it is wrong to therapeutically direct someone to accept the intolerable."

Angelique used the name she had given Johanna years ago when they began their friendship. It meant "sister" in the words of her people, who had successfully guarded their language despite targeted assimilation and unimaginable genocide. A word and a relationship her friend did not use lightly.

Johanna nodded thoughtfully. "You're right. Nathan was her champion. That's what she needs most from me now."

Both women dropped into a comfortable silence, each dwelling in their own thoughts. The sounds of the cafe seem to grow louder as some of the crowd stood up, scraping metal chairs against the wood floors. Some were leaving, and some were newly arriving with sounds of laughter, cups clattering and plates being placed in wash bins by the exit doors.

"Last night, I had an unexpected journey at the campsite. It ended with a visionary healing ceremony for Norah," said Johanna, breaking their silence. "One for me as well."

Angelique set her coffee down on the table and leaned forward.

"Tell me about it," she said softly.

Johanna set down her cup as well. She began telling her dearest friend how she was woken in the night by a mountain lion spirit guide, then led along a mountain trail under a shaft of sparkling stars that should not have been in the sky. She told her of meeting her grandmother on the Isle of Skye.

When she finished her tale, Angelique sat back. "A journey is always in non-ordinary reality," she said. "It is not in human time. It is always an expedition to your purest nature. I knew that mountain lion would find you a worthy student. Aila was your father's mother. Am I right?"

"Yes. She was born and raised in Scotland before her family moved to Nova Scotia. That's where she met and married Alistair Gordon, my grandfather."

"You're a Gordon, not a MacIntosh?"

"You know that story." Johanna reached over and lightly touched her friend's hand. Her voice dropped to a whisper. "I had to change my name. But for the Scots, it's all lineage."

"I know," Angelique said gently. "I am trying to understand why your grandmother is teaching you right now."

"She was a powerful influence in my life growing up. My mother had Scottish ancestry as well. Her people, the Rosses and the Campbells, were clans of the Cape Fear Scots that fought for Bonny Prince Charlie and deported to the

Carolinas for rising against the King of England. He gave them the choice of prison or land ownership in the New World as a reward for allegiance. They and others fought for the King during the American Revolution. I spent summers in Nova Scotia with my grandmother Aila. She told me I was like her, born under the caul."

"You mean with the veil of an unbroken amniotic sac?"

"Yes, to the long-ago Scots, it was a sign of having Second Sight."

"And to native peoples, it has many special meanings as well. Healing gifts. Intuitive knowledge."

"Some view it as evil, like left-handedness was once seen."

"We both know better than that."

It was suddenly silent. Both women looked around the cafe. The lunch crowd had left, leaving only two older men chatting at a table by a window. They had the place all to themselves. Even the wait staff was gone.

"This is about you and Scott," Angelique said gently. Her dark eyes bespoke a softness and her face a depth of compassion rarely experienced in the dominant culture. "This is about your past."

"I can never be sure of him."

Angelique sighed. "For a really smart person, you have a lot to learn about wisdom," she said affectionately. "I notice how he looks at you when you aren't paying attention. You carry his heart and he was afraid you would hurt him again."

"A woman has a lot of power over a man," she continued. "Once he falls for her, she can manipulate him. Disempower him. It's like your stories about Sampson and Delilah. A woman can truly wound a man, shattering his spirit irreparably. Such a woman uses him to get what she wants and he's willing to do anything for her. Like a drug."

"There are women who could wield that power but don't. They form a bond of undying trust and yield their spirit to the man they love. He knows you could manipulate that trust if you wanted to. But a woman like you, Johanna, would never compromise her bond. Scott knows this."

"But I always feel I might lose him. How can you say I have that kind of power?"

"That's the catch. You would only feel the power I am talking about if you used it. Then it would be too late for both of you. He would know it was power over him you sought, not his love or devotion. Women feel love and devotion, or don't. Men are love and devotion, or not. Their love can empower them to achieve great things, not just shallow accomplishments. Love like that is rare."

"But I only made him angry, distant, and dismissive when we separated. I had no power over him."

"That's because he thought he had already lost you. For him, it was over. Now, it is enough for him to know you could hurt him badly if you chose to."

"He is my heart."

"And he knows this," Angelique explained. "You are like two acorns fallen side by side from the same Mother Tree. Your roots and bases grew together, so intertwined you couldn't tell one from the other. You were one tree but grew as two. Yet you grew under one another's shadow. As you became taller, your branches reached for light in two different directions. You desire both connection and independence, thinking you must choose between the two. It's not what it takes to be together that's your problem. It's in wrongly believing being free means being separate."

"Was this Aila's message through the blessing bundles and healing ceremony?"

"She wants you to claim your lineage inheritance. You are a Seer and a Healer, in traditions as ancient and as sacred as my own people's ways. But first you must heal your fear if you are going to access the kind of power a shaman can wield. People who seek this knowledge using psychedelics, like mushrooms and ayahuasca, usually believe this power is the ability to dominate others and situations. We know it's power over ourselves and the integrity of our actions. Fear is an obstacle to true impeccability."

Tears fell from Johanna's eyes. She turned her face to the wall as if the truth in her friend's words was too painful to bear. She remembered Scrag telling her that fear could be her strongest ally.

"Remember Netuksq," said Angelique softly. "No one said this path was an easy one. Our actions and beliefs shape how we perceive others, regardless of theory of mind. What we judge others to be is usually within ourselves. Some people overlook danger and deception by only focusing on the good in others. Some people judge others to be bad or worthless when it's their own faults they are actually seeing. I have walked this road myself. It's difficult, but we must walk a road of truth if we are to have any real peace or happiness. However uncomfortable that road may be."

Johanna nodded, turned to face her friend, and looked deeply into her eyes.

"To truly see another means having the ability to be ruthlessly honest with oneself," Angelique said gently. "In this Freud and indigenous wisdom are aligned. We say, to see the world through the piercing eyes of an eagle and the compassionate heart of a deer is to know the truth about oneself and others."

"If it wasn't for you," said Johanna, "we would never have gotten back together again."

"Make no mistake," Angelique responded strongly, "Spirit brought you back together. Spirit has many forms and, like Nature, it's more-than-human. It has a peculiar sense of humor and a very refined sense of justice. That's why we need spirit guides to teach us the ways. Our evolution as two-leggeds took us away from these truths. We need to learn to live wisely in the realms of intellect, form, and energy."

They held hands across the table. Their bond was one of truth and a sisterhood of spirit that went beyond blood and cultural differences. They cleared the table and left the cafe.

"Please give my gratitude to your brother," said Johanna as she hugged Angelique, "for sharing you with me today."

"Ah, I will," laughed Angelique. "He will enjoy hearing one of our own, a spirit being, is out stalking a white person."

"Let's hit the road to Tiadaghton."

She yawned, baring her sharp teeth. She extended her claws to lick them. Fear, she thought. How utterly human. Her kind had no fear. The scent of rose was a nice touch. It reminded the woman of devotion. A necessary quality in a student. Without devotion, there is no courage. Touch not the cat, indeed, but with a glove. A fearless heart is a strong one.

A Forest of Opportunity

As Angelique pulled into the farmhouse parking area, they could see a van parked next to Johanna's car with a Hennessy Locksmith and Alarm Company sign on its side. There was a man dressed in blue jeans and a hunter's camouflage jacket kneeling on the font porch by the door. Norah was standing beside him with her arms crossed, impatiently observing his work when she noticed the red truck.

Johanna rolled down the passenger side window as Norah approached them. "What happened?"

"Right after you left, someone broke into the farmhouse while I was at the farm market. When I got home, the hallway chandelier was on the floor," Norah said. "Someone cut the electrical wires. I was only gone a couple hours. The back door was open. I know for sure, I locked it. But it was wide open."

"Are you alright?" asked Angelique.

"I was in shock at first. The sheriff's department sent out a deputy and Samuel came right away. The Herbary was also broken into, but there was nothing stolen or damaged from what I could tell."

"Why didn't you call me? We would have come right back," said Johanna.

"At first I was frightened. This is way out in the country. But then I got angry. Who breaks into a house and pulls a chandelier out of the ceiling? I'm having all the locks changed."

"That's very opportunistic. Someone had to have known you were gone," said Angelique. "Vandalism, not theft, seems to be the motive. But what might have happened to you if you'd been here?"

"Pete Mitchell, the deputy, believes it was some kids from town."

"That's not exactly comforting," responded Angelique. "I would think everyone around here knows one another."

"That's mostly true," said Norah. "But there has been an influx of people moving in from out-of-state."

Johanna got out of the truck, retrieved her backpack and duffle bag.

"Are you heading up to the Boundary Mountains Preserve, Angelique?" asked Norah.

The dark-haired woman nodded.

"Please let the elders know I'll be starting some cold-hardy herbs in the greenhouse in March. I'll bring a box or two up to them in the spring."

"They would appreciate that," said Angelique. "If either of you need anything, just leave a text message with Jake at the Trading Post in Eustis. He'll get it to me. There's no reliable cell coverage up in the Preserve." Angelique shared the cell number with them.

Johanna gave her friend's hand a squeeze through the open driver's window. Their eyes met. Angelique's face expressed her concern.

"Be careful Netuksq."

"I will."

After Angelique drove away, Norah helped Johanna carry her things into the kitchen.

"I'm glad you're back," she said. "I've made a few decisions. New locks and a new outlook. Eli Mittleman is coming over late this afternoon. I asked him to draw up some papers for me to sign. It's good you're on hand."

"Norah, how could they have known you weren't here? It's too coincidental."

"I don't know. Neither Pete nor Samuel could explain it, either."

Joe Hennessy came into the kitchen and placed four plastic bags holding two keys apiece on the table.

"I changed the locks on the greenhouse, the shop door, the back and front doors of the farmhouse. I labeled the bags and recommend you have copies made at the hardware store. You should keep them in a different place than the others. Who knows how these hoodlums got in?"

"Pete said there was no sign of forced entry on any of the doors, so it's a mystery."

"What if they'd been here before, Norah? When you left a door open? What if they took a key for later?" said Johanna.

"Anything's possible, I suppose," responded Joe. "I've lived here all my life and the only vandalism I've ever seen is a few kids tagging a wall with spray paint. Their own parents turned 'em in and they did a month of community service, pulling weeds outta the sheriff department's shrubbery."

It was about 3:30PM by the kitchen clock when a black sedan pulled into the parking space beside the Crosstrek. A tall, older man got out and smoothed his suit before grasping his brief case. He ran his fingers through a shock of white hair before deciding to walk to the front door. Norah greeted him in the driveway.

"I would like you to meet Johanna Kincaid, Eli," she said. "We can meet in Mina's office over the barn."

"Eli Mittleman," he said, introducing himself as he offered his hand to Johanna. "I'd prefer your dining room table, Norah. We will need some space to work on."

Norah nodded and led the way through the back garden and the kitchen entrance door.

"Samuel told me about the break-in," he said. "Nasty business. You must feel victimized. I worry about you here all alone now." He placed his briefcase on the dining table and unsnapped its locks.

"Not alone. Johanna is here for a while and I have new locks on all the doors. I put an extra key under the shingle marked 'x' by the front porch in case I forget mine. I am having multiple copies made and choosing a new place to put them. It won't be so easy to break-in the next time. No one but us knows about the shingle."

"I drafted the documents you asked about. We need to review them before you sign. Everything should be in order. I'll set them out."

"Would you like some tea or coffee, Eli?" asked Norah.

"Sure, coffee would be nice."

"I'll make some," offered Johanna.

"Better make some for all of us," said Norah.

She waited for Johanna to leave the table. When she heard sounds of coffee dripping and cups clinking in the kitchen Norah turned to the older man.

"Was everything clear, Eli?"

"Perfectly. Does she know yet?" He nodded toward the kitchen.

"No, I haven't had time to tell her."

"You need to propose it first before signing the documents."

"I understand."

"You're sure about this, Norah ? It's a big step. You've had a major shock."

"I've been thinking about it for quite a while. The break-in sealed it for me."

Johanna returned with a tray bearing three cups of coffee, cream, and sugar. She sat down next to Norah.

"Johanna, I've done a lot of soul searching lately, thinking about aging and impending challenges. You've helped me understand that my forgetfulness isn't out of the ordinary and that I can still make sound business decisions. Eli is older than me by ten years and he's still sharp as a tack."

Johanna reached over and placed her hand over her friend's.

"Instead of feeling intimidated or unsure of myself, the break-in strengthened my resolve. Today I am signing the acceptance notice to be the trustee of the Albert and Mina Minsky Legacy Trust. I'm also going to make some Trust changes Nathan didn't have time to do before he died."

Eli rustled the papers as he spread out four consecutive document piles on the table. He glanced over his shoulder at a painting on the dining room wall, momentarily. Then refocused on the task at hand.

"But first, I need to ask you, Johanna, if you would stand as my ower of attorney in case of incapacitation? You can run the Minerva's Meadows business enterprise as no one else could do. Eli needs to be free to retire from his official watch in these matters."

"Of course I would." Johanna fully understood the gravity of the situation and what her friend was asking of her.

"There's more."

Norah looked at Eli, who nodded and pushed a pile of documents toward her. "You should read them thoroughly first before signing."

"According to the current rules of the Trust," said Norah, "the properties gifted to Nathan, Samuel, and Eliana can be transferred only to their heirs. Without the approval of the Trust, it is not possible to sell or use the properties as collateral. Nathan wanted to end that stipulation. I have asked Eli to prepare a document stating that each property, its assets and profits are to be transferred over to the holders in their entirety to do as they see fit. They will no longer be required to submit financial statements to the Trust."

"What this means," said Eli, "is that Eliana and Samuel would each own the hay and blueberry fields and the textile mill building with no encumbrances. And that you specifically, Norah, own the entire twenty acre farmstead property and everything on it, to sell or transfer as you see fit." He raised his voice as if to proclaim the decision was final.

"There are implications for this decision, which I fully explained to Nathan," he continued. "I believed it went against my uncle's intentions, but I understand times have changed. The stipulation seems more stringent than necessary given the current economic horizon."

"That said," continued Norah. "As you know, Johanna, Nathan and I did not have any children. It would please him to know I am choosing to name you as sole beneficiary of my business holdings, properties, assets, lands, and intellectual property. This includes Mina's book of garden secrets and any franchising opportunities you believe would benefit the Minerva's Meadow and Tea Gardens Trust. I name you its trustee, as of today. Upon my death, these assets automatically transfer to you, to do with as you wish."

Johanna looked shocked.

"You're certain you want to do this, Norah?" she asked.

"Absolutely certain."

"The mail orders we are working on now will complete the fall business. Knowing you are attending the herb business financials while I focus on the Legacy Trust is more reassuring than I can say."

"At some point," said Eli, "we are going to have to explain to Samuel, Evelyn and Eliana that the family board they've been sitting on all these years is merely an advisory board for business assets owned entirely by the Legacy Trust, subject to your executive decision making for all operations. They will not be too happy finding out the seat on the Board occupied by you isn't what they thought it was."

"We can vote Samuel chairman of the Board as he wanted," said Norah. "That's only a small part of the Trust holdings. A tiny portion."

"I'm confused," said Johanna.

"Eli, can you explain the situation to Johanna while I review the documents?"

The older man looked uncomfortable.

"As you probably know, when he came to this country, my uncle bought forests and built logging mills and a railway. That empire was just the beginning. When he came from Germany, he brought bars of gold and silver with him that he used for those purchases. A year later, my father, Ari, joined him and Albert appointed him his right-hand man. They formed the Mittleman Gold and Silver Company, with Albert as a silent partner. That enabled them to trade in precious metals, creating a solid financial basis of real money from which Albert could invest in struggling businesses and international investments."

Eli stopped to sip some coffee and gather his thoughts. Norah signed the official document proclaiming her acceptance of the role of trustee to the Minsky

Family Legacy Trust. She pushed the paper across the table to Eli authoritatively, indicative of her new role in command.

She reviewed the documents severing Albert's stipulations on the three property holdings that dictated the restrictions his grandchildren agreed to uphold.

"When Albert and Mina escaped Hitler's grand plan to exterminate the Jews, they believed God had blessed them in the same way He honored the Prayer of Jabez. This became Albert's driving motivation and created a path of wealth that is practically unheard of."

"What's the Prayer of Jabez?" asked Johanna.

"There is a story in Chronicles, the Old Testament, that tells of man honored by God because he was a righteous man. The specific words are to be memorized and used by each successor trustee as their guiding light. It goes, *'Jabez cried out to the God of Israel, O that You would bless me indeed and enlarge my territory! Let Your hand be with me and keep me from the evil one.' And God granted his request."*

Norah looked up from the document she was reading and added, "For Albert and Mina, their escape from death meant that God had favored them. They believed it was because Albert was a righteous man, and he wanted his son and grandchildren to live that kind of life. Not because he dictated it, but because they were just naturally good people who gave back because God had blessed them with a good life."

"In that way, Albert and Ari were both men of integrity," said Eli wistfully. "Real Mensches, as Mina would often say. I aspire to that, but probably won't ever be the kind of men they were."

"Nathan was," said Norah firmly. "He took to heart his grandfather's belief that integrity was the measure of what you would not do. He lived it."

"And Morris did not," said Eli. "He believed, as do the treasuries of failing nations, he could spend his way out of debt. My father took his place as successor trustee and trained me. I, in return, trained Nathan who was his grandfather's choice. See, in Albert's eyes, the enlargement of those gifted properties was proof of God's favor in a righteous man. Hence the test of gifting properties with the stipulations that Norah just dissolved. If one could not use the principals of expanding wealth and generosity with a small gift, what would one do with the responsibility of greater wealth?"

"So Albert and Mina put their grandchildren to the very test their son failed?"

"Yes," replied Eli. "Being born to wealth is seductive; it offers temptations and the ability to do harm with impunity. Albert saw that as the basic reason that evil rose into power. Unbridled greed and a sense of being better than someone else. A righteous man did good things, made the world a better place, because it was in him to do so. An unrighteous man used his leverage for personal gain and was therefore temptable. Capitalizing on another's man's misfortune is an inevitable outcome of business. What you do with that opportunity is a measure of your integrity. Albert was a brilliant man who did not want to see that kind of power in the hands of weaker men."

Norah passed the signed documents detailing the Trust changes to Eli.

"It seems he found a business strategy that never failed to accumulate more wealth," said Johanna. *A hidden secret,* she thought.

"And each trustee had to train their successor in just that secret formula," continued Eli, as if he read her mind. "The books in Mina's office contain the tenets of those strategies. There's a family legend that Albert amassed far more precious metals than were included in the inventory of Ari's vault. Albert supposedly put some aside in case political turmoils ever threatened the Minsky holdings, undocumented wealth, as it were."

Norah looked up from the final documents she was signing, authorizing Johanna as her Power of Attorney and trustee of the Minerva's Meadows Trust.

"Nathan once mentioned he had heard of a cache of gold that was hidden away," she said, "But his grandfather never confirmed it."

"I think it's just a rumor," said Eli. "I believe he was referring to the fact Albert thought mental fortitude and integrity were the genuine gold behind the Minsky Legacy. I think Albert believed the true Minsky legacy was an inheritance of the mind."

And that is when Johanna knew Mina's book of garden secrets held far more than the wisdom of garden girls.

Independent Means

The next morning Norah and Johanna worked in the vegetable garden. They added the last of the late carrots and parsnips to a wicker basket. Johanna pulled vines and plant stems from the beds while Norah sprinkled quarry dust and shredded leaves on top of them. They brought roots, withered plants and gone over vegetables to the compost pile, then wound up the watering hoses to be stored in the shed.

Norah pointed out some mounds of dirt by the raised beds. "Let's get some shovels to sift through the dirt," she said. "I'm pretty sure we'll find some late season potato stragglers in there."

"There are shovels and pitchforks in the shed," the older woman said. Minutes later, they were digging and turning over the soil. Norah lifted the new potatoes as Johanna dug with her hands, uncovering even more.

"Of all the harvesting," laughed Johanna, "I love potato picking the most. They are like little hidden treasures. You never know how many you'll find."

"I know," said Norah. "The pleasure of 'putting by,' as they once called it, was the unexpected bounty of the gatherings. If we add some of these gems to the carrots we just pulled, with some sweet onion, celery and string beans, we could make vegetable stew or roasted vegetables tonight."

"'Garlic?"

"Of course."

"I'd love roasted vegetables."

"Let's get these baskets up to the kitchen and wash 'em up."

After stowing their equipment in the shed, the two women carried the basket between them into the farmhouse. In a modern world where quickly changing technology often dominated one's life, there remained only a few dependable ways to bring food in from the fields; agribusinesses cutting the fields with big machines or field hands digging and pulling the harvest from the earth.

"Garden girls," said Norah. "It's like belonging to a sisterhood. People can be territorial about their gardens. But when you feel you are part of a tradition, your gardens become part of a community of well-being. You share your seeds with other farmers and build stronger crops."

"Out in Cross Fork, we have a seed share. Some people grow better tomatoes on their land, some people grow better corn or beans. We like to share the hardiest seeds with one another."

"I'll put on the kettle, if you wash these up," said Norah.

"I noticed you were your old self yesterday, full of determination and confidence."

"I know," said the older woman, pulling Mason jars of loose tea down from the shelf. "It felt good to take charge. I think I lost that for a while."

"You weren't a fragile person to begin with," said Johanna. "But losing someone you love makes a person very vulnerable."

"I'm not sure why, but getting angry seemed to make a difference."

Johanna placed the scrubbed vegetables in the dish drainer. She dried her hands and turned to face the older woman.

"You were wounded," she began. "When we are hurting, we see the world through a lens of pain. We wonder when the next blow will come. It's hard to be strong when you're enduring the pain of losing someone you loved."

"I wondered if I could ever be strong again," said Norah. "But after I saw the chandelier on the floor and the senseless ruining of something so beautiful, something snapped inside me. How could I become someone so weak and afraid Nathan wouldn't have recognized me?"

"What do you mean?"

"Nathan once told me he admired what I had done with my life. He said my mind was stronger than most people's. We had been talking about how people often succumb to social pressures and influences. He reminded me of the battle

I fought in the world of science as a woman. He said, "you never back down. You are fearless when you have a purpose."

"It's true. I remember how difficult it was for you to get funding for the greenhouse research in the beginning and how you persevered."

"After the break-in, I thought it through. I decided I would not become a person Nathan wouldn't have admired."

Johanna protested, but Norah held up her hand.

"By that, I mean I have to be true to myself. Something happens to me when I'm afraid. It trips a trigger in my mind that causes me to stand up to it, almost irrationally," she explained. "I get combative. Sadly, it was never one of my finer attributes."

"Angelique might call it strength of character."

"Being hurt or confused, now that's different," Norah continued. "It puts my mind in a tailspin. I think I've been in free-fall since Samuel came to the college to get me that day. But I will never let some cowardly little vandal get in the way of what Nathan and I built together."

Johanna walked over and put her arms around her friend. "Oh Norah, we need a ceremony to honor your decision. I have just the right ritual."

"Isn't that what Angelique always says, ' sometimes you just need a good ceremony,' right?"

Before Johanna could reply, Norah's cell phone buzzed on the table, alerting her to an incoming text.

"It's Lisette."

Could you please call me at this number?

"She knows our cell service is spotty. Let me step into the driveway and call her back."

Johanna reflected on the older woman's remarkable change in attitude. She was actively confronting her grief, honoring her loss and encountering a depth of fortitude Johanna felt she, herself, did not have. She remembered a time in her own life when she felt she was losing control. For her, fear was a paralysis, not a catalyst.

"What makes the difference?" she wondered.

Norah returned to the kitchen. "Lisette was contacting me on Evelyn's behalf to invite us both to high tea this afternoon. Four o'clock at the mansion. You can attend, can't you?"

"Yes. I'd love to meet Evelyn. But I'm not sure I have anything to wear."

"I'm taller than you," responded Norah, "but I can sew threads as well as I can sow seeds. Let's just hem up one of my lecture outfits."

"I brought some dress slacks in case we went out to dinner. Will that do?" said Johanna. "At least I have a nice pair of shoes."

"That should be fine," Norah laughed. "They will treat us to scones and Russian tea cakes. I said we'd bring some of the new Lady Evelyn's Assam tea for her approval. The last time I went to the mansion things didn't go very well."

Norah chose the black wool dress and scarf she had worn the day they had turned her away from the garden party while Johanna wore a pair of dark slacks with a borrowed crimson sweater. They made an elegant, if not somber, pair as they walked up the steps to the mansion's front door.

Evelyn's home was a Gilded Age mansion made of granite with a carriage house at the front of its circular drive. A New York City investment banker had built it in 1895 as a get-away cottage in the country for his family. Albert Minsky purchased it at auction in the mid-1930s, after the stock market collapse of 1929 decimated the fortunes of many wealthy families. Evelyn was used to living lavishly and spent many summers in the Jameson's Bar Harbor cottage on millionaire's row. But it had burned down along with all the rest in the 1947 fire that swept through the city.

Lisette answered their ring and took their coats. She noticed Norah's outfit and nodded her approval.

"This is my dear friend Johanna Kincaid. Johanna, this is Lisette Gagnon. She runs things around here."

Lisette offered her hand and smiled. "As smoothly as if it were my own."

"How's Stephen?"

"He graduates from business school in the spring. We are all so proud of him."

"Please tell him to use my name on any references he needs."

"I will do that. They are having tea in the sitting room."

"Here is a jar of the tea we brought. Could you have Cook make a pot to serve?" Norah took a jar of loose tea from the basket and handed it to Lisette.

"I will make sure of it."

Norah led Johanna down a dark paneled hallway, past an elegant, mahogany walled living room with a stone fireplace so large she could have stepped into it. The room was richly furnished with modern couches and chairs, marble end-tables and a large, square coffee table on which stood a tall Chinese vase. It contained an exquisite floral design of fresh chrysanthemums and eucalyptus. Tall windows and French doors looked out onto a yard lavishly landscaped with multiple gardens and a reflecting pool.

"Nathan offered a letter of recommendation to Lisette's son, Stephen, to attend Harvard Business School because his grades at UMaine were so exemplary. Lisette and her husband raised a bright young man who has a promising future."

Further down the hallway was a smaller room with rose and vine wall-papering and comfortable chairs that surrounded an ornate central coffee table made of carved oak. As Norah walked into the sitting room, Evelyn rose to greet her.

She was a tall woman, well into her nineties, dressed in a tweed skirt and matching tan cashmere sweater. Her thin, grey hair was swept into a twist and held with an antique tortoiseshell comb that sparkled with tiny sapphires. Small diamond earrings twinkled in her ear lobes. She smiled and held out both her hands to Norah.

Norah clasped her mother-in-law's hands as she turned her cheek for a light kiss.

"I'm so happy you could come," Evelyn said. Her voice was low and husky, authoritative but polite. "So good of you to get past that other unfortunate business."

"This is my dear friend and former student Johanna Kincaid. Johanna, Evelyn Jamison-Minsky, Nathan's mother."

Johanna took the elderly woman's proffered hand and clasped it in a gentle hold. She smiled and offered her greeting.

"Please sit down. The others will be here shortly. What have you brought me, Norah?" she said with mock surprise.

"Minerva's Meadows has crafted a signature new blend. With your approval, I would like to name it Lady Evelyn's Assam Tea." Norah gave her the basket.

"What's this?" Evelyn held up the jar of jam.

"Rose petal jam," replied Norah. "I thought it might go well with the scones."

"And so it might." She opened a second Mason jar of loose tea and sniffed. "It smells lemony, a little floral with mint, yes?"

"Lemongrass, mint and dried honey with a fine, imported organic Assam. If it meets your approval, we can create a label."

"Wonderful, I am honored. Thank you." She laughed. "Lady Evelyn? It's about time!"

That moment, Samuel arrived with his wife. "Eliana will be along. She's in the kitchen, as usual, surveying the goods."

"Sampling, I'm sure," said Ann. "I'm Ann Jameson-Minsky, Samuel's more gregarious half." She reached for Johanna's hand.

"Ann, this is Johanna Kincaid," said Evelyn, "Norah's friend."

"Samuel said you were visiting. So good to know she isn't alone after that horrible break-in."

An attractive woman in her mid-fifties entered the room. She wore a dark, mid length dress and low heels that understated her vibrant personality. She seemed able to command a room with very little effort.

"Well, Mother, I can attest that tea is underway and will be served momentarily."

Ignoring Norah, she walked over to Johanna. "You must be Norah's house guest, the social worker."

"Psychologist, retired," Johanna responded holding out her hand.

"Ah," said Eliana. "Such an extensive field. I have my doctorate in organizational psychology. My company offers career strategies and leadership coaching for some of the nation's most successful chief executives."

"It's a good thing you conduct your consulting from a distance now, El," said Samuel, "instead of all those business trips to Boston and Manhattan."

"Don't let her fool you," said Evelyn, gazing at her expertly manicured nails. She flicked her long fingers and a large diamond sparkled. "My daughter is also a professor of business psychology at Colby, her father's alma mater."

"Someone needs to teach the newcomers how to deal with privileged corporate executives."

"Johanna used to work at The Glen, El. Pretty sure she's had her share of privileged clients with all their stress and angst."

"Different caliber of service, I'm sure."

"My experience is that stress hits us all with the same weaponry, the same effects," Johanna said. "The buttressing may be different. But I have found the most marginalized people in the most socio-economically disadvantaged sectors have a fundamental resiliency that my wealthiest and most successful clients would envy."

"Checkmate, El," laughed Samuel.

"We coach our executives in game-theory strategies for specifically targeted outcomes," said Eliana. "It's extremely profitable. We teach them to use language, not only to merely communicate, but to obtain a certain calculated effect."

The differences between the imagery of Second Sight and a sudden flashback are slight. The surge of adrenaline that raced through Johanna's body provoked the only distinction between the two, a memory.

Her mind flashed back to her training after college in a form of mind control referred to as psy-ops. Business game-theory differed dramatically from the practice of psychological manipulation. One was information that provoked a call to action. The other targeted disinformation to reinforce disempowerment. Eliana's form of management training involved a subtle form of manipulation. Most people did not know the difference. Johanna wished she didn't.

"I think you just quoted Edward Bernays and Goebbels in the same sentence," responded Johanna.

"Ah, then you are familiar with the process." Eliana laughed.

To those in the room, it sounded like intellectual banter, but the sparring was very real. Johanna knew instinctively Eliana was positioning herself as an adversary. In her line of work, it was well known, there were those who needed to broadly establish their authority because their egos were fragile. They were far more dangerous due to that very vulnerability.

"You must be a formidable chess player," said Johanna, defusing the moment with a feint worthy of a master swordsman. She had been taught by the best to appear bested. It was necessary to carefully leverage a psychological advantage.

Eliana smiled graciously.

Bullseye, thought Johanna.

Lisette entered the room carrying a large, stainless steel warming carafe. A maid followed her with a silver tray, which she placed on a low serving buffet counter against the wall. Lisette put the carafe on the tray, then opened a cabinet beneath the counter, revealing several shelves containing a variety of English bone chinaware.

"Which pattern would you like to use today, Miss Evelyn?"

"Let's use Spode, the Lancaster."

Lisette took the elegant cobalt blue and white bone china tea pot from the chest and placed it on the silver tray. She poured the freshly brewed tea from the carafe into the china pot. She then placed cups, saucers and dessert plates for a serving of six on the top of the buffet. The maid returned with another silver tray. It held plates of scones and round, powdered sugar tea cakes. A silver bowl containing red grapes on the vine was the centerpiece of the tray.

Johanna noticed the family's natural ease with wealth and status. Their acquaintance with old money and time-honored traditions were integral elements of the social adhesive that sustained them. What would they become, she thought, if their access to wealth was challenged or diminished?

Lisette poured the tea and served each one of them. The maid placed a smaller tray of orange slices, lemon wedges, with sugar and cream in cut crystal containers on the oak coffee table.

Evelyn received hers first, taking a sip of the Assam tea without cream or sugar. "Quite nice, just as it is, Norah."

Lisette offered Johanna and Norah their cups of tea next, followed by Ann and Eliana. She served Samuel last. They approached the buffet table, each taking a Spode dessert plate and made their choices of scones and tea cakes.

"Did you say the tea is lightly sweetened with dried honey?"

"Yes, Evelyn. Lemongrass and mint to lighten the somewhat heavier taste of Assam."

"Well, I must say, Norah," said Eliana, "this is quite nice."

"Lady Evelyn's Assam," said Ann. "I think it's wonderfully creative."

"Well, there you have it," said Evelyn. "Fully approved. It's a go!"

"Thank you Evelyn. I will send you some artwork for the labels to approve as well."

"I have another announcement to make," said Norah. She set her plate on the coffee table. "As you all know, Eli took back the chairman's seat when we lost Nathan. Since the beginning, it was a dual role. Chairman of the Board and trustee for the Minsky Legacy Trust. However, the two positions are separate, and only the chairman position is elected. The trustee appointment is carefully and specifically noted in the Trust documentation."

Evelyn put her cup of tea on the marble end table by her chair and leaned forward. Samuel leaned back in his chair and gazed momentarily at the ceiling.

Eliana tightened her shoulders and casually sipped her tea with a look of indifference.

Johanna quickly noticed their shifts in body language, but it was Ann's look of concern that informed her the most. Ann looked back and forth from Samuel to Eliana, as if she needed their reaction to guide her own. Uncertainty was the mood, regardless how well some could mask it.

"Are you saying it's time to elect a new chairman of the board?" asked Evelyn.

"Yes, that, of course, but I need to tell you more about the appointing of the trustee." Norah's voice was authoritative as she continued. "Albert appointed Ari the trustee of the Legacy Trust until his grandchildren came of age. At that time, Ari trained Eli to mange the Trust with the express knowledge he would train his successor. Albert chose Nathan, as you are all aware. After Eli stepped down, Nathan took his position as both trustee and chairman of the board."

Samuel nodded, and the ghost of a smile passed across his face.

"We know all this, Norah," said Eliana. "Get on with it."

"The Trust states each trustee is to choose their successor at the beginning of their tenure, then train them during their period of management. That way, when it's time to take over the helm, their successor is fully prepared."

"Albert was a wily curmudgeon," said Evelyn. "Typical of him, to keep us all in the dark." She sat back and resumed taking her tea.

"Nathan chose me," said Norah. "I met with Eli yesterday to sign the official acceptance."

"Well, that changes everything," remarked Samuel.

"In many ways, yes," said Norah, missing his point. "I promptly signed an executive amendment to the Trust. It was a change Nathan had wanted to make. You all know the terms of the individual gift properties and their stipulations. Nathan believed your grandfather's original purpose had been served. As of today, each of the properties, all rights and profits, all decisions therein, belong to entirely to each of you. You can sell or leverage the properties as you wish. There is no need to produce financial statements for the Trust."

Ann looked astonished as Samuel bit his lip nervously. Eliana crossed her arms over her chest and looked down at the floor. Only Evelyn nodded in approval.

"It took a woman to put a stop to the family competition, now didn't it?" she said.

"Who owns the real estate, logging and transportation division?" asked Samuel.

"The Minsky Legacy Trust owns it," responded Norah. "I believe the chairman position should be held by Samuel. I cast my vote for him. It makes sense that his legal expertise guides the advisory board."

"Well, thanks for your confidence," he said. His tone was dry and condescending, but Norah didn't notice.

"Let me get this straight," said Eliana. "I now own all the hay and blueberry acreage to do as I want. Samuel owns the Jameson Mills, to do whatever he wishes?"

"That's right."

"And you own the farm homestead property and meadows to do whatever you want with it. Even though the stipulation originally stated if there were no family members to receive it as inheritance, a property would revert to the Trust."

"That's right."

Eliana abruptly stood up, spilling tea on her dress.

Evelyn passed her a napkin, but she refused it.

"I'll be right back," she said coldly. "I have to take care of this."

She walked out of the room.

Johanna could see Norah was bewildered.

"I'll go see if she needs any help." Samuel stood up and left the room.

So much for game-theory, thought Johanna. In the end, family dynamics beat executive maneuvering, hands down.

"Would anyone care for more scones?" asked Ann. "Evelyn?"

"I believe I'll have another cup of tea, if you're pouring," she responded with an amused expression on her face.

"She's lying! She's not telling us everything she's planning."

Eliana wiped her dress furiously with a dampened cloth.

Samuel stood next to the sink. They were the only ones in the kitchen.

"What she's saying is accurate. The chairman and trustee positions are two separate roles."

"That's not what I mean. Before her petty little act of power, the meadows, all twenty acres of it, would revert to the Trust because she and Nathan were childless. Albert wanted to keep all the holdings in the family."

"Right. Blood line inheritance."

"Now it's up for grabs. She has no idea what she has."

"I know," said Samuel calmly. "The situation is not ideal."

Ann handed her mother-in-law a freshly poured cup of tea and placed a plate of scones on the coffee table. Johanna reached for one just to break the awkwardness.

"I'm not sure what just happened," said Norah. "I thought they would be relieved."

"Surprised, I would say," said Evelyn. She looked out the window, sighing as if she felt Norah's concern was boring.

"So Johanna," began Ann. "You're helping Norah with the tea blending orders, right? What do you think of Mina's fascinating garden book?"

"I'm amazed to see how much those women knew without the benefit of science."

"Did Norah tell you about the family legend of hidden gold? I heard Albert hid all his gold during the 1930s when the government outlawed US citizens from owning precious metals!"

"Oh Ann, stop it," said Evelyn sharply. "We all know Nathan made up that story when he was a boy. He imagined there was a treasure buried in Mina's backyard."

"Oh, that's right," said Ann. "The secret garden."

Samuel and Eliana returned to the sitting room. Eliana's dress displayed a large wet spot which was hidden in its folds as she sat down.

"Well, Norah," she said. "How quickly can we get to business?"

"If you mean calling a board meeting, Eli is coordinating it right now."

"I'll call him in the morning," said Samuel.

"That wasn't quite as bad as the last time," said Norah, opening the Jeep's driver side door.

"I tend to agree with Evelyn," responded Johanna as she settled into the passenger seat. "They were surprised."

"That's an understatement."

Undo Influences

Eliana, Samuel, and Ann remained in the sitting room after Norah and Johanna had left the mansion. Evelyn had gone upstairs to rest before dinner. They sat around the coffee table eating the remainders of scones and tea cakes.

"Well, this really changes everything," said Eliana.

"I will ask Eli about the legal ramifications," said Samuel.

"Your mother seemed perfectly fine with the decision to end the stipulations," offered Ann.

"We need to work on her some more," said Eliana. "It's an unfair distribution of our inheritance and I'm furious." She turned around in her chair and noticed the doors to the sitting room were wide open.

"Ann, can you close the doors? This should be a private conversation."

Ann walked across the carpeted floor and peered down the empty hallway before pulling the oak slider doors together. She had almost secured them when she thought of something that seemed important to say. She returned to the gathering, leaving the doors slightly ajar. They were too caught up in their discussion to notice.

"It seems to me your grandfather gifted the properties in a manner that was perfectly suited to each one of your skills and interests," Ann said. "Nathan was the businessman who could turn around the farm. You both would have hated to prove yourselves with that obligation."

She took Samuel and Eliana's silence as a cue to continue.

"The hay and blueberry fields are prime real estate. It's as if Albert knew the homestead operation would overwhelm you, Eliana, as well as the textile mill. He knew you were cut out to work with corporations and you would hire a great manager to improve the yields."

"And I did," said Eliana. "It's true. They are worth a lot more, now that I can sell them."

"Samuel," continued Ann, "the mill operations have always been a burden to you. But your skills in contract law enabled you to do exactly what your grandfather wanted and what your father could never do. You made it into a lucrative, profitable business and were able to develop and maintain your own law practice as well."

"It's all true, Ann," said Samuel. "We can sell those properties now without the legacy interference."

"But that's a drop in the bucket," fumed Eliana. "As trustee, she can distribute the legacy assets whatever way she wants. Besides, she lied. She withheld significant information."

"How do you know she lied?" asked Ann.

Lisette was approaching the sitting room to retrieve the carafe and trays when she overheard their voices. She hesitated by the gap between the doors, wondering if she should knock and offer coffee. But their agitated conversation stopped her. She struggled between knowing she should close the doors for their privacy and concern that something involving the mansion and Miss Evelyn was very wrong. She listened at the door.

"I need to ask Eli about the extent of the trustee powers," said Samuel quickly.

"I'm sure he would tell you." said Ann. "Even though the arrangement is some sort of big secret, he must realize how distressing this must be for the family."

"Tell him Mother is upset," said Eliana.

"We have to reclaim the family fortune for our heirs," said Eliana. "It's not like Nathan had any kids to pass it down to."

"It really burns me that Norah used her sneaky 'Lady Evelyn's Assam Tea' ploy to get on Mother's good side," she continued. "She succumbs to flattery so easily."

"What did you think of Norah's friend, the psychologist?" Ann attempted to sip some tea, but it was too cold. The cup rattled in its saucer as she set it down. "Will she be an obstacle?"

"Her soi-disant degree is of no consequence," responded Eliana, with contempt. "Clinical people look for mental health disturbances. It's not like she is some forensic detective or behavioral profiler."

"Soi-disant?"

"It means 'so-called,'" offered Samuel.

Eliana slammed her hand on the arm of the chair.

"We may not be able to remove her from our grandfather's Trust, but we can convince Mother to disinherit Norah from the Jameson Family Trust. She was never a Jameson. She needs to be cut off from as much financial resources as we can manage."

"It won't be easy because your mother sees Norah as an extension of Nathan. She may have her faults, but being unfair isn't one of them," responded Ann.

"If we persuade her to amend the Jameson Family Trust to per stirpes with Nathan's share being split only between his siblings," said Samuel, "then Norah can't inherit Nathan's portion. I could make the case that the value of the meadows homestead property far exceeds the values of the distributions allotted to us from Albert's trust. Appeal to her sense of fair play. Use her own Trust to right the wrong, as it were."

"If she thought Norah was crazy, you know, and made unsound investments, she might be more willing to distribute her inheritance between the surviving siblings," suggested Ann.

"That's what we're hoping," said Samuel. "When the deputy arrived at the farmhouse after the break-in, I told him we were all concerned about Norah's state of mind. I said we had seen a rapid decline in her memory."

"It took very little to convince him she probably left the doors open, accidentally, so the vandals could get into the farmhouse," he continued. "I told him she might not be safe living alone. He could see she was nearly catatonic when he arrived. I even suggested she needed a competency evaluation."

"Good work," said Eliana. "Our objective is to have her stability questioned. I think there is enough evidence to convince Eli she needs to step down from her position as trustee."

"You still didn't say how you know she's lying," said Ann.

"Because we put an audio recorder in her house," said Eliana. "We listened to her meeting with Eli. She neglected to tell us she named that sidekick of hers Power of Attorney or that she made her the sole beneficiary of the farm."

Ann gasped. "You bugged her?"

"Yes," said Samuel. "Norah withheld telling us Minerva's Meadows and all its property value will fall out of the Minsky legacy holdings when she passes away. Mother would have objected to that decision. We can use that little omission to our benefit."

"All that matters is that we have a clear shot at a trustee appointment," responded Eliana.

"I'm the best fit for that," said Samuel. "I always have been."

"I would love to see you at the helm," said Eliana. "It would perfectly execute all our plans."

"You work on Mother. I have a plan that'll secure Eli's support. It can't fail," said Samuel.

Lisette stepped away from the doors. She had heard more than enough to understand what needed to be done. Miss Evelyn might be a fixture from the past with all her pretentious aspirations, but she did not deserve to be manipulated by her own children. She needed to tell Norah what had just transpired, along with the other discoveries she had made.

She felt uncomfortable eavesdropping on the family, yet knew with great conviction, where her loyalties lie.

Mail Order

N orah turned the key in the new lock of the Herbary's front door. It was a brisk day in late October. Their warm Mackinaws braced them against the chill wind that gusted around the building. Behind the farmhouse, the trees that lined the mountain hillside became more barren each day. Gold and crimson leaves swirled in a flurry of wind before settling on the ground. The chill of the night still held in the light of day.

As soon as they entered the building, Norah squatted down by the woodstove and opened the firebox door. She stacked some fatwood sticks and lit the tinder before adding logs from a basket of wood.

"It'll catch in a minute and we'll soon be warm as toast in here," Norah said.

Johanna began taping flat shipping boxes together as they prepared to mail out the orders they had crafted last week. She hadn't taken off her jacket yet, as the room was extremely cold.

"How many shipping boxes should I make?"

"The mailing labels and invoices are on the counter by the register. I think there are about twenty-five different shipments. Most contain an order of about fifty assorted tea boxes. We have to match the inventory to the individual orders and pack them as we go. But getting the boxes ready first is really helpful."

The room warmed up as Norah opened the slider doors into the wildcrafting room.

"I'll bring in all the bins," she said. "When the woodstove gets cranking, I'll put a kettle on top for tea."

A three-sided oak cabinet nestled in a corner. It contained an old tea-kettle and mugs with the Minerva's Meadows logo on its shelves. Johanna looked at all the single tea box samplers that filled the Herbary's display shelves. Years ago, visitors to the Herbary must have had a wonderful experience being treated to a tea sampling, thought Johanna.

Norah closed the slider doors, trapping the heat in the shop. She placed the last of the bins on the back counter and filled the teakettle with bottled water.

"What do you do with all the single samplers now?"

"When we first started the Tea Gardens, we had an open house on the first day of summer. The parking area would be full with cars lined up all along the road to the boat house. Nathan would put tables and chairs out in the ornamental garden. People would come for the free sampling and leave with seed packets and tea box purchases. We called it the Summer Tea Festival."

"That sounds like great fun, but a lot of hard work."

"It wasn't hard then at all. The meadows were in full growth. People could tour them if they wanted a hike or just enjoy the ornamental garden. We almost always sold out of stock. I took anything that was leftover to Susan, my herbalist friend, for the farm market."

Norah put the kettle on the stove and joined Johanna at the shipping table. She handed Johanna an invoice. "Start by putting the label on the box first," she instructed. "Take the corresponding order and fill the shipping box. Add some packing material, then seal it up."

After a few minutes, the room became much warmer, and Johanna unbuttoned her jacket.

They heard the rumbling sound of an old pickup truck coming up the drive. Norah glanced out the window.

"It's Jost Bergman, the ice man. He's here to shred leaves with his chipper. Better keep your coat on."

They went outside to greet him.

Jost was an old Swede who had lived in Maine for as long as anyone could remember. How his wife, Delphine, an Arcadian French woman, managed to put up with his constant crankiness and Scandinavian oddities was anyone's guess.

"Morning, Jost," said Norah, waving the man down. "Meet my friend Johanna. She's here to help with the fall tea orders."

The old man rolled his window down reluctantly. His face was lined with wrinkles and none of them were laugh lines. His pale blue Nordic eyes blinked in the cold air as he zipped up his tan colored Carhartt work vest.

"What'd you say?"

Norah repeated herself as he nodded and peered at Johanna.

"Nice to meet -," she began to say.

"Hard to know that yet," he grumbled. "Glad you're helping the doc out. Stayin' long?"

"Probably til Thanksgiving."

"Give Delphine a call, Norah. She wants to have you over for Thanksgiving dinner. Bring your friend."

"Thanks, Jost. So thoughtful of you," said Norah.

"Make of it whatcha will."

"The high school students made some pretty big piles up by the vegetable gardens."

"That's where I plan to start," he said. "Right fine day for some leaf shredding." He rolled up his window and drove up toward the farmhouse. They watched as the dilapidated trailer carrying his leaf chipper bounced and creaked behind the old truck.

"Ice man?"

Norah laughed. "Jost Bergman sells ice in the summer and Jotul woodstoves in the winter. He has the market cornered around here. No one wants to compete with him."

"He believes in neighborly reciprocity," she continued. "He shreds 50% of your autumn leaf piles for free and takes the rest in barter for the privilege. He lets them 'winter over' in his mulch bins. 'Seasoned mulch,' he calls it and people come from miles around to buy it for their gardens."

"Wow, 100% profit for him."

"He sells them an empty bag too, so they can pack their own."

"Self-serve garden mulch?"

"Yes, he is very resourceful."

The two women returned to filling the tea orders when the kettle on the woodstove whistled. Norah poured the boiling water over nettle leaves in a porcelain teapot and set it to brew while they finished more order packing.

"When did you stop having the tea festivals?"

Johanna placed a completed order on the floor and took more invoices and labels to continue.

"In the late 1980s, we became more of a supplier than retailer. Nathan had the idea of blending our leftover stock with community service. Our accounting method is 'last in, first out,' so we always shipped the freshest tea blends first. We always had some back stock to fill the orders throughout the year. After we finished the fall orders, around Thanksgiving, Nathan would contact our regional high school."

Norah poured two mugs of steaming nettle tea and gave one to Johnna. They stepped away from the shipping table to take a short break.

"Tiadaghton has an annual holiday fair and Nathan would secure a booth for our herb farm. He took high school students interested in the trades and taught them a partnership business model." She sipped her tea, then continued.

"They had to count our leftover tea inventory and set up the booth at the fair. Two of them would do a loose tea brewing demo, handing out freshly made hot tea to passersby. Two more would sell the tea boxes to the fair goers. The last one would oversee the cash box. After cleaning up, Nathan would meet up with the students and show them how to complete the accounting. They learned a quick lesson about gross revenues, breakeven analysis, cost of sales, operating expenses and profits. They learned about percentages too because he divided the proceeds equally among the students."

"He believed in hands-on learning, didn't he?"

"Yes. He also believed in giving back. He not only taught the future business men and women of Tiadaghton how to make a profit, but also the value of giving back to their community."

"The Minsky Way?"

Norah nodded.

They could hear vehicles coming up the drive. Norah wiped the condensation from the steamed up shop window with the edge of her sweater and looked out.

"It's the sheriff's department's SUV. Granger himself," said Norah. "Pete Mitchell too. There's a van from the UMaine extension service."

A third vehicle pulled in behind the others. It was the public health department.

"What on earth could this be about?"

Danse du Mal

The two women quickly put on their coats and joined the group of people gathering in the driveway. Phil Granger, Tiadaghton's sheriff, was a tall man, wearing a brown uniform and a heavy gun belt on the outside of his service jacket. He had a serious expression on his face. Known to be fair but stern, he had served the county for more than a decade. The sheriff took a folded document from the inside pocket of his jacket and approached Norah.

"Sorry to be here under these circumstances, Dr. Minsky," he said. "I have a search warrant for your premises." He handed her the document, then turned to the people assembling in the parking area. He nodded to the university extension group, which then separated into three teams and fanned out across the property, each accompanied with a deputy. They headed to the ornamental gardens, the vegetable gardens and Norah's backyard carrying cameras, shovels, and evidence bags.

The public health official, a middle-aged woman with a dour look on her face, walked up behind the sheriff and glared at Norah. "Where do you want me?" she said.

"Just stand by, Alice, when and if we find what we're lookin' for."

He nodded to Pete, who handed the roll of crime scene tape to another deputy, then entered the herb shop.

"What's this all about, Phil?" Norah's voice wavered as she held the warrant tightly in her hands.

A brisk wind gusted through the parking area and whipped around the building. They could hear the whirring sound of Jost's leaf chipper in the distance. Then it suddenly stopped.

"I'm sorry to tell you this, Norah ," the sheriff said softly. "A resident's dog was poisoned by your pet spray last week. We have to confiscate any remaining bottles of your pet spray and take samples of your products, just in case there is any other contamination."

"How is that possible?"

"I don't know, but for now, we have to shut down your operations."

"But we have orders to ship, Phil!"

"Sorry, but not today." As a look of shock passed over her face, he added, "It's a matter of public safety, Dr. Minsky, you understand, right?"

"Do I need a lawyer?" she asked.

"I'd get one if I were you," said Alice.

"Can I make a call from the barn office?" Norah asked.

"Mitchell," the sheriff called out. "Go with Dr. Minsky and make sure they don't move anything while she makes her call."

The sheriff entered the herb shop as Norah, Johanna, and the deputy walked over to the barn. Alice stamped her feet in the cold air before retreating to the warmth of her running car.

Norah and Pete went up to the office, followed by Johanna.

"Just the phone, Norah," he said.

"Can I use the bathroom?" Johanna asked.

The deputy nodded while he watched Norah call Samuel on the landline.

She walked down the hallway, closed the bedroom door as quickly as she could and locked the door behind her. Mina's garden book was on the end table where she had left it. Holding it in her arms, she wondered where she could put it where it didn't look hidden on purpose.

There was a small, empty closet with an overhead shelf by the bathroom. The book would be visible there to anyone who was looking around the room. The end table by the sitting area presented the same problem. Putting it under a chair looked intentional, as well as under the bed or its mattress. It needed to be placed out of plain sight, where, if found, would look perfectly normal.

Her gaze fell on the two steamer trunks on either side of the bed. Johanna started toward the trunk on the right side of the bed that faced the door. She felt suddenly pulled toward the other trunk, between the bed and the wall.

She quickly took the lamp off that trunk and opened it. The scent of lavender and roses wafted up into the air. The trunk held folded quilts and dried flower sachets. This, she guessed, was the trunk that had held Mina's belongings when she traveled from Germany.

As she placed the garden book between the quilts, she saw an image in her mind. The garden book had once traveled in this trunk as well, shielded between soft, quilted folds of secrecy. There was a small bouquet of dried flowers on the bottom of the trunk.

A sprig of white petals with a cluster of florets was entwined around a stem with tiny, faded green leaves and shriveled purple flowers that reminded Johanna of honeysuckle. They must have been wound around one another when they were fresh and supple, then left to dry and bind together as one. Edelweiss wrapped in hyssop. She picked it up and held it carefully in her hands.

Images, sensations, and feelings suddenly flooded her mind. They came quickly, randomly. Frost flowers on cold ground, a crack line expanding outward across a frozen lake, a kiss stolen under a graceful linden tree. Absolute trust.

An angry woman's face contorted in contempt, shaking her fist. Condemned, vilified, hunted. Fear cloaked in unbearable sadness. Hands grabbing clothing and pushing them into a trunk on top of the garden book and a sack of seeds.

And there, momentarily, a singular thread of devotion wove itself into the shadows of Johanna's mind. Love and longing for a forest, an alpine meadow, and a cerulean blue sky.

Of one thing Johanna was now sure. The hands that had twisted together this bouquet of love and devotion were the same hands that urgently pressed together the pages of the garden book.

Replacing the lamp, she remembered to flush the toilet before returning to Mina's office.

"He's on his way, Johanna. Samuel is coming."

That brought little comfort to Johanna's mind.

"He said to cooperate with the sheriff's department."

Johanna nodded and followed Norah and deputy Mitchell out into the yard.

"Why don't you go wait in the farmhouse, Norah?" he said kindly. "I'll walk you over."

They passed through the backyard where three men were shoveling dirt in the gardens, photographing and overturning the herb rock garden. Norah went from shock to anger.

She turned on Pete Mitchell the moment they stepped into the kitchen.

"You know I would never plant anything poisonous on this property, let alone use it in a herbal blend." She was shouting, and the deputy had the grace to look down at the floor.

But it was the look of pity on his face when he looked back up at Norah that punched Johanna in the gut.

"What are you looking for? I know everything that's growing here!"

"You may wish to stop talking, Norah," said Pete. "Everything you say will go into a report." He left the farmhouse to join the team in the herb shop.

Norah shook uncontrollably. Johanna led her into the living room and helped the older woman sit down. She took her coat and wrapped her in the afghan. She went into the kitchen to make a pot of strong coffee.

Through the kitchen window she could see the men suddenly congregate by the Moon Garden. One gestured excitedly. As the coffee maker finished its brewing, Johanna stared at the lattice. Withered vines hung stiffly and not a flower remained. At the base were four separate plantings, some shriveled and drooping, others, a faded, unappealing shade of green.

Something's different, she thought.

Alice, the public health worker, joined the team in the backyard, kneeling down by the lilac hedge. She nodded, and they began excavating something from the ground. More workers from the extension group arrived, and Johanna could no longer see what they were removing. She poured two mugs of coffee and returned to Norah's side.

As she sipped the strong coffee, Johanna fought with her mind. The intuitive struggled with the clinical. She went back and forth between the power of the Sight and her rational view of the world. *What part of me does Norah need most? she wondered.*

There was a knock on the front door. Johanna answered and let Phil Granger and Pete Mitchell enter. They remained standing as she sat back down next to Norah and held her hand.

"Dr. Minsky, are you familiar with a plant called datura?"

"Yes, of course."

"Pete is going to show you some pictures, and I want you to try to identify the plant in the photo if you can."

"Should you wait for Samuel?" asked Johanna.

"He said to cooperate and I've done nothing wrong."

Norah leaned over and looked at the photo on Pete's cell phone.

"It's growing close to the ground, arrow-shaped leaves," she said. "The seeds are encased in spiky burrs, the petals are closed because it's no longer viable in the cold. They look like they were once white. Did the plant smell unpleasant?"

"Hard to know. It was wilted," answered Pete.

"I would say, it's possible it's datura. No one touched it, right? It's quite poisonous. Where did you find this?"

"In your backyard, Norah. We are taking the plant to the lab to be tested. But it looks like this might be the plant that poisoned the dog. You are very lucky it didn't poison its owner, too."

"That's not possible. I would never plant datura. Where in my backyard was it found?"

"At the foot of the lattice by the lilac hedge."

Johanna went back into the kitchen and looked out through the window over the sink. The gardens were a mess of overturned soil. She stared at the Moon Garden. She could hear the sheriff talking to Norah in the living room.

"Listen Norah, no one is accusing you of doing this on purpose. But I'm sure you understand the severity of the situation. They did an autopsy on the dog. He was killed with an overdose of atropine."

"No, no," said Norah. "That's horrible, the poor thing."

"The dog's owner bought an anti-insect, flea and tick remedy with your company's label from Susan Chambers at the farm market earlier this fall. They tested it and found that it contained atropine. The lab has to test all the remaining bottles in your inventory, as well as the contents of your tea blends, to determine if anything else is contaminated."

As she stared at the empty area in the dirt, Johanna remembered a jasmine bush had been growing in that spot. *What plant did they just pull out?*

"Until we can determine the safety of your products, Alice is posting a public health notice shutting down your entire herb farm operation. No one may cross the crime scene tape or remove it."

"That's it!" Johanna walked quickly into the living room. Norah was looking at the floor, holding her head with her hands.

"Sheriff Granger," she said. "Did anyone take a picture of the Moon Garden before they started digging up the datura?"

He looked at Pete Mitchell, who began scanning back through the camera roll on his cell phone.

"I was out in the backyard in the beginning of October doing yoga in front of the Moon Garden. I know what was growing there. The only white flowers I saw were moonflowers climbing the lattice with the morning glories. At the base of the lattice were four plantings; a night-blooming jasmine bush, some gone-over four o'clocks, a few straggling lavender-colored wild bergamots, and some purple violets. Datura looks somewhat like moonflowers, but it's not a vine. It's a ground plant. Besides, it stinks. I would have noticed it if it had been there."

Pete handed his phone to Johanna. She zoomed in on the ground beneath the datura plant.

"The jasmine bush is gone. It was right where they pulled out the datura," Johanna said.

"What?" said Norah.

"And look at this," continued Johanna. "The ground beneath the plant is disturbed," she said, pointing excitedly. "This is what it looks like when you transplant something new, then tamp down the soil to support fresh growth. Someone removed the night-blooming jasmine shrub that was growing there and replaced it with datura. Their leaves are completely different. Jasmine have shiny, elliptical leaves and datura's are arrow shaped. Someone planted the datura recently, to discredit you, Norah!"

Both men crowded around the photo to see what she had pointed out.

"When did they buy the inspect spray?" asked Norah.

"At the farm market in September."

"How could someone extract atropine from datura that hadn't been planted yet?" she asked.

"May I see that picture?" asked Norah.

Johanna hurried to the guest room and rummaged in her backpack. She found the spray bottle of 'pest be-gone' from her camping trip. She read the date on its label. The spray bottle was noted as Batch 43019, meaning it was made on April 30th, 2019. She returned to the living room.

"I'm sorry, Norah," Granger was saying. "It looks like the dirt is disturbed but we only have your friend's word that something else was planted where we found the datura. Her observation is just hearsay. We found a plant in your garden that produces the substance our lab determined killed a dog. A substance that came from a bottle labeled Minerva's Meadows. This is still a public health issue. A serious one."

Joanna held up the bottle of pest spray.

"Is this similar to the bottle that killed the dog?" she asked.

"Uh, yes," said Pete.

"You need to give that to me," said Phil, struggling to pull some nitrile gloves from his pocket.

"Sure," said Johanna with a smile. She sprayed it on her hands, immediately filling the room with a pungent scent.

"Stop!" Phil reached out, then quickly moved back.

"My husband and I used this spray camping last weekend. Many times, I might add. If it had atropine in it, we would both be dead or in the hospital. If the bottle that killed the dog has the same batch date as mine, then someone tampered with Norah's supply at the farm market, not here in Norah's shop. They did it purposely, intending not only to discredit Norah but potentially kill someone with it. It's used with both people and animals. Not only that, they came onto this property and switched plants so you would have further reason to believe the poison was grown on her land."

Pete stepped forward with an empty evidence bag and Johanna added the spray bottle.

"I wish you hadn't done that, ma'am," said Granger. "I'm going to need both of you to come down to the station to make formal statements."

The front door opened and Samuel walked into the farmhouse.

"Are you ok, Norah?"

She nodded and handed him the search warrant.

"Sheriff Granger?"

"Hi Samuel. I can fill you in, but it's important that both Norah and her friend make a formal statement tomorrow. There's a good possibility, given what just happened, that someone tampered with Norah's stock. Poisoned it. Until we can confirm that with this recent evidence, we still need to suspend her operations." Granger held up the bag with the bottle of pet spray.

Samuel looked shocked. "I'll make sure she's there if I have to drive her myself."

After Granger and Mitchell left, Samuel looked out the window. The university extension van and public health department vehicle drove away. The herbary, greenhouse and barn were surrounded by yellow crime scene tape. He turned to Norah.

"You may not want to hear this Norah," he said, "but I think you should have a competency evaluation. It shows taking responsibility for the situation. Better to schedule it yourself than to have this incident provoke a court order. No one would ever believe you did it on purpose, but if you aren't mentally sound, well then... you aren't liable for any damages."

Norah stared at him, speechless.

"I'll come back tomorrow to drive you to the Sheriff's department. Please consider my suggestion." He left without acknowledging Johanna's presence.

"What just happened?" Norah stared at her empty coffee cup.

There was a knock at the door.

"What now?" Norah asked.

Johanna opened the door to find Jost Bergman standing on the porch, his wool hat in his hand.

Johanna invited him in with a sweep of her hand.

"Norah?"

His gruff demeanor was replaced with softness and concern. "There's no way you would let datura grow on this property."

He kneeled down and took both of her hands in his own. He looked into her eyes.

"Delphine and I, we stand behind you, no matter what. People in this town are not going to let you be railroaded, no way."

"Thank you Jost," she replied. "I don't know what to say. This is a nightmare."

"Nathan's not here to watch over you, sure. But I am and I will. You call any time, day or night. I'll come right over. I was the last person to see that fine man alive. I owe him this. I won't let them do this to you. You need anything at all. You just call this old Viking, hea-uh?"

She nodded.

He looked up at Johanna.

"Make sure of it?"

Johanna nodded and tears flooded her eyes. This man, as gruff and cantankerous as he was, lived daily with a sense of loss she could barely imagine. He was the man who drove Nathan back to the boat house on the day he died. He was the ferryman.

Power Plays

The next morning Norah and Johanna left the sheriff's station house. The building was a modern red-brick building with a green standing metal roof. Carved into the white plaster frieze over its entrance were the words 'Town of Tiadaghton.' Johanna had driven them to Granger's office to give their statements before Samuel could insist on accompanying them. Norah needed a clear mind and right now, she felt her brother-in- law was confusing her.

Phil Granger had listened to their complete stories, asking only a few questions.

"*Did you make all the pest sprays you gave Susan Chambers at the same time?*" he asked.

"*Yes, it's easier that way,*" Norah explained. "*I make them all in the spring. One batch only. Johanna had a bottle from that batch. They all have the same label. There were a few left in the Herbary because I hadn't distributed them all yet.*"

He turned to Johanna. "*Let me confirm. You are here to help Dr. Minsky with her autumn herbal tea orders and you are an herbalist as well?*"

"*No, I'm not,*" said Johanna. "*I'm a retired psychologist. I have gardening experience and I came to offer support to Norah. This is a difficult time for her. Nathan would have helped with the harvest blending and mail orders.*"

"*I see, so you don't know anything about poisoned herbs.*"

"*Datura is a flowering plant, with medicinal use in pharmacology. It's seeds and flowers produce atropine which is used to treat bradycardia, a dangerously low heart rate. Every gardener knows the plant is poisonous.*"

Granger looked confused.

"*An overdose of atropine can cause the heart to beat too fast,*" said Johanna. "*It can cause delirium or death.*"

He cautioned them to not contact Susan Chambers or try to find out the name of the dog's owner. They got into Johanna's Subaru and discussed Granger's response to their only question.

"There's nothing we can do until the lab confirms the contents of all the pest spray bottles. If the bottle sold to the pet owner was the only one containing poison," said the sheriff, "it would seem to indicate someone added it after the bottles left your property. I can see my way to allowing you access to your shop and barn if that is the conclusion of our investigation."

"Do you want to get some coffee?" said Johanna, "There's a nice cafe in the center of town."

"I feel like everyone in town will be looking at me like I'm crazy."

"I'm going to text Scott to let him know what happened."

As Johanna contacted Scott, Norah's cell phone beeped with an incoming message.

"It's Lisette. She wants to know if she can meet me at the farmhouse. It's important."

"Tell her we are on our way and will meet her shortly."

Johanna drove away from the sheriff's department toward the outskirts of town. They drove by the river landing and fishing pier. They passed the hardware store, which had just opened for the day. The grocery store parking lot was filling up with cars and the roadside nursery still had a large display of pumpkins, although Halloween was only a day away.

All Hallow's Eve would come on a full moon this year. The night sky over Mt Katahdin was already boasting its brilliant harvest moon. The town was hosting a community trick-or-treat parade with businesses staying open to greet children in their costumes, offering candy and other snacks. Social events ranged from summer fishing tournaments on the town pier to a Christmas celebration at the Nordic Ski shop on the hill. It was a close-knit rural farming community with very little tourist appeal.

The people seemed to enjoy their anonymity and a degree of trust in their neighbors. The shutdown of Minerva's Meadows for a health department violation would soon spread like wildfire and rupture its longstanding reputation.

Within a half an hour, they were driving up the access road to the herb farm. As they drove into the parking area, the crime scene tape around the herb shop and barn doors fluttered in the breeze. Lisette Gagnon stood by her car, staring at the closed business. Johanna parked beside Norah's Jeep.

"Sorry to keep you waiting," said Norah, fumbling for her keys. "Let's go inside where it's warmer."

"No, let's stay out here," Lisette stated firmly. "You'll understand in a minute."

Johanna joined the two women in the drive way as Lisette began her explanation.

"This is very difficult to say, but I must. I overheard a conversation after you both left the mansion and it's been troubling me. I think they are taking advantage of Miss Evelyn, and I don't know what to do."

"How can I help?" asked Norah.

"It's about you. We can't talk in your house because they bugged it. They are eavesdropping on all your conversations. They know you made Johanna your beneficiary."

"Who?" asked Johanna.

"Samuel and Eliana," Lisette said. "They are trying to get Miss Evelyn to disinherit you, Norah, and make you look crazy. Something about a competency evaluation."

"Good grief," said Johanna. "This is a serious invasion of your privacy Norah!"

"There's more," said Lisette. "When I took Miss Evelyn's phone to invite you to tea last week, I saw someone had blocked your name on her new cell phone. It also sent your email to spam. I restored both."

"Wait a minute," said Johanna. "Norah, you said your calls to accept the invitation to the garden party a few weeks ago went immediately to Evelyn's voice mail, right?"

"Yes, the first two calls. The last one returned a busy signal but no voice mail."

"Didn't Samuel say the voice mail hadn't been set up yet?" said Johanna.

"I set up her voice mail when she first got the new phone," said Lisette, nervously. "Someone blocked your number."

"It was a setup, Norah," said Johanna. "They didn't want you to be at the garden party. They wanted to discredit you in your mother-in-law's eyes."

"Samuel said he had a plan to convince Mr. Mittleman you are too mentally unstable to run the business," said Lisette. She looked down at the ground.

"If they bugged the house, Norah," said Johanna, "then they overheard your meeting with Eli. They know I'm your Power of Attorney and the beneficiary of your personal Trust."

"Do you know where they put the listening device, Lisette?" asked Norah.

She shook her head. "No, they didn't say. But please believe me, Miss Evelyn doesn't have a part in all this. She doesn't know she's being used."

"I'm sorry you got put in the middle of things," said Norah. "This is all so sad."

"And so illegal," said Johanna. "We have to find that listening device."

"I need to call Eli," said Norah. "He can put this straight."

"Possibly," said Lisette, getting into her car. "He seems to have a great deal of influence with the family."

After she drove away, Johanna turned to Norah. "It took a lot of courage to reveal what she overheard."

"Lisette has integrity. Albert sponsored Lisette and her husband, Etienne, to come to this country from Quebec years ago. They were highly recommended as landscape manager and housekeeper from a wealthy businessman in Toronto," Norah explained. "Mina helped them become citizens of this country because she herself came here as an immigrant. She wanted them to succeed, even if it meant leaving Albert's employ. Etienne eventually started his own landscaping business but Lisette continued to run the mansion for Mina because she was getting too elderly to manage."

"She stayed on after Mina passed away?"

"Yes, Evelyn couldn't run the place on her own. Lisette is a brilliant manager. She hires the staff, orders the supplies, and runs the household accounts. Ironically, Evelyn refers to her as the French maid."

"Sounds like entrepreneurial skills run deep in the Gagnon family."

"They do indeed."

Johanna and Norah entered the kitchen to began their search. Scott had still not responded to Johanna's text.

Remote Viewing

"I'm going to brew a pot of tea," said Norah, putting her shoulder bag on the table. She raised her voice unnaturally, very aware that somewhere in her home an intrusive listening device had been recording her most personal conversations. *When did they start? she wondered. Before Johanna arrived? Maybe they wanted to catch me talking to myself out loud.*

"Sounds good to me," responded Johanna, nodding her head toward the dining room. After she put the kettle on to boil, Norah began a systematic search under the kitchen sink and in the cabinets. She did not know what she was looking for, but she knew what did or didn't belong in that room.

Johanna began her search in the dining room, looking under the oak table and chairs. She tipped the chairs over and ran her fingers over the edges, trying to be as quiet as possible. She didn't know how small an audio recording device could be. Neither woman wanted to imagine when it was installed.

The kettle boiled and Norah poured the water over a strainer of lemon balm leaves to steep in the Royal Albert Country Rose teapot. She completed her search of the cabinets, on top of the shelves, and the refrigerator, standing on a kitchen chair.

Norah looked at the kitchen table and other chairs, having already searched their undersides. Her gaze drifted down to the floor.

Hiding something low on the floor doesn't seem like a good idea, she thought. Just naturally, she looked up at the ceiling. She looked at the lighting fixture and smoke alarm. Standing on the chair under the kitchen light, she felt around its edges. Nothing. The light on the smoke alarm was not blinking. Moving the chair over quietly, she detached its cover.

There was no listening device, but someone had removed the battery.

"Johanna, check this out," she called.

Johanna came into the kitchen. "Is the tea ready?" She hoped her voice didn't sound as fake as her question was, in case she was being recorded. She found Norah standing on a chair, gesturing toward the smoke alarm.

She pointed to the empty battery holder. "Tea should be fully steeped. Go choose a teacup." Norah got down and rummaged through a drawer to find a fresh battery. Moments later she installed it in the smoke detector.

Johanna used the excuse of getting a cup to search the china cabinet. She looked under each shelf to see if any devices were taped underneath. The cups rattled as she jostled them in order to look in the back. Nothing. She randomly chose a cup, one delicately painted with a pink lotus. Choosing an Emerald Forest cup for Norah, she walked back into the kitchen.

They sat down at the table. Norah pulled over a sheaf of bills and flipped over an electric bill to write a note on its blank side.

[*where should we look next?*]

[*I'm not finished in the dining room, yet*] Johanna wrote.

They quietly drank the tea.

In moments like this, Johanna thought, she wished she were psychic. But her Second Sight didn't work that way. She used to believe her gift would forewarn her of trouble or provide a straightforward answer to difficult decisions. But experience had shown her it was no crystal ball. It had its own timing.

But she knew someone who did have a crystal ball, of sorts. Two people, in fact. Jayne and her partner Marti, whose involvement enabled law enforcement to crack the sex trafficking ring, combined their detective skills with an unusual array of non-ordinary means. Marti read Tarot cards and Jayne used an amethyst pendulum. She texted Jayne.

Got time for a consultation?

Norah looked distressed. Johanna reached over and gently touched her hand, then nodded toward the dining room. She left Norah at the table to make incidental noise while she resumed her search.

If they hid the device in the hallway, the chandelier was the only obvious choice. But now, only wires dangled from the ceiling. She wondered if Samuel had a hand in that as well. The missing keys now made sense. It was how they maintained access to the farmhouse.

Maybe they needed to switch out the listening device occasionally and used the cover of Norah's forgetfulness and a break-in to gain access. *Then they had to move swiftly, she thought. Get in, switch the device, get out.*

Her eyes drifted to a painting on the dining room wall. She was attracted to the colors of its vibrant blue sky and gradient earth tones. She walked over to get a closer look.

Norah followed her into the dining room. "That's a reprint of Joan Miro's, The Farm. He was a master of surrealism. The detail of the original is spectacular, from the tiniest farm bucket to the pathway with its paw prints, ladders and plots of ground ready to receive seedlings."

Johanna ran her fingers across the wooden frame and reached behind it. She felt something. Hard and small.

The two women lifted the painting from the wall and laid it on the table. Taped to the top edge was a small black device.

Johanna carefully peeled back the tape. It was a thin square, less than two inches long. There was a tiny switch on its top; in the 'on' position. It appeared to be a voice-activated recorder, not a wireless transmitter. Such a poor signal inside the farmhouse would have rendered it useless. *No, she thought, someone has to come get it, which was even more disturbing.*

Norah took the device and switched it 'off.' She sighed. "We need to bring this to Granger."

Johanna nodded.

Her cell phone buzzed. It was Jayne texting her back.

Anytime, dear. Is it a Feng Shui consult or 'other'

She responded.

> Other.

> *We have some free time this afternoon. 2PM. Zoom, I expect*

Johanna confirmed the time.

She read Jayne's responses aloud. "I can Zoom with them in Tiadaghton, where I can pick up a better signal."

"We should put it back the way we found it on the picture frame and snap a photo before bringing it in to the sheriff," suggested Norah.

Moments later, they sat at the kitchen table trying to piece together the significance of Lisette's information and what they had found.

"Do you feel safe here?" asked Johanna.

"Yes, of course. I think this is all about Eliana and Samuel feeling threatened by my appointment as trustee. I can't for a moment believe either of them means me any physical harm."

"What about the break-in? The chandelier?"

"We don't know for sure. We have no evidence either of them did that," said Norah. "They're essentially good people."

Johanna made a mental note to pose that very question to Jayne and Marti.

"Norah, bad people do bad things and they don't care. Good people don't think they are doing bad things. All it takes is for them to act is to feel justified in doing so."

"Do they believe I have an unfair advantage or that I would purposely manipulate the Legacy Trust as the trustee?"

"Possibly. They are definitely behaving as if they feel threatened."

"I have always been the outsider."

"Well, bugging your house seems an overreach. People only do that when they think someone has secrets," Johanna said. *Or they are paranoid.*

"Well now, we know they overheard our conversation with Eli."

Johanna turned the device over in her hands. It was slim enough to conceal in a shirt pocket. If they had already known at the tea party that Norah made me both her Power of Attorney and beneficiary, then they heard it on a previous device. *They must have been switched out days ago, she thought. They still believe Norah is withholding things from them. When will they return for this one?*

Her thoughts turned to Mina's garden book. It was out of reach behind the crime scene tape. For some reason, The Sight was more active around that book than focused on the trouble Norah was facing. *Unless...*

"Before you call Eli, let me tell you something that happened during Granger's search yesterday," she began.

Johanna described the hiding place where she placed Mina's garden book when she and Pete Mitchell were in the office over the barn.

"When I opened the trunk, I knew it was Mina's travel trunk from Germany. It smelled of lavender and roses."

"Ah, Mina's dried flower sachets. She gave them out to people she loved. She called them flower notes. It was her way of showing affection. There is an entire language of flowers, you know."

"I found a sprig of dried edelweiss wrapped in hyssop in the bottom of the trunk. When I touched it, I saw memories. A woman's angry face, fear and a great love for the land."

"Edelweiss stands for nobility, devotion and great bravery. The Hebrews used hyssop to cleanse an offering. It stands for purity, the cleansing of the soul," said Norah.

"You said she sketched flower drawings and inserted them like little notes in the garden book when the intern was putting the translations on the computer, right?"

"Yes, she did." Norah sipped her tea thoughtfully.

"I need to get to the garden book," said Johanna. "I think she may have been leaving you messages."

"Messages?"

"She didn't put them in the binders, right? Only in the original leather-bound book."

"Right," said Norah. "How are you going to get past the crime scene tape?"

"Maybe Granger will think the recording device is proof someone is sabotaging your business."

"By someone, you mean Samuel or Eliana."

"Possibly."

"I'm going to call Eli right now and tell him what's happened. He will confront them."

"I'll clean up here," said Johanna, "and join you in a few minutes."

Norah went out to the driveway while Johanna put the painting back on the wall. She carefully hand washed the china cups and teapot. *What if they came back for the recording device? They seemed to know when Norah wasn't there, she thought. What else will they do?*

When she joined Norah outside, she overhead her mentioning the listening device and Mina's garden book to Eli. She was asking him to intercede with Granger so she could have access to the barn apartment. A text message from Scott popped up on her phone.

> Scott: This is getting out hand. Do you need me to come?

> Johanna: We're okay here. We aren't in any danger. I will keep you posted, promise.

She made the decision not to tell Scott about finding the listening device. We aren't damsels in distress, Johanna thought, it's all under control. Certainly Eli can influence the sheriff to intervene, now there's explicit evidence of tampering.

A Taste for Chai

For the second time that day, Johanna was parked in the sheriff's department parking lot. She watched Norah enter the door in the red brick building, through the rear-view mirror. She held up her cell phone and chose the Zoom App she used with its confidential and encrypted communications and sent an invitation to Jayne Cullen.

They had met at the Glen, a wellness spa in the Berkshires of Massachusetts, where she had worked for many years as a psychologist to the wealthy and privileged. Johanna's unique blend of western mind-body medicine and eastern contemplative therapies offered tremendous benefits for corporate executives harried by high-level stress. Jayne was a successful architect whose troubled marriage brought her no end of distress and confusion.

But now, she had found love, passion, and partnership in a new venture, operating a detective agency. The Zoom connection opened up, and it was Marti who answered.

"How can we help, sweetie?" she said. "Where are you?"

"I'm at my old friend's herb farm in Maine, outside a police station."

Jayne appeared in the video's background image. She stood behind Marti, bending down to hug her. Marti held Jayne's hand to her heart with a contented smile. These two women were meant for one another. It was as if the universe itself ordained their love.

"You two give me hope," said Johanna. "Hope for the world. Love like yours is rare. It's like rain for the soul."

"I wish you were here," said Jayne. "I made chai."

Jayne was famous for a lot more than her chai, but on a day like this, the thought of sipping her deliciously smooth and perfectly balanced blend of hot black tea and spices was comforting.

She handed a cup of chai to Marti and set next to her, so they could share the video screen.

"We've got a problem here," said Johanna. "I guess I should start with the farmhouse break-in and vandalism. Then someone poisoned Norah's pet spray blend with datura, which killed one of the townspeople's dog. The sheriff shut down her business. There's crime scene tape around her shop."

Johanna took a breath. Marti and Jayne looked at one another. As humorous as the pair liked to conduct both business affairs and personal relationships, they didn't find the situation at all funny.

"Sounds like vengeance to me," said Jayne.

"Personal," said Marti, "Who hates your friend?"

Johanna explained the complexity of the Minsky Legacy Trust and Norah's appointment as trustee. She let them know there were considerable assets involved.

Jayne was no stranger to wealth and the trouble it could cause in families. She had inherited quite an amount of money from her parent's investments.

"Money has a way of straining so-called brotherly and sisterly love," she said. "You really think they are behind this?"

Johanna filled them in on Lisette's revelation and finding a tiny audio device.

"Now, that's a bit over the edge," said Marti. "What did they hope to discover by bugging their sister-in-law's home?"

"We think they believe she is hiding something from them."

"Is she?" asked Marti.

"Norah is so above-board and ethical, its hard to imagine anyone believing she is conniving."

"That's because they are the conniving ones, Johanna," said Jayne. "They suspect other people of doing what they do. I think I learned that once, from a psychotherapist I used to see."

"Yes, when you are trained in psychopathology, it's what you look for in situations like this. But sometimes, it's just people feeling threatened and acting out. It may be disruptive but not lethal, if you know what I mean."

"Yeah," said Marti. "You need some help to decide if they are sociopaths or just a pair of blue-blood schmucks."

"Exactly," said Johanna. "Norah thinks they are good people caught up in feeling wronged by the choice their grandfather made, to run the business. Like I said, there is a lot of money involved."

Jayne looked at Marti. "Where do you want to start? The cards or the pendulum?"

"Cards. We'll use the pendulum to dowse for confirmations."

Johanna looked up at her rear-view mirror. The steps of the sheriff's office were empty. She hoped Granger took Norah seriously.

Marti shuffled her deck. "I want you to think about the situation. Bring to mind your fears and concerns while I cut the cards."

Johanna closed her eyes. She wished Second Sight offered the definitive directions that Tarot cards could often do. In Marti's hands, things were nicely sorted out, with a blend of the mystical and her understanding of the criminal mind. She used the cards to open up lines of inquiry and her incisive policing skills to infer the rest. She was usually spot on.

The garden book lying within its secret folds came into her mind. What does that have to do with anything, she thought.

"Good enough. I am going to pick three cards. One for the main provocateur and one for any henchmen involved." She cut the cards, selected one, cut again and selected another. She put them face down on the coffee table. She aimed her iPad in such a way that she and Jayne were off camera and the layout was on the screen.

"Now," she cut and selected again, "for any ally you can count on to assist."

Johanna hoped it was Granger.

Marti put the last card face down by the others. She turned over the first one, the Devil reversed.

"You've got to be kidding," said Johanna.

"You are dealing with someone who likes to kill. Enjoys it, actually."

Marti turned the next card over. "Emperor, reversed. This represents someone who has had a setback. They were once a respected authority, admired even. But they are caught in deceit and financial manipulation."

"Is that a different person?" asked Johanna.

"Ask the pendulum, my love," said Marti.

Jayne leaned down so Johanna could see the motion of her amethyst crystal on its delicate silver chain in the Zoom window.

It quickly swung back and forth over her palm.

"That's a yes."

"They are in it together," whispered Johanna. It swung back and forth even more widely.

"It's safe to assume you have a pair of evil knaves in your deck," said Marti.

"What about the third card?"

Marti flipped it over. "The Father of Stones in the West. I use the Haindl deck. We call him Old Man."

Johanna froze.

"So who the heck is Old Man?" asked Jayne, noticing her reaction.

"He's a helper spirit for the earth, the leader of the pack," said Marti. "You have a powerful ally here."

"Johanna?"

"I know who that is," she said slowly. "But I don't know why he would show up here."

"You know this person?" asked Marti.

"Very well."

"What's your next step?"

"I hope I can convince Norah they are not just plotting to remove her as trustee. If she stands in their way, they don't appear to have much restraint. They might do anything. And if Old Man is involved....."

"Are we done with the cards?" asked Marti.

"The pendulum says no," said Jayne. "Um, do we need a card for the energy Johanna brings to the equation?"

"Good question," said Marti, shuffling the cards.

"Pendulum says yes."

As Marti cut the deck, a card fell out, face up, onto the table.

"Strength, upright," Johanna whispered.

"This is a card of insight and revelation. It changes everyone involved," said Marti. "It is completely balanced between calm energy and ferocious courage. It is the ability to restrain one's impulses or unleash incredible power."

"And it's what Johanna will have to draw upon in whatever situation is transpiring," said Jayne.

Norah was coming down the police station steps. She didn't look happy. In fact, she looked rather angry.

"Keep us in the loop, Johanna," said Marti. "Please, we're worried."

"I might need your law enforcement skills."

Johanna signed off just as Norah got into the Subaru. She gave the listening device to Johanna.

"He can't use it. Nothing proves Samuel put it there. It only has a recording of our conversation from dinner last night. He said they can't use audio recordings for evidence. I think Granger believes I've lost my mind."

"So we can't get into the barn?"

"Nope."

Johanna put the device in the Mackinaw's pocket, wondering if they should put it back in its hiding place.

If they came for it and didn't find it, what would happen? The jig would be up and that wouldn't be such a good thing, she thought.

All Souls Day

Two days after Halloween was All Souls Day, November the second, a day of commemoration and prayer for the souls of those who have passed away. Norah had lit a small candle on the dining table. She was wearing blue jeans, her Teamster shirt and a white chef's apron tied around her waist, making a light breakfast when Johanna joined her.

"Are you up for a walk to the top of the meadows?"

"Not really," said Norah. "I think I'm going to distract myself today by baking. If I keep thinking about the shut-down, I'll just get more frustrated."

"Will you work on more trial recipes from the garden book?"

"No, that will make me feel depressed. I was thinking of some hot chocolate with amaretto and some cookies."

"I think I'll have some yogurt and fruit, then my yoga practice. I noticed your votive candle on the table. For Nathan?"

"Yes, but it's actually his Yahrzeit candle. I burn it on the anniversary of his passing, a Jewish tradition. But this morning I felt, if only he was here, he would know what to do. So All Souls Day felt appropriate."

Johanna nodded and went to get her yoga mat. When she returned, she could smell the hot chocolate as Norah stirred her home crafted recipe of cocoa, sugar, almond extract and milk on the stove.

"Cooking and growing things calms you, doesn't it?" She sliced some apples and bananas to put in her yogurt.

"Being in my blending lab is the best," said Norah. "I have a fast mind and sometimes it covers more territory than I would like. Keeping my hands busy in the wild-crafting room or in the gardens helps slow it down. If I focus on sounds and smells, textures and producing tangible results, I won't feel so helpless."

"Not being able to get into the Herbary must be difficult."

"If I think about it too much, I'll go into a tailspin."

A tailspin is Norah's version of a melt-down, Johanna thought. How brilliant of her to find her own antidote for a cacophony of sensory neurons flashing in her brain like neon lights.

A bottle of amaretto, along with almond flour, tahini paste and baking powder, were on the table. Norah had set out mixing bowls, spoons and measuring cups. From what Johanna could tell, her kitchen wasn't all that different from the wild-crafting room. Norah poured the hot chocolate from the saucepan into a stainless steel thermos by the sink, then added a quarter cup of amaretto. She smiled.

"Who needs marshmallows when you have fine liqueur?"

"What cookies are you going to bake?"

"Sesame tahini with slivered almonds and cranberries."

"I've never tried tahini cookies," said Johanna.

"You are in for a treat. I should have a batch coming out of the oven after you're done with yoga."

Norah stood for a moment and looked at Johanna affectionately. "Having you here is helpful beyond measure. Being with you is like sitting at the top of the meadows. You are like gentle winds and softly scented flowers. A bestowal of grace."

A rosy blush brightened Johanna's cheeks as she touched her friend's hand lightly. She would have given her a hug but she knew how difficult it was for Norah to experience physical signs of affection. Hugs were uncomfortable unless Norah, herself, initiated them. For autistic people, affection was more often shown by acts of caring, rather than risking a sensory overload.

Norah went to her spice shelf and retrieved cardamom and cinnamon. "The secret is using ginger paste instead of ground ginger," she said.

Dressed in black yoga pants and a purple t-shirt imprinted with the words, 'Bliss is a Kiss,' Johanna spread her yoga mat on the floor in the living room. The contrast between Norah's Bauhaus furnishings and the gentle poses of a five thousand year old tradition was striking. Reaching up into mountain pose, then dropping into Goddess, rising outstretched arms in warrior, and balancing one leg in tree pose, Johanna moved silently amidst the vibrant colors and geometric shapes of Miro and Klee. She came down onto the floor into child pose, arms outstretched with prayer-locked fingers beneath O'Keefe's giant scarlet poppy. It was as if she bowed in reverence to artists whose minds created images of which others could never even dream.

As she rested in her pose of surrender, she thought of Norah's vibrance and resilience in the face of such losses and setbacks. Even now, in her mid-seventies, her body was strong and willowy. She strove to understand nature. Norah surrounded herself with colors, textures, scents and tastes that brought peace and fulfillment to a mind that in another person would be too turbulent to function. She had spent her life in sun-filled activities, growing healthy foods and focusing her inquisitive mind on objective reasoning. These things, Johanna thought, kept Norah from the rapid aging and mental decline she had seen in so many of her wealthy clientele.

She heard footsteps on the front porch, followed by a sharp knocking on the door.

"Who could that be?" said Norah, nervously. She stood in the hallway, beneath the dangling ceiling wires with flour smudged on her face.

"I'll get it," said Johanna. She stood up and looked out the window that faced the barn. There was a sheriff's department SUV, and another car parked in the driveway behind it. She could not identify the second as the SUV partially blocked it.

She steeled herself as she opened the door. Pete Mitchell, hat in hand, nodded to her.

"Mornin' ma'am," he said, peering around her to see Norah standing in the hallway. "Mornin' Norah. We have some news for you."

"Come in Pete," Norah said.

Alice Derosier, the public health official, followed him into the farmhouse. Johanna wondered if a scowl perpetually twisted her face. They stepped into the living room and Johanna closed the door. The woodstove gave off a warm glow and heat filled the room. Johanna noted she needed to top off the log basket from the woodpile outdoors.

"I'll be brief, Norah," he said. "The lab reports came back. The only pet spray bottle that was contaminated with atropine was the one Susan Chambers sold to the dog owner. All the others and the herb tea samples we took from your shop were perfectly fine."

Alice stood with her hands on her hips as if she disagreed with the findings, and Pete had dragged her along unwillingly.

"What does this mean for my business?" asked Norah.

"It means I'm here to take away the crime scene tape and Alice will remove the closure notice. You are free to ship out your orders."

"What about her reputation?" said Johanna.

"Phil Granger has instructed Alice to write up a notice for the local newspaper, in her official capacity, declaring your products safe and free from contaminants."

Alice looked none too happy to comply with that directive.

"I'm sorry we put you through this Norah," he said.

"What about the listening device we found?" asked Johanna. "Is the department going to talk to Lisette?"

"Phil has plans to speak to her, but he has to tread lightly. The Jameson and Minsky families are influential. If there is any involvement we can prove, we need to be careful about our chain of evidence."

"I understand, Pete," said Norah. "I'll look for that article in the paper, Alice. I would appreciate you writing an official letter to Minerva's Meadows, clearing my business operations from any health concerns. I may need it for my customers."

Alice nodded.

"We'll be on our way now," Pete said.

Norah returned to the kitchen. Johanna watched from the living room window as Pete removed the tape. She could smell the cookies as Norah pulled them from the oven.

"Hot chocolate, to celebrate?" Norah called out.

Norah and Johanna spent the next three days packing and shipping orders from the herb shop. No one returned the samples of pet spray or tea blends that were confiscated in the investigation. Johanna wondered whether someone had thrown them out or if the lab workers consumed them.

The weekend loomed ahead of them. Norah did not call Samuel to tell him the investigation was over and that they'd cleared her business to continue its operations. Johanna was concerned about the outcome of Granger's visit with Lisette. Neither Eliana nor Samuel were inclined to admit wrong-doing. If a listening device itself was inadmissible, what about a servant's statement she overheard them saying they installed it? Would the sheriff believe Lisette over the statements of a prestigious lawyer and a successful businesswoman?

She thought about the petite, dark-haired French woman. She and her husband had come to this country, hoping for something better. The willingness to work hard and provide a better opportunity for their son was commendable. Many of the adult children of industry and corporate wealth she had counseled during her career had forgotten, they too, descended from immigrants coming to this country for opportunity. There was a difference between opportunity and access. So many people she knew, like Lisette and her husband, strove for the first, while often being denied the second.

She hoped Phil Granger was an astute judge of character. *Lisette will be lucky to keep her job, Johanna thought uneasily.*

The Carrabec

*I*n *her dream, Johanna crouched on the ground. She could feel the palms of her hands on the rocky path, her fingers splayed as if she gripped her yoga mat. Her shoulders shifted side to side as she moved forward in the pale, silver light of a waning moon. Her hips swayed in synchrony with her shoulders as she moved. She felt a finely tuned, tightly held balance in her movements. Catlike.*

Before her on the moonlit path was another creature. The muscles of its soft, yellow body rippled as it moved. Its tufted tail swung back and forth. Johanna's eyesight was unusually sharp in the subdued light as they prowled through the forest. The trees glimmered with a soft glow. The muscles in her face tensed as she picked up a sharp, acrid scent. It smelled as if someone was burning newspapers in a fireplace.

The creature turned to look at her. Its golden eyes glowed, and it bared its teeth. It hissed, and she suddenly woke up.

Johanna sat up and looked out the window. Orion rode high in the western night sky. The time was 3 AM on her cell phone. She rolled over and drifted back into a light sleep.

A sound in the house woke her up. A rustling sound, like the crinkling of paper. She heard the sound again. Her bedroom door was open, to make the most of the heat from the woodstove in the living room.

Was Norah lighting the woodstove, she wondered. Had it gone out? She slipped on her moccasins and walked silently into the hallway. She could see a reddish glow coming from the living room. The woodstove seemed to be working fine.

Johanna heard the kitchen door close. Spinning around, she felt her hair prickle on the back of her neck. She rushed back into the bedroom and grabbed her pistol from the nightstand. She flicked off its safety. *One in the chamber,* Scrag had said. If she had needed to rack it, the intruder would have been forewarned.

She crept toward the kitchen as quietly as possible, holding the gun poised to fire, her left hand tightly gripping the trigger guard and her right forefinger alongside its barrel. It was a nanosecond away from the trigger. She held her hands steady.

Johanna listened. She heard a sound, like the intake of a breath.

Light flickered and shadows danced on the walls as she stepped into the kitchen. She had just enough time to realize the intruder had been leaving, not entering, when she saw a potato chip bag on the kitchen counter burst into flames. It made a puff, then exploded, engulfing the wall like a silent incendiary bomb.

Old walls, she thought, panicking. They have horsehair and newspapers for insulation. She dashed down the hallway to Norah's room.

"Fire!" she screamed. Then she saw that the glow from the living room was not from the woodstove. The couch was on fire as well, blocking their way to the front door. Flames climbed up the living room walls and thick, black smoke roiled out along the ceiling of the hallway. Norah stumbled out of her bedroom.

"Quick, this way!" Johanna pushed Norah into the other bedroom and slammed the door as the living room burst into flames.

"Out the window," Johanna yelled. Norah lifted the window casement. Johanna grabbed her sweatshirt and Nathan's Mackinaw jacket from the coat tree. She shoved her cell phone and pistol into her backpack and tossed them all through the opened window. Holding onto Norah's hands, she carefully lowered her to the ground in the backyard.

Smoke poured over the top and sides of the door, filling the bedroom. Holding her breath, she climbed onto the sill, then jumped. She landed on all fours.

They heard an explosion in the front of the house as the windows in the living room blew out.

Johanna jumped up and ran with Norah through the backyard, clutching everything in their arms, and escaped through the gap in the lilac hedge. They kept running until they reached the back gate to the meadows. Norah shivered in her pajamas and bare feet as Johanna tore through her backpack.

"What on earth happened? Why didn't the smoke alarm go off? I reset it!"

"Yes, you did. Norah, someone broke in and set the house on fire! I heard them in the kitchen. They must have taken the battery out again!"

"This is carrying vandalism too far," Norah said angrily.

"It's arson. Someone wants to kill you," said Johanna. She kicked off her moccasins and handed them to Norah. "Here, wear these." She stripped off her sweatpants, which were big enough to fit the taller woman. "I have my sneakers and extra blue jeans from the camping trip in my backpack."

She handed Nathan's jacket to Norah, then struggled into her blue jeans. She quickly shoved her feet in her sneakers and pulled the heavy sweatshirt over her head. They were as warm as they were ever going to get that night. She tucked her Sig Sauer into its concealed carry holster and wedged it by her belly, behind her belt.

"Let's go up the hillside, where we can see what's happening. Maybe I can get a cell signal higher up. We can call the fire department," Johanna said, shouldering her backpack.

The moon was a waning gibbous orb in the sky, casting just enough light for the two women to see the path leading to the upper meadows, and just enough shadow to shield them. They stopped at the first rise, where they could see over the barn and into the driveway.

The farmhouse was blazing but contained. It had not spread to the barn or to the three vehicles in the parking area.

"What's Samuel's Range Rover doing there?" said Norah.

The call would not go through. Johanna frantically typed a text message to her daughter, who was on duty that night in a 911 dispatch center three states away.

> *Norah's house on fire. Call Tiadaghton Fire and Rescue*

Even though there were only a few bars, the message might still get through, she thought. She clicked the 'send' arrow.

When she looked up, she saw Samuel walk to the far side of the driveway by the barn. He watched casually as flames engulfed the farmhouse.

Norah stood up. "I have to let him know we're ok."

Johanna pulled her back down on the ground.

"He started it! Norah, we need to get somewhere safe before he figures out we aren't in there."

Norah started shaking as she began to realize he had intended them to die in the fire.

"Jost! If we get to the top of the meadows, we can take the old logging road out to the main road. He has a landline we can use to call for help," she said.

Johanna shook her head. "If Samuel leaves, he would drive right past us on the road that goes to the Ice House."

Norah thought a moment, then said, "The boat house. We can take kayaks down the Carrabec to the fishing pier. We can get there through the woods."

"Right, he won't see us. But it's almost pitch dark. How can we paddle a river in the dead of night?"

"He's not the only one who knows the Carrabec like the back of his hand. I can paddle it blindfolded. I know every bend. The river is so low, we can walk the kayaks over Step Falls."

"What about the Thresher?"

"We port around. Now, Johanna! He's walking to the back of the farmhouse. If he sees the open window, he'll know we got out!"

Norah pulled Johanna to her feet.

They ran toward the path that led through the forest. The darkness shielded them from being seen and there was just enough moonlight filtering through the trees to illuminate the path to the river. Just as it was in her dream.

When they reached the boat house, there were three kayaks on the rack. Johanna grabbed two sets of paddles.

"If he comes to the boat house and sees two kayaks gone, he'll know we took to the river," said Norah. "Quick, help me." She struggled with an orange kayak.

"It's Samuel's. We can't sink it, but we can set it adrift in the river. Let's not make it easy for him!"

They dragged his kayak into the river and pushed it off into the swirling black water. It drifted for a moment, then got caught by the river's flow. It spun around, then quickly disappeared into the darkness.

Norah and Johanna pulled the remaining two boats to the water's edge. Norah put in first, settling into a long, gray kayak. Johanna handed her a long oar with paddles on both ends. She pushed the shorter, yellow kayak into the edge of the river. Securing her backpack under the deck, she got in and pushed off the riverbank with her paddle.

The moon was behind them now, casting a pale, silver swath of light which illuminated their path through the water. In the western sky, Johanna could see the belt of Orion, with its three bright stars in a row as it lowered toward the horizon. It seemed to be chasing Taurus over the rim of the earth. And yet, she remembered an ancient Greek myth with a different outcome.

It was the responsibility of Artemis the Huntress, Goddess of the wilderness to protect young girls from harm. When Orion pursued and raped Merope, one the seven sisters, she turned the girls into a cluster of stars, the Pleiades. She formed a bull into the constellation Taurus and set the ring of stars upon its back. Arming it with a piercing eye, the star Aldebaran, Taurus forever stood between Orion and his prey. What seemed to be one thing, pursuit, Artemis turned into the ability to protect. Johanna could only hope their escape into the wilderness of the night held such an advantage for she and Norah.

"We stay in the middle of the river, it's fastest there," said Norah.

As they rounded the first bend in the river, they saw headlights flickering through the trees. He was driving down the access road.

"There are more kayaks in the boat house," Norah said. "He's coming for us."

The Thresher

"**C**an he catch us on the river?" said Johanna.

"The river flows as fast for him as it does for us. We have a good enough head start."

Another bend came up and Norah expertly guided her kayak to the right. There was just enough moonlight to see the 'vee' in the river that showed where the deepest water flowed.

Deep water is swift water, Johanna thought. Her heart was racing, and she knew they were not out of danger yet. She gripped her paddle, dipping right again, then left, keeping a safe distance behind Norah. It was one thing to travel on a river in full daylight, being able to see rocks and the water passages around them. It was quite another to paddle in the darkness, seeing only inky black waves rising and falling before you, indistinct and dangerous.

She could see Norah's back in the moonlight. Sitting so low in her kayak, she looked as though she was gliding on top of the water. She had to trust Norah's ability to read the river and her own ability to follow her. She tried not to focus on what Samuel's plans would be if he caught up with them.

Her mind was clear and methodical. She knew that stress like this could highjack the part of the brain responsible for strategic planning. At least, that's what she told her clients in the past. Fight or flight was good for one important thing; deciding which way to run and how fast. Adrenaline served a purpose. Nature designed it for just this kind of situation.

But fear was also an unreliable asset. *It can turn on you, she thought.* The waves bumped against her kayak, rocking it. She tightened her grip on the paddle and stabilized the craft by balancing her body. It would be too easy to turn sideways against the river and start spinning.

She panicked. Her heart pounded. She forced her mind to concentrate on the river and her paddle while keeping Norah's back in sight. *We're safe now, she reasoned. We're ahead of him.*

She heard the sound of trickling water in the darkness. It was like the coming together of multiple streams flowing over a creek bed.

"We're coming up to Step Falls," said Norah. "When it gets louder, just dip your paddle down in the water to see if you're near the bottom."

Her voice sounded confident and calm. Johanna dipped her paddle and scraped the riverbed. The flow of the river had slowed.

"I'm getting out on the rocks," said Norah, calling back through the darkness. "I'll wait for you. We can walk them over."

Johanna felt the bottom of her kayak go aground in the dark. She stood up and stepped out into the cold, shallow water.

"Hold up, Norah. I think I have Scott's flashlight and duct-tape in my backpack. I didn't unpack it when we got back from the camping trip."

She dug in the bottom of her backpack and identified them by feel.

"We can tape it to your kayak!" She flicked on the Maglite and helped Norah secure it to the top deck of her kayak. A pool of yellow light filled the area ahead. Johanna could see both sides of the river now, bathed in a swath of light.

"Nathan painted three white circles on a boulder on the left bank after the bend where the river widens, so boaters would know exactly where the portage is. They will shine up nicely with this torch."

They carried both kayaks over the stones and pebbles that shaped the rapids of Step Falls when the river ran high. As they eased back into their seats, Johanna saw a glowing ball of red light through the base of the trees lining the eastern side of the river.

"What's that? Lights from Tiadaghton?"

"No, it's the sun coming up. At this elevation, the sun looks like it's rising from the forest floor. It will lighten up the sky within an hour."

They moved into deep water again and paddled a little faster. Both women shivered with the cold and an urgency to make up for lost time. The river began moving faster. Johanna felt relieved. She could see distinct shadows now on both sides of the river bank. Trees and undergrowth stood out as darker impressions against the paler spaces between them.

She could hear a thundering sound in the distance, like diesel powered logging trucks powering up a steep incline. Norah spun her kayak around, still paddling, and waited for Johanna to come up beside her.

"That's the Thresher," she said, loudly. "When the river widens, be prepared to follow me quickly to the left bank. There is a swift under-tow in the river, which can pull us over the cliffs and into the Thresher. I don't know if it's strong enough now or not."

"I don't want to find out," shouted Johanna.

Norah spun her kayak around and power-paddled past Johanna, taking the lead again.

As they approached the waterfalls, the thundering sound grew louder. The cliffs at the Thresher gorge were thirty feet high. In the spring, a much faster river plunged over their stark rock walls. Even now, with a low river, a sluice of water poured over the ledges, creating multiple waterfalls that crashed onto the rock pinnacles below.

The Thresher itself was created by the force of the river pouring over the cliffs into pools of various depths and thunderous back washes of water at the bottom. At one point, the river lurched backwards toward the rock cliffs with five-foot high standing waves.

Norah suddenly tilted her kayak as she leaned to the left, with a powerful draw of her paddle. She darted across the river and skimmed into the eddy behind a boulder with three white circles painted on its side. It was as if Nathan himself guided her in. The portage point was muddy incline on the bank of the river where Norah grounded and got out of her kayak.

Johanna leaned over, using the weight of her body to tilt the kayak as she planted the paddle deep in the water. She curved it around her paddle and headed for the eddy. Giving a last gentle stroke, she guided the tip of the kayak into the still water as the force of the river spun it around in a smooth eddy turn. She came to a stop, facing upriver. Up to her knees in freezing cold water, Norah waded to the stern of Johanna's kayak and pulled it up onto the muddy embankment.

"Let's port your kayak first," said Johanna as she leaped into the frigid water and helped Norah pull her craft up to the portage trail.

"We enter the river again below the cliffs," shouted Norah over the sound of the falls. "This way!"

She pulled on the front of her kayak and lifted it as Johanna pulled up the back, gripping the grab handles mounted on the front and rear. They lifted, tugged and carried it on the path that looped around to the base of the falls. Nathan and Samuel had cleared a path through the forest that did not require roping down a steep elevation. But the portage was a longer route, and they were running out of time.

Within five minutes, they came to the base of the falls where they would put into the river again. The older woman gasped, trying to catch her breath. They put her kayak down by the edge of the cascade pool at the bottom of the waterfalls.

"Rest here in the clearing. I can carry the other kayak by myself," said Johanna.

Norah sat down and leaned against a tree as Johanna disappeared into the darkness. She gazed around the portage area as the shadows receded in the light of the rising sun. It was 5AM, and they had at least another hour of flat water paddling ahead of them. It would be slower going from here on.

Johanna reached her kayak, tipped it on its side and lifted it, holding the edge of the cockpit. She struggled as she pulled it up to the path and headed to the portage point. *That was the thing about fight or flight, she thought. You have more strength at your disposal.*

As she came into the clearing, Norah was bending over something in the thicket. She cried out.

Johanna set her kayak down and reached Norah just in time to catch her as she slid to the ground with a sob. She was clutching a mud encrusted shoe in her hands.

"It's Nathan's," she cried out. "It's one of his Sperry topsider boat shoes!"

"What?"

"It was under those bushes."

Johanna reached into the underbrush. Something else was sticking out of the ground. It was a broken paddle shaft. She held it up.

"He made it here! He didn't go over the falls," cried Norah.

"What if his paddle broke, and he tried to continue with a broken half, like a canoe, and that caused his accident?"

"He would never have chanced that. He would have walked out through the woods. They said he drowned, most likely from going over the falls and hitting his head while submerged," Norah continued. "But he must have died here on the portage trail, not in the river!"

"Samuel must have killed him here," said Johanna.

"But Samuel was in a meeting that morning," insisted Norah.

"What if he followed Nathan that day on the river and caught up with him here? Or what if he was waiting here all along?"

"I can't believe he would murder his own brother. And for what? Money? A seat on the Board? To be the trustee?"

"Norah, Samuel just tried to kill you," Johanna said softly. "We are running out of time. You need to get Nathan's shoe and the broken paddle to Granger. It's hard evidence. Quick!"

They ran to the river's edge. Johanna helped her friend into her kayak. They stowed Nathan's battered shoe and paddle under the deck.

"Here, take my phone. When you reach the pier or get a signal, text Scott. Tell him to come as quickly as he can!"

"You're coming too, aren't you?" Norah shouted to be heard over the crashing torrents.

"No!" Johanna yelled. "I'm going to delay Samuel by shooting a hole in his kayak. He'll be stuck here!"

At Norah's shocked face, Johanna leaned down and shoved her friend's kayak into the churning waters at the base of the falls. The river grabbed the boat and pulled it into the flow. Norah had no choice. She had to maneuver herself through the cascades.

"I'm a good shot!" Johanna called out after her.

The rising sun painted the river in liquid golden light as she pulled her own kayak onto the lower ledge of the Thresher falls. She dragged it over rocks worn smooth by the river's actions for eons of time and hid it behind a stand of boulders on the other side of the falls.

A flicker of shadows in the trees on the upper portage trail caught her eye. He was coming through. She crouched down behind massive rocks between two separate waterfalls that spilled down from the cliffs. She had an advantage. He would never imagine either woman would have stayed behind. And he didn't know she carried a pistol.

She had time to gage her target area. There was a narrow opening between the rocks where kayaks and canoes entered the river. It sloped down to a pool of calm water, just short of the Cascades. He would have to lower his kayak, as she had helped Norah lower hers. The bottom of the cockpit would be an easy target when he tilted it.

She could not shoot a person, not even a murderer. But she had no trouble putting a bullet through his hull. The put-in was about twenty feet away. More than twice the distance she had practiced shooting with any accuracy.

It's a bigger surface area than a paper target, she thought. All I have to do is put a hole in it. He'll duck because he'll think I'm shooting at him. I'll get away in my kayak on the other side of the river. He won't be able to follow.

Her mind went cold, but her fingers were colder as she thumbed off the Sig's safety. She took aim at the edge of the river bank. She waited.

Samuel came through the woods carrying a kayak. The rock walls of the cliff were turning bright red in the blazing light of the sun. The river shimmered like molten gold, as if it was smelted in a cauldron of fire. Her trigger finger rested along the barrel of her pistol, as she steadied her hands.

He leaned down at the river bank, righted the kayak and lowered its bow into the water.

Johanna fired. The shot went wild.

The kickback wrenched the pistol out of her hands and it dropped over the ledge. It landed in a small pool beside a torrent of water falling overhead from the cliffs.

Samuel yanked the kayak back up onto the bank with superhuman strength and reached into the cockpit. He pulled out a hammer and headed through the boulders in her direction.

She backed away, trying to calculate if she could make it across the ledge to her kayak before he got to her.

She turned and scrambled up the rocks.

This is how he killed Nathan, she thought. He came at him with a hammer on the portage. His brother never stood a chance.

She was fast.

He was faster. Samuel grabbed her braid and viciously pulled her back onto the ledge, slamming her against the side of cliff wall. He raised the hammer.

She spun around, ripping her hair out of his grasp. She attacked him like a wildcat, clawing and screaming.

Surprised, he slipped backwards and dropped the hammer. He leaned forward like a skier on a snow jump and recovered his balance. He had her, then, and he knew it. Rage contorted his face in a skeletal sneer.

She could not say how she smelled the fear in him that moment. A stench filled her nostrils like something caught in a snare. She saw his shocked face as he suddenly realized she had lain in wait for him while Norah was on her way to Granger, who would soon know the full extent of his actions. His rage came from utter fear.

He reached for her throat.

Johanna lunged at him with a guttural howl as a more-than-human power surged through her. She pushed him backward over the ledge and into the roiling waters of the Thresher.

He bounced off two rocks before landing in white water. It swallowed him whole, then spit him out to be swept through the Cascades. His body bashed against the bones of the Carrabec river and he died the death he wanted everyone to believe his brother had suffered. Samuel Minsky was killed by the river, by the Cascades; by the very rocks he had named as a young boy.

She backed away from the edge. His terrified face as he plunged to his death became indelibly etched into her mind. It took its place beside the birthplace of another horror in her brain, never to be forgotten.

Shaking, Johanna climbed down to the lower ledge, retrieved her wet pistol and returned to pick up the hammer with the edge of her sweatshirt. She climbed over the rocks to the other side of the waterfall and pulled her backpack out of the kayak.

Wrapping the hammer in a T-shirt, she then dried off her pistol and wedged it back into its concealed location under her belt. *It's over, she thought*. Placing the hammer in her backpack, she then pushed her kayak into the river and paddled around the shallower side of the Cascade rocks.

On any other day but this, a magnificent dawn ride down a pristine river, curving around tall sentinel stones like these, would have been a pleasure. The river was serene, yet Johanna's body shook violently and she struggled to hold onto the paddles. She felt as if she were still being chased. Her heart pounded and her mind was as turbulent as the waters she churned up behind her with each stroke.

She lost all sense of time. Though she knew the events at the Thresher happened quickly, she felt as if time had come to a standstill. All she could do was keep paddling forward. There was no need for Norah's river guidance, as the water only led in one direction.

The river itself was her guide now, so she focused on letting it carry her to safety. In the distance, at a bend in the river, she saw a fallen tree half submerged in the water. She would have to paddle between the tree and the left bank of the river. As she got closer, she saw something pinned in its branches.

His arms were bent at impossible angles and his blackened eyes stared sightlessly from his chalk-white shattered face. A bloodless gash across his forehead marred his once handsome features. The tree held Samuel's battered body tightly against the current, trapping it against the river's fury. As Johanna floated by, she was close enough to touch him. His body suddenly moved as the river tugged at it.

She recoiled as the river pulled at him, fiercely trying to dislodge him from the tree's grasp. That is when Johanna suddenly realized how Samuel did it.

He went with Nathan that day, as they had planned. He hit his brother with the hammer on the portage path and threw him in the river beneath the falls. The rocks would have smashed Nathan's body, making it appear as if he had been injured and drowned in an accident. Samuel must have shattered Nathan's paddle, throwing part of it into the river along with his kayak to be found down stream as if it had gone over the Thresher falls.

He must have used his brother's cell phone to text the messages back and forth, then threw it into the river as well. Leaving behind the other broken shaft with Nathan's shoe on the path was proof that adrenaline can highjack even a murder's reasoning.

She heard sirens in the distance. Firetrucks heading to the farmhouse, she hoped. Norah must have gotten to the pier by now. Johanna was paddling in slow, flat water and saw the picnic area on the left bank. The last bend before the town was coming up. She noticed a small landing at the base of the hill leading up to a grove of trees where the picnic area was located.

And dirt access to the main road, she thought. Samuel must have kayaked down here to the picnic area that day. Did he walk back to the boat house, pick up his car, then return here to retrieve his kayak? Or was there someone waiting there to help him? Did he act alone or did he have help?

She had no answer to that question.

As she rounded the last bend, she saw strobe lights flashing. She could see the sheriff's department vehicles and an ambulance on the fishing pier. Uniformed men and women were moving on the dock. A motorboat came up alongside her and Pete Mitchell called out.

"Are you alright, Johanna?" He reached for the grab handle on her kayak's bow as it bobbed on the choppy waves. He secured a line and towed her up to the dock.

Investigation

"Where's Norah? Is she ok?" asked Johanna. She stood on the dock, shivering.

"We had her transported to Urgent Care. She's in shock from exposure, possibly hypothermia. Granger is with her now, getting a statement," said the deputy. "She was incoherent when she showed up at the pier. One of the fisherman called 911."

An EMT wrapped a blanket around her and guided her to the back of the ambulance, where someone handed her a cup of coffee. The warmth of the paper cup felt soothing to her nearly frozen fingers. Townspeople gathered by the parking area, but the deputies had barricaded the pier with yellow tape.

"Did she give you the evidence?"

"What evidence?" asked Johanna.

"We found one of the shoes Nathan was wearing the day he died and part of his kayak paddle on the portage site. He was murdered!"

"Right now, I need to ask you some questions."

"Samuel set the farmhouse on fire! Was the Fire Department dispatched?"

"Yes, they're probably there now. Norah tried to tell us what happened, but all she could tell us was about the fire and the two of you escaping down the river. She said you stayed behind at the portage to shoot Samuel."

"No, not him, his kayak."

"First, Johanna." Pete held up his hand, signaling her to stop talking. "Are you carrying a weapon?"

"Yes."

"Are you the registered owner of the firearm?"

"Yes."

"Did you fire it?"

"Yes."

"I'm going to need to take your firearm. But do not reach for it."

"It's my protection. I have a conceal carry permit."

"We'll get to that," Pete said. "You discharged it and we need to take it in evidence. I am going to ask you to stand up, and raise your arms while I take your weapon."

Pete nodded to a female deputy, who stepped forward with an evidence bag.

"It's in a holster, concealed under my belt by my stomach," said Johanna. Her whole body shook uncontrollably.

Pete Mitchell stepped forward and took her gun. He noted the safety was on and placed it in the evidence bag.

"How many rounds does it hold?"

"Seven."

"How many rounds did you fire?"

"One."

"Ok, you can put your arms down. Have some coffee and tell me what happened. Start at the beginning."

Johanna sat on the back bumper of the ambulance and began to the tell the events of the night, waking up to the sounds of paper crinkling and of someone in the kitchen. She told of escaping out the window with Norah, seeing Samuel in the yard and realizing he set the house on fire.

Pete put his hands on his hips. He leaned forward, listening intently to her story. She continued explaining they had to take the kayaks down the river and Samuel followed them. She explained what they found at the portage and why she sent Norah ahead with the evidence that Nathan had been murdered, not drowned in an accident.

"Where's that 'evidence' now?"

"If Norah didn't give it to you, it's still in her kayak." Johanna stood up, but Pete gently pushed her back. He nodded to the deputy.

"You say your shot missed the kayak? Did you shoot Samuel?"

"No, I told you. It went wild into the trees. He came after me. We struggled on the cliff edge," she said. She looked away from Pete's eyes. "He went over into the Thresher and I got away."

Pete said nothing. The silence between them grew. Johanna knew silence was a technique to get her to say more. She had used it often in her sessions. She waited, then spoke.

"I saw him later, pinned under a tree in the river, right before the picnic area."

"He was dead?"

"I believe so," she responded. *He could not have survived, she thought.*

The deputy returned holding two large evidence bags, containing Nathan's Sperry top-sider and the shaft of his broken paddle.

"We found them in the dirt at the Thresher portage site, partially buried," Johanna said. "It's proof Nathan did not go over the falls. He was killed on the path, not on the river." Her voice dropped to a whisper. "No one goes on a river without a paddle."

"I need you to understand this, Johanna. I have to take you back to the station. We need to find Samuel's body. We need to be sure you didn't shoot him. Your story needs to be corroborated."

"Am I being arrested?"

"No."

"Can I call my husband?"

"Absolutely."

Johanna looked down at her backpack. "Then you better get the hammer Samuel used to try to kill me."

"What?"

"It's wrapped in my T-shirt in my backpack." She nudged it with her wet sneaker. "It's got his finger prints on it, not mine."

Pete used nitrile gloves to open her backpack and withdrew an object. Unwrapping it, he saw both the hammer and the writing on the T-shirt.

"Really?" he said. It was a National Park Service T-shirt with a moose logo saying, *'stand your ground.'*

"Yes, really," she replied.

"Wait'll Granger sees this."

Wrapped in the blanket given her by the EMT, Johanna sat in an uncomfortable chair at the station. To her right was a small cubicle, framed in plexiglass. A uniformed woman, the county dispatcher, was wearing a headset and sat at a desk with three large monitors. She kept looking over at Johanna, then averting her gaze.

The female deputy who had taken the evidence bags at the pier walked by Johanna and entered a room at the end of the hallway. She was a tall, muscular woman, with dark curly hair cut short. She looked like she worked out in a gym. When she returned, she asked Johanna if she wanted more coffee while she waited.

"Thanks, I've probably had enough, and my heart is still pounding from paddling down the river."

"I'm Sophie Gauthier," she said. "Let me know if we can get you anything."

"Do they know anything about the farmhouse? Did the barn and herb shop burn too?"

She thought about her Subaru and Norah's Jeep. What if the out-buildings were destroyed? What if Mina's garden book had gone up in flames?

"I'll see if we know anything yet," the deputy said. She walked into the dispatcher's room.

Johanna watched the two women converse through the glass window. She felt disheartened to see the dispatcher shake her head. Johanna inhaled softly, trying to still her agitation. Her body shivered.

Pete Mitchell came into the station and walked over to her.

"Were you able to contact your husband?"

"No, I gave my cell phone to Norah. I.. I can't remember his number."

"Hold on. Be right back." He went to a desk at the back of the station.

Gauthier returned. "No news yet. They are still at the scene." She touched Johanna briefly on the shoulder, then walked down the hallway.

Pete came back.

"I got ahold of Sheriff Granger. He is leaving the hospital now. I asked him to bring back your phone."

"How is Norah?"

"They sedated her. She is being treated for exposure. She'll be ok."

Johanna relaxed against the chair, looked up at the ceiling and braced her head against the wall for support. She sighed.

"I still can't believe she ran the river in the dark," he said. "A woman her age. You too. The search team is out on the river now, looking for Samuel."

"Are you going to talk to Eliana? She may have been involved too," said Johanna.

"Depends on what we find. We have a procedure to follow."

He walked back to his desk.

What if they don't find his body? she thought. I can't prove I didn't shoot him. What if I get arrested for killing Samuel? She saw his face again, as he plunged to his death. *But I did kill him. Didn't I?* She tried to remember the sequence of events.

Her head still hurt where Samuel yanked her hair. She remembered grabbing at the rocks when he caught her. *But what happened next?* He slipped and dropped the hammer. In her mind, she saw the hammer on the ledge by her feet. She vividly remembered picking it up with the sleeve of her sweatshirt. *But he had already gone over the edge by then, hadn't he?*

She saw his face again. She saw a flash of her hands on his chest. *I pushed him over, didn't I?* Images swirled in her mind. Reaching into the pool of water to retrieve her pistol. The horror of seeing his body move as the river water bumped against him by the tree. Dark, black smoke swirling around the bedroom door as she jumped out of the window. *Edelweiss wrapped in hyssop.* She felt the panic rise again.

The door to the station opened and Phil Granger walked in.

"Are you ok, Johanna?" he asked.

"I'm not sure."

"Here's your phone. Call your husband," he said. "I'm going to have a word with Pete, then we need to talk."

"Gauthier!" Granger called out.

The deputy stepped out of a back office. Granger nodded toward Johanna. Sophie sat down at her desk and began reviewing some papers. The dispatcher looked up, then looked away. Phil Granger went into Pete's office and closed the door.

Johanna looked down at her phone and saw two red indicators for incoming messages. One was from Kaye, confirming she had called Tiadaghton Fire and Rescue and urging her mother to call her back. The other was from Scott, whom Kaye had also alerted, saying he was on his way. She pressed the call button for Scott's cell phone in her contact list. He answered while on the road from Belfast. Her voice shook as she told him what had happened.

Juxtaposition

Johanna was putting her phone in her backpack as Sophie got up from her desk.

"We will need to take your phone for a while," she said. "Just procedure. You'll get it back."

Johanna nodded dully and wondered if she needed a lawyer. Fatigue suddenly hit her and her mind felt like it was lost in a fog bank. She handed it over.

The door to Pete's office opened, and Phil Granger stepped out.

"We need to go over what happened again," he said. "Follow me to our interview room."

Pete accompanied them as Johanna walked behind the sheriff, entering the room beside the one that contained the evidence bags.

He indicated a chair on one side of the table for her to sit in while he and Pete occupied two seats across from her.

"I'm going to ask you some questions. Pete, here, is gonna take some notes."

She nodded wearily.

"Start at the point where you woke up hearing someone in the kitchen. Try not to leave out any details, even if you think they're not important."

She told everything she remembered, again, in chronological order to the best of her ability. Her voice broke when she described firing her gun at the kayak and missing, then scrambling up the rocks to get away from Samuel as he came after her with the hammer. She concluded her recollection of the events to the point of seeing him pinned by the tree.

"So you dropped your firearm after shooting it once."

"It flew out of my hand from the kickback."

"Samuel slipped on the ledge, dropped the hammer, and fell over the cliff?"

"He grabbed my hair and pulled me off the rocks when I tried to get away from him, I fought back."

"Then he slipped off the ledge?"

She nodded.

"You did not shoot him?"

"No. My gun was in the puddle."

"I need you to understand there is a big difference between using personal protection for self-defense and using it to shoot someone who is not imminently about to harm you. You have a right to defend yourself. But when you are clearly escaping a threatening situation and you decide to go back and wait for an attacker, to shoot him... well.... that's something else entirely."

She shivered. Her mind began spinning.

"I had to go back. Norah was exhausted. There was no way to know what he would do to us if he caught us on the river. If he had a gun, we were sitting ducks with our backs to a shooter."

"We are having a hard time understanding a motive here. Might he have seen you escape the fire and wanted to render assistance? What if he wanted to help by taking you and Norah to a safer place? What if you had it all wrong?"

"Samuel tried to kill us. He knew we were in the farmhouse. He set it on fire. I heard him leave the kitchen!"

"How can you be so sure it was him?"

"Because he stayed to watch the farmhouse burn. There was nobody else there!" *How could they not believe her?*

"You shot at him, why wouldn't he defend himself?" Granger asked, pointedly.

"If he didn't set the fire, then who did? Why was he standing in front of Norah's house at 4AM watching it burn to the ground?" Johanna shouted. She started to shake uncontrollably. *What if they didn't find him?*

"Well, that's a problem. What's the motive for such a desperate action?"

"You already know," her voice dropped. "We found a recording device in the farmhouse. Norah discovered that someone had removed the battery from the smoke alarm. It's obvious they planned this."

"But why? What does Norah have that Samuel wanted? Why kill her, and you too, for that matter? That's the motive we're having trouble with."

"He killed Nathan over a year—"

"We don't know that," said Granger curtly. "There is a lot we have to investigate here. We need a motive."

"Maybe Eli Mittleman can help with that," said Johanna. "He knows what Samuel stood to gain if Norah was out of the way."

"Pete checked your firearm. There are six rounds left in the magazine, which is pretty wet, by the way. We just learned a few minutes ago, they got the fire under control. The farmhouse is gone but the rest of the buildings look like just smoke damage. Our county fire inspector's going out there tomorrow. The area is being cordoned off and we'll have an officer on the scene, around the clock."

Someone knocked on the interview door. Pete opened it and stepped out.

When he came back into the room, he said, "They found Samuel. They are taking him in for an autopsy, but so far, no sign of any gunshot wounds."

The sheriff reached over and touched her arm.

"You did ok, Johanna," he said calmly. "You're a very brave woman. I just need you to understand what's at risk here and what avenues we have to follow."

"Am I going to be charged with killing Samuel?"

"I believe your story, Johanna," Granger responded. "But there's a lot here that doesn't add up and I'm going to get to the bottom of it."

"Do you have a place to stay?" asked Pete.

"Scott's coming. I need to see about Norah."

"She is anxious about you," said Granger.

"You need to keep us informed of where you're staying," he continued.

"I need to contact Eli, the family's lawyer. I'm her Power of Attorney," said Johanna. "She's going to need emergency housing, clothes, and other things. She is going to need protection. Samuel might not have been acting alone."

"Understand," said Phil. "You're free to go. Stay in contact with Pete, here. We need to complete the investigation."

"Will I be able to get my car, see what's left in the barn, and Herbary?"

"I will be in touch with the fire inspector," said Pete. "Here's your phone. I will call you and let you know when you can go out to Minerva's Meadows."

Johanna nodded and returned to the chair in the front office to wait for Scott. Her clinical training with its triage procedures and protocols helped her focus despite the fatigue that threatened to overwhelm her. She chose to call Eli's office first, then the hospital to get a status on Norah. There hadn't been time to file a medical proxy note with her primary care doctor, so getting around the privacy regulations at the hospital would be a challenge.

"If you need a phone charger, Dr. Kincaid," said Sophie, "We got an extra you can use."

She'd left a message for Eli on his voice mail. The hospital put her through to Norah's room without hesitation. Her name, it seemed, was on the list. Norah answered immediately. Her voice sounded weak, but relieved.

"They told me you were ok," Norah said. She spoke hesitantly, trying to catch her breath. "The Bergmans are ...... here with me... now. I am going to go stay with ..... them after the hospital.... releases me."

"Scott is on the way," said Johanna. "They might let me go to the farmhouse to see the damages. Do you want me to handle all that?"

"Yes, please. All the house... records are in the barn office. Insurance coverage.... documents. Business papers. Oh, Johanna... I can't stop seeing Nathan's shoe! There is nothing left... now. Nothing we built... remains."

"Certainly the farmhouse is gone," said Johanna. "But we don't know about the rest, yet." Her voice was gentle and soothing.

Another voice came on the line.

"Johanna? This is Delphine Bergman. Norah needs to rest. If you handle the business affairs, Jost and I will take care of her. I will text you my cell number so we can stay in touch."

"Thank you."

"They are releasing her soon. We'll take her back home with us. You can come over whenever you want. I know it would do her good to see you. I can't imagine what the two of you have been through."

Moments later, two texts came through to Johanna's phone. The first was a message from Delphine Bergman with her contact information and the second was a message from Scott.

> *I'm an hour away. I booked a room for us at the Greenwood*

The Greenwood Inn

S cott helped Johanna into the Tahoe, then closed the passenger door as she buckled herself up. She leaned back against the headrest and sighed. He slid into the driver seat, gripped the steering wheel and turned to face her.

"I'm really angry," he said. "You should have told me how dangerous it was getting. If I had been there, I would have -"

"Samuel took us all by surprise. There was no way anyone could have predicted what he was planning to do." Her voice sounded weary.

"I nearly lost you."

"I know – " Johanna reached out for his hand, then stopped.

"I thought we were in this together."

"I didn't want to worry you. It's just that -"

He started the vehicle. "Don't take this the wrong way," he said, "but you have to stop pretending you're so independent, you don't need me. We need each other."

"You're right. I should have called you." Clumps of hair had come loose from her braid, sticking out in random wisps where Samuel had grabbed it. There was a streak of dirt over her left eye and a cut on her hand.

Scott nodded, then gently touched her shoulder.

"You know, you look like a drowned cat." He put the vehicle in gear.

"I feel like one."

"How about we buy you some toiletries, then check into the hotel? A hot shower would do you good."

She nodded and texted Kaye she was safe and headed to a hotel with her father. She agreed to fill her in as soon as possible.

The Olde Greenwood Inn was a few towns away from Tiadaghton. It was an old ski lodge from the 1970s nestled between mountains that were later overshadowed by the Sugarloaf and Saddleback ski resorts. It had been re-discovered by ATVrs and cross-country ski enthusiasts who enjoyed its backwoods charm and anonymity.

The owners had renovated the check-in lobby with a woodsman motif that was more authentic than decorative. A red and black cloth covered a table, which boasted a pot of freshly brewed coffee and a plate of just-baked chocolate chip cookies.

A young woman with a pierced nostril, wearing a flannel shirt, quilted hunter's vest, and wool ski cap processed Scott's room charge. She handed him a key with a green tag.

"Room 102. Down that hallway. Go past the Great Room with the large stone fireplace and go down the steps. You're in the back wing down by the river. Pretty quiet down there."

"Thanks," said Scott. "I haven't seen a key like this for forty years."

She laughed. "It's older than that, I promise you."

"Any events going on?"

"This Friday and Saturday night we have a guitarist who plays folk music, and that's when our cafe is open. Home-style foods, nothing fancy. Other than that, well, that's why our rooms have kitchenettes. It's fend for yourself."

"Just the way I like it," said Scott, taking a couple of cookies.

The hallways were much wider than modern hotels from the days when guests maneuvered themselves into their rooms wearing ski boots and carrying skis on their shoulders. It was easy to find the room. It was the last door at the end of the wing, across from a well-stocked potbellied woodstove they were surprised to find in the hallway.

The suite featured a living room area, kitchenette, and a bedroom with a kingsize bed. The bathroom was spacious, with a wide tub and shower enclosure. It was cozy, containing all the essentials for people whose visits focused on outdoor recreation. Scott opened curtains to reveal large windows overlooking the forest.

"Best kept secret?" Johanna asked.

"It looks to be," he smiled. "I'm filling up the tub for you. While you're soaking, I'll bring in some supplies. I stopped off for groceries on my way to break you outta jail."

"You are amazing!"

"No one's gonna find you out here, my love. This is as safe as it gets." He patted his holster. "And if they try, it will be the last foolish thing they'll ever do."

He shut the door behind him as Johanna lowered herself into the bathtub. The mirror fogged up with steam. She found a bar of hand-milled floral soap lying on top of the thick white towels supplied by the Inn's staff. The scent of roses filled the room. She let both her fatigue and her fear melt away as she sank down in the hot water. Her body let go of its memory of the cold, black river water and the image of a body bumping against a submerged tree. Samuel's face, with its visage of horror, receded as she basked in the realization that she and Norah were alive.

"You look refreshed," Scott said.

She had swept her hair up in a twist and clipped it with a new barrette. She nodded.

"Let's go shopping," he said. "You need some clothes and I'm thinking Cabella's."

Within a few hours, Johanna left the outdoor outfitter and apparel store carrying several shopping bags with jeans, shirts, sweaters, a couple sweatshirts, and several pairs of thick socks. She wore a newly purchased fleece-lined jacket with a woolen scarf and a pair of suede boots. She had insisted on getting clothing for Norah as well.

They drove to the Ice House to drop off the bags of clothing at the Bergman's. Jost took Scott aside while Johanna visited with Norah. She was doing better, but still weak from the exertion of kayaking the river.

"I don't know how you two did it," said Delphine.

"It was Norah who led the way," said Johanna. "I would never have attempted it, certainly not alone."

Norah thanked Johanna for the gift of clothing.

"It's a good thing Delphine and I wear the same size," she said. "I'm going to call Eli and see if he can get my bank to issue new cards and a checkbook. I need to replace some essentials."

"Scott and I are meeting up with the fire inspector at some point. We will survey the damages."

"Oh, Rufus?" said Delphine, looking out a window with a view of the driveway. She shook her head. "Well... well...well."

"Rufus McCoy is a good man," said Norah. "The county is lucky to have him. If he approves, why don't you and Scott stay in the apartment over the barn? If it's....."

"Good idea," said Johanna.

Delphine turned back to face the other two women, a look of amusement on her face.

"That ole Swede has taken a liking to your husband," she said. "He's opening up the Ice House to give him a tour."

Norah smiled. "Didn't he always say you can't trust a man till you've known him for twenty years?"

"Yes," responded Delphine. *"Cuz by then ya'll have seen all his good sides and all his bad sides and if you lend him a saw, whether or not he'll sharpen it before he gives it back."*

The two women laughed.

"Now that's a phrase Scott would appreciate," said Johanna. "He judges men by how well they take care of their tools."

As Johanna stood up to go, Norah hugged her. "Your quick actions saved us. Thanks to you, I have something left. Nathan's Mackinaw. Here, for you." Norah reached into its pocket and retrieved the audio recorder.

"Just in case, Granger sees his way to testing it for prints."

Johanna slipped the thin, black device into the pocket of her new jacket.

Her cell phone buzzed. It was a text from Phil Granger.

> *Can you meet the Fire Inspector and me out at the herb farm on Wednesday? 9AM?*

Thunder Ponies

Two days later, they arrived at the herb farm before the sheriff and fire inspector. Scott parked beside Johanna's Subaru. The farmhouse was burned to the ground. The backyard had burned all the way to the lilac bushes, which were scorched and drooping. The odor of burned wood, metal and plastic filled the air. The fire department had cordoned the area off.

They determined Norah's Jeep and Johanna's vehicle were covered with ash, but otherwise undamaged. Walking up the meadow path, they saw the vegetable garden bed was untouched by the ravage of the blaze.

"This is where you ran to?" asked Scott.

Johanna nodded. "Through the lilac hedge to the back gate. Then up into the meadows."

He nodded, then took her hand. "You and Norah were very lucky. You could have died."

"He meant us to. Both of us."

By the time they walked back to the parking area, the sheriff and fire inspector had arrived. Johanna pulled her jacket collar up against the stiff wind that blew around the side of the barn.

Not a Wind Sister, she thought, not today.

"Mornin' Johanna, Scott," said Phil. "This is Rufus McCoy. County fire inspector. Rufus, I'll let you handle the fire business."

Rufus McCoy was an older man of medium height, a firm handshake and blue eyes that twinkled when he spoke. Well-defined laugh lines and a handlebar mustache barely concealed his rakish grin. This was a man who had seen horrors and yet still kept his humor intact.

He smiled. "You are lucky to be alive, Miss."

Johanna nodded.

"I have a couple questions for you, then I can wrap up our investigation."

Rufus was a man that moved a lot. He shifted back and forth as he talked. It could have been habit, thought Johanna, but more likely, it was years of always being ready to jump into action.

"This guy was an amateur," said Rufus. "It was arson, to be sure. But he left signatures all over the place that made it easy for us to see what happened. Tell me, from the beginning, what woke you up?"

Johanna began her story from the moment she heard paper crinkling. She mentioned the red glow from the living room she thought was the woodstove and hearing the kitchen door close then ended with seeing the potato chip bag explode into flames and leaping out the window before they were overcome by the smoke.

"Ah. Exploding potato chip bag. It's undetectable. The oils in the potato chips act like an incendiary device and the bag itself disappears, so it looks accidental. We found charred candlestick holders in the kitchen and by the burned couch. He started the fire on the couch, first. Those worn polyurethane cushions combust immediately. Then he probably lit a small candle stub and put it by the potato chip bag on the kitchen counter by the wall. That gave him time to get out."

"So that's what I saw," said Johanna. "Shadows on the wall from the candle flickering when he closed the door."

"Those old walls caught on fire like a blaze in a hay barn. Fast and hot. Lots of air trapped in old newspapers and bunched up horse hair. The perfect formula. Taking out the battery in the smoke alarm made sure the occupants would be trapped," he said. "Yeah, we found the melted smoke detector, but without a melted battery."

"Not just arson, Rufus?" said Phil. "Attempted murder?"

"Ayuh."

"When will we be able to get a demo crew out here?" asked Scott.

"Need to wait a couple weeks to make sure all the heat is gone. Shouldn't take long with the colder weather. Is Norah going to rebuild?"

"Not sure, yet," said Scott. "I'm a retired contractor, so I thought I'd give her some options."

"Is it possible to occupy the apartment over the barn?" said Johanna.

Rufus nodded. "All the out-buildings were untouched. Other than ash and smoke. Ya might want to wash the windows and maybe toss out any herb stock she had stored in the shop. It's up to Norah, but smoke damage can be pervasive. I'd leave those apartment windows open for a while."

"Can we take a walk around the property, Rufus? I'd like to see what needs to be done," said Scott.

The two men walked toward the cordoned off area and Granger turned to face Johanna.

"Our investigation is complete," he said. "I can return your firearm. By the way, we know how Samuel knew when Norah wasn't at the farm. Rufus' team found a hidden, motion-activated video camera mounted by the barn garage doors. It was a camera hunters use to see deer movement patterns."

Granger reached into the front seat of his SUV and took out an evidence bag. It contained her Sig Sauer and an empty magazine. He handed it to her.

"Your bullets are in our evidence locker, as proof only one shot was fired. But it looks like Samuel operated on his own. There wasn't enough evidence to support that Eliana was involved. We interviewed Evelyn Jameson-Minsky and found no evidence of undue influence. She has not changed her Trust and denied her daughter or son suggested she do so."

"But what about the housekeeper? Lisette said...."

"We talked to Mrs. Gagnon and what she overheard was not evidence of wrongdoing, except bugging the farmhouse. She did not overhear any plans to set fire to the farmhouse or plots to murder Norah or yourself. We know someone tampered with the pet spray, but can't prove any involvement by either Samuel or Eliana."

"Mrs Jameson-Minsky believes what the housekeeper overheard was a misunderstanding," he continued. "Her daughter and son were upset about the new Trust amendment that Norah put into place. She was unconcerned about their blocking Norah's calls and called it merely a family matter. It may have shown intent, but without hard evidence, Samuel is the only person we can prove burned the house. And that's because you and Norah witnessed his hand in those events."

"What about Nathan's murder?"

"It looks like someone killed him, but there is no hard evidence it was anyone other than, possibly, Samuel. In that case, there is no one to prosecute."

"You said yourself you had trouble coming up with a motive. Doesn't that mean others could have been involved?" said Johanna. "What about Eliana? She stood to gain as much as Samuel."

"Eliana was in Boston at a conference the day Nathan died. She returned Saturday afternoon and there is no proof she was party to Samuel's plans to burn down the farmhouse. We talked with Eli Mittleman. He confirmed Samuel was in financial difficulty. The textile mill wasn't offsetting some of his investment losses. So we found our motive."

"He was counting on the farm going back to the Legacy Trust so he could sell it to cover his losses," Granger continued. "By sabotaging the farm's operations, he could put Norah out of business. Then the Trust, under his trusteeship, would have taken it back. He would then have the power to sell the property and underwrite his personal losses. When Norah terminated the stipulations, killing both of you and making it look like an accident was the only way to get the property."

Granger looked away to give Johanna time to process the gravity of his words.

"What a deranged plan," said Johanna.

"No one said he was the sharpest tool in the Minsky shed."

"What about bugging the house?"

"It's not breaking and entering, because he had keys. I will speak to Norah, but again, there is no one to prosecute."

Johanna nodded.

"Can I go up to the apartment now? I need to get insurance papers for Norah." *And something else, I don't want to leave behind, she thought.*

"Sure," said Granger. "I'm going to have a word with Rufus. The property can be occupied safely, and that's what matters to me."

Johanna looked up at the sky. She could see the peaks of the Katahdin range just over the pine tree spires. Wispy clouds scattered across the skies like the flowing manes of wild horses running across the plains. *Thunder ponies, she thought. Something is in the winds. It's coming this way, and it's not the weather.*

A few minutes later, she joined Scott in the driveway. Rufus and Phil had already left. She carried a folder with the farmhouse insurance documents and Mina's leather-bound book of garden secrets.

"We can come back tomorrow and wash the vehicles," said Scott, as Johanna got into the passenger seat. "We can move into the apartment and start taking care of things for Norah."

She sat on the ground in the upper meadows. The scent of fallen rugosa rose petals and charred wood filled her sensitive nostrils. From this vantage point, she had watched all of them. The woman was perfecting the art of stealth and the man was fiercely protective of her.

There were two ways to make fear one's ally, the Shapeshifter thought. One was to become something others feared. The other was to use the feeling of fear, to fuel a more-than-human strength that rose from the earth itself; the power of elemental allies. Beings that had never been, nor would ever become human. On the river, the woman had nearly found the second way.

She saw the Thunder Ponies running in the distance. The regalia of the Wind People. It was the wind that night that kept the out-buildings safe from the fire. This woman had powerful allies and she was just beginning to know how to call them up.

The Rhinemaidens

J ohanna laid the garden book on the coffee table at their room in at the
Greenwood Inn. Scott sat down beside her and placed a cup of coffee on a
side-table.

"Norah said Mina not only translated this book by hand, but left little notes
with flower drawings between its pages. I keep feeling something is hidden in the
book."

"Whatever it is was worth killing Nathan over," said Scott. "Granger was right
about one thing. Samuel must have had a powerful motive to kill you and Norah.
But it seems to me, a little financial difficulty doesn't really add up."

She opened the leather-bound book to the front page and showed Scott the
Yiddish greeting. She read it out-loud and paused at Mina's words.

> *Food is medicine, you will see, and a healthy life makes one as wealthy as
> a fortune of gold and silver. Between these pages, you will find more treasure
> than ever you could imagine.*

"You're right, there's something hidden in this book," he said.

"When I put it in Mina's trunk, I found a sprig of dried flowers in the bottom:
edelweiss wrapped in hyssop. Norah said Mina liked to craft flower sachets and
bouquets using the language of flowers."

Scott raised his eyebrows and sipped his freshly brewed coffee. He shrugged his
shoulders.

"Never heard of that," he said.

"For example, when I opened the trunk, I could smell roses and lavender. Look at this," she said. She searched the Internet on her cell phone, then held a webpage up for Scott to see.

"Red roses mean beauty and, umm… lavender symbolizes peace and happiness," he said as she flipped to the second webpage. "And, so?"

"Norah said edelweiss stood for bravery and devotion, while they used hyssop in Biblical times to create sanctity through purification. What if the flower drawings are like her sachets? Little messages written in the language of floral bouquets?"

"That's as good a guess as any," said Scott. "Where do we start?"

She turned the pages in the planting section, slowly, one by one. She came to the first note. "Here," she said, "we start here."

They easily identified the Moon Garden by Mina's drawing of the morning glories, twisting their way up the lattice among fully bloomed moonflowers. At its base were night blooming jasmine, 4 o'clocks, wild bergamot, and violets. The names of the flowers were in English, but at the top of the drawing were the German words; 'Mondgarten' and 'streben.'

"It looks like she drew this sketch of a flower grouping for a garden design layout. It's the Moon Garden, which Norah later planted. But what's the message?" said Johanna.

Scott handed her a blank notepad and a pen that were lying on the side table.

"Courtesy of the Greenwood staff," he said. "It's a full-service hotel."

She used a Translation App on her phone and found that 'Mondgarten' was German for moon garden and 'streben' meant 'to aspire.' She then searched for the flower symbolisms. Within a few minutes, she translated the entire note, using Mina's unique combination of German and the language of flowers. She wrote a phrase on the notepad.

Moon Garden. Aspire to unconditional devotion and affection, make time for love, hope for a new day, prosperity, and faithfulness.

"Sound advice," said Scott.

Johanna continued to turn the pages of the garden book until she came to another note with a drawing of flowers and the word 'vorsicht.' She had drawn the flowers as if grouped like a planting in a floral design layout. The words identifying the drawings were written across the bottom of the page; begonia, geranium, bird's foot tre-foil, and a yellow rose, tinted by a colored pencil. This was the first flower drawing that included color.

She consulted her Translation App and learned 'vorsicht' meant 'beware,' then looked up the meanings of the flowers and wrote down what was rapidly becoming Mina's secret messages. She then read it out-loud to Scott.

> *Beware of a fanciful nature, folly, revenge and betrayal.*

"More sound advice," said Scott.

Johanna replaced the note in the planting table section where she had found it, as she had replaced the other note so Norah could see where they had been placed. She continued for several pages and went beyond the drawing of the Rhine Maiden fountain that separated the two general sections of the garden book. This time, she didn't tremble or feel anything when she handled the pages.

Johanna continued to turn the pages when she came across a third secret note. A single word, 'hingabe' was written across the top and it included five flower drawings which were crowded together on the small note paper. Beneath each flower, Mina had written their names: rhododendron, marigold, columbine, hollyhocks, and an orange lily, using a colored pencil.

Again, Johanna consulted the App and the internet to translate and decipher the message. She wrote another phrase on the notepad and read it.

> *Abandon dangerous jealousy, foolish ambition and hatred.*

"Sounds to me like she knew all her grandchildren pretty well," said Scott.

"Maybe so," said Johanna. "She tucked this note into a herbal formula for heart health. It's well known in the psychology of mind-body medicine that holding resentment is implicated in the development of heart disease. "

"If the shoe fits, love."

She punched Scott on the arm, teasingly.

Johnna replaced the note and moved forward through the book. She found another one, folded and tucked into the binding on a page for sleep remedies. She unfolded it and found five flower drawings, some of which included a German word between the English words identifying them. On the top of the note, Mina had written the word, "suchen."

The order of the flowers, from left to right, were black-eyed susan, calla lily, [und] honeysuckle, [mit] edelweiss [werden] hyssop. A shiver ran through Johanna's body as she consulted the App and the symbolic meanings of the flowers.

"Oh," she said with surprise. She then read the phrase aloud.

> *Seek justice, beauty, and the bonds of love with courage and devotion - become sanctified.*

"It's a blessing, Scott!"

"Keep going, Jo," he said. "She is giving the prerequisites for living a fulfilling life."

"She is describing what it means to be a righteous person."

Scott nodded. "It's about Nathan. He's the righteous man."

Johanna replaced the note, but left it unfolded. She continued to turn the pages. She was coming to some recipes. When she got to the page with instructions to make dandelion bread, she discovered a note Norah must have seen many times. It began with the German word, 'kultivieren' on the top of the note. Then it included an herb and three flowers; camomile, lavender, a rose,

colored in red, and a dandelion. She looked through the flower symbolism links
and typed the German word into the App.

"More wisdom from Mina," she said, then translated the phrase.

> *Cultivate patience in adversity, happiness, beauty and love, and overcome*
> *hardships.*

"Why do you think she left so many messages?" Scott said,

"I think it's her legacy to her grandson. It was a way to tell him she already knew
the man he would become," Johanna said. "She knew he would find value in her
words, not merely want to possess the prize she had in store for him."

Scott nodded. "I think you may be right. I would have cherished each one of
those notes had they been from my grandmother. I never got a chance to know
her. You can feel Mina's love and respect in those messages."

"There must be more, maybe hidden in the recipe sections," said Johanna.

She continued to turn the pages of the book. The cake recipes included
frostings made with dyed plant colors and topped with edible flowers as
decorations. She found another note. It had a yellowish stain. This time there was
an entire sentence written in German, followed by a drawing of a single herb and
three flowers. *'Du wirst einen sehr grossen Schatz erhalten.'* The words under the
drawings were coriander, a tiger lily, a poppy and buttercups. Mina had painted
the poppy with yellow dust that looked like pollen to Johanna. She rubbed it and
her fingertip turned yellow.

"Pollen is the stuff of life," she murmured.

She consulted the App and the internet webpage on flower symbolism, again.
Then translated the message, writing it down on the notepad.

> *You will receive a very big treasure, hidden wealth, success and riches.*

Johanna paged through the rest of the book and but didn't find anymore notes.
She looked over at Scott. He shrugged.

"Is that it?" she said.

"What if Samuel murdered Nathan and tried to kill you and Norah, believing in a legend of tangible wealth when, all along, it was all a big recipe for right livelihood that paid out in the end with happiness and a life well lived?"

"That's entirely possible," Johanna said.

"What a tragedy."

In her mind's eye, Johanna saw wrinkled hands pressing together two pages in the garden book. She backtracked through the garden book, holding each page between her hands. She waited for it.

It came. *A tingle. A shiver.* Johanna was holding a page with instructions for planting a rain garden. According to the book, it should be a natural depression in the land, shaded, about twelve feet by twenty-four feet and filled with an assortment of plants and flowers that didn't mind getting their feet wet. Along with its description was a comprehensive list of rain garden plants: rhododendron, cardinal flowers, meadow rue, and wild columbine. The other side of the page was a carefully drawn landscape plan. But those weren't the plants Mina had drawn on that page.

Instead, she had sketched mistletoe, red roses, gladiolus, meadowsweet and nettle, along with buttercups. Johanna knew these flowers did not belong in a rain garden. She quickly consulted the flower symbolism webpage and wrote the message on the pad. Looking up at Scott, she passed the notepad to him. Instead of leaving a note inserted in the book, Mina put this message right on the page itself.

In a place where no violence can occur, beautiful warriors guard and protect riches.

"Whoa!"

"It's as if the notes were just a key to the use of flower language, but the hidden message was right on the pages of the book, itself."

"Hidden in plain sight," said Scott.

As Johanna held the page in her hands, she could feel something wedged inside it. Mina had carefully glued together two separate pages. The weight of the garden book over the years had effectively sealed the two pages as one.

"Are there any scissors in the kitchen?" Scott asked.

"These old pages are delicate," she responded. "We should use something like a razor blade to cut the edges."

"I have a knife with a box cutter attachment. I'll put a fresh blade in it."

Scott retreated to the bedroom as Johanna rose to search the kitchenette's utility drawer. She found a knife with a dull, serrated edge and butterknife that had a flat, spade-shaped blade.

"This'll do," she thought.

Moments later, Scott returned with a workman's utility knife. They carefully laid a bread board under the rain garden page, tucking it as tightly as possible against the spine of the book.

"Let me cut the corner of the page, then you pry it open," said Scott.

Johanna carefully slipped the butterknife between the sealed pages, sliding it through the small opening Scott had cut. She worked it gently around the margin edges, loosening the dried-out glue. As she pulled the pages apart, a thin onionskin paper was revealed, wedged between them.

She slowly removed a fully rendered drawing of the Rhinemaidens fountain. Mina had sketched mistletoe along the edges of the fountain and each maiden held a single flower. The maiden sitting in the fountain gazed dreamily at the sky and held a yellow iris in her hand. The maiden leaning against the fountain's column was looking at the first maiden and held a yellow rose. The last Rhinemaiden held up the fountain bowl with one arm and looked over her shoulder. She held a sprig of white edelweiss in her other hand.

"Three warriors protecting riches," whispered Scott.

Johanna was shaking. No wonder Mina sealed up this drawing.

She consulted the flower symbolism webpage. She translated the meanings of the flowers in Mina's last message.

> *Trickery, greed, courage and devotion.*

"Trickery and greed leads to the fountain," said Scott. "Courage and devotion points the way to the riches."

Johanna looked at Mina's drawing closely. "It's a map, Scott."

"So what's over the shoulder of this Rhinemaiden?" He pointed to the statue holding the white edelweiss.

"The wishing well."

True Colors

I t was still dark the next morning when they parked the Tahoe in the barn at Minerva's Meadows. While Scott searched for tools on Nathan's workbench, Johanna went to Mina's office and put the garden book on the bookshelf so Norah could review it. She felt it was safer in the office than in their hotel room. They would move into the apartment later today. She turned off the lights behind her.

By the time she rejoined Scott, he had outfitted himself with a headlamp, a shovel and a crowbar. He stowed his firearm in the Tahoe's center console and Johanna did the same. Excavating packed earth while wearing their pistols seemed foolhardy.

Daylight slowly illuminated the pathway as they walked to the ornamental gardens. It was cold, overcast and boded an unpleasant excursion which might not prove fruitful at all. They weren't really sure what they were looking for.

The rain garden was beyond the rose arbor. In its center was a marble fountain with the three Rhinemaidens positioned exactly as they were on Mina's drawing, yet none of them held any flowers. A stone carving of mistletoe circled the edge of the fountain's upper bowl.

The beautiful warrior holding up the bowl with one arm was easy to identify. She gazed over her shoulder to an area behind the fountain. Directly behind her was the stone wishing well, with its shingled roof and decorative bucket.

Courage and devotion.

The well was constructed with rounded river stones and covered with moss. When they looked into it, they saw it was lined with brick. Scott dropped in a rock. It struck the dry earth below.

"I think we have it," he said. "There's an iron ladder bolted right into the mortar between the bricks. Hand me the shovel when I go over the side."

He secured the headlamp to his forehead and slung his leg over the side of the well. Assuring himself the iron rungs were sturdy, he nodded to Johanna. Within moments, he was out of sight. She could only see a small pool of light illuminating the walls as he descended.

Eliana drove toward Minerva's Meadows in Evelyn's silver Mercedes. During their last conversation, he told her he had learned the secret of Mina's Garden Book when he listened to one of the audio recordings. He played it back for her. She remembered hearing Norah's voice say:

> *"When she was translating the instructions, she left little notes and drawings in the garden book. While the intern worked on the translations, Mina would write something on a notepad then insert it in the book."*

He had not only been clear; he had been decisive. He believed the clues lay on the various pages. She only needed to find the notes that were scattered throughout the book and read the pages they were on, to find out where the real Minsky wealth was located.

Who would have guessed? She gunned the car's engine as she drove up a mountain back road. He had also made very clear the actions she would need to take. If Norah were to die now, all of it would go to that woman. The Jameson's would never get their hands on the real treasure. Even though she now knew the full extent of her grandparent's legacy holdings and what she stood to inherit, it was not enough to stop her from wanting more.

If Samuel hadn't screwed up, they would all have been a great deal richer than they could ever have imagined. If they had persuaded Norah to step down, it would have forced Eli to appoint her brother trustee to the Minsky Family Legacy Trust. Samuel would have then activated Albert's safety clause: declare there were no suitable family successor trustees, then disband the Trust by separating it into four equal parts; Samuel's, Evelyn's, Norah's and hers.

Now her only choice was to recover the treasure before Norah returned to the herb farm or Johanna figured it out. They must have taken the garden book from the herb shop, because it wasn't there during the break-in. She hadn't thought to tell Samuel to look for it in Mina's old homestead office.

Eliana smiled. Telling him to leave the door to the herb shop open was a stroke of genius. The datura was all Samuel's idea. Planting it in the Moon Garden should have shut the whole business down. Their plan to require Norah to get a competency evaluation had failed.

Her sister-in-law's strange behavior, along with a poisoned animal and tainted products, would have cast enough suspicion on her mental stability to remove her as Nathan's successor. But no, Johanna had convinced the sheriff it was sabotage instead.

Hence, Samuel pulled out all the stops. Burn her out, making it appear she forgot to change the battery in the smoke alarms and was careless with a candle. What an idiot. Mina's book could have been in the farmhouse. We might have lost it in the fire.

Eli was the current trustee in place and she knew he was ready to declare there was no family member prepared to take it over, since Samuel was gone and Norah seemed emotionally incapable. Now, her mother, Norah, and herself would split the proceeds of the entire Minsky Legacy Trust. That rankled. To be sure, she would talk to Eli about a financial settlement option to take care of Ann. Her sister-in-law wouldn't jeopardize that income by telling anyone what she knew. I will make it worth her while, she thought.

She turned the car onto the access road to Minerva's Meadows. Both the Subaru and Jeep were parked on the far side of the barn, still coated with gray ash from the fire. Yellow tape cordoned off the farmhouse from the rest of the property. Seeing the burned-out house was a bit of a shock. *Too bad about that, she thought.*

Oh Samuel, you played a long shot with that idea. Just like losing everything gambling at a casino craps table. I would never have made that mistake. She parked the Mercedes in front of the barn, blocking the garage doors. She had been very careful to make sure anything Norah remembered was attributed to Samuel acting alone. The sheriff had closed the case. She climbed the back staircase to Mina's office and unlocked the door to the apartment with the newest set of keys Samuel had managed to take.

She went to the bookcase beside the old antique desk and found her grandmother's garden book. *I'll take it down to the car, she thought. I can bring it back later after I find the entries. If anyone comes by, I can duck it under the seat and leave.*

She had a proven skill in game theory. While writing her doctoral thesis, she minored in it and was passionate about designing counter-strategies. She found it compelling that one could win an objective by accurately predicting the motivations, intentions, and actions of another, then defeating them with a countermove, much like a game of chess. Only with much larger stakes.

It was well known successful businesses used various game strategies to bolster their bottom lines. *It's best to mix up your moves, she thought, be unpredictable. Do the unexpected. Calculate what other people will do, then beat them, whatever way you can.*

Eliana had taught these strategies to her most successful corporate coaching clients. It was easy to develop game theory tools with those who possessed a devious character, less so with those executives who espoused a sense of general goodness and fair-play. She remembered one in particular who believed the height of negotiating skills occurred when everyone walked away from the bargaining table, feeling they had won.

Her training tableau was to put him into several compromising scenarios where winning the negotiation was based on achieving a signed contract, even though making the entire delivery on time was impossible. She pitted him against competitors who were less morally aligned than himself.

She quickly discovered it was fairly easy for a winning negotiator to base their strategies on what good intentioned people won't do, find their ethical boundaries and push them beyond their limits. But it was almost impossible to predict what a good person would really do under pressure, then find a counter-strategy. Varying degrees of bully bargaining remained their last resort.

She remembered her grandmother as a poorly educated, old woman who spoke broken English. She couldn't negotiate business deals or manage social events. Mina Minsky had been no better than a yard laborer whose skills were barely more than weeding or a kitchen cook who baked by following other people's recipes. How clever could she really have been?

Using her game theory skills to solve the problem of the garden book's secrets should be easy. Moments later, sitting in the Mercedes driver's seat, she opened her grandmother's leather-bound book and started turning the pages, looking for the secret notes. She failed to look in the barn or she would have seen the Tahoe.

As she turned the pages, she came across the first inserted note: the Moon Garden drawing. As Johanna had done earlier, she identified the lattice with its twisted vines of morning glories and moonflowers and the four plantings at its base. The words "jasmine, 4 o'clocks, wild bergamot and violets" accompanied the perfectly rendered line drawings. She saw the words "Mondgarten" and "streben" written across the top of the paper. *Of course, the old lady wrote her clues in German, she thought.* She quickly opened the Translation App on her cell phone. Aspire.

Eliana read the two pages that held the note. The location had to be written in the book, didn't it? He had been so sure. But the word "aspire" had nothing to do with instructions for preparing soil. There were no plantings she could distinguish that pointed to a location designated in the book itself, at least not on these pages.

She turned the note over in her hand, then turned it over again to the drawing. The Moon Garden was in Norah's backyard and Nathan had always called it the

Secret Garden. She wouldn't let any crime scene tape deter her if what they were looking for was buried there.

But her puzzle-solving mind said *no, not the right place.* If there were more notes, then there were more clues. She carefully turned the pages until she found the next one.

This note had four line drawings of intricately drawn flowers: begonia, geranium, bird's foot tre-foil and a yellow rose. Her grandmother had written the word "vorsicht" at the top of the page, which translated to the word - beware. She looked at the pages it was tucked between, which detailed generic planting schedules. These descriptions could refer to anywhere on the property. She kept turning the pages of the garden book.

Another note, tucked between two medicinal recipes, both for heart health. Her grandmother had drawn five flowers on the note with more labels. Mina had written the word "hingabe" at the top which, according the App, meant to abandon.

What if it's the order of the words, not in the pages of the book itself? Aspire, beware, abandon? *I need more notes; she thought.*

The next note made a little more sense. "Suchen" or seek. She looked carefully at the flowers her grandmother had drawn. She wondered if there was a landscape design plan that identified all the gardens. Eliana remembered Nathan handed out ornamental garden brochures at their tea festivals. She ran back up to the office.

An old handout was on the bookshelf beside the seed catalogs. She brought it back to the car and unfolded it on the dashboard. After scrutinizing the layouts, she found nothing that designated plantings with the particular flowers in any of the notes, so far.

But I'm onto something, she thought. Keep looking.

She found another note with the word "kultivieren" written on the top: cultivate. Four additional flowers were drawn and labeled. But again, the brochure design did not include any groupings that contained those plantings.

Eliana felt frustrated. This wasn't going well.

It's right in front of me, but I can't see it. Maybe the flowers don't mean anything, she thought. *What if they were just doodles, meant to confuse someone?*

She turned more pages of the garden book and found another cryptic note. But this one was different. The words, *'du wirst einen sehr grossen Schatz erhalten,'* were written across the top of the note. Eliana translated the phrase to say; "you will receive a very great treasure." There were four flower drawings below it.

Yes! I've got it, she thought. Her grandmother had simply strung the notes in a meaningless series. Unless you persevered and found all of them.

Eliana held all the notes she'd found in her left hand as she turned the pages of her grandmother's garden book. Then she came to the Rain Garden note and its drawings. Mina had drawn and labeled four plants. There was a rain garden in the landscape brochure. *This is it, I can feel it, she thought, excitedly. I was right, the flower drawings are irrelevant.*

The onionskin drawing of the Rhinemaiden fountain was next to the note. Each maiden in the drawing held a bouquet in their hands. Eliana sat back, stunned. Of course. In Wagner's opera the Rhinemaidens guarded the Nibelungen treasure. Her grandmother loved the myth of the Rheingold. She had commissioned a fountain with their statues to be built in the ornamental gardens. She looked at the brochure again.

They buried the real Minsky Legacy in the fountain, she thought. I solved it. I'm the only one who knows. We'll have to get a crew out here to break up the concrete. I'll hire someone privately. As long as I pay them a lot more than they ask, they'll do it and keep quiet about it. Everyone has their price.

Eliana laid the book on the passenger seat, then walked down to the Rain Garden. She planned to survey the fountain and take pictures with her cell phone. *I have to get an estimate for the work before Norah returns to the property.*

All That Glitters

Scott tested the hard-packed earth at the bottom of the well with the tip of the shovel. He had been digging for a while but had found nothing. He stopped to wipe the sweat from his forehead when his headlamp caught flashes of light reflected from the brick walls. He looked closer and saw what appeared to be metal end-caps with pull-rings between some of the bricks, he hadn't noticed before. He climbed up the iron ladder to get the crowbar and break up the old mortar. He told Johanna what he'd found.

"It's possible Albert walled up metal boxes, decades ago. If that's what's attached to the plates, those boxes are strong enough to hold precious metals. They look to be set into the brick walls at chest level height. The roof protected the well hole from filling up with precipitation, rain and what-not, over the years."

"How far down does it go?" she asked.

"Not deep enough to hit water," he responded. "Old Albert knew just how far to dig. This well was never meant to produce any water."

Johanna handed Scott the crowbar, then he descended back down into the well. She turned around, hearing someone coming down the pathway.

"Someone's coming," she said, leaning over the well. She had just enough time to walk toward the fountain when Eliana walked through the arbor into the rose gardens.

The last thing Elaina expected to find in the rain garden was Johanna standing by the Rhinemaidens statues.

"What are you doing here?" Eliana demanded.

"I might ask the same of you, Eliana," Johanna said loudly. She hoped Scott would hear their voices and stay hidden in the well.

"Norah asked me to check on the gardens after the fire inspector cleared access to the property," said Johanna. She walked closer to the statues. "I've never seen them before," she said. Walking to the front of the fountain, she kept her gaze on the Rhinemaidens. *People tended to follow someone else's gaze and points of interest, she thought.*

"My grandmother loved the Wagnerian opera Das Rheingold," said Eliana.

Her tone was conversational, Johanna thought, too friendly.

Eliana came closer.

Johanna reached down into her pockets, trying to appear casual and non-assuming. She found the audio recorder. She switched the tab to the 'on' position and took her hand out.

She pointed to the Rhinemaiden that was sitting in the fountain. *The one Mina labeled Trickery.*

"I'm not sure I am up on the story of that opera," she said.

"The Rhinemaidens guarded the Nibelungen treasure," said Eliana. "A cache of gold hidden in the Rhine river."

"Do you think Nathan's story about his grandfather's gold had some truth to it?"

Eliana walked closer to the fountain, leaned over and took a cell phone photo of the maiden leaning against the center column.

The one labeled Greed.

"Don't tell me you haven't thought about that," said Eliana. "Ann told me your eyes lit up when she mentioned it at the tea party."

"I'm here because Norah wants me to be," said Johanna.

"No, you're here because you want my grandfather's legacy," said Eliana.

"Well, you're wrong about that."

"Norah, too. She's not a blood descendent of Albert and Minerva Minsky," said Eliana. "She deserves no more than what she got from being Nathan's wife."

"You'll have to work that out with Norah," said Johanna. "This is her property and if there is anything valuable buried here, your grandfather meant for Nathan to decide what to do with it."

"I'm the only remaining inheritor in my grandparent's direct lineage," said Eliana. "By rights, it's up to me."

Her tone was cold and curt.

"Maybe Nathan was chosen to be the trustee because he was a fair man who would have divided equally whatever your grandfather had hidden," said Johanna. "Did you ever think that might have been the case? Either you or Samuel? When you bugged her house, blocked her phone, and tampered with things so she would question her sanity?"

Eliana stared at her with contempt.

"Even now," said Johanna, gently. "Norah would probably consider it the fair thing to do. That's if there is anything here at all." She used her calmest therapeutic voice, the one she used to reassure suicidal clients.

She felt Eliana stiffen, so she drifted away from the fountain and walked toward the rose beds. She heard someone else coming through the arbor.

Eli walked into the gardens. Dressed warmly in heavy khaki pants and a wool overcoat, he moved with the limberness of a much younger man. Johanna felt relieved. Here at last was a voice of reason that might make an impact on Eliana.

He approached the fountain where Eliana stood. She snapped another shot of it with her cell phone.

"Did you find it yet?" he said, completely ignoring Johanna, He rubbed his hands together, warming them from the cold.

"I figured it out," she said. "Albert buried the gold in the Rhinemaiden fountain. I'm trying to figure out exactly where before I get a demolition guy."

"Give me the book," says Eli. "It can't be that hard. Pardon me, Eliana, if I need to see for myself."

"The book's in the apartment," lied Eliana. "There is no X that marks the spot. We will have to break up the concrete if we want to get to it."

Johanna suddenly realized Eli had been a part of the scheme to gaslight Norah, all along, and convince her she was incompetent. But why mentor and support her trusteeship? Something's terribly wrong here. I can't let them know we've found the location. I can't let them know where Scott is. *He's a sitting duck, she thought.*

"So that's why you're here. You don't trust her," stated Johanna.

"Of course I do," he replied. "She followed my instructions to the letter. It's Samuel who improvised. See how that ended up."

"Norah seemed to think that Albert buried something in the rose gardens," said Johanna. "Nathan told her Albert excavated the ornamental gardens himself when Mina designed the layout years ago. She thought there might be clues in the order of the rose plantings." She walked toward the arbor where the rose beds began and pointed to a grouping.

"So you think if you help us," said Eliana, "you'll get a share? Think again. We have no use for you. That should have been clear the night of the fire."

"No need to stoop to murder," said Eli with a chuckle. "Just a little restraint."

"Buy her out?" asked Eliana.

"Everyone has their price," he responded.

"You are forgetting," said Johanna impetuously. "All of this legally belongs to Norah."

"If you walk away now, Johanna, I will make sure all of this will belong to you. With the exception of a little glitter."

"Norah already made me Power of Attorney and in the case of her death, I inherit all of this, as you said, so there are no bargaining chips here."

"Only if I actually file her Trust changes," he responded. "You lose everything if I don't and if I do, I can say I counseled Norah against it. You see the problem here, right?"

Johanna started to understand the full implications of the situation. That document could implicate her as an instigator of indue influence on an emotionally fragile friend.

"I think you see where this could go," said Eli.

Eliana crossed her arms with a smirking smile. She swept her right arm in a wide circle. "See, we found you here in the garden looking for a secret cache of gold while Norah was incapacitated. It was obvious what you were doing, and we had to stop you. After all, everything started happening after you came to visit," said Eliana.

Johanna ran.

She bolted through the arbor and raced through the gardens. She leaped over twigs and branches that were strewn across the path. She heard Eliana running after her.

Tripping over a root, Johanna fell head-first into the boxwood hedge that separated the ornamental gardens from the driveway. Her long hair got tangled in its branches. The brambles scratched her face as she freed herself. She had to get off the path. Pushing through the shrubbery, she slipped down the hillside and stumbled onto the paved driveway. She heard Eliana running on the garden path and knew she would catch up with her in moments.

Johanna could see their two vehicles blocking the garage doors. She could not use the Tahoe to escape. She quickly entered the side door of the barn and locked it. She could get her pistol from the Tahoe but her mind froze. *She remembered trying to shoot Samuel's kayak on the riverbank. She couldn't even hit that, let alone him.*

No time.

There was a landline in Mina's office. The entrance to the apartment was joined to the barn through a narrow hallway. She ran to the stairway. The side door burst open.

Eliana blocked her way. "Don't you know I have all the keys?" she laughed.

Johanna turned and ran back into the barn. She had to reach her pistol. As she put her hand on the vehicle's door, Eliana grabbed her from behind, wrenching her arm and twisting it up behind her back.

Johanna cried out.

Eliana punched her shoulder, spun her around, slapped her, then shoved her against the wall. She lunged for Johanna's throat.

Grabbing her wrists, Johanna forced her backwards, pushing her away.

A surge of fury raced through Johanna, an ice-born rage. For a moment, she saw white. There are those for whom anger is a fire, seething with hatred and retaliation. There are others, whose rage is cold, decisive and far more deadly.

Eliana grabbed a sledgehammer by Nathan's work bench and came at Johanna. Its weight added a lethal momentum to her murderous lunge. As she struck out, Johanna stepped aside, put her hand on Eliana's shoulder and pushed. Eliana slammed full force into the barn's side wall, then slid down onto her knees and the sledgehammer crashed to the floor. She pitched forward, hitting her head with a dull thud. Eliana lay still, unconscious and bleeding, on the floor.

Johanna pressed the automatic door opener. If she ran now, she could get to the Ice House. Jost would help. As she started down the driveway, Eli stepped off the path, aiming a gun at her. He walked toward her.

"I think not," he said. Looking into the barn, he saw Eliana on the floor.

"I see you have made our position even easier, Johanna. Aggravated assault. The jury will see I had no choice."

"Why, Eli?" she implored. "What is worth all this deception? Murdering Nathan? Destroying Norah's mind? Why would a decent man like yourself do this?"

"Taking out Nathan was Samuel's idea, and he executed it perfectly. If Norah wasn't so single-mindedly obstinate, this could have had a much more hospitable outcome."

"She would have gotten her little farm business," he continued. "Samuel would have put Albert's fail-safe clause in effect, liquidated all the Minsky holdings, then distributed the cash to himself and Eliana. All problems solved along with an extraordinarily large, unaccountable cache of gold that isn't documented anywhere."

"That still doesn't explain why a man of integrity like you would have done this. You have nothing to gain. You aren't named in the legacy, are you?"

He laughed. "Fifteen percent of the entire legacy distribution goes to the lawyer who handles the dissolution as proper compensation. My father was a fool to let Albert use him the way he did."

She was surprised she felt no fear; the adrenaline that now coursed through her body served to unexpectedly focus her mind in razor-sharp clarity. *He feels justified in his actions, she thought. He is justifying them to me right now. He wants me to think he has no choice other than what he's preparing himself to do.*

"He held the right to buy at spot and sell at premium, whenever he wanted to," Eli continued. "My father's vault held the precious metals that Albert liquidated and replenished every time he ran a business deal buy-out, including the textile mill loan, all of it. My father only netted five percent of those deals for himself, but he took all the risks. When Roosevelt signed the Executive Order in 1933 making it illegal for US citizens to own gold, my father was the one who stood to go to prison if it was discovered."

This wasn't the first time Johanna had encountered someone who was escalating their level of violence. She had sat across the room from clients who were descending into psychosis. Her only advantage was using a well-honed clinical skill of unconscious mirroring. She intentionally relaxed her shoulders and softened the muscles in her face. It sent an immediate and powerful message to Eli's conflicted mind.

His hand wavered causing him to slightly lower the gun on his outstretched arm.

"My father adored his uncle, and it was his biggest failing. Sure, Albert paid for my education, but he owed my father a bigger debt. Loyalty was the true asset on the books and it was never accounted for properly. My father was owed a great deal more than he was ever paid, and for what? So Minsky got richer. Later, the gold disappeared. My father assumed Albert transferred all his gold to one of his Canadian companies. I am only claiming what is owed me."

Behind him, Johanna saw Scott standing on the path to the ornamental gardens, the crowbar in his hands. *I've got to keep him talking, she thought.* She looked down at her feet and sighed. Eli's gaze followed hers. Then he tightened his grip on the gun. It was pointed at her heart. He stood nearly seven feet away from her. If he fired, he wouldn't miss.

"I managed the Minsky empire for decades," Eli said. "Nathan was just dabbling. I orchestrated some back alley deals that netted a huge profit for the Minsky fortune. So what if they weren't entirely above board? Nathan always insisted on looking a little too closely at the books. Samuel would have looked the other way."

He is talking himself into pulling the trigger, but he's no sociopath. He's desperate, she thought.

"Unfortunately, Albert had already dictated Nathan was to succeed me when I stepped down," he continued. "There was an age limitation in the trustee designation. A step-down was required at age eighty-one. Nathan had to go and something needed to be done."

She saw Scott moving forward slowly, in her peripheral vision, but Eli's gun was still pointed at her chest.

"When the dust settles on this," he said, "you will look like an opportunist who attempted to discredit your old friend and persuade her to assign you power over her affairs. I will make sure of it."

"There is something you don't have control over," Johanna said, knowing full well the effect her words would have. He was motivated by greed and power, no matter how justified he believed his actions to be. "And it's going to blow up in your face. Phil Granger knows Samuel killed Nathan. We found his shoe and broken paddle at the portage site. He is investigating you right now." She grabbed at the last straw available and played a psychological maneuver from Samuel's own playbook. Three truths then a lie.

He stepped back. "What do you mean? My hands are clean."

That's when he sensed something behind him. Eli spun around. Scott slammed the crowbar on Eli's hand, smashing the bones in his left wrist and the pistol fell to the ground.

Johanna dived for the gun.

Scott ran at Eli but the older man knocked him off balance with an astonishing amount of strength. He pushed him down, grabbing the crowbar with his uninjured hand and swung it at Scott who scrambled in the dirt to fend off the attack.

Kneeling in the dirt, Johanna aimed upwards and fired.

The bullet pierced Eli's shoulder and the impact threw him facedown onto the ground. A pool of dark, red blood soaked through his coat.

Scott rolled onto his feet and quickly removed his belt to use as a tourniquet.

"Call 911, get Granger out here and an ambulance!"

As she turned toward the apartment, she stumbled.

"Put the safety on, before you shoot yourself," he called after her.

Stunned, she realized she had just shot a man. She had automatically aimed at a non-lethal area and the bullet struck exactly where she wanted it to. He would live to stand trial. And so would Eliana.

Moments later, Johanna placed Eli's pistol on the desk, called 911 and stated the emergency clearly and concisely. She grabbed some towels from the bathroom, then ran back to join Scott in the driveway. He had been able to put enough pressure on the wound to staunch the bleeding.

"There's a medical kit in the Tahoe," he said. "See if she needs any help."

She heard moaning coming from the direction of the barn. Eliana had pulled herself into a sitting position, but her head wound still bled profusely. Johanna handed her the towel and turned to the Tahoe. Eliana grabbed her wrist.

"Please, let's make a deal," she said. "It was Eli's plan from the beginning. He told us the legacy trustee had the express power to make investment decisions, including liquidating any assets he deemed necessary. He told us Nathan knew about the gold his grandfather had set aside and planned to keep it for himself. He would not distribute a share to either Samuel, me or our children."

"You believed him without even confronting Nathan?"

"He would have lied."

"You were so sure of that you killed your own brother. Whatever happened to due diligence?"

"Please, I have two children in prestigious private schools. Having their mother in prison would mar their opportunities, their social connections. Besides, Johanna, I didn't kill anyone, I just wanted my share of the inheritance."

"Unless I'm mistaken, you were about to kill me."

"If you change your story, we can say I came to help you locate the gold. Eli tried to kill both of us. I can say that he did this to me." She indicated the wound on her head. "Instead of you."

It's a veiled threat, thought Johanna.

"You made a serious mistake, Eliana. In your game theory gambits, your scenarios always succeed because your clients are role playing. You never imagine failure," said Johanna. "That's the difference between your kind of coaching and mine. My clients came from some of the world's most successful investment firms and they always hedged their bets. They always had a plan for losing. You didn't."

They heard a siren in the distance. Eliana pressed the bloody towel against her head.

"I can make it worth your while, Johanna."

"Not on your life, Eliana. As your grandfather said, integrity is measured by what you will not do."

Just Deserts

Gauthier and Mitchell arrived first, followed by an ambulance. They drove to the far right side of the driveway, so Emergency Services had full access to the area where Scott kneeled by Eli's side. He periodically loosened the tourniquet as Eli groaned in pain.

Granger pulled in behind them and parked in the farmhouse's front yard. The emergency medical technicians attended Eli, assessing and treating his gun-shot wound. A paramedic went to the barn to attend the gash on Eliana's head.

Phil followed, to take her statement and review the assault scene. Pete took Scott over to the ruins of the farmhouse to obtain his statement of what occurred. Sophie took Johanna aside.

"The gun's in the office, upstairs over the barn," said Johanna. "I wanted it out of reach."

"Understand," said Sophie. She ran her hands through her hair. "Can you take me to it?"

Johanna led the way up the back stairway and through the apartment's kitchen. Her hand shook as she opened the door to the office and pointed to the pistol laying on the desk.

"This is the phone you used to call 911?"

"Yes," said Johanna.

"Your firearm?"

"No, it belongs to Eli Mittleman. Or, at least I think it does. He pulled it on me. He was -"

"Hold on, I'll take a full statement in a minute. I have to secure it and take it into evidence. Are there any other weapons?"

"We stowed our Sig Sauer pistols in the center console of Scott's Tahoe."

"I need to see if they've been fired."

Johanna nodded. "And a crowbar."

Gauthier raised her eyebrows. Wearing blue nitrile gloves, she released the magazine from the 22 millimeter Smith and Wesson, ejected the round in the chamber, and placed it all in evidence bags.

"You may find this useful," said Johanna. Again, her hand shook as she removed the small audio recorder from her jacket pocket. "I recorded the whole thing, right down to Eliana, begging me to change my story."

Sophie offered another evidence bag, and she dropped it in.

"I didn't erase the conversation Samuel recorded between Norah and myself. Tell the Sheriff to keep listening to the end."

Sophie nodded. "You want to tell me what happened here?"

Johanna started from the point where she and Scott were excavating the bottom of the well at Norah's request. She described Eliana showing up in the rose garden, then Eli, whom she had initially believed to be supportive of Norah's claim to whatever was buried there.

She told of running for help and Eliana's attacking her with a sledgehammer. She described how Eli confronted her with a gun, then Scott disabled him with a crowbar. She told how she shot Eli to prevent him from killing her husband.

Johanna finished her story with a tone of weariness in her voice.

"We'll get the sledgehammer too," Sophie said. "You should sit down and catch your breath."

Johanna sat down in an office chair. She could feel the adrenaline drain from her body.

"We need you to come down to the station, get fingerprinted and give a formal statement."

"There's something you need to know," said Johanna. "I'm right-handed. The thumbprint on the left side of the barrel is mine. Eli is left-handed. He may have left his thumbprint on the right side."

"Smart girl. Do you mind if I ask a personal question?"

"What's that?" said Johanna.

"You're a psychologist, right?"

Johanna nodded. "Retired."

"You seem like a peace activist to me. Why all the gun slinging?"

"Years ago, I worked for an agency that dealt with domestic violence and sexual assault victims. I helped a particular woman escape an abusive relationship." She paused.

"Yeah?"

"She was married to a very influential guy, lots of money. Our team at the agency was part of an underground escape system for abused women. In those days, women had to fend for themselves. There weren't any protection laws on the books."

"Her husband hired a hit man to find out where she went, so he came to the agency first. I will never know how he knew the woman was my client, but he grabbed me in the parking lot and put a gun to my head. Our agency director called the cops. When he heard the sirens, he let me go and left before they got there."

"My God!"

"Yeah. It was bad. I was terrified. Trauma. PTSD, the whole deal. I had to leave the agency and work in a different area of psychotherapy. I took a self-defense course in gun training. I learned to shoot and carry a concealed weapon," Johanna continued. "This is the first time I had to shoot someone."

"My advice?" said Gauthier. "Don't try to do this yourself. Get a therapist to work through the shock. It's gonna hit you hard later, real hard. Even seasoned officers have to go through assessment and counseling after a shooting."

Johanna nodded. "Good advice."

By the time they got back to the driveway, the EMS team had already left, transporting Eliana and Eli to the hospital, under guard. Pete returned from the ornamental gardens, where he had taken photos of the rain garden and the Rhinemaiden fountain. Norah and Jost had arrived and were standing with Scott by the ruins of the burned-out farmhouse. Phil Granger walked over to them.

"What are you going to do about the contents of the well, Norah?" asked Granger. "When word of this gets around...." He shrugged his shoulders.

"I have a friend with a hoist," said Jost. "If Scott here can get down theyah and pull the boxes outta the walls, I can lift 'em outta the well."

"If the Sheriff will let me."

"You and Johanna need to come to the station to make formal statements as soon as possible. But if you can remove those boxes today, I'll assign Gauthier to stay here and guard against any unwanted intrusion."

"If we load the boxes into your Tahoe," said Norah, "we can bring them to Nathan's office in the Minsky Building. There's a vault there. I'll alert our security team, and we can use the back alley entrance and service elevators."

Ceremony

Johnna woke to the smell of freshly brewing coffee in the barn apartment. She snuggled deeper in the Amish quilt and wrapped her legs in its soft folds. She could hear Scott rummaging in the kitchen cupboards.

Two days ago, they had transported six metal boxes to the vault in the Minsky Building. Each box contained five hundred, one-ounce Saint Gaudens double eagle gold coins, that had never been in circulation. While the spot price of gold was currently nearly fifteen hundred dollars per ounce, these flawless coins had been minted in 1925. Worth nearly $24,000 each, Albert's wishing well contained a fortune in precious metals.

She gazed through the overhead skylight. Sunlight filtered through the icy morning frost on the glass and scattered shards of light on the walls of the small bedroom. Her body was still sore from Eliana's attack; her face hurt, and her sleep had been restless. She thought about her use of lethal means to stop an old man from harming the man she loved. In the flash of a moment, she discovered, she could deliberately harm another human being. Before this, she would never believe herself capable of such a thing.

Had fear become her ally, as Scrag had suggested? She wasn't sure. She recalled the cold, white rage that rose up in her body. Being a person who embraced peace and compassionate actions, it was disturbing to discover she had such darkness buried within her.

A deadly darkness, she knew she would eventually have to face.

Norah was now solely responsible for the fate of the entire Minsky empire. Her first decision was to have the remains of the farmhouse demolished and removed.

She had asked Scott and Johanna to winter-over in the apartment, so he could design a rebuild.

"I'm not sure I can bear to live there again, so please design a structure that pleases the both of you," said Norah. "Whatever you want, whatever materials you want to use, please take full rein."

Scott brought Johanna a cup of coffee and announced he and Jost were going to visit a solar energy company in Lewiston. "We're going to build an off-grid farm here, and Jost wants to tag along." Scott laughed as he sat down on the bed beside her. He ran his fingers through her hair, avoiding the reddened scratches on her face.

"He's giving Norah a deal on a new Jotul woodstove for a backup heating source."

"Of course he is. Swedish opportunist."

"A Viking, through and through. I like what I saw in his showroom," said Scott. "Are you meeting up with Norah?"

"I'm bringing her Mina's garden book," she said. "It's a good thing Granger let me take it from the Mercedes. Apparently, they didn't consider it evidence."

"Delphine dropped by earlier with some cranberry scones," said Scott. "They're pretty good."

"Between Norah and Delphine, I'm going to have to seriously start working out in a gym."

He gently kissed her forehead, to the left of a purple bruise. "You gonna be ok? After Delphine left, Granger brought back our firearms. I put your pistol on the kitchen table."

A dark shadow passed over her face, her body tensed.

"Busy morning," she mumbled.

"It's gonna take a while, love," he said. "But it's like getting back on a horse. You saved my life. You need to keep practicing and training. You did good."

"If only it felt like that..." her voice trailed away in a whisper.

She ran her thumb across his lips then swept her fingers over his face. She buried her fingertips in his hair, pulled him close, and inhaled. The scent of wood smoke filled her nostrils. His body smelled of fire-tending and sandalwood soap; earthy, and refreshing. She realized she had nearly lost him. This time would have been forever.

He kissed her then left the apartment.

She ate one of the scones. *Home-baked goods are vastly underrated, she thought.* Real food has healing power; it's baked with love. Dressing warmly, she locked the apartment and went to the herb shed. She needed a few things before she joined Norah at Delphine's house.

Minutes later, she drove to the Ice House and parked her Crosstrek by Norah's Jeep. There was so much to decide. She wanted to hear Norah's plans. Johanna knew offering Scott the opportunity to design and possibly rebuild the farmhouse was something he would love to do, but where did that leave Elk Run Farm in Pennsylvania? A rebuild would take quite a while and winter was coming. It wasn't the time of year for construction.

It was Scott's decision, after all, she thought. She gathered the packet of tea blends and Mina's garden book, then closed her car door. *Was it really over?* What was Evelyn going to do, now that she had lost two sons and her daughter was likely going to prison?

Delphine greeted Johanna at the door and led her to the kitchen. It was a country kitchen with wide pine counters. Pots and pans hung from an iron rack. A bright yellow, linen cloth covered the table where Norah sat with a legal size notepad. Her long legs stretched out under the table and she sipped a cup of tea.

Johanna placed the garden book and the packet of tea on the table, then sat down.

"You look like you're immersed in curriculum planning for a new botany course," said Johanna.

"I've been thinking," said Norah. She smiled and laid down her pen.

"I'm putting on a fresh kettle of water to boil," said Delphine. She placed a plate of cranberry almond cookies on the table, then joined them.

"I've made a few decisions. Thanks to Delphine's practical suggestions and a long discussion with Evelyn, I've arrived at a preliminary plan."

"You've spoken to Evelyn already?"

"I called her after we came back from the Minsky office building. I felt she needed to hear from me quickly, after she learned about Eli and Eliana's arrests. I'm not the only one betrayed. She was manipulated by her own children and has effectively lost all of them."

"At her age," said Johanna, "that could be a death sentence."

"Indeed. She was very upset. Phil Granger informed her about an hour before I called. Her biggest concern was for her grandchildren. Samuel's sons were already dealing poorly with their father's death. Imagine finding out he died while attempting to murder someone. She hasn't told them he likely murdered their uncle."

"It seems Phil talked with Eliana's husband, as well. Her children are a wreck, as is he," Norah continued. "I've come to a big decision. Let me lay it out for you, then I want your professional opinion." Her tone was decisive.

Johanna nodded. She took a freshly baked cookie.

"The Jameson-Minsky family might be pretentious, but Evelyn values her family more than anything. She realizes that Samuel's and Eliana's actions may have destroyed their children's opportunities. No one loves a scandal more than the rich and privileged," said Norah. "I've decided to enact Albert's Trust clause and liquidate all the holdings, sell the investments, and subsidiary businesses. I will then distribute equal shares to Evelyn, Samuel's sons, Eliana's children, Ann and Eliana's husband, Roger, and myself, as Nathan's portion. Evelyn and I agreed we should set aside funds for Eliana's legal defense to ensure she receives fair representation. I hope that doesn't offend you."

"No." said Johanna. "Eliana needs to be tried by a jury of her peers. She needs to understand how society views her actions. They charged her with assault with a deadly weapon. I will probably have to testify."

"If she has good representation, her lawyer may persuade her to take a plea deal and serve a reduced sentence," Johanna continued. "Eli is another matter. He actually conspired to commit murder. He played on Samuel's hatred and jealousy. The prosecution may use the audio recording as leverage. I don't know the legal ramifications here. I think it's whatever the district attorney can prove in a court of law."

"It seems, according to Eliana, the metal boxes containing the gold Scott unearthed from the wishing well originally came from Ari's vault," said Norah, reaching for a cookie. "When it became illegal for US citizens to own gold, Ari and Albert hid it all away. Eli used that fact to persuade Eliana and Samuel to discredit me in order to remove my trusteeship with the taint of mental unfitness. He promised them, if they found it, they could split the undocumented wealth amongst themselves."

"It turns out that Eli knew something that Eliana and Samuel didn't," she continued. "All trustees of the Legacy Trust were informed there was a fortune in the Minsky Canadian offices when they accepted their leadership position. The vaults in Toronto hold King George the V British gold Sovereigns, minted in 1925 as well. I was aware of this because Nathan told me. Eli planned to liquidate those holdings for himself without revealing its existent to Samuel and Eliana."

"So that's why Eli seemed to support your trusteeship, he didn't want Samuel to find out about the Canadian gold," said Johanna. "It's like a weird, sinister puzzle in which Eliana and Samuel thought they had all the pieces, but Eli only showed them what he wanted them to see."

"Sadly, it was the real motive behind Nathan's murder and why it was so easy to convince Samuel to kill me. I stood in the way of the hidden gold, to Samuel's way of thinking. I wasn't a Minsky and I didn't deserve it. When I made you my beneficiary, Johanna, you ended up in the crosshairs too. I am so sorry." Norah reached for Johanna's hand.

"Eli was cheating the very people he set up to do his dirty work," said Delphine.

"That's the true nature of greed and power," stated Johanna. "They are cannibalistic and would eat their own kind as easily as their targets."

"Pete Mitchell told me Eliana confessed she knew Samuel kept stealing my keys," said Norah, softly. "He turned back the kitchen clock so I'd be late to Evelyn's garden party. She admitted to tampering with my invitation but it was Samuel who switched it back to the real one so I'd believe I was losing my mind. Earlier in the fall, she said he poisoned a bottle of pest spray in the herb shop. He left it in a box that I, unknowingly, brought to the farm market. He even staged the break-in and destroyed his grandmother's chandelier."

"Killing an animal or a person didn't seem to bother him," Delphine said. "It's hard for me to understand how a person who had so many opportunities in life, cared so little for the lives of others."

"He planted the datura in the Moon Garden, believing it would prove me incompetent." Norah's face tightened. "According to Pete, Eliana insists she had no idea Nathan's death wasn't an accident. She is holding to the story that Samuel acted entirely on his own."

"There is an audio recording in her own voice, suggesting something quite different," Johanna said. She finished eating the cookie and took another.

"As Phil Granger said, the only person who could have killed Nathan is now dead," Norah said sadly.

"How could he have done it?" asked Delphine. "He must have grown up in Nathan's shadow and hated him for being the golden boy in his grandfather's eyes. I'm so sorry, Norah." Delphine gently laid her hand on Norah's wrist. "I didn't mean –"

"It's ok," Norah responded and covered Delphine's hand with her own. "I understand. It's a strange relief to know he didn't die because of a stupid mistake or a miscalculation. I can understand that Samuel hated him. Albert never meant for them to compete with one another. He gave each of his grandchildren an opportunity to succeed in their own way. He needed to know who could be trusted with the family finances. He had amassed wealth of such magnitude, he needed to protect it from greed and mismanagement. "

Delphine turned to Johanna. "But I still just don't understand how Samuel could hate Nathan so much he could murder his own brother so brutally. You're the psychologist, Johanna, how do you explain it?"

"I don't think Samuel grew up in Nathan's shadow. I think they all grew up in the shadows of two very different kind of men. Albert was guided by spiritual principles and a discerning mind. Morris grew up having advantages that were simply his for the taking. He saw no value in reciprocity or generosity. Nathan found a kindred spirit in his grandfather's values. Samuel and Eliana were attracted to wealth and access so they were more aligned with their father. Not to mention the Jameson attraction to social standing."

"Nature or nurture?" asked Norah.

"It's always both."

"But to kill your own brother for personal gain?" Delphine shuddered. "And what about Evelyn? Didn't she play a role in her children's ruthless actions? She is their mother, after all!"

"Evelyn has always orchestrated her own ambitions behind the scenes," said Norah. "It's true she favored Samuel and believed Nathan was too soft. But he always had his grandfather's approval. For Nathan, that's what mattered most. She has always been most proud of her daughter. I suppose it's because Eliana achieved the kind of career success Evelyn, herself, could not. The times being what they were." Norah's voice trailed away.

"I know how hard it was a generation later, to get recognized as a woman in the field of science," she continued. "It couldn't have been easy for Evelyn to know she was smarter than many of the men around her, but denied the reins of the business world she was raised in. It must have, well, rankled her."

"Even so, the level of callous disregard for others exhibited by Samuel and Eliana has a real consequence, not just a moral one," said Johanna. "Regardless of the circumstances, in the end, we all make a choice about our willingness to harm others. Evelyn is suffering for her role in shaping what they believed the world owed them."

"Samuel paid with his own life. It's as if the river exacted justice for his crime," said Norah. "This family has suffered enough."

Johanna thought about her part in that form of justice. She saw Samuel's face again. His shock and disbelief. Then, seeing the river sweep him away. Her mind burned with more images; the hammer raised at her head, being pulled off the rocks by her hair and thrown against the cliff walls, his body bumped and pushed by the river, trapped in tree branches that seemed to snarl with malevolence. Her body stiffened as she fixated on whirling scenes in her mind.

The tea kettle whistled. Delphine's chair scraped the floor as she stood up. A cabinet door shut loudly. Spoons clinked in tea mugs. The sharp sounds jarred the hypnotic hold with which Johanna's mind grasped those images.

Norah's voice resumed its authoritative tone as she continued discussing her plans.

"Evelyn has agreed to put her share in a Trust for her grandchildren, which I will do as well. We will assign an administrator for each Trust to ensure that the children do not dissipate the funds irresponsibly."

"Good plan," said Johanna, struggling to focus her mind on the present.

"I am going to create a new business, the Nathan Minsky Foundation. I will fund it from periodic sales of Albert's Rhinegold, as needed. It's mission will be to develop sustainable business practices that are aligned with Nathan's standards and his grandfather's legacy of integrity. It will include scholarship awards and business plan funding for those students who adhere to sustainability practices in the state of Maine. It will also include a payback clause in which each supported business plan must show how it will develop generative community involvement."

"The Minsky Way?"

Norah smiled.

"What about Minerva's Meadows?"

Norah put her hand on the garden book. "I have decided not to franchise the tea blending, as Samuel suggested. I am going to have the entire book published, recipes included."

"What about the Rhinemaidens drawing?"

"I'm keeping the original divider page, but I will add Mina's flower messages. They are sound advice for living a good and prosperous life, written in flower language."

"It's your first example of a sustainable business," Johanna said.

"Speaking of flower language," said Johanna, reaching for the tea packets. "We need a good ceremony. I brought the Heart Soother blend, from my grandmother's blessing bundles."

Johanna explained the concept to Delphine. "Hawthorn, rose petals and lavender in a tea blend for mending a broken heart, and moving forward, accepting peace and happiness in one's life."

"It's time," said Norah. "I may have lost everything in the farmhouse that I shared with Nathan, but I can never lose his love."

"May I join in?" asked Delphine. "I don't know how much time I have left with that cantankerous old Swede. I'm sure someday my heart will be broken too."

"I'm ready to believe that love can be strong enough to withstand whatever tries to destroy it," said Johanna. "Nearly losing Scott again was enough for me."

"And you," said Norah, softly, "we so nearly lost you."

Delphine poured hot water over their tea strainers and they sat in silence while the hawthorn, lavender and rose steeped. Scents of summer filled the kitchen while they each thought of the man they loved and the courageousness required for true devotion.

Sunlight streamed through Delphine's kitchen windows. In the distance, Katahdin with its snowy crags and windswept peaks, stood as both guardian and witness. Devotion is that which weathers all storms; like a mountain range, unbreakable. They sipped their tea, illuminated in golden light.

A few minutes later, Johanna broke the silence.

"Norah, there's something I need your permission to do."

The Boundary Mountains

A few days later, Johanna woke Scott in the early hours before dawn. The previous night they received an answer to the text message they sent to the Trading Post in Eustis.

> *Angelique will meet you here at 1PM tomorrow. Bring snowshoes and dress accordingly. -Jake*

They poured hot coffee in a travel thermos. They made sandwiches for the road. As the sky lightened with the coming dawn, they walked down to the boat house. It was the first time Johanna had been there since the night of the fire. There was something she needed to do before they left for the Boundary Mountains.

The harmony of the land was broken. The river, the mountain, the meadows and gardens now carried seeds of hatred, jealousy, and greed. Only a good ceremony could restore their seamless beauty. This was an integral part of the wisdom traditions that Angelique had taught her. A simple act of restoration in which she herself was both agent and recipient.

Angelique's people believed victims were powerful; they had survived. The evil they encountered had not defeated them; they had not perished. To consider oneself irreparably harmed was to truly be vanquished. Angelique had taught Johanna how those who were wounded could be transformed into conduits of healing.

"Our lives are an inextricable part of the earth," she taught. "We are part of an undefeated chain of harmony and beauty. The trees, waters and land, the sky, four-leggeds and winged ones are our family. All our relations carry the threads of life."

"If one part of the thread is damaged, the rest must seek to restore it to wholeness. In our ways, we do not isolate or shun victims because of the evil they endured. The community embraces them. See, the survivor holds the thread that was broken. Your people isolate and medicate your wounded ones. You leave their wounded spirits to fend for themselves."

"Be it a broken mind or shattered body," she had continued, "you separate yourself from them. It's as if, by having endured harm, they are tainted. But we say, if they survived, it's because Spirit honored them. They have a new gift; one that is desperately needed. If we shun them, the community will have a gap. If it's not restored by Spirit, that gap will eat away and destroy the culture."

"The Creators brought that person into the tribe for a reason," she taught. "The tribe needs them."

Scott and Johanna came to the boat house. Scott found the padlock in the dirt, where Samuel had thrown it when he broke in to take one of the kayaks. He locked up the boat shed. Together, they walked to the place where Norah revealed what had happened the day Nathan was killed on the river.

Scott sat on a flat boulder and waited.

The river was now so shallow, Johanna found it easy to walk into the riverbed itself on stones that had once been covered by water.

The bones of the river, she thought.

She knelt on one knee and put her hands in the muddied soil of the riverbed. She sifted through patches of sodden leaves; leaves that would decay and later become soil. It would then harden into ground so strong it could bear the weight of a spring runoff. Each spring, as the mountain snow melted, the Carrabec became a river once more.

This river had seen evil, murder, and violence. The water flowing around her in trickles and splashes were talking about it. They had stopped their laughing. Johanna closed her eyes and listened.

She heard the flow of the water around her and felt a momentary spray of mist on her face. Sadness filled her, even deeper than her own. It was tears she heard in the narrow streams. They had worked together, the river and the woman, and both had been tainted by evil.

The river was crying.

Tears flowed down her face and fell into the rivulets that flowed around the stones in the riverbed. It was true, she had pushed Samuel to his death. But it was the river itself that had taken the threat away. It had claimed Samuel's life and prevented him from killing her.

She reached down into the riverbed and took a stone; rounded and softened by thousands of years of spring runoffs. Water had carved it into a river-bone. She held it in her hands. It was icy cold; an ancient remnant of wind and mountain flung into a ravine and tumbled over and over in water that became a river.

Not once, but four times, she had escaped death in the past few weeks. She had survived a burning house, a hammer aimed at her head, Eliana's attack, and a gun pointed at her heart.

There was another time she remembered, long ago. She survived death, but a friend did not. Johanna clasped the stone, stood up, and walked over to Scott. He waited for her patiently.

They walked through the woods into the meadows toward the barn.

Johanna went into the Herbary for the last of the things she needed to bring Angelique. Locking the door behind her, she put a small willow basket containing the river-stone and a package of herbs and flowers in the back seat.

Scott packed the Crosstrek, adding a pair of borrowed snowshoes and poles from Norah, and a duffel bag of cold weather gear Johanna would need to navigate the Preserve. The Boundary was rugged country. Sometimes the roads were impassable by anything other than foot, snowmobile, or all-terrain-vehicles.

Checking to ensure the door to the apartment and barn were locked, he parked the Tahoe in the driveway to deter visitors. They drove down the long driveway, turning onto the Tiadaghton road. Johanna noticed Scott had taken down the Minerva's Meadows Herb and Tea Garden sign. An empty post stood at the end of the access road. It was the end of an era.

Norah had come by the apartment the day before to say Evelyn had invited her to live in the mansion. The property would go back into the Trust when Evelyn passed away. The two women decided the mansion would best serve as the headquarters for the new foundation with its possibilities of ethical, sustainable business practices.

"I will offer Lisette the position of building manager with a salary and retirement package more in line with the job she has already been doing," said Norah. "She has given a lot to the Minsky family and I want to provide for her future as well."

Johanna's face was downcast, her demeanor somber, as Scott drove toward Rangeley Lakes. They traveled the back way along meandering mountain roads and drove through rural townships. It was a four-hour drive to Eustis.

Scott reached over and took her hand. They traveled in silence. He focused on driving as she watched the trees whip by the window.

"I'm glad you're seeing Angelique," he said.

"I don't know what to do with this sadness."

"Can you talk about it?"

"I keep seeing his face, his shock. I see his body bounce off the rocks, then being sucked into the water. I kept thinking he was gone, til I saw his body trapped in the tree branches. I see it over and over again."

"With all your training -"

"It's no good. I know what to do if a client is traumatized, but I can't do this for myself."

He squeezed her hand.

"Nothing prepares you," she said.

"I know people who accidentally killed someone," said Scott. "They are usually pretty clear about the circumstances. Did you push him over the falls?"

"He was falling back, trying to catch his balance. He went over the edge."

Scott waited.

"Yes, I pushed him. I killed him."

She wept.

"You protected yourself."

"I have blood on my hands."

"I understand," he said softly, "in more ways than you can imagine."

As they drove further into the north Maine woods, the elevation became higher and the air colder. There were windswept patches of snow along the forested roads. The towns were further apart and the countryside more rugged as they passed the Sugarloaf Mountain ski resort town of Kingfield. They shared sandwiches while driving.

When they entered the Rangeley Lakes area, Scott drove to a local coffee shop. It offered fresh roasted, brewed coffee and Scott wanted to replenish their thermos. He returned to the Crosstrek with some packages of their signature coffee brand as well.

Eustis was another thirty-five miles northwest and could take nearly an hour, with icy roads and blowing snow. Thanksgiving was only a few days away and cold weather was moving in. The shimmering blue lakes mirrored the cloudless depths of the sky. The mountains looked as if they had been born from the expanse of lakes and risen to pierce the skies with their rugged, forested peaks.

They arrived in the small mountain town of Eustis and Scott found the Trading Post without difficulty. It was an indigenous owned general store that sold supplies for camping, hunting and wilderness living. It had snowed the night before and the air was very cold. They had arrived a few minutes before 1 o'clock.

A woodstove burning in the corner filled the trading post with a sweet scent. One area featured staple food supplies with milk, water and other refrigerated items. Another area had racks of parkas, heavy coveralls, hats, gloves and boots. In the back of the store was a long, glass-covered counter featuring pistols, rifles, and ammunition. The walls featured compound bows, arrows, snowshoes and cross-country skies.

It was an outfitter's general store without the commercialized branding of a national franchise. It smelled of apple pie.

A tall, muscular man with a dark complexion and a long black braid walked through a door behind the counter. He wore a red flannel shirt with blue jeans and knee-length deer-hide boots.

He carried a pie plate with mitt-covered hands. Steam curled from its pastry vent holes. The smells of vanilla, cinnamon and baked apples wafted through the shop.

"You, Johanna?"

"Yes, and this is my husband, Scott."

"I'm Jake. Can I get you anything? Fresh apple pie?"

The tone of his voice was solemn but his eyes shone like sunlight flickering in pools of dark water. He grinned and Johanna could see the distinctively mischievous laugh lines of a person used to joking around.

"Just pulled it out of the oven," he said.

"It smells delicious."

"Slices are on-the-house. We keep fresh bakery goods here. First come, first served," said Jake. "Angelique should be here anytime now."

"Thank you for passing our message along to her," said Johanna. "Can I use your dressing room to change into my outdoor gear?"

"Sure, over there." He tilted his head sideways and nodded toward a wall with heavy flannel shirts hung on pegs. "We take lots of messages here for folks in the Preserve."

By the time Johanna returned from the car with her duffle bag, Scott and Jake were talking by the gun counter. She entered the changing room, put a thermal shirt under her ski sweater and pulled on heavy woolen socks. She stepped into her snowmobile suit, then zipped it up. Catching an image of herself in the mirror, she laughed. With its bright crimson color, she looked like a cardinal on a tree branch.

If they were going to snowshoe today, she would need ski goggles too. The cold air could freeze extremities quickly and most people forgot to cover their eyes. She transferred an extra t-shirt and jeans into her backpack, then added ski-gloves and a hat. She pulled a balaclava from the duffle bag and added it as well. Johanna then shrugged out of the arms of her snowmobile suit and rolled the top half down to her waist. It wasn't a good idea to get overheated in the warmth of the store. When Angelique arrived, she would zip it back up. She folded her long silver hair in a twist and secured it with a barrette.

She longed for one of her friend's healing ceremonies but felt unsettled. There was no way for her to know what to expect. This was uncharted emotional territory, or was it? In a way, it was more familiar than she wanted to acknowledge. When she gathered the items in the willow basket, she had been listening to her heart. Now she felt uncertain.

Johanna stepped out of the dressing room and handed her empty duffle bag to Scott.

He looked into her eyes and kissed her forehead.

"It will be alright," he said softly, "Angelique will know what to do."

"Where'll you hang out till I get back?"

"It turns out there is a firing range in the back of the store. Jake told me the lanes are twenty-five bucks an hour if I buy the ammo from him."

Johanna smiled. "I get a healing and you get some training time."

"Even better, I'm going to try out a new hunting rifle."

Bells jingled on the door as Angelique entered. She stamped the icy snow from her feet and waved.

"*Kwe'* Jake! " She said in a traditional Mi'kmaq greeting.

"*Pjila'si,* "he responded in kind and laughed.

"I see you two are getting some apple pie," she said. "But, around here, it's fry bread he's really famous for."

She wore a jet black snowmobile suit and a knit headband of white wool with a black thunderbolt design. The contrast with her hair was as if shards of daylight had wrapped itself around the darkest of nights. Her long black braid plunged down her back.

"Can I bring some pie back to my brother in the Preserve?"

"Take the whole thing," Jake laughed. "There is another one in the oven."

While Jake wrapped the pie in tinfoil, she turned to Johanna. "Did you bring your snowshoes? We have to trek in."

"In the Subaru," Johanna responded, "with a small basket."

"Let us go, then."

Angelique touched Johanna's face. She caressed her friend's pale, somber cheeks with soft, dark fingers. Johanna felt wheels of energy spinning within her. Compassion flowed like a warm liquid throughout her entire body.

"We are going up to the Chain of Ponds, then into the Preserve area, Scott," said Angelique. "We will park and snow-hike in. We take the Red Trail up around Ice Lake."

Jake nodded.

"We should be back by sundown."

Jake turned to Scott. "You want to rent a cabin for the night?"

"Sounds good to me."

"Rustic, but I promise indoor plumbing."

"I've snowshoed my way to an outhouse in Colorado. Sounds like luxury to me," said Scott.

Angelique drove north on Route 27 toward Chain of Ponds for about half an hour. If they had kept going, they would have soon reached the Canadian border crossing at Coburn Gore. Johanna told her what had transpired since they met at the Blueberry Cafe. She recounted the story of Samuel setting the farmhouse on fire, their escape down the river in kayaks, and the shocking realization that Nathan had been murdered.

She lowered her voice to tell her plan of staying behind to shoot a hole in Samuel's kayak only to miss, then struggling with him on the ledge above the Thresher.

"I pushed him over," she said in tears, "and the river swept him away."

She completed her story with the discovery of Albert's hidden gold, Eliana's attack and shooting Eli with his own pistol.

Then Johanna was silent. Angelique had listened without commentary or any attempts to comfort her.

"It is good you have come to the Preserve," she said.

Angelique turned into the deserted trailhead parking area. They leaned against the tailgate and attached snow-shoes to their boots. Johanna adjusted her ski goggles over her woolen hat. Angelique tucked the willow basket into the backpack that was secured on Johanna's back.

Extending their poles, they set out to find the Red Trail that led up the mountainside. The sun was bright and a stiff wind swirled around them, knocking off pockets of snow from trees.

The trail was hard to find at first. Hiker's maps listed it, but there were no markers identifying the trail. Johanna could see a single set of snowshoe tracks ahead of them, heading in the same direction. They were recent. This was not the path that led to the camps where Angelique had been staying. She was taking her somewhere else.

"It will be better when we get in the lee of the mountain," said Angelique. "The wind will not be coming off the ponds. Best not to talk. Save your breath." She led the way between the pines.

They came to a cross-trail and continued to follow in the tracks of the person who came before them. Johanna thought about the contents of the willow basket that she had assembled as a blessing bundle. Norah had given her permission to bring Mina's sprig of edelweiss wrapped in hyssop along with some meadowsweet, nettle leaf, lavender and red rose petals for an offering. It was a message written in the language of flowers, held within tightly woven willow branches. The stone was part of the offering.

> *Devotion and courage blesses, guards and protects strength, resilience, and beauty, wrapped in rebirth.*

It was a gift for the preservation and protection of the Boundary Mountains. What was wounded in the Carrabec, had the power to strengthen the Preserve lands. The stone was both a river-bone and a mountain-bone. It sought to become part of a mountain once again. Johanna was merely its carrier.

Ahead of them was a large body of water reflecting the icy blue sky overhead. It was called Ice Lake because it was the first to ice over, so people could travel across it. It was too soon in the season for that yet. They could hear the frigid waves lapping against the shoreside as they snowshoed around it. Rolling hills, mountains and emerald forested lands surrounded the lake.

They followed the trail around the western side and began an upward climb. The elevation was not strenuous, but it demanded one's complete focus. *The best meditation, Johanna thought, was the one that commanded all your attention, moment by moment.* Snowshoeing was meditation in motion.

The Red Trail led up an incline that ended abruptly in a clearing of old growth pine. A log cabin stood at the edge of the tree-line with a curl of sweet-scented smoke wafting from its chimney. To the right of the clearing, another path led into the woods toward another mountain that ringed Ice Lake. Two skids containing quartered wood for fuel were beside a lean-to where someone had parked a snowmobile.

They approached the porch where Johanna could see a pair of snowshoes hung from pegs driven into the chink. Unlatching their snowshoes, they hung them, along with their poles, from empty pegs. Angelique rapped on the heavy oak door.

The two women entered the cabin and stowed their snow-frosted boots in a boot-tray by the door, then hung their outerwear on pegs fixed to the log hewn walls. Johanna placed her backpack by the door.

An old Franklin woodstove glowed with flames and filled the small cabin with its flickering warmth. A man was sitting in a chair before the fire with his back to them. He stood up and smiled as he turned to greet them.

He was a tall, wiry old man. His thin, white hair was combed back from his high forehead. Dark eyes sparkled above the heavy creases and wrinkles that time and age had weathered into his face. He had the lanky build of a lumberjack and the strong upper body of man who had worked outdoors all his life. He wore a red and black plaid flannel shirt, faded blue jeans and thick red woolen socks.

Johanna met Old Man over thirty-five years ago after a tragic event that resulted in her living with her grandparents in Nova Scotia. She had returned to the United States and attended university where a single act of integrity brought her to the attention of an agency that used her compassionate predisposition for their own agenda. She had been young and impressionable.

When she finally realized the agency was using her to infiltrate student activist groups on campus, she resigned. They forced her to sign a non-disclosure contract declaring she would never reveal her involvement with their group. They threatened her with imprisonment, stating their program involved national security. For weeks afterward, she was followed on campus.

That was the first time Old Man rescued her mind. It was said he was of French and Abenaki descent. No one knew which tribe and he would never say. He spoke fluid English, Mi'kmaq, and Acadian French. When he was a young man, he had married a Passamaquoddy girl. They had only been married for fifteen years when she died from a white man's disease, a simple infection for which her people had no immunity.

As a younger man, he had been a hunter and a fur trapper. The US Forestry Service hired him to walk the mountain trails, making sure logging operations stayed in the legal areas. The forests of the Preserve were a vast wilderness under management protection. Native tribes held those lands in trust and enforced the use of sustainable practices. In those days, he was called Francois Le'Tourneau.

It was said he understood the language of the mountains, rivers, and trees. It was also said he spoke to them and they spoke back. He was a mountain man who knew some of the old ways; ancient ways. That's why the People called him *Gisigu-qasgusi,* Mi'kmaq for Old Man Cedar. He was as much of the boundary lands, the ridge-lines, valleys, lakes and woods as he was of the human race, perhaps more.

These days, he lived at the edges of the Preserve. The people of the lodge camps made sure he was stocked with plenty of food, wood, and natural medicines. He was a revered elder. Today, he stood before her, old and thin; not the younger, stronger man Johanna remembered. Yet his eyes still had a familiar effervescent sparkle riding over his high cheeks, shaped by years of laughter and generosity.

"Grandfather asked to see you," said Angelique.

"Come here Little Sister," he nodded. "We have a lot to talk about."

They sat by the woodstove and Johanna repeated the story of the events she had disclosed to Angelique. He listened to her words the way he listened to trees; the stories of which were often punctuated by the sound of birds, then whispered on the winds and carried over lakes and mountains.

He tilted his head while she spoke; to better hear the words she said and the words she didn't say. In this manner, he heard the entire story and saw everything that had happened. He saw the things she didn't see.

He put his large, dark hand on her knee. It was a wrinkled old man's hand, with ropey veins wrapped around strong bones. She felt warmth flow into her leg; a kind and tender warmth that flowed down to her toes. She felt he understood her sadness.

"The last time you could not prevent a death," he said. "This time you prevented someone from killing another." He paused, allowing silence to fill a space for Spirit to enter.

"Whether a person walks a good road or a bad road in their life, at the end of the trail, there is only light. It is the same light for all beings. The difference is that the person who has walked a bad road will fear it. For one who walks a good road, the light feels like they are coming home."

"You are not haunted by your actions. You are haunted by what he saw when the river took him. He saw the light at the end of his trail. You saw and felt his fear. It does not belong to you." He paused again.

"You need a drum journey to help you find your own good road again," he said.

He stood up and nodded to Angelique. Together they went outside and brought back six long cedar branches, which he had left on the porch in preparation. He spread a tattered Hudson Bay trading blanket on the floor in front of the woodstove. Angelique helped him place two branches, cut end-to-end, on the floor. She helped Johanna lie down on top of the branches, her head and feet resting on its cedar fans.

Johanna closed her eyes, rested her arms by her side, and relaxed as Old Man and Angelique placed two more cedar branches on top of her legs. They placed the last two fans of cedar over her heart and hands, then over her face.

The branches had been freshly gathered from a secret and sacred place. Years ago, Old Man found a stand of northern white-cedar trees in an old growth forest in the mountains. It was part of a pastureland that had been abandoned after the higher elevations were no longer farmed. To prevent their being exploited by loggers or shifting regulations, he never marked the grove on the Forestry Service maps that had been entrusted to him. He honored a more sustainable harvesting plan. He thinned the stand himself and left most of the healthiest and oldest to prosper. Therefore, Old Man's wood pile contained white-cedar intermingled with logs of oak and spruce.

Johanna smelled the sweet fragrance of cedar burning in the woodstove. The scent relaxed her body gently, slowly. It was the scent of good medicine. Cedar was as sacred to the indigenous woodland people as sage was to the plains nations. It was used to cleanse and sanctify, so gathering was only done with permission from Spirit.

Old Man took an old deer-hide drum from its hanger on the wall. He sat on the floor by her feet. He drummed a familiar rhythm; a powerful beat. Her heartbeat just naturally followed the cadence of his drum.

At first she fought what her heart had already joined. It felt as if she was being pulled away from the room, from her body, from the tender, familiar boundaries of her own mind. Angelique sat on the floor and cupped her hands around Johanna's head. She placed her thumbs under the cedar fronds and over her friend's eyes.

"Follow the drum," Angelique said in a tone so soft it could have been the wind.

Johanna's field of vision plunged into darkness. Swirls of energy flowed in, down, around, and through her. Then, all she saw was light.

Warm tears flowed down her face and into the palms of Angelique's hands. Perfect light bathed her and held her within the heart-bone beat of Mother Earth. Her sense of time and place evaporated like mist in morning sunlight, as a Presence filled her being. She recognized her surroundings as a place she had visited in vision journeys many times before. She was in the cave behind the waterfalls and the Lady of Rainbows was now placing her wrinkled, dark-skinned fingers on Johanna's forehead. Swirls of energy flowed throughout Johanna's body.

She was an ancient woman with eyes that glittered like starlight and wild black hair, tied with crow feathers that floated around her head. It was if she was just now, but barely, changing back and forth from a crow to the shape of a woman. She leaned over Johanna and whispered.

"Kindness is your sharpest arrow."

Johanna saw the words in her mind take the shape of feathers, then they floated away. The Lady was gone.

After a while, Old Man drummed her back. He helped her to sit up and readjust to the room.

Angelique gave her valerian tea that tasted like she was drinking the earth. Its pungent, woodland scent filled the room as she drank from a chipped cup with a broken handle.

They rolled the cedar branches up in the blanket.

"You will take these back and throw them in the river, the one that carried away the man," said Old Man. "It is the nature of a river to be soft, to laugh, to run and jump. Yet it knows fury and wildness, icy coldness. It is strong enough to lift boulders and tumble them for miles but gentle enough to form a peaceful eddies where the four-legged and winged-ones can safely drink. This river needs to remember how much it is loved."

Johanna retrieved the willow basket and gave him her offering. She explained the message written in flower language. She placed the river stone in his hands.

Old Man held it for several minutes, then placed it on the woodstove's hearth of blackened iron.

"This river reached up and gave its strength to protect you and your friend from death. It still has a lot to teach you," he said. "I will take this basket and the river stone to the mountain. It will become part of a stone ledge where it will be greeted by the dawn every morning."

"There is a wildness in your soul," said Old Man. "It is fearless. You are afraid of it because it has caused you great suffering. This wildness is not foolhardy or impulsive, it's the true nature of a human being. Just as a river and a mountain have the nature to maintain and restore harmony, so do human beings. The difference is that the natural world cannot forget it."

He paused a moment. A cedar log cracked in the searing flames of the fire.

"Rivers, trees, and creatures don't have to be fearless to act within their nature. They simply do it. For humans, it requires fearlessness to act with integrity. That is why so few people have it. It is why so many people harm those that do."

Johanna began to understand the full meaning of the gifts she had been given. As a child, she never questioned them. But as an adult, she had sought to hide them so they could not used against her will.

Old Man's eyes shimmered in the firelight. Their dark brown pools momentarily reflected the luminous golden flames. His shape wavered between being an old man and being something else. He showed her his own wild soul; a being so ancient it remembered every form it had ever taken. As the firelight wavered, so did the procession of forms. First, a Mayan priest wearing a headdress of iridescent Quetzal feathers, then the Quetzal bird itself with piercing eyes, then briefly his skin turned into anaconda scales before he quickly shifted into the shape of an eagle.

Old Man's familiar features returned, along with a kind gaze and he smiled at her. "Nothing is ever what it seems."

"When you are true to yourself," said Angelique, softly, "you become fiercely genuine. You fear nothing and nothing of real value can ever be taken from you."

"We become what we give to the world," said Old Man. "If we give hatred and harm, we become that. That is what enters the spirit world when we pass on. If we give love, compassion, care and respect, we become that. Who we truly are in this world, is what we carry with us into the world of spirit. It can be no other way."

"Is there no hope, then, for those who carry forward the trauma they experienced in life?" asked Johanna. "So many people repeat to others what was done to them."

"We have many opportunities to exchange compassion for harm. That is why our people believe our souls return for another earth walk. Each rebirth is forgiveness. It is another chance to fill the world with light. The goodness people bring to life, is actually the pure light of spirit. It fills the world. It is always there, if you have eyes to see it."

"There are many ways a person can heal the harm that was done to them," said Angelique. "That's why we are grateful to the Creators. We just need a good ceremony."

"It is time for you to return to your people," he said. "It is not important if they don't understand you. What they have forgotten will be restored in its own time. When you recognize your own wildness, you must embrace it. Then you will never forget who you are. You are a storm and you are a summer breeze. You bring the ability to feel again to those who have been hurt, like the refreshment of raindrops. You find the lost ones and bring them back home. Your one true name is *Calls the Wind.*"

She felt bewildered.

Old Man laughed. "And you thought it was psychotherapy you were doing all these years!"

He slapped his leg.

"All along, you were calling up winds in people who had forgotten their way."

Johanna felt a jolt, a shock to her heart. Then she saw the truth about herself. She realized she could never un-see it. What had been done to her, long ago, was finally undone.

"Thank you, Grandfather," Johanna bowed her head.

"You carry my song," he said softly.

Angelique put her arms around Johanna's shoulders. The two women held one another tightly.

"Wanto'ti, Granddaughters," said Old Man. [Peace]

"Aqueneh, Grandfather," said Angelique. [Peace] "Come, Netuksq. It is time to go back."

They suited up against the cold and lashed their snowshoes firmly to their boots. They hiked away from the log cabin in the clearing as the sky displayed a swirl of red and purple clouds over the mountain range. High in the atmosphere, white wisps streamed like the manes of wild horses running across the plains.

"Look," said Angelique, "thunder ponies!"

The Shapeshifter watched them from the forest as they snowshoed down the Red Trail. Her golden tail swished back and forth, as they disappeared around a bend on the path. That woman is one of us now, and she knows it. She has a heart made of rainbows and a fierce storm in her eyes.

Three days later Scott and Johanna arrived at the Carrabec River, parking at the picnic area in the bend, where Mina had watched her grandsons kayak past so many years ago. The setting sun was a blazing orange orb making flickering, knife-edged reflections on the tips of the waves.

The sky began to darken as Scott unrolled the trading blanket on the Subaru's hatch back. Johanna helped him remove the cedar branches that Old Man used in her healing ceremony. Together, they walked down the steep embankment. One by one, they laid the branches in the river. The cedar fans floated, spun, then swirled away. She felt her sadness recede as the river took their offering.

Scott raised Johanna's hand to his lips and kissed her fingers. Remnants of sunlight flickered across her storm-gray eyes and illuminated them like shimmering diamonds. Her face seemed to waver. Then momentarily, she appeared to him as she had been long ago: a young girl with long blonde hair streaming down her back. She closed her eyes.

"Unbreakable," he murmured.

The Wind Sisters blew through the trees, lifting Johanna's long, silver hair in the air, then whipped the strands around her shoulders like wild fringe on an ancient shawl. They spun across the ground, skittering leaves in a golden whirlwind. Then they danced off into the sky, sealing an unspoken promise, and wrapped it in clouds.

Afterword

Some of these events are true. All of the wisdom is real. My stories are written using a traditional literary storyteller device, called writing the braids. Each story is a braid woven by three independent stories, or strands, that come together for a central theme. The central theme is like the ribbon that binds the braids together. The ribbon that binds CLOUDS OVER KATAHDIN together is *respect*.

The first strand of the braid is the story of Albert and Mina Minsky who escaped Germany before the Holocaust and built a financial empire. The second strand is the story of murder, greed, and an attempt to destroy another person's mind. The third strand is the story of Johanna's development as a reluctant detective and the ability to trust herself again after grievous harm.

Notes

- *The Tarot card selections really happened during my research consultation with fellow mystery writer, Erica Shay. Her character Marti O'Neil drew the Emperor and Devil cards, reversed. She drew the Strength card for Johanna. Then, unexpectedly, the Father of Stones in the West card (Otherwise known as Old Man) fell out of the deck and landed upright on the table. That is how Old Man got written into the story.*

- *My original research in herbal wild-crafting started with some organic seeds and a small summer garden. I crafted all the herbal tea remedies mentioned in the Herbary and Mina Minsky's Herbal Tea Compendium. My favorite is Lady Evelyn's Assam.*

- *Many of the vision journeys I include in the Johanna Kincaid Mystery Series actually occurred. In particular, meeting my ancestor on the Isle of Skye who then imparted the wisdom of making Blessing Bundles filled with herbal tea packets and poultices.*

- *Good research is necessary for designing a good plot. Hence, finding Orion, The Hunter, on the horizon with my Solarium software became a daily practice. Was he rising or setting in the western skies at daybreak? He can be found in the night skies in the northern hemisphere from November to March so he is a winter constellation. Clouds Over Katahdin takes place in Maine beginning in October, with mysterious events, sabotage and interference that extend throughout November. So when does Orion become a night-riding constellation?*

- *At 6AM on October 10th, 2023, when I was writing the chapter, "Clouds Over Katahdin," Orion was riding low on the western horizon. Below him was Taurus and the Pleiades. As I finished writing the book, in mid-March 2024, Orion rode high, overhead, in the evening sky. I liked the prospect of adding the myth of Artemis the Huntress opposing Orion the Hunter in the universal conflict of good versus evil.*

- *The Boundary Mountains Preserve is a large continuous forest that stretches over 260,000 acres from the White Mountains in New Hampshire to the western Maine mountains and beyond, to Quebec. The lands of the Preserve are held in Trust by the Passamaquoddy Tribe and the Penobscot Indian Nation for care and stewardship. There remains significant old growth northern white -cedar forests in the Preserve. I took creative license when writing about the Eustis Trading Post and Lodge Camps.*

The Herbal Tea Compendium

Nettle, Tulsi & Meadowsweet with lemon and honey: This tea blend is anti-inflammatory and an antioxidant while helping reduce hypertension. It is an analgesic and anti-allergy. Helps boost immune system with respiratory support, heart health, and is a cold and fever reducer.

Lady Evelyn's Assam: Assam tea with Lemongrass, Mint and dried honey.

Summertime Iced Tea: Lavender, Rose Petals and Jasmine tea.

Nighttime: Valerian, Sweet Violet & Green tea; helps with insomnia, anti-anxiety, relaxation, congestion, anti-inflammatory.

Relax: Ginseng and Turmeric in Green tea:. Useful for stress reduction, energy boosting, muscle soreness, and it's anti-inflammatory.

Black Birch Bark Tea: can be hot tea or iced. Helpful for pain, arthritis and it's a diuretic to help flush kidneys.

Heart Health: Hawthorn, Hibiscus, and Meadowsweet. A blend to strengthen cardiovascular function and helps reduce joint pain.

Heart Soother: (Aila MacDonald of Skye) Hawthorn, Lavender and Rose Petals. A tea blend for managing loss and grief. Helps restore hope and happiness.

Dandelion Detox: Dandelion Root with Milk-thistle, Lemon Zest, and Feverfew. This blend assists in detoxifying and supporting liver functions. Milk-thistle is a precursor to glutathione, a natural anti-oxidant which helps neutralize toxins. This blend includes digestive support, and relief for headache. It is also antiseptic.

Wild Bergamot & Rose: Bee Balm and Rugosa Rose tea. This is a calming tea blend with a gentle aromatic scent. It helps relieve anxiety, promotes better sleep, regulates chi (energy centers), nourishes the liver, improves blood circulation, and is an antioxidant.

Winter Health Blend: Hawthorne, Nettle tea with Lemon, and a teaspoon of Elderberry syrup. Strengthens immune function, it's anti-viral. It promotes respiratory ease, and detoxification.

Acknowledgements

When I decided to become an independently published writer, I had no clue what a learning curve it would become. I surround myself with fellow writers, friends, colleagues, and associates who won't hesitate to tell me like it is, when it comes to my manuscripts. My stories are so much the better for their incisive commentaries and suggestions. Indie-authors have to be more courageous than I ever imagined and often lonelier, too.

I would like to acknowledge the many people who help research and validate the information in this book. The seeds for the plot of this story began many years ago, when I helped with the spring planting at an organic farm at Pumpkin Hollow in Craryville, NY.

It continued in the gardens of Celeste Longacre in New Hampshire. Thank you, Celeste, for letting me learn in your gardens and for your magnificent overview of all things herbal and flower related. Thank you for your enthusiastic willingness to "vet" Minerva's Meadows Herb and Tea Garden. (All errors are my own). She is the real deal! I recommend readers follow this link for her website, classes, and kvass demos. https://www.celestelongacre.com

Many thanks to Lisa Hawkins, whose delight in the natural world contributed to the tone of respect for the land that I strove for in writing this book. Her involvement in the Common Ground Fair, Maine Organic Farm Growers Association in Unity, Maine and interest in straw-bale home building inspired my research and the use of sustainable agriculture methods as the backdrop for this suspense story. She taught me the proper way to see the natural world, the emotional value of seeking peace in a meadow, and joy in a songbird. In all the world, there can be no more majestic a moment than seeing a great blue heron rise from the marsh and sail into the sky.

I am grateful to my dear friend Ahanecqa, for sharing her wisdom, friendship and sisterhood. *Aqueneh, Netuksq.*

Thank you, Naomi Lake, for your teachings, drum journeys, and for your impeccable wisdom and healing light. Good Medicine.

Retired Pittsfield, MA Fire Inspector, Lieutenant Randy Stein, was my fire consultant. My deepest gratitude for your years of service and good humor in helping me devise the farmhouse fire scene. Rufus McCoy was fashioned after you!

Accurate police procedures and law enforcement scenes are vital assets in a writer's toolbox. I'm lucky to have a daughter who was a 911 emergency dispatcher. Kerrie Peters, you are awesome. Thanks for your legal research and late night texts. I salute the Thin Gold Line!

All references to the Ojibwe language in this book are due to the language lessons of James Vukelich on Facebook and Instagram. Thank you for your gift of teaching the Ojibwe language lessons and for offering your book: <u>Seven Generations and Seven Grandfather Teachings</u>

I wish to thank the Mi'kmaq online translation project for assistance in using traditional language at: https://mikmaqonline.org/

Much appreciation to Diana Beresford- Kroeger for her book: <u>To Speak for The Trees.</u>

I highly recommend readers learn more about precious metals, inflation, and the history of the gold standard. History tends to repeat itself, and the wisdom of being prepared cannot be understated. Just ask Albert Minsky. Mike Maloney on YouTube offers excellent informational videos and his Hidden Secrets of Money series is unparalleled. It can be viewed at: https://www.youtube.com/watch?v=DyV0OfU3-FU

A shout-out to the descendants of Horace (Scrag) Baker. Orleans, MA, a Cape Cod fisherman, for letting me use his name and profession.

I am grateful to my cousin Frank McDonald Burt (Mack). Vietnam Veteran, US Army, Bronze Star recipient. Thank you for your service, your stories and in memory of your struggles. I finally told your battle story with all its fear, anger, and sadness. I will always remember what you could never forget.

My BETA readers, editors, and Street Team participants are the strength behind my writing successes and not to be held accountable for my blunders. Their commitment and eagle eyes are precious beyond measure. Lisa Kearley Elder, Robin Goodman (and their magic red pens!) Louise DeSantis Deutsch, Claire Wagner Kimball, Shari Lynch, Barbara Stein, and Melanie Masdea-Dignum.

To the Wednesday Writing group, HUZZAH! Constance Wilkinson and Mary-Elizabeth Briscoe, fellow authors, poets and therapists. Cheers to the art of murdering one's darlings.

Thank you, Jess Kielman and Gayle Andrew for the late night plot jams, blueberry pie, and the sweetest of baklava; not to mention some of the most excellent chai and, of course, scones, but that's in the next book!

I would like to thank Erica Shay, author of the Tarot Mystery series, for allowing her characters Marti O'Neil and Jayne Cullen to appear in this book. Look for further involvement in future Johanna Kincaid shaman mysteries. Meanwhile, I recommend reading:

The Ace of Cups: Her First Time Out by Erica Shay

and

Two of Swords

Thank you Granddaddy. I carry your song.

Anneka Lowrie writes the Johanna Kincaid Mysteries—psychological suspense stories drawn from real-world crimes, human behavior, and ancestral insight, delivered through twisty, high-stakes investigations. In addition to writing mystery thrillers, Anneka Lowrie is a retired psychotherapist who worked with victims of violent crime. Her Johanna Kincaid novels draw on professional insight into trauma, ethics, and the consequences of silence.

Her first book in the series, A Convergence of Crows, was a Quarterfinalist in the Booklife Critics Prize for the Mystery & Thriller category. When she is not writing psychological thrillers she is traveling the country with her husband, hiking, exploring, and camping under the stars.

You can connect with her at:

www.annekalowrie.com

Follow her Substack for Case File Notes and more

https://substack.com/@annekalowrie

Join her mailing list for New Releases, Book Deals and Discounts

https://bit.ly/FollowAnneka

LITERARY PRAISE

A band of strong, capable women determined to take down a child sex trafficking ring with the aid of First Nations and other mystical wisdom is a powerful combination in this important story. Lowrie's sweeping natural imagery gives space for readers to process difficult subject matter. While sex trafficking is an oft-explored topic, a seldom celebrated, fierce female presence lights up this book—an antidote to its brutal truths. The infusion of spirituality and its intersection with the natural world provides an impactful additional layer of meaning. Lowrie's characters are vibrant and easy for readers to connect to, despite populating an uncommon, strikingly realized setting. Their backgrounds are fully examined and nicely inform the events unfolding in the present. ~ **Booklife Prize Critic's Review**

This debut novel interlaces a murder mystery, injustices to indigenous people, violence against women, and misuses of power--all suffused with a mystical overlay of spirituality and nature. Johanna Kincaid, retired psychologist and budding Shaman, uses her several skills and friendships to unpack crime, while challenging readers to confront a range of contemporary social issues. Marked by lucid prose and fast paced action, this novel is the first of a series. Look forward to journeying with Johanna along future mysterious ways. ~ **4 Star Amazon Review – Louise A. DeSantis Deutsch, Professor Emerita, Dep't of Language & Literature, Cape Cod Community College W. Barnstable, M A**

What sets "A Convergence of Crows" apart is its fusion of psychological intensity with a mystical twist. The narrative keeps readers on the edge of their seats, unraveling a complex tapestry of secrets and revelations. Fans of the Joe Leaphorn Series by Tony Hillerman are sure to find a kindred experience in the intricate twists and turns of Johanna Kincaid's mysteries. This mystery series is a must-read for aficionados of psychological thrillers seeking a narrative that skillfully blends the visceral with the mystical. ~ **Emilee Jackson Reviews, Instagram**

I enjoyed the way Anneka Lowrie weaves together the story of Johanna Kincaid's journey into shamanic training and her ability to help a victim of human trafficking. Lowrie explores the horrific underworld of high ranking, privileged desire, and the difficulty punishing crimes against indigenous people. Don't miss this psychological thriller with a shamanic twist! ~ **5 Star Amazon Review – Barbara Stein**

Incident on the Right of Way

Book Three of the Johanna Kincaid Psychological Mystery Series

Accident... or murder? A psychological mystery where truth is manipulated—and the cost of seeing clearly may be everything. When a decomposed body is discovered in a storm-swollen creek beside a controversial gas pipeline, the response is immediate: local, state, and federal law enforcement. It's a murder case. But with no identification, no clear motive, and time working against them, the truth should have stayed buried. Drawn in by a father unwilling to accept the official story, Johanna Kincaid begins to examine what others are too quick to dismiss. What she finds is not a single death—but a narrative already taking shape. One designed to deceive.

Set against the backdrop of environmental politics, this third book in a series of mystery stories explores the intersection between ancient wisdom and the devious nature of human greed. With Johanna Kincaid at the helm, readers will be taken on a thrilling journey filled with multiple twists and turns.

Subscribe to Anneka's mailing list for New Releases, Book Deals and Discounts

https://annekalowrie.com/